O9-ABI-394

ARMS OF MERCY

Also by Ruth Reid and available from
Center Point Large Print:

Abiding Mercy

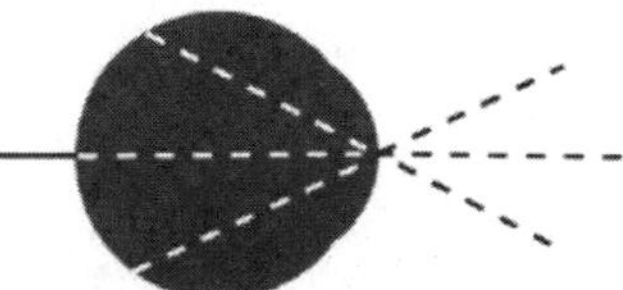

ARMS OF MERCY

AN AMISH MERCIES NOVEL

RUTH REID

CENTER POINT LARGE PRINT
THORNDIKE, MAINE

This Center Point Large Print edition
is published in the year 2018 by arrangement with
Thomas Nelson.

The text of this Large Print edition is unabridged.
In other aspects, this book may vary
from the original edition.
Printed in the United States of America
on permanent paper.
Set in 16-point Times New Roman type.

ISBN: 978-1-68324-853-8

Library of Congress Cataloging-in-Publication Data

Names: Reid, Ruth, 1963- author.
Title: Arms of mercy / Ruth Reid.
Description: Center Point Large Print edition. | Thorndike, Maine : Center Point Large Print, 2018. | Series: An Amish mercies novel
Identifiers: LCCN 2018014376 | ISBN 9781683248538 (hardcover : alk. paper)
Subjects: LCSH: Amish—Fiction. | Large type books. | GSAFD: Christian fiction. | Love stories.
Classification: LCC PS3618.E5475 A88 2018b | DDC 813/.6—dc23
LC record available at https://lccn.loc.gov/2018014376

To my daughter Lexie.
As I'm working on the final edits for
Arms of Mercy, you are traveling the world—
China, India, Indonesia, Malaysia, Ireland,
London, France, Amsterdam, and Iceland—
and I am praying night and day for your safety.
Adventure awaits! But never forget that
God is the one who lights your path.

In all your ways acknowledge him,
and he will make straight your paths.
PROVERBS 3:6 ESV

Love, Mom

Show me the right path, O LORD;
point out the road for me to follow.
Lead me by your truth and teach me,
for you are the God who saves me.
All day long I put my hope in you.
PSALM 25:4–5 NLT

Glossary

ach: oh
aenti: aunt
Ausbund: Amish hymnbook of praise
boppli: baby
bruder: brother
bu: boy
daed: dad or father
danki: thank you
daudi haus: house for grandparents
doktah: doctor
Englischer: anyone who is not Amish
fraa: wife
geh: go
guder: good
guder mariye: good morning
gut: good
haus: house
hiya: a greeting like hello
icehaus: icehouse
iss appeditlich: is delicious
jah: yes
kaffi: coffee
kalt: cold

kapp: a prayer covering worn by Amish women
kinner: children
kumm: come
maedel/maed: unmarried woman/women
mamm/mamma: mother or mom
mammi: grandmother
mann: husband
mei: my
nacht: night
narrish: crazy
nau: now
nay: no
nett: not
onkle: uncle
Ordnung: the written and unwritten rules of the Amish; the understood behavior by which the Amish are expected to live, passed down from generation to generation. Most Amish know the rules by heart.
Pennsylvania Deitsch: the language most commonly used by the Amish
reddy-up: clean up
schweschaler: sister
sohn: son
wedder: weather
welkum: welcome
wunderbaar: wonderful
yummasetti: a traditional Amish dish made with noodles, hamburger, and cheese

Chapter 1

Posen, Michigan

Finally, he arrived.

Catherine Glick placed the jar of pickled eggs on the serving table, then pretended to straighten the other dishes so she could spy Zachariah Lantz pressing through the crowded entryway of The Amish Table restaurant.

Removing his snow-covered coat, Zach looked her direction and smiled. Even from across the crowded room, his deep blue eyes had a way of warming her insides and melting the balled-up tension. Thoughts of him sliding into the ditch somewhere had invaded her mind. Sure, icy roads were typical this time of the year in northern Michigan, and Zach owned an exceptional horse, but not knowing if her boyfriend of nearly five years was stranded someplace had knotted her muscles. Now it didn't matter how much snow accumulated. Zach was here, safe, and just in time for their district's New Year's Eve supper.

Catherine stepped away from the food table to greet Zach at the door but was stopped when his sister, Mary, sidled up beside her, a vegetable tray in her hands.

"I see *mei bruder* finally made it."

Catherine smiled. "Better late than never."

Mary set the tray on the table. "You'd think being a clockmaker he would pay more attention to all those chiming reminders around him in the shop and be on time."

"*Jah*, you'd think," Catherine echoed while following Zach with her gaze as he joined the other unmarried men in the corner of the room. He was a talented clockmaker, meticulous with details, but he was certainly not a timekeeper. He'd missed several functions in the past, citing work-related reasons. But she wasn't about to complain about his punctuality now and ruin this fine evening. Her heart had been pounding with anticipation of their sleigh ride home tonight.

The women filed out of the kitchen, carrying various plates and bowls of food to put on the long buffet table. Roasted turkey, sliced pine-apple ham, sauerkraut and pork, and venison made up the meats, and *yummasetti*, baked yams, mashed potatoes, green beans, and peas made up the side dishes. The feast was like Christmas all over again. Even the children had flocked to the cheese and pickle trays, their tiny hands snitching a few samples before the meal was blessed, while their mothers hovered nearby, chiding them for their actions.

A niggle of jealousy stabbed Catherine's heart. One day she would have a few sticky-fingered culprits to wag her finger at. Of course, she'd told herself *one day* for years and it hadn't changed the fact that at twenty-nine, she was the oldest *maedel* in her district.

Don't dwell on such negativity. Everything could change after tonight's sleigh ride. She wrung her hands, suddenly eager for the meal to get started and, more importantly, for it to end.

The bishop's wife, Alice Zook, was the last to come out of the kitchen. She placed a steaming dish of brown gravy on the table, then nodded at her husband, who stepped forward.

Bishop Zook cleared his throat, signaling everyone's attention. "Shall we bow our heads and ask the Lord's blessing over this *wunderbaar* food the women have prepared?"

Catherine closed her eyes. *I know You hold the future, Lord. I pray it's Your will that Zach wants to include me in his future.*

The bell over the door jingled, and a gust of cold air sent a shiver down her spine. Boots stomped, muffling the tune the latecomer whistled as he entered. Catherine didn't have to open her eyes to know who it was. She recognized the man by his off-pitch tune.

Elijah Graber.

The latecomer blew into his fisted hands. His hat, coat, scarf, and pants below the knees were snow covered. As Elijah stood at the entry, his gaze flitted across the room and stopped on Catherine.

Sharpness seized her breath. After six years, why would he search her out in the crowd first? Years of wondering what it would feel like to see him again flooded her senses, and for the split second that their gazes connected, everyone else in the room disappeared.

Rein it in. You feel nothing. Nothing.

Catherine narrowed her eyes on the man. *At least be respectful of others, Elijah, and bow your head.*

As if reading her thoughts, he dropped his hands to his side and lowered his head for the final seconds of the blessing.

Once the bishop cleared his throat again, his way of signaling the end of the silent prayer, conversations and activity around the room resumed. Except for Catherine who was frozen in place.

Elijah shivered and snow fell from the brim of his straw hat. Removing the knitted scarf from around his neck exposed his big red ears, which contrasted with the pale, purplish tinge on his lips. But what caught her off guard was his beard.

She focused on the puddle that had formed from his stomping snow off his boots, a hazard that needed to be addressed immediately. As other members greeted Elijah, Catherine dashed into the kitchen, grabbed the mop from the utility closet, then returned to the dining room.

Still standing at the front door, Elijah looked up from brushing snow off his pant legs as she approached. "*Hiya*, Cat." He smiled as if there'd never been a moment of distance between them.

Before she had the chance to return a formal greeting, Bishop Zook came up to Elijah and patted his shoulder. "It's *gut* to see you again, Elijah."

"Same here."

The bishop glanced at Catherine a brief second, then continued. "I trust your trip to Posen went well."

"The roads were snowy, and for a while there was talk that Mackinac Bridge might close due to high winds, but we made it fine."

"How long will you be staying?"

This time it was Elijah who looked at her uncomfortably. "I'm, ah, *nett* sure."

This was agonizing. She expected any conversation she might have with Elijah to be stilted, but she hadn't expected Bishop Zook to guard his words. Why didn't he just go ahead and ask Elijah about his wife and children?

"Again, it's *gut* to have you home. Hopefully we'll have a chance to talk more later." Bishop Zook motioned to the table of food. "*Nau* don't be a stranger. Jump in line and fill your plate while the food is hot."

"*Jah*, I'll be sure to join you shortly."

Once the bishop left to rejoin some of the other married men, Catherine mopped up the trail of water he tracked across the floor. Elijah hadn't moved from the doorway when she went back to finish cleaning up the entrance area.

Elijah lifted one snowy boot, then the other. "I made a mess, didn't I? Would you like me to mop it up?"

"*Nay*. I'll get this." She motioned to the other married men filling their plates. "You should go eat. I'm sure a hot meal and mug of *kaffi* will warm you up."

"That's nice of you to be concerned. I've been meaning all week to stop by your *haus* and say hello."

All week? Catherine harrumphed. "It's a little late to tell me you got married."

He scratched his whiskered jaw. "*Jah*, I've been meaning to—"

She glared.

"It's a long story."

"I'm sure." Obviously he hadn't changed. He was always itching to tell long stories. Well, this time she wasn't interested. Six years ago when he'd told her he needed to visit an out-of-town friend, she hadn't expected to read in *The Budget* newspaper a few weeks later that he'd gotten married. She redirected her attention to the wet floor and shoved the mop around.

"I'll get out of your way," he said, yet didn't move. When she purposefully swabbed the area next to his boots, he finally sidestepped the mop. "Nice seeing you again, Cat."

She stopped cleaning the floor and straightened her posture, but just as she unclenched her teeth to speak, he was swarmed by other members welcoming him home.

"*Mei* name is *nett* Cat," she muttered to herself.

She finished sopping up the melted snow, then returned the mop to the utility closet in the kitchen. After taking a moment to relax her breathing and slow her racing heart, she turned to head back to the dining area, but a shadowy figure moved out from behind the row of storage shelves.

She clutched her chest, hissing his name in a sharp gasp. "Zach!"

"Were you expecting someone else?" Zach stepped closer.

"I—I wasn't expecting someone to be lurking in the shadows. I thought you were in line getting food with the others." Her hands trembled as she wiped them on the side of her dress.

"*Jah*." He lifted his plate, dumbfounded by her sudden lack of observation skills. "I did." He hoped catching her off guard was all that was wrong and her jumpiness didn't have something to do with Elijah's return. "I didn't mean to startle you. I figured I'd say hello and tell you that I'm looking forward to our sleigh ride tonight."

"You are? I mean, I'm looking forward to our ride too." She tucked a stray strand of her honey-colored hair under her prayer *kapp*. "When you didn't arrive right away I started to think something had happened."

"I had an important business matter to take care of and lost track of the time." He stabbed his fork into a chunk of carved turkey, his mouth watering. He'd been so preoccupied tinkering with a customer's antique pocket watch that he'd skipped lunch. Although his stomach complained, he was happy that word had started to spread about his clock and watch repair services.

"Business on New Year's Eve?"

"I'll tell you all about it later. But now you should get something to eat. I don't want to stay long." He had to wake up earlier than normal tomorrow morning. The man was coming to the shop to pick up his watch, and Zach wanted to give himself enough time to adjust it if it wasn't keeping perfect time.

"*Jah*, I'm sort of anxious to leave early too." Catherine's cheeks turned a rosy shade before she spun around, her dress hem swinging around her ankles with her quick turn.

He took another bite of turkey and followed Catherine through the swinging doors, but as she went toward the food line, he veered over to the table where his long-lost friend Elijah was seated.

Zach clapped Elijah on the shoulder. "Nobody whistles like you."

"You mean off-key."

"Exactly." Zach set his plate on the table, then plopped down beside him. "I heard you were in town."

"*Mammi* guilted me into being here for her birthday. She told me, 'One doesn't turn one hundred years old every day, you know.'"

Zach chuckled. "I'd say *nett*. How long do you plan on staying?"

"A week, maybe two—maybe all winter if I can't get *mei mammi*'s buggy out of the ditch. The driveway was like a big frozen pond. The buggy skated into a pile of snow at the bottom of the ditch—at least I think it's the ditch."

Zach opened his mouth to take a bite of food but lowered his fork. "The mare didn't get hurt, did she?" He recalled Elijah always trying to race his family's horse and goading Zach into doing the same. But on snowy nights like tonight, no way. Even with runners on his buggy, Zach always went slowly.

"The old mare is fine. I put her back in the barn. Hey, you think you could give me a ride back to *Mammi*'s when this is over?"

"Ahh . . ." So much for Catherine and his moonlight sleigh ride. "*Jah*, sure."

"I can find someone else to take me, or I'll walk

if you have other plans," Elijah said, buttering a dinner roll.

"*Nay*, that's okay. But I want to make it an early *nacht*. I have to work in the morning." He ate a spoonful of buttery mashed potatoes while pondering how he'd tell Catherine their plans now included driving Elijah.

"Still making clocks?"

Zach nodded. "I repair watches *nau* too."

"That's great. I always knew you would do well." Elijah pushed his empty plate aside and picked up his coffee mug.

"What about you? I seem to recall you wanted to train horses."

"Still want to . . . one day," Elijah muttered as he stood. He motioned to the dessert table. "I think there's a piece of apple pie calling *mei* name."

Zach continued eating. When Elijah didn't immediately return to eat his dessert at the table, Zach scanned the crowd and found him standing with the married men and engaged in a conversation with the bishop. A scene all too familiar to Zach. His other friends had migrated to the married side of Sunday services and gatherings after they married, too, as if an unwritten rule forbade them from hanging around their unmarried friends once they passed over to the other side.

Sure, he could join the group by marrying

Catherine, and several of his friends had encouraged him to do so, but he wasn't one to do things to appease others. Besides, up until the other day, his business wasn't stable; he couldn't support a wife. But for some reason, watching his once best friend huddling with the others irked him. Elijah—his so-called friend—had never bothered to tell him he'd gotten married. Zach read the announcement in *The Budget* same as everyone else. Zach finished cleaning off his plate, then picked it up and went to the buffet for seconds.

Catherine approached the serving table from the opposite side. "Have you tried the pork pie?"

"I haven't yet. Did you make it?" Catherine's grin told him she had before she confirmed it with a nod. Zach reached for the spoon.

Usually he asked Catherine what she brought and selected those dishes first, but tonight she'd been busy cleaning the floor when he was in the serving line selecting his food. He scraped the bottom of the dish to get the last few morsels of pork gravy and crust. "This looks *gut*."

"I hope you like it."

He smiled. "I don't think you've made anything I haven't liked." He took a bite and nodded. "It's *gut*." Just as tasty as when she had served it to him a few weeks ago when she invited him for supper at her brother's house.

A gust of cold air filled the room as several men went outside, then reentered a moment later.

Bishop Zook raised his hand. "Folks, may I have your attention? The weather appears to have gotten much worse. I suggest we conclude the evening activities as soon as possible."

Zach wasn't concerned about the amount of snowfall. The runners he'd mounted on an old open buggy would glide over anything. Besides, he had a blanket for warmth and lanterns to help guide the way. Perhaps the get-together ending early was a blessing. He did need to get up early and double-check the watch he'd been working on.

Within minutes the women had the tables cleaned off and the place tidied up. As children were dressed in their outerwear and shuttled to the buggies, the room emptied quickly. Zach shoved his arm into his coat sleeve. He spotted Elijah being handed a covered dish by the bishop's wife. Knowing Alice Zook's motherly concern over the flock, she would insist on them giving Elijah a ride to his grandmother's house once she heard about him going into the ditch. Zach smiled at the thought of not having a third passenger in his sleigh tonight after all.

He scanned the area for Catherine and spotted her talking with her cousin Faith. He sidled up beside them as they were discussing restaurant operations.

"Last winter we struggled badly," Faith said. "Closing is for the best."

"You're closing the restaurant?" Zach divided his attention between Catherine and her cousin, who looked equally somber.

Faith nodded. "We don't do enough business in the winter to pay the fuel bill, and the township won't allow us to install a woodstove. *Mei* parents and I have prayed about it, and . . . it's only for a few months. We plan to reopen in April or May."

"That's *nett* so bad." Zach studied Catherine's strained expression. She was no doubt worried about her loss of income. She'd been a cook at the restaurant for more than fifteen years, and since both of her parents had died, she had given most of her paycheck to her brother to help with household expenses.

"Perhaps we can get together and sew. I want to make a few things for *mei* hope chest." The blush on Faith's face said there was more, but with Zach in the midst, she wasn't about to blurt what he already knew. Gideon had asked him to make a grandfather clock for a wedding gift Gideon planned to give Faith. Of course, Zach had promised to keep their news a secret until an official announcement was made.

"Sure." Catherine's voice cracked. Did she suspect her cousin was engaged? She was always fast to get choked up at weddings. *Maedel* tears.

Faith glanced over her shoulder in Gideon's direction. "Gideon is putting on his coat. I'd better get mine on too." She turned back to Catherine and reached for her hands. "I'm going to miss talking with you at work every day, but we're going to get together regularly, right?"

"*Jah*, for sure." Catherine had gained better control over her voice now that she had time to think about it.

Zach leaned closer to Catherine as her cousin walked away. "The months will go by quickly—you'll see."

Elijah joined them. "I just need a second to grab *mei* coat and I'll be ready." Elijah faced Catherine and extended the covered dish the bishop's wife had given him. "Do you mind holding this?"

Her hands remained at her side.

"Please," he added after her brows puckered in what looked like confusion.

Accepting the dish, she faked a smile. When the corners of her mouth twitched, it wasn't because she was happy.

As Elijah crossed the room, a steeled expression replaced her smile.

"He needs a ride," Zach said.

"And there's no one else?" Her gaze traveled around the room. "Isn't one of his cousins here? Why couldn't Elijah—?"

"He's staying with his *mammi*, and her *haus* is only a couple miles down the road from your *bruder*'s place. Besides, I'd hate for someone else to go out of their way on a *nacht* like tonight."

If she hadn't just received news of the restaurant closure, he would have thought she was still holding on to the past the way her voice quivered saying his name. "Do you want me to hold the dish?"

"*Nay*, I'm fine."

Guilt wiggled through him like a hooked worm. Expecting those two to sit side by side on the same bench peacefully might have been foolish. He scanned the dwindling crowd for his sister, but Mary and her *bu* had already left, which was too bad. Elijah would have made a perfect chaperone for his younger sibling. Still, even they would be going out of their way—on icy roads. Catherine would understand. She was a practical woman. Besides, Elijah was married. What could they hash out now? "I'll take you on a sleigh ride another day—just the two of us. Okay?"

Disappointment flickered in her eyes, but she nodded, then immediately dropped her gaze to the floor.

"I'm ready whenever you are." Elijah broke the silence with his upbeat tone.

Catherine handed the dish back to Elijah, then wrapped her knitted scarf around her neck and head, covering her entire face except for her eyes.

Outside, the restaurant sign flapped in the wind. A few inches of snow had collected on the buggy bench in the short time Zach had been inside.

He swept the snow off with the small broom he kept under the seat, then held Catherine's hand as she climbed onto the bench. The lap quilt he'd stowed under the bench was cold and snowy, but he offered it to her anyway. She declined. Apparently, being sandwiched between him and Elijah had given her two windbreakers.

Elijah did the majority of the talking on the ride, mostly about the changes he'd noticed in the community since he'd been home last. "Was your *bruder* there tonight, Catherine? I didn't see him."

"George and Gwen decided to stay home. *Mei* niece wasn't feeling well."

"Bit by the flu bug?"

Catherine shrugged.

"And your *mamm*, how is she?"

"Elijah." Zach cleared his throat hard. "Catherine's *mamm* went on to be with the Lord three years ago."

"I'm sorry. I didn't know."

"You don't live in Posen. How could you know?" Not waiting for Elijah's response, Catherine pulled her cloak up higher around her neck and lowered her head, a sure sign she was finished with the conversation.

Silence fell over the three of them during the last few miles of the trip. Zach pulled into Catherine's driveway, stopped in front of the house, then jumped off the sled. He reached for her hand. "Watch your step. The runner is slippery."

"*Danki* for the ride home," she said through chattering teeth.

"I'll walk you to the door." He wanted to be out of earshot when he apologized again for the change of plans and told her good night.

"*Nay, danki.*" Instead of going inside, she sprinted to the barn.

Cold air numbed his senses. He stared at the space she'd fled, his brain taking several seconds to register what had just happened. Nay danki? *When had she become so formal?* He headed to the barn.

A soft glow of lantern light flickered on her face as she removed a horse blanket from the wall peg and took it inside the mare's stall. "It's going to be a *kalt nacht*, Cocoa." She hooked the lantern handle on a nail, then placed the cover over the horse.

Zach entered the stall, squatted down, and helped tie the straps under the horse's girth. "I wish you weren't upset with me." He rose when she did.

"I understand Elijah needed a ride to his *mammi*'s . . ."

"But?"

"But I'm a bit surprised you dropped *me* off first. Shouldn't it be the other way around? I thought this being New Year's Eve . . ."

"Your *haus* is the closest. I'd have to double back if I took him home first."

Catherine pivoted so her back was to him.

"This isn't like you," he said. "What's wrong?"

She was silent a moment, then her shoulders lifted with a raspy inhale and sank again as she released her breath. She faced him. "I thought you were going to propose on Christmas, and when you didn't, I thought maybe you would surprise me on Second Christmas. But I was wrong—again."

He opened his mouth, but she continued.

"You made a point to tell me how much you were looking forward to our sleigh ride tonight, so of course I figured for sure this was the *nacht*—the *nacht* you would propose."

He swallowed hard.

She placed her hands on her hips and stared into his eyes. "We've courted almost five years. I'm ready to get married. Are you?"

Chapter 2

Shock registered across Zach's face. "You're proposing . . . to me?"

Catherine lowered her head, and despite the draftiness in the barn, her cheeks and neck blazed with embarrassment. She should have thought this through. Maybe if she'd waited he would have come to the decision on his own—eventually.

"Catherine, is that what you're asking?"

She lifted her head. "*Jah*, Zachariah Lantz, I asked you to marry me. To be *mei mann*."

His brows furrowed. "What's gotten into you? You sound . . . desperate."

She gulped. Her words spurted out similar to how blood gushes from a fresh cut. Only she didn't have a tourniquet for her mouth. Perhaps Elijah showing up unexpectedly and then asking about her mother had pushed her over the edge. Had he thought nothing changed since he'd left the community? Many things hadn't; she was still working at The Amish Table, still living at home, and still single. Seeing him again highlighted her stagnant life.

Catherine shifted her attention to Cocoa and adjusted the blanket a little higher on the horse's neck. The mare's thick winter coat would keep her warm, but the blanket would make Cocoa more comfortable against the wind that howled outside the barn. And adjusting the blanket gave her something to do to help relieve the pressure from Zach's stare.

"Can you name one other woman who has proposed? Did Annie, Agnes, Doris, Phoebe?" As if driving a nail, he continued hammering out the names of her friends, cousins, and any other married woman in the district.

"*Nay*," she muttered, focusing her complete attention on Cocoa. "Just me—the desperate one."

"Catherine." He drew her name out in a pitiful tone.

She cringed. Couldn't he just let it go? She'd already made a complete fool of herself.

"I'm merely trying to point out how unacceptable it is for a woman to be so . . . so bold."

"Point taken." Her friends and relatives were right when they teased about her old-maid status. She never wanted to believe she wasn't marriage material, but nothing had worked. Even her cooking hadn't won Zach over. She'd invited him to supper numerous times, prepared his favorite meals, but his praise for the tastiness of the food hadn't encouraged a proposal from him.

Oh, Lord, this isn't how I wanted to start the

new year. Will I ever be able to forget this nacht? *Will he?*

Zach cupped his hands over her shoulders and turned her to face him. “Patience, Catherine. Don’t fret over the future.”

She forced a smile, but her mouth twitched after a few moments. Anymore it seemed patience had become part of her name. *Patience Catherine.* Zach should understand why her patience had worn thin. Why she was desperate to get married. She wanted children—lots of children. But obviously he had no inkling how pressured women her age were to get married. Especially those living under their brother and sister-in-law’s roof—imposing on their family time. In a few months, she would turn thirty, and even she understood that the invisible timeline of someone marrying her was fading. She’d be an old maid, living out the rest of her life in her brother’s house, under his care.

“It’s getting late, and Elijah is probably freezing by *nau*. I should go.” Zach leaned closer and planted a soft kiss on her forehead. “Happy New Year.”

“*Jah*, Happy New Year to you too.” She stepped back, distancing herself from the warmth of his closeness, and straightened her shoulders. “I don’t want to keep you.”

He placed his hand on her lower back. “I’ll walk you to the *haus*.”

She planted her feet. “I’d rather stay here awhile longer.” The old barn was cold and drafty, but she wasn’t ready to go inside yet. She dried her eyes with the edge of her wool cloak, flinching as the scratchiness irritated her skin.

“I’m sorry to disappoint you.”

“No need to apologize.” Hearing his deep sigh, she turned to Cocoa and gave the mare a pat on her neck. “You don’t need to worry. I won’t be so bold as to propose to you again.”

The clanging sound of a metal bucket skittering across the barn’s cement floor drew her attention. She spun around to find Zach’s mouth hanging open in stunned silence.

“Sorry.” Elijah stepped out from the shadow of the equipment room. “I tripped over a grain bucket.”

“You were spying on us!” Catherine rasped.

“Well, *nay*. *Nett* intentionally.” He pointed his thumb over his shoulder in the door’s direction. “It’s freezing out there.”

“I left you a blanket,” Zach snapped.

“It’s wet, and . . .” He looked at Catherine with those penetrating blue-gray eyes of his, which had a way of seeing straight through her. “I, ah . . . I think I’ll . . .”

Silence hung between them before Zach snipped, “You’ll what?”

Elijah stared a half second longer at Catherine

before turning his attention to Zach. "I'm gonna walk the rest of the way to *Mammi*'s."

Catherine couldn't do much about how puffy and blotchy her eyes must look, but she stood straighter and squared her shoulders. "You don't have to walk home. Zach was just leaving."

She stormed past Zach, then Elijah—the two men who had broken her heart.

Elijah trudged through the snow toward the sleigh alongside Zach. "What was that all about?"

"Nothing."

It wasn't nothing. Elijah climbed onto the sleigh and sat on the bench. "You made her cry."

"Like you haven't?" Zach ground the words under his breath, but Elijah knew enough to clamp his mouth shut and leave things alone. He didn't need anyone reminding him how badly he'd hurt Catherine. Past decisions had plagued him with daily reminders. Still, it pained him to see tears clinging to her lashes—especially when she was trying so hard not to show her emotions.

Elijah wished now he hadn't gone to The Amish Table for the get-together. Other than his parents and *mammi*, Catherine and Zach were the main people he wanted to see, and neither of them offered much welcome. Now he wished he had slipped into the district, spent a few days visiting his family, then hopped the first bus out of town without seeing anyone else.

"I'm sorry. I shouldn't have *kumm* into the barn," Elijah said.

Zach tapped the reins and the sleigh lurched forward.

Something was eating at his friend, but Elijah wasn't sure if he should bring it out in the open or leave things alone. Besides, it wasn't like he could offer relationship advice; he'd certainly made a mess of his life.

"I think the temperature has dropped more."

"Probably," Zach muttered.

Neither spoke until they reached *Mammi*'s farm, and then Zach only muttered something about the tracks leading into the ditch as he stopped the sleigh. Without verbalizing his thoughts, he unhooked the lantern and climbed off the bench.

Elijah circled around the back of the sleigh. "What do you think?"

Zach shone the lantern over the area. "Doesn't look damaged."

"That's *gut*." The old buggy had seen better days. The worn top was cracked to the point of seeing snow flurries inside the buggy before the accident, and he couldn't imagine riding in it during a rainstorm. Even so, he would have felt awful if he had bent a wheel or done major damage. His grandmother didn't go out by herself anymore, but she did lend the horse and buggy to neighboring youth who offered to go into town for her groceries and supplies.

"I don't think it'll be difficult to pull it out. I'll *kumm* by tomorrow," Zach said.

"*Danki*, I appreciate it."

"It won't be early. I have someone coming by the shop in the morning to pick up an order."

"So, you're open on New Year's Day?"

"Every day but Sunday."

"*Nett* much free time."

Zach snorted. "It's the only way to build a business."

Elijah hadn't meant to sound judgmental. Lately he had *too much* free time on his hands. He wished he had clear goals again—and a horse training business to build.

Thankfully when Catherine went into the house all was quiet. Her older brother, George, and his wife, Gwyneth, had already put the children to bed and had turned in themselves. Otherwise they would have been full of questions. Especially Gwen, since earlier Catherine, in her excitement, had slipped and shared how she hoped Zach would propose tonight during their sleigh ride.

Catherine tiptoed upstairs and went into her bedroom. The moment she stepped into the room, she flopped onto her bed and buried her face in the feather pillow to muffle her sobs.

Lord, I'm so confused. If I'm nett *to marry Zach, then what is* mei *purpose? To cook at The*

Amish Table the rest of mei *life?* She cried harder as the prospect of her thoughts coming true cemented in her mind.

"Closing is for the best." Faith's words mocked Catherine. Only moments ago she'd whined about being a cook the rest of her life—forgetting that she was jobless. *Ungrateful.* She sobbed harder. Now how would she be able to help George with the bills? He'd taken the brunt of their mother's financial responsibility when complications from diabetes had claimed her foot, then her leg, and finally her life. At least the money Catherine had earned working at The Amish Table helped pay the household expenses.

She reached for the box of tissues on her bedside table and yanked one out, then blew her nose. "No job. No *bu*. No purpose. *Nau* what?"

Catherine pushed off the bed, changed into her nightdress, then crawled back into bed, burying herself under the covers. Her eyes filled with tears once more, and the tissue couldn't absorb them fast enough.

The door creaked open, and her five-year-old niece poked her head inside. "*Aenti* Catherine, are you awake?"

Catherine coughed to push down the lump clogging her throat. "*Jah*, *kumm* in, Julie."

The child padded over to the bed.

"Are you *nett* feeling well?" Her niece had been feverish earlier. Catherine placed her hand on the child's forehead. "You don't feel as hot as you did earlier."

"I heard a noise. Can I sleep with you, *Aenti*?"

Catherine flipped back multiple layers of blankets and patted the mattress. "*Kumm nau*, before you wake your parents."

Her niece snuggled next to her under the covers, warming her cold feet on Catherine's legs.

"Where are your socks, child?"

Julie simply giggled and wiggled her toes more against Catherine's skin. Her playful gesture brought a smile to Catherine's face. At least her niece seemed to be feeling better. It wasn't long before Julie fell asleep.

Catherine wished she could close her eyes and not see the scorn on Zach's face. After the blunder she'd made, she wished she could move to another district and start a new life—if only that were possible.

Chapter 3

The following morning Catherine slipped out from under the bedcovers and gasped at the sudden chill. Sleeping next to Julie had been like sleeping next to the cookstove. The poor child's fever still lingered, even after a night of alternating sweats and chills.

Catherine sat on the edge of the mattress with her feet dangling to postpone the initial contact of her bare feet on the plank floor. Cold winter mornings such as today made her wish she could crawl back under the covers and stay put the entire day.

Yawning, Catherine glanced over her shoulder at Julie. Her niece had ended up tossing in her sleep for several hours, not settling until her tiny arms were wrapped around Catherine's neck and she was blowing wisps of nasal-clogged breaths next to Catherine's ear. She studied the girl's rosy cheeks and red lips. Thankfully she hadn't awakened Julie when she untangled herself from the child's grip.

Catherine eased her toes onto the floor first, then tiptoed over to the chair where she had removed her wool socks and left them to dry last night. Shivering, she shoved her feet into the woolen footwear. While some people splashed cold water on their faces in the morning to get their blood flowing, all she had to do was step on the chilly floor.

Catherine changed out of her nightclothes without opening the curtain or lighting a lantern to illuminate the darkened room. She wasn't even sure what dress she had selected off the wall peg, but it didn't matter. She wasn't going into work today. It wasn't important to look her Sunday best. Then again, if Zach dropped by for a visit—and he probably would, to apologize for his brash response last night—she would want to look presentable. After all, he would have had time to think about her proposal, and perhaps he changed his mind.

Catherine opened the curtains and took a good look at what she was wearing, then decided to change into a better dress. She carefully brushed her hair and formed it into a bun, then fastened her prayer *kapp* in place. Yes, she wanted to be ready when Zach came calling.

She padded down the stairs, the warm air greeting her as she neared the kitchen. Her sister-in-law had already stoked the cookstove and was busy preparing breakfast when Catherine joined her.

"Well?" Gwen stirred pancake batter. "I want

to hear all about your evening. Did he ask?"

Catherine shook her head. She wasn't prepared to share that she'd been the one to propose to Zach, or how he promptly rejected her.

"I'm sorry."

"*Jah*, me too." She opened the cabinet door and removed a stack of plates, then counted out the utensils for the three adults and three children.

"How was the get-together? I suppose everyone showed up but us."

Everyone plus one unexpected out-of-towner. "It was better that you stayed home with Julie. It ended early because of the weather." Catherine went to the window and glanced at the snow blowing across the driveway.

Gwen came up behind her and peered over her shoulder. "Do you see George?"

"*Nay*," she said with a yawn. "I was just interested in how much snow had fallen overnight. It's gotta be below zero. If you listen closely, you can hear the wind howling."

"Poor George. I'm sure even with all the hay insulating the barn, he's still *kalt*. I probably should have made oatmeal."

"We still have time. Do you want me to put a pot of water on to boil?"

"*Nay*, I already mixed the pancake batter, and there's no sense making both." Gwen covered her mouth with her hand as she yawned. "Your yawning is catchy. I take it you didn't get much sleep last *nacht*. What time did you get home?"

"Early." She went to the stove to check the percolator. She needed a mug of coffee to wake her up. In time, she would tell Gwen. Then again, Zach would stop by later, and they would be able to smooth things over between them.

Gwen placed the cast-iron griddle on the stove and added a few pats of butter while Catherine filled two mugs with coffee. She handed a mug to her sister-in-law. "Would you like me to wake the *kinner*?"

"*Nay*, let's give them a few extra minutes." Gwen took a sip of coffee, then set her mug back down on the counter while she worked the melting butter over the surface of the skillet. Once the pan was coated, she poured the pancake batter.

The kitchen door opened and George stepped into the house, bringing in a gust of cold air with him. Clumps of snow fell from his boots as he stomped them on the rug. Even so, snow trailed his stocky frame over to the counter where he placed the galvanized milk canister. "It's another *kalt* day. The milk is already chilled." He removed his coat, gloves, and hat and hung them on the wall hook. George glanced around the kitchen with a frown, then poked his head into the sitting room. "Where are the *kinner*?"

"I thought they could use more sleep." Gwen readied her husband's plate with a stack of golden pancakes.

George's frown deepened. "Are they all sick *nau*?"

Catherine couldn't help but wonder if the worry lines marking her brother's forehead were of a financial nature. George had worried almost nonstop ever since the crops failed. It was bad enough to lose them to drought the season before last, but this year the harvest yield wasn't enough to feed the livestock all winter let alone bring in extra money. The crop catastrophe on top of *Mamm*'s unpaid hospital bills had put a hardship on the family and was probably what caused her brother's hair to gray prematurely. Catherine had gladly offered her paycheck each week to help with the household expenses, but her brother rarely took it all. He insisted she have spending money of her own.

"Jimmy started coughing and became feverish in the middle of the *nacht*," Gwen said, stacking the golden pancakes on a platter. "I think this bug is going to run through the entire household before it's over."

Lord, let it nett *be so.*

George washed his hands at the sink. Her brother was a stickler for the entire family getting up at sunrise and sharing the morning chores, whether it be assisting Gwen and herself with meal preparations, as ten-year-old Leah was tasked to do while five-year-old Julie wiped the table, or bringing firewood in from the woodshed, as seven-year-old Jimmy did each day. By the time George finished the morning milking, hands were washed, breakfast was on the table, and everyone was ready to eat.

George took his place at the table, and Gwen was quick to place the plate of pancakes before him along with a small jar of warm maple syrup.

Catherine poured him a mug of coffee, then sat next to Gwen. They bowed their heads in unison and silently asked the Lord's blessing over the food. Catherine asked for the children to be healed of the flu and a made a special request that she find another job. Because, unlike Faith, she wasn't planning a wedding, and it wasn't as if she had pot holders to sew for her already-full hope chest.

"How bad do you think the roads are?" Gwen asked once they were eating.

He shrugged. "The end of the driveway is drifted shut, but I noticed the Kings' buggy heading toward town earlier and saw Bishop Zook going in the opposite direction. The county plows must have cleared the main roads. Do you need to go somewhere?"

"I was hoping you would be able to pick up a few things in town," Gwen said.

"Does it have to be today? I don't want to be away from Jasmine when she starts calving. We nearly lost her last time she delivered."

Catherine poured maple syrup over her pancakes. "I can go. What is it you need?"

"I have a list started. Mainly cough and cold products for the *kinner*."

"There's supposed to be another snowstorm coming through later today," George said between bites of food. "Another foot or two is what I heard."

Catherine ate a little faster. More snow meant the roads would be slippery. If she waited too long, George would insist she stay home. She couldn't risk the children going without medicine.

A few minutes later, her brother finished his pancakes, drained his mug of coffee, then pushed away from the table. He put his coat, hat, and gloves back on. "I'll shovel the driveway and hitch the buggy for you."

"*Danki.*" Catherine braced for the rush of cold air that swept inside with his exit. She sipped her coffee.

Gwen scooted across the room and came back to the table with pen and paper. "I'm adding a few packets of yeast to the list. If we're going to get another storm, I don't want to be without bread." As she made the notation on paper, she said, "You never told me how your sleigh ride with Zach went."

Catherine frowned. "He offered to drop Elijah Graber off at his *mammi*'s *haus*—and *mei* stop was the closest, so he dropped me off first."

Her sister-in-law's eyes widened at the mention of Elijah's name, but as she opened her mouth to speak, Leah lumbered into the kitchen holding her belly and complaining of a sour stomach.

With Gwen distracted with checking her daughter's forehead for a fever, Catherine stood and collected the dirty dishes.

Her nephew staggered into the kitchen next, yawning.

Catherine set the dishes in the sink. She spotted George at the end of the driveway shoveling a path through the snow. It would be a while before she could leave. Catherine set the frying pan on the stove, added enough butter to coat the pan, then poured little pancakes from the leftover batter. "Your breakfast will be ready in a minute."

"*Nau* Leah has a fever." Gwen removed the liquid acetaminophen from the cabinet, eyed what little remained, then measured the dose and tossed the empty bottle into the trash.

Julie toddled into the kitchen and sat down just as Catherine was setting the pancakes on the table, but the children only picked at their meals.

Gwen sighed. "I think they'll all be heading back to their sickbed for sure." She winked at her youngest. "Maybe I'll join them for a nap."

"I hope you're *nett* getting sick too," Catherine said.

Gwen placed her hand on her belly. "Didn't I say it would go through the *haus*?"

"I'm keeping *mei* distance," Catherine teased, covering one hand over her nose and mouth and snatching the supply list off the table with her other. She went to the door and put on her boots, wool cloak, scarf, gloves, and winter bonnet. "I'll try *nett* to be too long."

Catherine gazed at the gray clouds hovering overhead. George was probably right about another storm looming. Snow crunched underfoot as she made her way to the buggy her brother had already hitched.

"Try to keep your eye on the weather." George handed her the reins.

"*Jah*, I will."

"Don't give the horse too much rein, and don't drive on the shoulder of the road where the snowplows have banked the snow."

She knew those things. George was overly cautious. She'd been driving a buggy on the main road during sleet, snow, and heavy rain without any issues for more than fifteen years. But since *Aenti* Irma and *Onkle* Mordecai's buggy accident last year, her brother had become increasingly more cautious.

Their narrow country road proved challenging, but once she reached the main road, the pavement had been plowed and salted. Their community was blessed to have one store open on New

Year's Day. Since the Yoders lived over the market, they were open year round except for Sundays and Christmas.

Catherine parked on the side of the brick building and hurried inside. The bell above the door jingled, alerting Melvin Yoder, the store owner, to look her direction. He waved, then resumed his conversation with the person at the register.

After tossing her handbag into a shopping cart, Catherine headed for the cough and cold aisle first. She scanned the shelves. There were so many products that all claimed to reduce fever, clear congestion, and relieve sore throats.

When Catherine was growing up, *Mamm* didn't use store-bought products. Instead she lathered up her *kinner* with strong-scented balms that never failed to open their nasal cavities. Catherine also recalled the licorice-tasting drinks that caused her eyes to water, not to mention the cayenne pepper that sent a ball of fire down her throat with each swallow. But Gwen didn't like using unproven remedies on the children, especially since she was convinced that *Mamm*'s death had something to do with the homemade concoctions interfering with her diabetes.

Catherine compared the prices on the bottles, chose the least-expensive brand, then continued shopping. As she placed the items in the cart, she mentally tallied everything together. Deciding she had enough money of her own to splurge, she selected a small bag of peppermint candy for the children while waiting in the checkout line.

"Tonight's snowfall is supposed to double last *nacht*'s," Melvin said to the Amish man he was ringing up at the register.

Catherine groaned under her breath as she placed the items from her cart onto the counter.

"Winter is *mei* favorite season," the man said. "It's yours too, isn't it, Cat?"

Her spine stiffened as the customer glanced at her. With a scarf wrapped around the lower part of his face and his straw hat pushed down over his ears, she hadn't recognized Elijah.

He loosened his scarf. "Do you still like to go ice skating on the pond, *Catherine?*"

She glanced nervously at Melvin, then narrowed her eyes at Elijah. If his memory was so keen as to recall her favorite season and her favorite pastime, then why didn't he remember that saying anything in front of Melvin was equivalent to talking openly at a quilting bee? Men were not innocent when it came to gossip and spreading the word about her talking to Elijah—a married man.

She cleared her throat. "I haven't skated in—" *In six years*. "I work full-time."

Melvin announced Elijah's total, which drew his attention away from her.

She unloaded the remaining items from her

shopping cart, and when Elijah said goodbye to her and Melvin, she pretended not to hear.

"The temperature is dropping. I hope you're heading straight home." Melvin repeated the same weather predictions to her.

"*Jah*, I am."

"Elijah Graber hasn't changed much."

Other than the beard. She waited for Melvin to give the total due, then handed him cash. "Are you hiring? The Pinkhams are closing The Amish Table until April or May, and as you know, I've been a cook there several years. I know how to use a cash register."

"Business is slow this time of year, but I'll keep you in mind."

"*Danki.*" She picked up the grocery bag and headed out the door. Rounding the corner of the building, she plowed into Elijah's chest. Catherine stifled a squeal but couldn't calm the quiver in her voice. "What are you doing loitering by *mei* buggy?"

"Waiting"—he placed his hand over the left side of his rib cage—"for you."

Chapter 4

Elijah hadn't expected Catherine to come flying around the corner of the building, let alone plow into him and steal the air from his lungs. He held his hand against his throbbing ribs and gingerly took a deep breath. "What's in that bag, a block of cement?"

"Flour." She clutched the grocery bag with both arms and stepped backward. "And sugar—and why are you waiting for me?"

Another bad start. "I'm sorry I startled you, Cat. I was hoping we could talk."

"This isn't a *gut* time. There's a storm moving in." She went to the back of her buggy and opened the latch.

"*Jah*, so I heard." As she placed the shopping bag inside the buggy, he moved closer, preventing her from being able to shut the hatch. "Catherine, couldn't you spare a minute or two? I promise *nett* to keep you long."

The woman was skittish. First scanning the area as if nervous about being alone with him, then avoiding eye contact by looking at the ground.

"Please?"

Catherine eyed him briefly, then lowered her head again. "Say what you came to say."

"I, ah . . ." The words caught in his throat. Starting a difficult conversation with someone unwilling to look him in the eye made the situation even more awkward. Partly why he'd stayed away from Posen so long was fear of not finding the right words. *You weren't the reason I left town . . . I liked where our relationship was headed . . .*

No, he couldn't lead with that. Their relationship was in the past—buried. Until a few weeks ago when memories too difficult to ignore hounded him. As though an inner voice was urging him to come home—to make amends with Catherine—he obeyed God's prompting. Yet here he was tongue-tied. Everything he'd rehearsed to say, he couldn't.

"It's snowing harder. We both need to get home," she said.

"I'm sorry about your *mamm*'s passing. What happened?"

"The *doktah* said she had multiple organ failure from being a diabetic."

She took a jagged breath, and his throat tightened. When she looked nervously around again, he said, "I hope I don't make you feel uncomfortable."

She huffed.

"When I asked for a ride home from the get-together last *nacht*, I didn't realize you and Zach were . . . courting." He'd been led to believe Catherine spent all her time cooking at The Amish Table. Elijah couldn't put his finger on what was wrong with Zach last night, but the tension between them made it difficult even to make small talk. Now he questioned if it was God who had prompted him to return to Posen. After all, this wasn't his home, but neither was Badger Creek.

"And you were surprised I moved on *after six years?*"

Her words caught him off guard, and he shook his head. "*Nay*. Of course I'm *nett* surprised. Zach's a *gut* man."

"Yes, he is." She nodded stiffly as if affirming her words as much to herself as to him.

The image of tears budding on her lashes last night had prevented him from getting much sleep. She had tried so hard to conceal her emotions in front of him that he couldn't help but wonder if his return had caused the friction between Zach and her. "I know you were upset last *nacht*. I'm sorry if it had anything to do with me."

"You? Why would you think—never mind." Muttering something under her breath, she marched to the front of her buggy where she untied her horse. "I'm going home, and judging by the amount of snow falling, you'd best do the same."

He reached for her arm as she was about to climb into her buggy, the simple touch sending shocks through his system. "I know I deserve your *kalt* shoulder, but part of the reason I returned to Posen was . . . to see you—to find out how you're doing."

Catherine looked him hard in the eye, then at his hand on her arm before returning her icy glare to meet his gaze once again.

Message received. Elijah released her arm, then opened the buggy door. "I won't be staying in Posen long."

"I didn't expect you to." She took the reins in her hands but paused before releasing the brake. "Did you *nett* think I would read about your marriage announcement in *The Budget*? After reading about your nuptials, I couldn't bring myself to pick up a newspaper again. You could have written me a letter and told me yourself." Without giving him a chance to respond, she released the brake, clicked her tongue, and never looked back.

As her buggy disappeared down the road, Elijah sighed. Catherine might not ever give him a chance to make amends. He ambled to the back of the building where he'd parked his buggy.

Lord, forgive me. I'm the reason she's bitter. She's stored up anger over the years, and I deserve her unleashing it on me. But, Lord, You know mei *heart. I never meant to cause her pain.*

When I married Edwina, I didn't even know our wedding made The Budget *until her* mamm *pointed it out.*

The road before her turned into a washed-out haze of whiteness as Catherine struggled to focus her tear-filled eyes. She'd never been one who embraced change, and recently she hadn't been given a choice—everything had changed. For all she knew, The Amish Table was closed for good. Faith could easily decide she wanted to stay home after she and Gideon married.

Lord, mei *life is unraveling. It's as though a rug has been pulled out from under* mei *feet. I'll be an old, unmarried maiden with no job—nothing to contribute to the household fund. I made a fool of myself to Zach, then bumping into Elijah, I made a fool of myself in front of him as well.*

Catherine clamped her lips together. Not that God didn't know her thoughts—she just didn't wish to voice what had been swirling in her mind since Elijah's return. Yet, try as she might, Catherine couldn't stop the deluge of buried memories from bubbling to the surface.

The rhythmic clip-clopping of Cocoa's hooves faded into the background as memories replayed of the last day she and Elijah had spent together.

A foot of snow crunched under their feet as they walked hand in hand down the snow-covered cow path toward the pond. Elijah was uncharacteristically quiet, and his slumped shoulders should have cued her that something was wrong. He hadn't engaged her in a snowball fight or found a reason to kiss her once they were out of sight of the house and barn as he usually did.

"Elijah, please tell me what's wrong."

Wisps of cold air lingered around his mouth with each exhale. Although he wasn't speaking, his lips moved, and then all at once his facial expression sobered—as if he'd lost a debate with himself. When they neared the edge of the water, Catherine pointed to the thin layer of ice that had formed over the surface. "Looks like it won't be long before I can try out the ice skates you gave me for Christmas."

Elijah smiled, but it faded all too soon. "I need to make a trip to Badger Creek."

"When?"

He tapped his boot on the icy shoreline, breaking through the layer and soaking the toe of his boot in the process. "I'm catching the bus in the morning."

Badger Creek, a hundred miles north in the Upper Peninsula, was the small district where he'd grown up. She'd heard him tell of how his father had worked for a local sawmill, but because work was scarce in the winter, he moved their family to Posen four years ago to become potato farmers.

"How long will you be gone?"

Elijah pulled her into his arms and, placing his hand on the back of her neck, gently brought her closer. "I'll be back before the pond freezes over," he said before capturing her mouth with his chapped lips.

His lingering kiss sent rippling impulses from the top of her head down to her toes and would have uprooted her had she not held on tighter when his kiss deepened. She broke from the kiss, her lips tingling and insides trembling. "You know the pond isn't that deep. It'll be frozen solid in another week or two."

"And I'll be back to watch you skate." He leaned in to kiss her again, but Catherine pulled back.

"You promise?" She blinked back tears that threatened to fall and reveal the depth of panic over his impending departure.

He held her gaze. "*Mei* heart is yours forever."

A car moved into the passing lane, splattering slush against the side of the buggy and jolting

Catherine back to the present. *Englischers* were always in a hurry.

Cocoa jerked her neck forward, pulling more reins and increasing her pace. *Pay attention to the road.* If Cocoa hit a patch of black ice at this current speed, the mare would lose her footing and the buggy would end up in the ditch or worse—in front of oncoming traffic.

Catherine regained her grip on the reins, determined not to let the horse have her way again. She had to somehow push these thoughts of Elijah aside. After all, wallowing in the past—over Elijah—would only bring her trouble. And yet the more she tried not to think about him, the more she dwelled on what he had done.

Elijah lied.

His intention was never to return. She'd been a fool to think his heart belonged to her. Why he decided to come back now was of no interest to her.

Now, *she'd* lied—to herself.

Her body stiffened. Elijah shouldn't have this effect on her. He chose his path. Listening to any of his explanations now was useless. Rumors would swarm. Folks would assume she was somehow tangled in his unfaithful behavior. Once Zach heard the scuttlebutt, he would assume the rumors were true. He would never change his mind about marrying her.

Had it been another baptized member of their

flock, the bishop would see that the individual stood before the members of the church and made amends for his actions. Even though Elijah was no longer a member of their district, he should still be made accountable. Perhaps someone needed to bring it to Bishop Zook's attention.

Chapter 5

Zach disregarded the bishop's dismissal of the congregation and tried to block the noise around him as members shuffled to their feet and conversations started. His heart had been heavy since Catherine's proposal, and he needed God to reveal why. He'd confessed to overreacting, saying hurtful things, making her cry, but even after asking God's forgiveness, things still felt unsettled deep in his soul.

Father, forgive me for not paying attention to the service. I didn't listen to any of the Scripture readings or the bishop's message. I shouldn't have allowed mei *thoughts to wander. I feel so ashamed . . .*

Elijah nudged Zach's shoulder. "You coming?"

Zach pushed to his feet and caught a glimpse of Catherine talking with the bishop's wife. The two women made their way to the side door of the barn and disappeared from sight.

"You look tired." Elijah elbowed him. "Late *nacht*?"

"*Jah*," Zach replied, determined not to share the reason. Let Elijah think what he wanted. Despite how at one time they were close like brothers, now they weren't even good friends. For whatever reason, Elijah had distanced himself from Zach and everyone else in the district, and apparently Elijah never felt it necessary to give a reason why.

Zach craned his head to look beyond Elijah. The benches on the women's side of the barn had emptied quickly, the women dashing off to the Pinkhams' house to prepare the afternoon meal. But the men's side of the barn was still congested with people blocking the aisle. None of the men seemed interested in leaving the barn, and for a good reason—the temperature outside hadn't risen above zero. Zach looked behind him. He'd make his exit through the milking parlor.

"Hey," Elijah said. "Where are you going?"

He stepped over the bench. "I'm going inside the *haus* to get in line for the meal." *And to ask Catherine what she was doing in the alley of Yoder's Market with Elijah.*

"*Gut* idea." Elijah followed. "I'm looking forward to trying the tuna casserole I noticed earlier on the table."

Zach weaved around a small group of teenagers.

Elijah continued to talk. "It's been a long time since I heard one of Bishop Zook's messages. It's nice to sit under his charge again."

Zach waited until they were inside the milking parlor and out of earshot of the other members before stopping to face Elijah. "I went by your *mammi*'s farm the other day to pull the buggy out of the ditch but was told you had gone into town."

"*Jah*, young Paul King next door ended up helping me dig out. I should have stopped by your shop to let you know. Sorry."

Zach shifted his stance and crossed his arms, his unspoken words burning a hole in the pit of his stomach.

"I knew you were busy," Elijah continued. "You mentioned on Friday *nacht* that you were meeting a customer in the morning, and I figured—"

"Did you go into town to see Catherine?"

Elijah stiffened.

"Did you?"

Elijah's cheek twitched. "I took a chance that The Amish Table was open and went into town thinking I'd have *kaffi* . . . And yes, I thought if Catherine wasn't too busy . . . But the restaurant was closed."

Zach furrowed his brows. "What went on in the Yoder's alley?"

Elijah flinched, but Zach didn't care how uncomfortable the man was feeling. He glared steadily at him.

"It's been a long time since I've seen Catherine. I just wanted a chance to catch up on old times."

"That's inappropriate—you're a married man."

Elijah closed his eyes and shook his head. "*Nett* anymore. *Mei fraa* went home to be with the Lord."

Zach's lungs emptied in one long exhale. Again, his onetime best friend didn't think to share that sooner. He recalled how he hadn't found out about Elijah getting married until Catherine stormed into his shop six years ago and cornered him with the newspaper, demanding that he—Elijah's best friend—tell her everything. Zach had nothing to share. Elijah had kept his plans hidden from them both.

But this wasn't the time to bring up any of that. Elijah had lost his wife, and by the way Elijah's eyes glazed over with tears, Zach could see that he wasn't dealing with the loss very well.

"I didn't know." Zach softened his tone. "I'm sorry for your loss. Did she pass away recently?"

"Elijah." The bishop stood in the entrance of the milk *haus*. "May I have a word with you, please?"

Elijah wiped the wetness from his eyes. He wasn't sure how much he could talk, being choked up the way he was, but the bishop's tone seemed urgent.

"I'll leave you two to talk." Zach turned to go out the opposite exit. Apparently his friend had picked up something in the bishop's tone as well.

Bishop Zook clasped his hands together. "As I said yesterday, your visit has made your *mammi* very happy."

Elijah braced for a "but" in the statement.

"I know technically you're no longer an active member in our district, but when there's a grievance between two members—"

"Grievance, you say?" Elijah groaned under his breath. *Zach.* He must have gone to the bishop after finding him with Catherine in the alley. No wonder he scurried off like a barn rat when the bishop asked to have a word. "I think I can explain."

"Please, do."

"Zach wasn't aware that *mei fraa*, Edwina, had gone on to be with the Lord. He saw me talking with Catherine in town and . . . jumped to the wrong conclusion." Noticing the bishop's brows anchored at a slant, he further explained. "After being gone so long, I was probably overzealous wanting to . . . reconnect with old friends. Under the circumstances, Zach believed his concerns were legitimate."

He stopped short of suggesting Zach had been motivated by jealousy. But if the bishop wasn't aware of Zach and Catherine courting, Elijah wasn't about to snap that trap. Especially since couples often kept their relationship a secret in the beginning.

"It wasn't Zach who voiced concerns."

"I see." Then it had to be Melvin Yoder, who could have glanced out one of his storefront windows when Elijah had left the parking lot shortly after her. Tongues had wagged for lesser offenses.

"Catherine spoke with Alice, who then brought it to *mei* attention."

Elijah lowered his head as heaviness filled his chest. He'd made a mess of things in the short time he'd been back.

Bishop Zook placed his hand on Elijah's shoulder. "Perhaps you need to consider sharing the news about your *fraa* with the others—when you feel ready, of course."

Elijah nodded. "If it's okay with you, I think I should do it *nau*."

After her conversation with Alice, Catherine lost her appetite. Guilt gnawed the lining of her stomach, and now acid was climbing the back of her throat. She'd deliberately fed information to the bishop's wife, knowing that Alice wouldn't hesitate to take the news directly to her husband. Sure, Elijah had blocked the back of her buggy so she couldn't close the hatch, in order to talk, but he hadn't actually cornered her in the alley as Alice might have concluded.

Catherine added a heaping spoonful of brown sugar into the crock of baked beans and stirred the mixture. Zach's sister, Mary, wedged in beside her and leaned closer. "You look pale. Are you feeling okay?"

Nay, she was sick, and not from the flu. She should have prayed about her decision to confide in Alice. "I—I'm roasting. I need some air."

"I'll go with you." Mary twined her arm with Catherine's as they stepped onto the back porch. "I have some news, and I want to tell you first."

Catherine took a deep breath, then coughed when the icy air seized her lungs.

"You okay?"

She nodded.

"Robert proposed on New Year's Day." Mary squealed. "I've been floating on air ever since."

"That's *wunderbaar* news!" Catherine smiled—until reality stole her joy. Come spring both Faith and Mary would be married. Catherine was the last of the trio, and judging by Zach's reaction, she wouldn't be sharing news of an upcoming wedding anytime soon.

"We haven't told anyone yet, so please keep the news to yourself." Mary's face held a warm glow. "I'm sure people will find out soon. You know how difficult it is for me to hold on to secrets."

"Floating on air"—must be nice. The resentment chilled Catherine to the bone. She shivered. "It's colder out here than I thought. We should *geh* back inside."

"*Jah*, let's." Mary practically skipped to the door.

Once inside, Catherine picked up a basket of yeast rolls off the counter and walked them into the sitting room to place on the serving table. Most of the men were milling around, talking in small groups. She spotted Zach a few feet away, but the moment their gazes connected, he turned his back to her. She had wanted to believe the snowstorm had kept him away the past five days, but his reaction was all too clear—she had really messed up by proposing the other night.

Oh, Lord, I see nau *how wrong it was to propose and* nett *trust Your plans for* mei *life. Please forgive me, Father, but please convict Zach of his shortcomings too.*

Catherine cringed. She couldn't expect God to work in Zach's heart when she was still carrying bitterness in hers toward Elijah.

The front door opened. Bishop Zook stepped inside, followed by Elijah. The bishop removed his coat, but Elijah did not. He stood stiffly with his hands clasped in front of him and his head down.

"Folks, if I could have your attention." Bishop Zook waited for the conversations to stop and for the women to file out of the kitchen. Once he had everyone's attention, he continued. "Before we pray over the food and enjoy our fellowship meal, Elijah would like to say a few words."

This should be interesting to hear. Catherine crossed her arms. Half expecting Elijah to hurl daggers at her when he looked up, she was taken aback by his doleful expression. The lines across his forehead crinkled as if he was searching hard for where to begin.

Elijah cleared his throat. "As many of you know, I used to live here in Posen. I've been gone a few years, but I still have strong ties in this community." He looked across the room, his gaze stopping on his grandmother, who had fallen asleep in the rocking chair next to the woodstove.

A faint smile appeared, then faded as Elijah turned his attention back to those gathered around him. "I didn't want *mei* visit to disturb anyone, but it's been brought to *mei* attention that tittle-tattle has reached some of your ears. Please know that I meant no harm when I tried to visit an . . . an old friend. I certainly never wished to taint that individual's reputation." He paused long enough to take a breath. "What most of you don't know is that while it's true I did get married in Badger Creek a few years ago . . ."

Six years ago, Catherine held back from voicing aloud.

"*Mei fraa* has gone on to be with the Lord. She was sick . . . several years." He forced a smile. "But she's in a better place—she's healthy and strong." He turned and coughed into his fisted hand, and when he looked up his eyes were brimming with tears.

Catherine's throat swelled with emotion. Guilt threaded her veins. Elijah standing before the congregation, baring his soul, was her doing.

Bishop Zook clapped Elijah's shoulder. "*Danki*, Elijah. I know talking about losing your *fraa* was difficult. We offer our support and prayers."

Elijah nodded. "If you don't mind, I'd like to say one more thing." His gaze locked on her. "I'm sorry I made you feel uncomfortable, Catherine. I hope you'll forgive me."

It seemed everyone's eyes had turned toward her, awaiting her response. She sought out Zach in the crowd, only to find indifference in his stare. Thankfully, the bishop broke the tension by asking everyone to bow their heads in prayer for the meal. Silence filled the room.

Catherine lowered her head, but it seemed forever before she could find the right words. *Had I given Elijah a chance to talk, he probably would have told me privately.*

The bishop cleared his throat, signaling the end of the prayer before Catherine had the chance to thank the Lord for the meal. Her eyes were still closed when someone nudged her arm. She muddled through a quick "*Danki*, amen" and looked up.

"What was that all about?" Mary raised her

brows. "How did Elijah make you uncomfortable?"

"I'll fill you in later. *Mei* head is pounding." Catherine pressed her hand against her temples. "I need a drink of water." She dashed into the kitchen, but instead of removing a glass from her *aenti* Irma's cabinet, she grabbed her cloak from the pile of winter wear and put it on. She needed more than water to dilute the acid clawing her throat.

Mary came into the kitchen. "Are you leaving already?"

"I'm *nett* feeling well. Will you tell Gwen I've gone home?" She wrapped her scarf around her neck.

"Should I get Zach to drive you?"

"*Nay*." She sounded a little panicked to her own ears. "Let him eat with the others." She reached for the doorknob. "I'll talk with you soon."

Catherine breathed easier once she was outside. The chilly air numbed her face as she hiked the mile-long route home. Normally she would have avoided the main road and cut through the fields that joined the properties, but today the snow would be too cumbersome and getting home would take too long. Even walking along the roadside was challenging. Approaching traffic forced her over to the shoulder and into a bank of thigh-high snow just to keep safe. She lost feeling in her toes.

Usually a quick walk helped clear her mind. Not today. She struggled to sort her thoughts—Zach's avoidance in particular. Questions popped one right after another like kernels of corn under heat. Had she proposed to Zach in some sort of panic? In fear of loneliness, or in desperation, as he had said? Was there more to Zach's cold shoulder?

Catherine's feet came out from under her and she fell backward. Her head smacked the ground. As she sat up, sharp, wave-like pulses radiated from the back of her skull to the front.

You have to move. Roll into the ditch if you must, but get off the road. Black spots filled her vision.

Chapter 6

"Are you hurt, miss?"

Catherine squinted up at the broad-shouldered man hovering over her and grimaced. Blinding light obscured her vision. It wasn't until he crouched beside her that she noticed his bushy red hair and his amber, almost glowing, eyes. Drawn to the glimmer of gold flecks dancing around his pupils, she forgot about the throbbing knot on the back of her head.

"Should I call for an ambulance, miss?" Lines in his forehead rooted his weathered skin. "Miss?"

A high-pitched buzzing sound filled her ears, blocking out the stranger's deep baritone voice. She cupped her hands over her ears, but the ringing didn't stop. If anything, the sound intensified.

The good Samaritan placed his large hands over hers. Despite lying on the frozen ground, being wet, cold, and shaky, the moment his calloused hands touched her, she warmed from within. He uttered a string of gentle, undecipherable words, then moved his hands away from hers.

The ringing stopped, and a sweet scent filled her senses.

She quickly pushed off the ground. "How did you—?" A wave of dizziness washed over her at the same time her knees went weak. The man must have sensed her wooziness, because just as her legs buckled, he reached out and steadied her with his strong hand.

"You need not ask how," the elderly gentleman said, "but instead, turn your eyes upon your loving Father in heaven and give Him praise."

Catherine closed her eyes. *Father,* danki *for watching over me, and for sending this stranger to help. Please continue to keep me safe. Amen.*

"'The LORD is good to all; he has compassion on all he has made.'" The man pointed to a young sparrow perched on the top of a fence post. "'Look at the birds of the air; they do not sow or reap or store away in barns, and yet your heavenly Father feeds them.'"

"Even in the winter," she added.

"Are you not much more valuable than they?"

Was she? Surely God had to be disappointed in the way she'd treated Elijah. She recalled Elijah at the gathering, standing in front of the members, how his eyes had moistened and how he kept touching his throat as though manually trying to push a lump aside in order to talk.

The songbird's chirping caught her attention. Perhaps the little bird was singing its own praises to God. "Don't you find it odd that it didn't migrate south for the winter with the other sparrows?"

When the man didn't reply, she glanced over her shoulder. The stranger was gone. *How can that be?* A shiver cascaded down Catherine's spine as she looked in both directions down the road. Had she hit her head so hard on the ice that she'd simply imagined the red-haired man? The sweet fragrance, which she recognized as lilac, engulfed her senses. For sure her mind was playing tricks. Lilacs didn't bloom in winter.

Prompted by a nudge on her arm, Catherine peeled back the covers without opening her eyes and made room on the mattress for her niece. This was becoming a habit. Julie had to learn to sleep the night in her own bed. But instead of feeling her niece's warm little body snuggle up beside her, Catherine felt a second, deeper poke on her arm. She opened her eyes a smidgen, but a flood of blinding sunlight prevented her from focusing on the five-year-old.

"It's time to eat, *Aenti* Catherine."

Catherine climbed out of bed. It had been two days since she'd fallen on the ice, and her head was still swirling and her joints ached as if she'd been trampled by a plow team. She touched the back of her head. The egg-sized bump hadn't gone down. She smiled at Julie. "Tell your *mamm* I'll be down in a minute. I have to get dressed."

A few minutes later Catherine lumbered into the kitchen. "I'm sorry for waking up late again, Gwen." She went to the sink and washed her hands, then tied an apron around her waist. "What would you like me to do?"

Gwen glanced up from the stove. "Aren't you going to be late for work?"

Catherine shook her head. "You didn't hear that *Aenti* Irma and Faith closed the restaurant for a few months?"

Gwen removed the pot of oatmeal from the stove. "When did they decide to do that?"

"Faith told me on New Year's Eve. I figured they would have said something on Sunday." She filled a mug with coffee.

"The topic of everyone's conversation wasn't the restaurant."

"Let me guess. Elijah?"

"And you." Her sister-in-law picked up her mug of coffee and motioned to the table. "Let's sit down and talk. George is tending the new calf. He won't be in anytime soon."

Catherine followed her to the table. "Is something wrong?"

Gwen shrugged. "I don't know what's gotten into Jasmine. Ever since she gave birth, she's been pushing the babe away. George has had to bottle-feed him every couple of hours."

"*Ach*, that's *nett gut*."

"I agree. The special milk it requires is costly." Gwen sighed. "I guess it is what it is."

"I'm going to look for another job. I asked Melvin Yoder, and he's going to let me know."

"Your *bruder*'s worried about you. So am I."

"I have some money saved up—"

"It's *nett* about the money," Gwen said. "Called out the way you were in front of everyone on Sunday, I would have expected your face to take on more of a beet shade, but yours turned as white as bleached sheets."

Catherine massaged her throbbing temples with the tips of her fingers with no relief.

"Is there something going on between you and Elijah?"

"*Nay*." Catherine shook her head for emphasis but stopped when what felt like shards of heated glass seared her head, making her cringe.

"Catherine, are you okay?"

"I have a headache." Gwen would ask too many questions if Catherine admitted to falling on the ice and a stranger stopping to help her, so she kept that information to herself. Besides, it wasn't just the lump on her head causing the pain. It had been a week since her proposal, and Zach hadn't so much as looked her in the eye. "Would you mind if I skip breakfast? I think I need to lie back down."

"Sure." Gwen's brows knitted. "Do you

need something for your headache—aspirin or Tylenol?"

"I think if I lie down a little while, I'll be fine." Medicine wouldn't dull her heartache. Only Zach could heal that pain. Catherine took her mug to the sink and rinsed it out.

"Before I forget." Gwen moved to the basket where she kept the mail. "A letter came for you yesterday. It's postmarked from Florida." She handed Catherine the envelope.

"*Danki*." Catherine glanced at her cousin's handwriting. She hadn't heard from Dawn since last fall. Heading up the stairs, Catherine opened the letter.

> Dear Catherine,
>
> I hope this letter finds you well. The weather here has been cool, some days only in the sixties and seventies. I suppose I shouldn't complain to a northern Michigander. I hear from some of our customers at the bakery (whom we call snowbirds down here) that your area has had a lot of snow this year. I so wish you would come stay the winter with me. I could sure use your help . . . Our bakery has expanded. We're open for lunch now, serving sandwiches and specialty salads, and we hope to add more items to the menu soon . . .

Catherine continued reading, but her thoughts had stalled on the sentence about Dawn needing her help. Maybe going to Florida was the answer to Catherine's dilemma. It would be an adventure, traveling so far away—a new journey.

Chapter 7

The following morning Catherine devoured a large stack of buttermilk pancakes, the thick maple syrup giving her a much-needed boost of energy. Last night she had stayed up late writing a letter to her cousin, and once the kitchen was tidied up, she planned to head into town to mail it. She half expected her brother and sister-in-law not to agree with her decision to go to Florida. Even she'd admit her response was rather spontaneous. Still, leaving town seemed the only answer to her problems, and she had prayed about her decision, although not with her usual fervency. Humming softly, Catherine slid the forked piece of pancake around her plate, sopping up the maple syrup.

"You certainly seem chipper this morning, Catherine. I'm glad you're feeling yourself again." Gwen passed the plate of sausages to George, who took a few small patties and passed the plate on to Leah.

Catherine swallowed the bite of pancake with a drink of milk. "*Jah*, I feel much better, *danki*." She glanced at Julie seated beside her and winked. Her youngest niece had once again awakened in the middle of the night and ended up sleeping with Catherine.

George pulled the pancake platter closer, then stabbed his fork into one and transferred it to his plate. Focused on eating, he'd been quiet since coming in from the morning milking. That wasn't unusual, but Catherine sensed something was lying heavily on his mind. Gwen must have sensed it too, because she finished eating faster than normal and was pushing the children to do the same.

Moments like this made Catherine wish she had her own place, then maybe she wouldn't feel as if she were imposing. Not long ago George had talked about converting one of the smaller sheds on the property to a *daudi haus*, only it wouldn't be fixed up for a grandparent but would become her home. Although she'd been grateful her brother offered to give up one of his equipment sheds, at the time she believed she wouldn't be living with them long since she and Zach had been courting seriously for more than a year. Refusing to revisit the latest turn of events, she pushed her chair away from the table, stood, and then collected the dirty dishes.

"Catherine, I'd like to have a word with you." George motioned to her vacated chair. "Please sit down."

"Okay." She glimpsed Gwen shuttling the

children out of the kitchen. No doubt Elijah's speech the other day had something to do with this meeting. Catherine set the stack of plates back on the table and returned to her chair. Her brother, ten years older, had taken on the fatherly role in her life at an early age, and over the past few years, he'd begun to look like *Daed*, often sharing the same deadpan expression.

She cleared her throat. "What would you like to talk about, George?"

"You know how fast gossip spreads in our district and the problems it tends to create."

She held up her palm to stop him. "Before you continue I just want to say that I"—she swallowed hard—"I don't know what came over me to *geh* to Alice. I knew she would tell the bishop . . . but seeing Elijah again had brought back so many hurtful memories, and he kept seeking me out. I didn't know his *fraa* had passed away."

George picked up his mug, brought it to his mouth, but paused. "I think Bishop Zook was the only person he'd told."

"I acted impulsively." She shrugged. "I was wrong. I'll speak with him and apologize."

George drained his coffee mug, then stood and went to the sink where he filled it with tap water. He gazed out the window a long moment before turning to face her. "The reason I asked to speak with you was to find out if it's true that you proposed to Zach Lantz. Is it?"

The muscles tightened in Catherine's neck and shoulders, sending a dull, pulsating throb to her head. *Not another headache.* It had taken hours for the last one to subside.

"Catherine?"

"*Jah*, it's true—I acted impulsively about that too." Heaviness filled her chest as Zach's betrayal sank in. Why did he tell anyone, especially her brother?

George sighed. "That impulsiveness is exactly what worried Zach. You haven't been acting yourself lately. Is there something else going on?"

Besides Zach's rejection, The Amish Table closing . . . Elijah? "I, ah . . . I need a change." She lowered her gaze to the breakfast crumbs on the floor.

"What do you mean by change? What sort of *change* are you looking to make?"

"Our cousin Dawn has invited me to *kumm* to Florida. She needs help in her bakery."

"You've never gone that far before."

"George, I'm twenty-nine years old. And I prayed about the trip. The change will do me *gut*."

He frowned. "Have you told Gwen?"

"I planned on telling her after breakfast." She leaned back in her chair to look into the sitting room. "I don't see her. Should I *geh* get—"

He shook his head. "I didn't want little ears

listening to our conversation. Leah is at an impressionable age, and I certainly don't want her getting it in her head that it's okay to propose to a man."

"Then *mei* leaving will be *gut* for everyone." Catherine picked up the stack of plates, walked over to the sink, and lowered them into the basin. More dirty dishes waited to be picked up from the table, but she couldn't face the disappointment she would see in his eyes. Instead she watched a pair of cardinals pecking at seed in the bird feeder outside the window. Such beautiful creatures with their bright red wings and black masked faces, a stark contrast to the snowy backdrop. It always amazed her how birds knew instinctively when to fly south, and how some, like cardinals, didn't migrate at all.

Snowbirds . . . Catherine smiled, recalling her cousin's description of Florida-bound northerners. Going to Florida to work wasn't technically a vacation, but who knew? Perhaps this snowbird would not migrate home at the end of the season. *Jah*, a one-way ticket was all she needed.

After her purchase, Catherine thanked the woman at the ticket booth, then proceeded across the small lobby while at the same time double-checking the departure date and time. The disclaimers at the bottom of the ticket caught her attention. Not that she planned to change her mind about going to Florida before Thursday, but she'd never taken a bus before and wanted to be prepared.

Her eyes strained reading the small print. *Nontransferable, nonexchangeable. Budget Bus has the right to cancel without prior written notification in accordance with—*

Catherine's arm brushed against something sturdy, and when she looked up, Elijah greeted her with a wide smile. The ticket fluttered from her hand to the floor, and he squatted down to retrieve it.

"I'm beginning to think there's something magnetic between us." He looked the ticket over as he stood. "We seem to be drawn to each other."

Ignoring his comment, she snatched the ticket from his hand. "I'll take that, *danki*."

"Who's going to Florida?"

"You looked at *mei* ticket?"

"Sorry." He opened his mouth as if to say more but didn't utter more than a few undecipherable syllables before clamping his mouth closed, his lips forming a tight line.

"I'm going to visit *mei* cousin in Sarasota." *Not that it's any of your business.* Catherine jammed the ticket inside her handbag. "What are you doing here anyway?"

"I told you I wasn't planning to stay long."

"You're leaving before your *mammi*'s birthday celebration? I thought that's why you came back."

He scratched his bearded jaw. "Things change."

"*Jah*, things change," she echoed absent-mindedly. "I'm sorry about your *fraa*." *About involving the bishop . . .*

"I didn't mean to make you feel uncomfortable. I hope you believe me."

She nodded. "I got that message—along with the entire congregation," she mumbled under her breath. Heat infused her face, recalling how everyone had shifted their attention to her.

"Making that speech wasn't exactly *mei* idea, but I am glad you know the truth *nau*."

Having been put in her place and not especially proud of her actions, she averted her gaze to the floor. "Elijah, I was the one who—"

"Ratted me out?"

Catherine looked up to find him grinning. "You knew it was me?"

He nodded. "I tried to find you afterward, but you had gone home."

"I wasn't feeling well."

"And here I thought you were just avoiding me."

Catherine smiled. She liked that he could joke with her again, especially after seeing how choked up he'd been on Sunday when telling everyone about his late wife. Questions still lingered as to why he promised to love Catherine forever yet married someone else, but she resisted the temptation to unearth his motives. The relationship they'd shared was buried long ago, and while digging it up could answer some questions, the pain of unearthing the truth might be more than she could endure at the moment.

He glanced toward the ticket booth. "I see there's no line. I should probably go purchase *mei* ticket. It was nice to see you again, Cat."

"You too." She took a few steps and turned. "Elijah?"

He spun to face her. "*Jah*."

"Couldn't you postpone your trip a little longer? You shouldn't miss your *mammi*'s birthday. Even if she sleeps through most of the celebration, it would still mean so much to her for you to be home."

"You think so?"

"*Jah*, I do. Unless you have somewhere important you need to be." She looked beyond him at the ticket booth, and even though he glanced over his shoulder, he didn't volunteer any information about his travel plans, and she couldn't bring herself to ask.

He stepped closer. "Will you still be in town?"

"I leave Thursday." The get-together for his grandmother was planned for Wednesday. Birthdays in their district were kept simple. Never before had the members come together for such an event, but since so many people talked about wanting to shower Irene with cards to celebrate her one hundredth birthday, an exception was made.

He wagged his brows in a teasing manner. “Maybe I’ll see you there?”

“Perhaps.” As a playful smile tugged at her lips, warning alarms blared in her head. Why couldn’t Zach have the same easygoing nature?

Chapter 8

Catherine's suitcase sat against the bedroom wall, packed since the day she purchased her ticket. The only thing left to decide was the items to take in her carry-on.

Catherine flipped through the informational brochure she'd been given at the time of booking the trip. Most of the items on the things-to-take list didn't apply to her. She wouldn't be listening to music, watching downloaded movies, or playing video games, so electronic devices, headphones, and batteries weren't necessary. Except for the *Farmers' Almanac* and the Bible, she wasn't much of a reader. Two full days on the road would be boring with nothing to occupy the time. She considered packing her knitting needles, but Budget Bus policy clearly prohibited sharp objects. Catherine ran her finger over the rounded end of her crochet hook, then slipped it into the carry-on tote bag along with two large balls of navy yarn.

The bedroom door opened, and Julie shuffled into the room, having just woken up from an afternoon nap. Her lips puckered into a frown.

Catherine lifted the girl's chin. "What's wrong, sweetie?"

"I don't want you to go, *Aenti*," Julie whimpered.

Seeing tears collect on her niece's lashes tugged Catherine's heart. "I won't be gone long, and I'll bring you, Leah, and Jimmy something back from Florida."

Julie swiped a tear off her cheek. "You will?"

"Absolutely, but you have to promise to be a *gut* girl while I'm gone and help your *mamm*."

"I will."

She reached for Julie's hand and gave it a tug. "Let's go downstairs and see if your *mamm* and *schweschaler* are ready to make cookies."

Always eager to bake sweets, Julie's face lit with a wide smile. The two of them descended the stairs hand in hand. Although Catherine was looking forward to baking cookies with her sister-in-law and nieces, she wasn't looking forward to going to the birthday celebration for Elijah's grandmother. She had too many things left undone, or at least that was the excuse she'd given Gwen earlier today when she arranged for Gwen to take the card and gift with her.

Under different circumstances, Catherine would have enjoyed watching Irene unwrap the scarf she had made, but staying home was for the best since in order to get to the bus station in the morning on time, she needed to leave the house before daybreak.

A sweet scent of cookies filled the air as Catherine and Julie made their way into the kitchen.

Gwen and Leah rolled small balls of chocolate chip cookie dough and placed them on cookie sheets. "We decided to make peanut butter, chocolate chip, and sugar cookies," Gwen said. "That way, you'll have some to take with you on your trip."

"*Gut* idea. They'll make a nice treat." Catherine washed her hands at the sink. She had planned to pack a couple of sandwiches, an apple or two, and whatever she could find that wouldn't spoil to take on the trip. The bus made regularly scheduled stops, according to the information packet, but she would cut down on expenses by bringing her own food.

Julie pushed a chair next to the counter and climbed up on it, but Gwen redirected her to the bathroom to wash up before helping.

Catherine tied an apron around her waist. She needed to remember to pack an apron to take to Florida. Once she arrived, she would be busy in her cousin's bakery. She looked forward to working with new recipes. The menu items hadn't changed much since she had started cooking at The Amish Table, and all of those she had already committed to memory.

Hands still wet, Julie climbed up beside Catherine and picked up a spoon. Her dress sleeves dripped from washing up in a hurry, but Catherine pretended not to notice.

Leah scooped a spoonful of dough from the bowl. "What type of sweets will you be making in Florida, *Aenti* Catherine?"

"Fancy pastries and turnovers. Maybe donuts. Dawn said she would teach me how to decorate cakes. Apparently their bakery sells a lot of special-occasion cakes to the *Englisch* folks."

"Best be careful *nett* to sample too much," Gwen said.

"*Jah*, I'm going to try *nett* to." Her sister-in-law's warning was a gentle reminder of the diabetes that ran in the family. *Mamm*'s sweet tooth in the end caused much more pain than pleasure.

Catherine handed Julie the eggs to crack over the bowl, then picked out the pieces of shell that fell into the batter. She took her time and let Julie do as much as possible. When it came time to sift the flour, her niece shook the sifter like a salt shaker, and flour went everywhere.

Gwen eyed her youngest daughter when the white powder landed on her.

"I should have demonstrated first." Catherine dabbed a white dot on the end of Julie's nose. "I think I'd better finish this part. You can make the crisscross pattern with the fork."

Julie relinquished the flour sifter and watched as Catherine measured out the rest of the ingredients. By the time they slid the first pan of peanut butter cookies into the oven, Gwen and Leah had started working on the sugar cookies.

It took most of the afternoon to bake several dozen cookies, and after sampling more than she should, Catherine had no appetite for supper. Gwen and the girls indicated they weren't hungry either, but they all worked to *reddy-up* the kitchen and get supper on the stove.

A short time later, the girls had the table set, and Gwen and Catherine had a pot of chili bubbling on the stove and a loaf of corn bread cooling on the counter. Like clockwork, George came in from doing the evening chores.

Gwen looked up from stirring the chili. "Where's Jimmy?"

"I sent him out to fetch the mail." George removed his coat, hat, and boots. As he took his place at the table, Catherine was ready with a mug of coffee. "*Danki.*"

"How's the *wedder*?" Catherine asked.

"*Kalt.*" He picked up the mug of coffee and blew over the steaming surface. "I don't think it'll snow tonight, if that's what you're wondering."

"That's *gut.*" If the bus trip was canceled due to a storm . . . She pushed the thought from her mind.

The door opened and Jimmy scooted inside, a

fistful of envelopes in his hand. He handed the mail to his father, then slipped out of his boots and coat.

George sorted through the stack, then set the mail aside except for an envelope he held up. “This letter is yours, Catherine.”

“Just set it by *mei* plate, please. I’ll get it in a minute.” She finished slicing the warm corn bread, then set it and the butter crock on the table. Gwen came behind her with the chili, and Leah and Julie with milk-filled glasses.

As Catherine sat down, she recognized Dawn’s handwriting on the envelope. Had her cousin changed her mind about needing help? Catherine’s stomach tumbled. Unable to eat more than a few nibbles of food, she pushed her bowl of chili aside.

Gwen motioned to Catherine’s bowl with her spoon. “You’re *nett* hungry?”

“Too many cookies.”

George shifted on his chair, straining his neck to look toward the jar on the counter. “What kind did you make?”

“Chocolate chip, peanut butter, and sugar,” Gwen replied. “But those are for taking to Irene’s birthday celebration. You didn’t forget, did you, George?”

“*Nay*, I didn’t.” He seemed less than enthusiastic as he slathered butter on another slice of corn bread, then took a bite.

"Is there gonna be cake?" Jimmy asked.

"None for you if I don't see you eat your supper," his father said.

Her nephew ate faster, as did the girls.

A few minutes later, George pushed his chair away from the table and stood. "I'll hitch the buggy."

Jimmy shoved the last spoonful of chili into his mouth, washed it down with a gulp of milk, then followed George outside.

"Finish up, girls," Gwen said, collecting the dirty dishes.

Catherine gathered an armload and met her sister-in-law at the sink. "I'll *reddy-up* the kitchen. You and the girls go get ready."

"What about you? Don't you need to change for the get-together?"

"I've decided *nett* to go. I have too much to do to get ready for *mei* trip tomorrow, and I don't want to be up late."

"What about Zach? Shouldn't you tell him goodbye?"

"He hasn't made a point to *kumm* visit, and he knows I'm *nett* working at the restaurant, so . . ." She shrugged. He wasn't interested in having a future with her—she wasn't marriage material. "It's for the best," she said, not realizing she had spoken her thoughts out loud until Gwen frowned.

Her sister-in-law leaned closer and lowered her

voice. "I'm sorry things didn't work out between you and Zach. You know . . . the proposal."

Catherine forced a smile. "'To every thing there is a season, and a time to every purpose under the heaven.'" She busied herself by plugging the drain and turning on the tap water. "It's just *nett mei* season for marriage, is all."

"I don't know what to say."

"That makes two of us, so can we please drop the subject?" Catherine turned her attention to Leah and Julie as they clamored over to the sink with their dirty dishes. "You can stack them here." She patted an empty space on the counter.

"Put on your coats and boots, girls. *Daed* should have the buggy hitched." Gwen covered a plate of cookies with foil. "Catherine, I wish you would change your mind. I hate that you'll be spending your last *nacht* alone."

"Don't worry about me. Like I said, I have a lot to do before tomorrow." Starting with reading the latest letter from her cousin. Her ticket was nonrefundable. Maybe she should have prayed more. Catherine mindlessly swabbed the bowl with the soapy dishrag.

"See you later," Gwen said as she and the girls left.

"Okay. Have fun." Catherine waved at the girls, pleased that Julie had been too preoccupied with her big sister to question why Catherine wasn't going with them. She washed all the dishes except for the chili pot and the corn bread pan, which both needed time to soak.

Catherine held her breath as she opened the letter and didn't exhale until she scanned past the greeting and down to the part where Dawn said she was looking forward to her visit. Excitement bubbled up as Catherine read more.

> . . . Trust me, winter here in Sarasota will feel odd at first. Most days are in the eighties. You'll find yourself confused over what month we're in because it always feels like summer. Also, you won't need to pack much. Other than to a funeral, we don't usually wear dark colors in our district. The darker colors absorb more sunshine, which then heats you up faster and makes for a miserable day, especially working in the hot bakery kitchen. Our dresses are pastel shades with white aprons. But don't worry, I'll let you wear some of mine until we can arrange a sewing day just for you! How are you at riding a bike? I've already secured one for you to use while you're here. I think you'll like it. It even has a basket attached to the front handlebars.

A knock at the back door pulled her attention away. She went to the door and was taken aback from the unexpected visitor. "Zach."

"You sound surprised." His jaw twitched.

"I suppose I am." She opened the door wider and stepped aside. "*Kumm* in."

Zach stomped clumps of snow off his boots on the mat, then entered. "How are you?"

"*Gut*, and yourself?" She motioned to the table. "Want to sit and have a mug of *kaffi*?"

He shuffled his feet and looked around the room awkwardly.

"George, Gwen, and the *kinner* went to Irene's card shower," she said.

"*Jah*, I saw them."

Without asking again if he wanted coffee, she went to the stove, placed a log on the embers, then moved the kettle to the middle of the stove. Even if he didn't want something hot, she needed something to divert her attention.

He cleared his throat. "Mary told me you left early on Sunday."

Why was he telling her now—more than a week later? She hadn't wanted to start this conversation on the defensive, but she couldn't hold her tongue either. "Did your *schweschaler* tell you I went home sick?"

"*Jah*."

Not heeding the inner voice of reason telling her to leave it alone, she asked, "What day?"

His brows drew together in what looked like confusion.

Catherine persisted. “What day did she tell you?”

He lowered his head. “Sunday.”

“Service Sunday or visiting Sunday?”

He groaned. “The Sunday you went home sick.”

Figures. Catherine opened the side compartment of the stove and poked the wood—not that it needed repositioning, as the fire was burning nicely.

“I should have *kumm* over sooner. You know how I lose track of time when I’m working in *mei* shop. I—”

Ignoring him, she went to the cabinet next to the sink and removed two mugs. “Do you still take cream in your *kaffi*?”

“You know I do.” He snorted.

Okay, so that was an unfair dig. Still, he deserved a little pushback, since he’d been the scarce one lately.

“Catherine, would you rather I leave?”

Is that what you want to do? In her brief moment of hesitation, his body stiffened and face hardened. He was probably feeling a little sting of rejection.

He headed to the door.

“*Nay*,” she said as he reached for the doorknob. “I’d like you to stay.”

Tension seemed to drain from his body right before her eyes. His ramrod-straight spine and squared shoulders softened. When he pivoted around, an impish smile filled his face. As if he'd gone from feeling rejected to feeling empowered, he strutted toward her with a demeanor that spewed confidence.

Catherine turned her attention to the whistling kettle. She poured two mugs of coffee, fixing his according to how she knew he liked it, then set the mugs on the table. She motioned to the chair opposite hers. "Have a seat."

He pulled the chair out from the table, plopped down, and crossed his arms. "When were you going to tell me that you're leaving town?"

"You were upset with me on New Year's Eve and haven't made a point to talk with me since. I didn't think *mei* leaving would matter."

"I've had a lot on *mei* mind—a lot to think about."

"Me too."

He picked up his mug, took a drink, then set it down. "I went to the get-together tonight, assuming you would be there." He looked down at the mug, gripped its handle, but didn't pick it up. "I drove *mei* sleigh. I thought we could *geh* for that ride I promised to take you on." He lifted his gaze to hers and held it unwaveringly. "Do you want to *geh*? I, ah—I'd like to talk to you about something."

A mixture of excitement and unease battled for control over her nerves. A shudder, starting at the hair follicles on her head reverberated down to her toes. “Okay. Do you want to finish your *kaffi* first?”

He took another drink, then stood. “We can *geh*—unless you want to stay longer and drink yours.”

Coffee wouldn’t sit right on her roiling stomach. “I’ll get *mei* cloak,” she said, stunned by his sudden eagerness. Catherine went to the wall peg and plucked her cloak off the hook. She tried not to think about what urgent matter he wanted to discuss with her. Had something been said earlier at the get-together? Was Elijah the one who told Zach about her leaving town?

She’d barely had the scarf wrapped around her neck and face when Zach opened the door. He grasped her elbow as they descended the porch steps and didn’t let it go until he assisted her into the sleigh. The evening wasn’t as nippy as she had expected for mid-January, but sitting on the cold bench did cause her teeth to chatter.

Zach lowered a blanket over her shoulders. “Better?”

“*Jah, danki*.” She sighed. He wasn’t one to show attentiveness often, but even a simple gesture like placing a blanket over her shoulders warmed her heart.

Zach took the reins and directed the horse over the snow-covered field, the steel runners gliding effortlessly as the sleigh whooshed over the snow.

The moon shedding light on their path reminded Catherine of the verse in Psalm 119: "Thy word is a lamp unto my feet, and a light unto my path." *Lord, I ask that, as You light this path for us tonight, You will also guide me in all of Your ways as I seek You.*

Zach pulled back on the reins once they reached the crest of the hill near the dense forest on state land where towering trees blocked the moonlight.

Breathing in the pungent, sappy scent of jack pines, hemlocks, cedars, and the various firs opened her sinuses much better than the greasy ointment she'd lathered on Julie's chest the night she was sick.

Zach shifted on the bench, lantern light flickering in his eyes. "This is where I wanted to take you on New Year's Eve."

She gulped. Was he leading up to another lecture of why she was out of place proposing?

Zach leaned back on the bench and lifted his gaze upward. "I find it interesting that people all over the world are looking at the same sky. Of course, it's daylight in some parts of the world, but we're still all under one big sky."

"The stars seem almost touchable," Catherine said, relieved he'd changed the subject from the night she'd proposed. Leaning back on the bench, shoulder to shoulder with Zach, she began counting the stars. This time tomorrow she would be somewhere en route to Florida, and the following night, if all went as scheduled, she would be stargazing in Sarasota.

For a long time neither spoke. If it wasn't for a nearby branch cracking under the weight of the snow and the sound of various trees creaking in the distance, there would be total silence. Catherine cleared her throat. "Earlier you said you wanted to talk with me about something."

His chest and shoulders rose and fell as he inhaled and exhaled. "Why are you going to Florida? Is it because of me . . . or does Elijah have something to do with your decision?"

She closed her eyes. *Lord, please give me the right words.* "It's a mixture of things." She opened her eyes. "When I saw Elijah again after so many years, I realized *mei* life hadn't changed. His had gone on, but mine had somehow stalled. After six years I'm still living with George and Gwen, still working at the restaurant, still—" She lowered her head. Telling him she was still single would be as useless as beating a dead horse.

"What were you going to say?"

"A soon-to-be thirty-year-old old maiden." She sighed. "I didn't realize the depth of *mei* bitterness. You were right to rebuke me the way you did. I never should have proposed."

His silence stretched into eternity, then he rubbed his gloved hands along his thighs. Either he was cold or nervous—she couldn't tell which.

"Do you want to get married?" he blurted.

Was he proposing? No, not the way his face had pinched and he was staring straight ahead. If this was a proposal . . .

His chest expanded, then deflated. "Is marriage what's most important to you?"

By what sounded like pent-up tension released in his heavy exhale, she wasn't sure if she was being set up to be scolded, but since he asked, she wouldn't withhold the truth. "It's what all young *maedels* dream about doing," she said softly.

"Then let's get married."

"What?" She'd heard him plainly the first time, but she needed to hear it again—she needed to hear some sort of declaration of love.

"We can get married," he said matter-of-factly. "*Nett* right away. I still have to build *mei* business, but sometime . . . in the future."

He droned on about how he'd received a large contract for grandfather clocks for a major franchised furniture store, but Catherine kept wondering why she wasn't, as Mary had said, floating on air. Just the opposite. A heaviness filled her chest and a lump wedged in her throat. Where was his "I've loved you forever"?

". . . Mr. Ziglar wants to buy *mei* clocks exclusively. He said I should expect—"

"Zach"—she held up her palm—"aren't you interested in *mei* answer?"

He smiled sheepishly. "I was rambling, wasn't

I? I'm sorry. Yes." He reached for her hand. "Let's make it official."

She held her breath, becoming light-headed.

"Catherine Glick, we should be able to get married . . . someday. Soon. That is, if you want to."

A sinking—no, a drowning sensation—overcame her. Had she been in the lake, she'd be sitting on the sandy bottom with lungs filled with water. Zach proposing, she becoming his *fraa*, was exactly what she had always wanted, so why didn't it feel right? Beyond her understanding, something was amiss.

She gasped for air, which he mistook as a yes, because he pulled her into a tight embrace. "It shouldn't be more than six months. Maybe a year or two at the most," he said. "I'm glad you won't be going to Florida."

"Zach." She pushed off his chest. "Are you only asking me to marry you because you don't want me to go to Florida?"

"Is there something wrong with that? Just the other day, you proposed to me."

"And we both agree *nau* that it was wrong. I already promised *mei* cousin that I would *kumm*. She needs help in her bakery, and I—I need time to think. And so do you."

Chapter 9

She had made the right decision, hadn't she?

Seated in the lobby of the bus terminal, Catherine stared at her ticket. Her cousin would understand if she canceled the trip, especially once Dawn learned Zach had finally proposed. But Catherine didn't understand why his proposal included an ultimatum—forgo the trip.

Catherine glanced at the large wall clock. The bus wasn't scheduled to leave for another forty-five minutes. Tightening her grip on the ticket, she closed her eyes. *Lord, I hope I'm* nett *just being stubborn. Please show me some sort of sign, and please make it something obvious, like sending Zach to the terminal to proclaim his love.*

Someone nearby cleared his throat, and she looked up.

"Do you mind if I sit here?" Elijah pointed to the empty seat beside her where she had placed her quilted tote.

She stared absentmindedly at him a moment, then moved the oversized handbag to her lap. The Lord had a sense of humor if this was His *obvious* sign. *Don't read anything into it.*

Catherine had seen him in the terminal the other day when he came to buy a ticket to go back to Badger Creek. Still, it was nice to have someone familiar to sit with while she waited for the bus.

He tossed his duffel bag under the chair and plopped down. "How long have you been here?"

"George dropped me off a couple of hours ago. I heard there were several people at the get-together for your *mammi*. I hope she had a *gut* birthday."

"She did, I think." He grinned. "She slept through most of it." He lounged back on the chair and cupped his hands behind his neck. "I thought you were going to drop by."

"I had packing to do." Catherine fussed with a frayed string on the seam of her tote bag. At one time, Elijah was her best friend, but things were different now. She didn't owe him an excuse for missing the party, and he certainly didn't need to know about Zach's visit, yet something compelled her to give account. "Zach stopped by the *haus* to see me last *nacht*."

His smile faltered briefly. "I hope you were finally able to go on that sleigh ride you two had plans for on New Year's Eve."

She arched her eyebrows and hoped he took notice. "The one you interrupted?"

"*Nett* intentionally." He grinned sheepishly, then angled his head to one side as if preparing to question her more about the night, but she cut him off.

"Yes, Zach took me on a sleigh ride. And the moonlight and snow-covered forest were . . . breathtakingly beautiful."

"*Gut*, because you won't find snow in Florida."

Finding herself drawn to his sweet smile and relaxed nature, she leaned back and hugged her soft travel bag close to her chest. "Zach proposed on our ride." Her words slipped out unchecked, and for half a second, she thought his breath caught in his throat, the way he rasped.

"I didn't think—I mean—well . . . congratulations?" His voice formed the statement into more of a question.

A question, because anyone who had become engaged as recently as last night wouldn't, or at least shouldn't, be sitting alone in a dingy terminal, waiting to board a bus that would take her hundreds of miles away. She chose to ignore his question and addressed what he didn't say. "You didn't think what?"

He shook his head.

"No, tell me." She elbowed his ribs.

He grasped his side and slightly recoiled, then chuckled. "Ouch, brutal."

His words were playful and overtly loud. Catherine smiled until she realized their antics had garnished the attention of the other travelers in the lobby. She shouldn't have drawn unnecessary attention to them by elbowing him.

"Elijah." Her strong tone captured his attention. She made an open-palm gesture, suggesting he finish his sentence. "You didn't think what?"

He resumed his previous position, hands linked behind his neck. "I didn't think Zach wanted to get married."

Her face froze as Elijah's words struck her like an ax.

Elijah sat upright, a grave look on his face. "Well, obviously Zach changed his mind from—"

"New Year's Eve when he rejected me?" An image of Zach's hardened expression from that night in the barn flashed before her eyes. *"Is marriage that important to you?"* His words echoed in her mind, and remembered humiliation heated her cheeks.

Elijah shifted in his seat to face her. "Zach was smart to get his head together. That's what I should have said."

Unable to acknowledge the pity in his eyes, she redirected her attention to the soda machine across the room. *Lord, am I supposed to take any of this as a sign from You? Did Zach get his head together and propose because he loves me or to keep me from leaving town?*

"Are you thirsty?" Elijah must have noticed her staring at the machine. "I'll buy you a soda."

"*Danki*, but *nay*. If I drink anything *nau*, I'll have to use the restroom, and I'm getting ready to board a bus for a very long—" *Enough rambling about yourself.* "You never said what time your bus leaves."

He glanced at the wall clock, then at his ticket. "They should announce boarding in a few minutes."

Her mouth dried. Catherine swallowed hard to force the lump down before it permanently lodged in her throat. His leaving was final. In a few short minutes, he would walk out of her life—again.

Zach proposed. Was it safe to assume Catherine turned him down? After all, what newly engaged woman would want to spend months apart from her intended? Plus, her brother had brought her to the bus depot—not Zach. If Elijah were in Zach's boots, he would have driven her to the bus station, seen her off safely—no, he would have talked her out of going so far away—had she been his future wife.

But Catherine wasn't pledged to him, and it was unlikely that she would ever trust him again.

Still, Elijah had found her sitting alone, deep in thought. She wasn't as distraught as she'd been in the barn, but . . . what? He twisted his hands, cracking each knuckle as thoughts of Zach and her future pelted him. Elijah rubbed his thighs. He had to know.

"What did you say?" he blurted.

She crinkled her nose as though she'd taken a whiff of something odd. "Just *nau*? I didn't say anything."

"*Nay*, to Zach. What was your answer?"

She stared at him a moment, then fiddled with a loose thread on her bag. "We didn't see eye to eye on me going to Florida." Her voice barely rose above a whisper. "I'll only be gone four months, and I had already promised *mei* cousin I would help in her bakery, so . . ."

"And you and Zach didn't work something out?"

Catherine shrugged. "We'll see what happens in May."

The hopeful, singsong ring in her tone and her overstretched smile didn't fool him. Her voice trembled and she'd forced her smile, the quiver at the corners of her mouth betraying her.

Knowing Zach, he'd pressured her to choose between Florida and him. In the past his friend second-guessed all his major decisions, even having buyer's remorse when he purchased a buggy horse at a very good deal. He hadn't been around Zach much over the last few days, but he doubted his friend had changed. Some sort of retraction probably immediately followed his proposal.

Four months wasn't that long to wait, and if Zach truly loved her, he wouldn't let time and distance stand in his way. Elijah glanced around the room, half expecting Zach to show up.

Elijah stood. "I need to stretch *mei* legs. Do you mind watching *mei* duffel bag?"

"I don't mind, but *mei* bus is leaving shortly."

"I'll be back." He needed a little fresh air to clear his head and put his emotions in check. She'd been part of his past—part of his heart. Had he not gotten the letter from Edwina's folks, he and Catherine would be married and probably trying to figure out how to keep food on the table for a houseful of kids.

He stepped outside and pulled in a deep breath, but when the frigid air reached the depth of his lungs, they spasmed. He coughed, then took in another cleansing breath before turning to go back inside. As he entered the lobby again, a call for boarding sounded over the speakers. Elijah checked his ticket.

"That's me," she said. She dragged her suitcase and his duffel bag to meet him. "I have to go."

His gaze locked on Catherine. She appeared strong, confident, eager to begin her journey—too independent for her own good.

She handed him his bag. "I'll see you—well, I guess I don't know when I'll see you again." Catherine's words ran together. "Take care, Elijah. I wish you well."

Focused on reading her expression, he almost missed the second overhead call for boarding. As she turned and headed toward the sliding glass doors, which led to the loading area, he hurried to her side. He unzipped his duffel bag and shoved his ticket inside, then reached for the handle on her traveling case. "Let me take this for you."

"You don't have to do that," she said, eyes blinking back tears.

Choked up, good sign. Elijah smiled and kept walking. He stopped behind another passenger in line with his bags.

"Elijah, the sign says you cannot be in this area without a ticket." Catherine pointed to the notice posted on a dangling overhead sign.

"I have a ticket." He leaned closer. "I told you I wanted to stretch *mei* legs before getting on the bus." He handed her case to the uniformed man standing beside the bus's underneath storage compartment.

"Ticket, please." The man held out his hand.

Catherine gave him her ticket. The employee tore off a section, fastened it to her case, then gave her back the ticket.

"Give this to the driver," the attendant said, then turned and bellowed, "Next."

Catherine moved out of the way of the other travelers. Glancing toward the line of people getting on the bus, trepidation filled her gaze.

"Do you want to change your mind about leaving?" Elijah held his breath. The last thing he wanted was for her to second-guess her trip—her decision to leave.

"*Nay,*" she replied, still staring at the boarding passengers.

"Then the apprehension you're feeling must be from *nett* knowing how to tell me goodbye, *jah*?"

She whirled to face him. "Elijah—" An overhead announcement calling for final boarding blared over her words.

"The seats are going to be taken if we keep talking." He motioned to the disappearing line.

"I have to go." She hurried to join the other passengers.

Elijah fell into line behind her. "You'll want to pick a window seat."

"I appreciate you walking me to the bus, but you should go back inside."

He lowered his duffel bag to the ground, unzipped it, then removed a ticket. "I hope you don't mind a traveling companion, Cat."

Her mouth dropped open.

He motioned with a nod to the person ahead of her climbing the bus steps. "Do you have your ticket ready?"

"You're going to Florida?"

"Yep."

"Why are you going to Florida?" She handed her ticket to the driver, who stamped it and handed it back.

"To visit *mei* cousin Toby." He gave the man his ticket. "At least I hope he still lives in Florida."

She stopped midway up the steps and glanced over her shoulder at him. "What's the real reason?"

Elijah smiled. "We have two full days to talk about that."

Chapter 10

Catherine chose an empty row in the middle of the bus and took the seat next to the window, nervous excitement feeding her veins. She placed her handbag on the floor at her feet, then pressed the wrinkles out of her dress with jittery hands.

Elijah shoved his duffel bag into an overhead compartment, then sat beside her. "You nervous?"

"A little. I've never been on a bus before."

"Trust me, sitting for hours on end will get old quick."

At least the cushioned seat was comfy, unlike the hard buggy bench. "It all seems unreal." *Leaving town, sitting next to Elijah.* "Did you tell anyone you were going to Florida?"

He shook his head. "You worried about Zach finding out?"

Zach had his chance to stop her before she boarded the bus.

The overhead speaker crackled to life. "On behalf of Budget Bus, I'd like to welcome you aboard," the driver mumbled into the handheld microphone. "I need to get a few things out of the way before we begin our journey. In case of emergency there is an exit located to my right and at the back of the bus." The man pointed to the designated areas.

A young child fussed in the seat ahead of them, making it hard for Catherine to concentrate on the emergency evacuation instructions given by the driver.

Fear must have shown in Catherine's expression, because Elijah reached for her hand and gave it a squeeze.

"I won't let anything happen to you." He smiled. "I promise."

Much as the warmth comforted her, she quickly slipped her hand out from his. "We both know you're *nett gut* at keeping promises."

His expression sobered. "Are you incapable of extending even a little mercy?"

"The driver's still speaking." She turned her attention to the short, pudgy man speaking over the loudspeaker but didn't hear a word he said.

Guilt niggled at her conscience as the words of the Lord's Prayer came to mind. *"Forgive us our trespasses as we forgive those who trespass against us . . ."* She couldn't hold his empty promise to her against him forever. Besides, he only meant to try to ease her fears about traveling by taking her hand. His gesture was sweet, protective, exactly how she remembered him being years ago. *Lord, help me see him through Your eyes.*

The driver concluded his speech, then took his place behind the wheel. As the gears ground and the bus moved forward, she watched the terminal fade in the distance. A few miles down the road, she settled back in the seat. This would be a very long, very agonizing trip if she and Elijah didn't clear the air once and for all.

She drew in a deep breath, let it out slowly, then turned to him. "Can we talk?"

"Sure."

The wide smile he flashed set her back a little. "I . . . I shouldn't have said what I did. You were just trying to be nice when you promised not to let anything happen to me, and that means a lot, because truthfully I am a bit frightened. I'd like to call a truce over our . . . past issues." She extended her hand, and he accepted it with a firm grasp that reached her core and instilled a measure of trust and safety.

"Truce it is."

He held her hand longer than necessary to seal their agreement, but she forgot about pulling her hand free when his mesmerizing blue-gray eyes caught and captured hers.

"I hope over these next few days you'll see me differently," he said.

See him through God's eyes. That had been her prayer. Catherine's throat dried. His gaze was too familiar, and so were the nervous tremors that rippled through her unchecked. *Get ahold of yourself.*

"*Danki.*" She let go of his hand. "I feel much . . . safer *nau. Nett* as . . . afraid." *Oh, Lord, I'm sputtering like a fool. Elijah's always had this effect on me.*

"I'm glad you feel safe." He sat up straighter and stretched his neck to look around the bus. "I've read that buses tend to draw a lot of transient people. It wouldn't surprise me if some of these passengers have criminal records."

Catherine leaned forward and looked up and down the aisles—until a man with a straggly beard and a bandanna wrapped around his forehead eyed her back. She slumped in her chair, scooting closer to the window.

Elijah relaxed, stretching out his legs under the seat ahead of him. "I can't believe Zach didn't insist on escorting you to Florida. This isn't the place for a woman traveling alone."

She ignored his edgy tone. "Zach has a new client. A furniture store owner wants to sell his grandfather clocks, and apparently the man owns more than one store, so it should mean increased revenue for his business." She recited almost verbatim the information Zach had told her.

"Hmm . . ."

"What do you mean by 'hmm'?"

He rolled his eyes and shrugged. "Seems odd to

me that he would value money above his future *fraa*'s—your—safety."

She narrowed her eyes. "You're implying he's greedy."

"Either that or his priorities are skewed. But that's for you to decide. You're the one who wants to marry him." He slouched down, crossed his arms over his chest, and closed his eyes. "I'm going to take a nap. Wake me when we make our first stop."

"Okay." She leaned her forehead against the cold window and watched the snowy landscape pass in a blur while replaying the conversation she had with Zach on the sleigh ride. *"We can get married."* Even today his choice of words made her cringe. She had waited so long for him to ask, and when he did, it was so matter-of-fact that it left her more confused than ever.

His response replayed in her mind. *"First I rejected you, and* nau *you're rejecting me? This was your idea. You're the one who was desperate to get married. If you want to marry me, then I forbid you to go to Florida."*

A sour taste rose to the back of her throat the more she rehashed the snippets of their conversation. Walking away from a marriage proposal—the possibility of never having a husband, a home, and a family of her own—was the hardest and yet easiest decision she'd ever made. Zach was the wrong man for her, or maybe she was just the wrong woman for him. Either way, God had given her wisdom to see the truth and the courage to walk away.

Catherine reached down, picked up her tote bag, and removed a ball of yarn and crochet hook. Living in Florida, she wouldn't need scarves and mittens, but she could get started on next year's Christmas gifts for her two nieces and nephew. Hopefully one day Julie would forgive her for not coming back to Posen.

Elijah opened his eyes as the bus slowed to turn off the road. The sign over the worn building read Buck's Truck Stop and Restaurant. Home-Cooked Food. He had closed his eyes to avoid saying more than he should about Zach and ended up falling asleep. Now his neck was kinked. He rolled his right shoulder, then his left.

Catherine stopped working on her yarn project. "Are you okay?"

"Just stiff." He repeated the stretches without much relief. "I'll be better once I get outside to walk around."

"I'd better put this away if we're getting off the bus." She picked up her tote bag and tucked her handiwork inside.

The overhead speaker squawked. "This route will resume in twenty minutes, folks. Please have your tickets with you for reboarding. We will leave at ten o'clock."

Someone's purse bumped Elijah's shoulder as people stood in the aisle waiting for the driver to open the door. He leaned toward Catherine. "We'd better wait until the crowd clears so we don't get trampled in the stampede."

She followed a few passengers with her gaze, then turned her attention back to him. "People do seem eager to get off the bus."

"It'll clear in another minute or two." He settled his shoulders against the seat and yawned.

"Do you want to stay on the bus and sleep longer?"

"*Nay*, I wouldn't be able to go back to sleep." Elijah wasn't about to let her get off the bus alone at a truck stop. Places like this weren't safe for someone as trusting and naive as Catherine.

"How late did the get-together last for your grandmother?"

"It ended sometime around nine, but I stayed up late talking with *mei* relatives. *Mei* parents want *mei* grandmother to move in with them in Metz. Their place is only a few miles away, but *Mammi* is resistant. It seems the older she gets, the more stubborn in her ways she becomes." He shrugged. "It'll be a challenge to get her to change her mind. According to her, she took her first breath in that *haus* and plans to take her last breath in it as well."

"That does make for a difficult decision. On one hand it makes sense why your *mammi* is attached to her home, and on the other I'm surprised she's lived alone for this many years."

"Things were working out fine with *mei aenti* watching over her, but *Aenti* Agnes is in her late seventies, and it's getting more difficult for her to cross the pasture dividing their *hauses*. Besides, she has her hands full since *Onkle* Silas had a stroke. As it is, the neighbors do most of the grocery shopping and errands and make the necessary arrangements with a nearby *Englisch* driver to take them to their doctors' appointments." He stood when the aisle cleared, and motioned for Catherine to go in front of him.

Once outside, Catherine resumed their conversation as they followed the other travelers meandering toward the building. "Maybe you should consider moving back to Posen. Your *mammi*'s farm is large enough to train horses like you always said you wanted to do."

He opened the door. "Maybe I will."

Chapter 11

The first stop lasted long enough to use the restroom, purchase a bottle of water, and line back up to board the bus. A sweet aroma filled Catherine's senses as she wandered across the parking lot alongside Elijah. "Do you smell that?"

Elijah curled his lip. "Gas station hot dogs? I'd rather *nett*."

"You don't smell lilacs?" She tilted her head up slightly and drew in a deep breath. *Springtime.* Her mind was playing tricks. They hadn't even crossed the state line. Besides, lilac bushes never bloomed in January in Michigan.

Elijah sniffed. "*Nay*." He chuckled. "All I smell are diesel fumes." He motioned to a group of women a few feet ahead of them. "You're probably catching a whiff of their perfume."

Working at the restaurant, she'd smelled lilac perfume and powder before, but this scent didn't carry the underlying hint of rubbing alcohol as many perfumes did. The wind shifted directions, and the same scent carried on the breeze.

"Do you have your ticket ready?" Elijah pulled his from his jacket pocket.

Catherine rummaged around her needlework to find hers in the tote bag, which doubled as her handbag for the trip. "Found it." She lined up behind Elijah, showed the driver her ticket, then boarded the bus.

Elijah stopped at their row and motioned for her to go first.

She hesitated. "Would you like to sit by the window this time?"

"*Nay*, I'll take the aisle."

It wasn't until Catherine had sat and the bus was in motion that she recalled smelling lilacs the day she'd fallen by the side of the road. The scent had been strong then too. An image of the red-haired man's gold-flecked eyes flashed in her mind.

Elijah leaned closer. "Is something wrong? Did you forget something?"

"*Nay*, it's *nett* that." She leaned forward and, sitting on the edge of her seat, arched her body so she could see the passengers seated behind, across, and in front of them. Her gaze stopped on a passenger a few rows ahead, but when he turned enough for her to study his profile, she realized it wasn't the same man.

"What's wrong, Cat?"

"I, ah . . ." Another man with pierced eyebrows and a fire-breathing dragon tattooed down his neck eyed her hard. She withered against the seat cushion, her breathing ragged.

Elijah shifted his body so his shoulder blocked the other passengers' view of her. "Tell me why you're trembling."

Catherine glanced at her shaky hands, then palm-pressed a fold in her dress. After she'd fallen on the ice last Sunday, she hadn't thought any more of the elderly man who had stopped to help or how he had placed his hands over her ears and they had stopped ringing. She clearly recalled how they were talking about a sparrow she'd seen perched on a fence post when the man disappeared as mysteriously as he'd arrived.

Catherine touched the back of her head where the lump had been. "Do you believe in angels?"

"Do you"—he glanced over his shoulder—"see one . . . *nau*?" Turning back to her, his brows pinched together as concern etched his face. "Do you, Cat?"

"Never mind." Leave it to Elijah to answer a question with a question. She played like it didn't matter and redirected her attention out the window. She'd fallen, hit her head hard enough to black out, and upon opening her eyes, a stranger was peering down at her. She had no logical reason to believe he was an angel. *"For he will command his angels concerning you to guard you in all your ways."*

He cleared his throat. "I believe in angels."

"Are you just saying that?"

"I haven't seen one, but I know that in Psalms

the angel of the Lord is encamped around those who fear Him, and He delivers them. What got you thinking about angels?"

His interest prodded Catherine to share her story. She wanted to tell someone about what had happened on her walk home from the church meeting, but could she trust Elijah? She hadn't even told Zach. If word got back to her family about this, after they were already disappointed in her judgment after her proposal to Zach . . .

"Why are you asking about angels?" Elijah's soft tone was comforting.

"On *mei* way home from church the other day, I slipped on the ice and hit the back of *mei* head hard enough to black out. I'm *nett* sure how long I was unconscious, but when I finally opened *mei* eyes, I had a horrible headache . . . and a man was hovering over me, asking me if I was okay."

"Did you recognize him?"

She shook her head. "He wasn't Amish."

Elijah's eyes widened. "You must have been scared."

"I was at first." She drew a breath. "I don't know if he was an angel or if *mei* mind was playing tricks on me."

"Why do you say that?"

"I was talking to him one minute about a sparrow he had pointed out, and the next minute he was gone. The man vanished." She studied Elijah carefully, scrutinizing every blink of his eyes, every twitch of his lips. "I also smelled lilacs."

"Like you did at the truck stop?"

She nodded. "Like I still do *nau*. The aroma is strong, and it's *nett* someone's perfume. I suppose you can't smell it, can you?"

"*Nay*, but *mei* nose is *nett* the most sensitive when it comes to flowery scents."

"Maybe it's all in *mei* head."

He cracked a smile, then sobered when he picked up on her underlying fear. "You did say you had blacked out. Are you still having headaches?"

"*Jah*," she said reluctantly. "Please don't tell anyone." The last thing she wanted was for her cousin to think she needed mothering. Dawn was the one who needed Catherine's help.

"I won't."

"*Danki*." Enough about her problems. "Why did you change your ticket to Florida?"

He smiled. "Who said I changed the ticket?"

"On the day we ran into each other in the bus terminal, were you there to purchase a ticket, or had you followed me?"

"Nope. I did *nett* follow you."

She studied him hard. "Ah, when I dropped *mei* ticket and you picked it up, you asked who was going to Florida."

His gaze dropped to her hands for a moment, then locked on hers. "I noticed Sarasota on the ticket, but I wasn't able to catch the name or the date before you snatched it out of *mei* hand. That's one reason why I wanted to know if you'd be in town for *Mammi*'s birthday party. I wanted to know what day you were leaving."

"And the other reason?"

He grinned. "I was hoping to see you at the party—and I was disappointed when you didn't show up."

Heat rose to her cheeks. Elijah's outspoken boldness could always cause her to blush. She had tiptoed around her real question—why did he follow her to Florida?

Catherine plunged ahead with her questioning. "Was it difficult to change your plans at the last minute—assuming you were headed somewhere else besides Florida when I first ran into you at the bus terminal?"

"It wasn't difficult because I hadn't decided where I was going yet."

"I don't understand."

"I had been praying for God to lead me in the direction He wanted me to go. I asked Him to make it obvious—and then I bumped into you."

He'd prayed for things to be made obvious? The same prayer I'd prayed. Her throat dried. Catherine opened the bottle of water she'd purchased at the stop, took a drink, then recapped it. "So you think going to Florida, *nett* knowing for sure if your cousin still lives there, is following God's *obvious* direction?"

"Do you *nett* believe in God's guidance or praying for direction?" Elijah hadn't realized how harsh he'd sounded until Catherine's shoulders sagged and she lowered her head. He softened his voice. "I've prayed for direction, and God's been faithful to provide it."

"You're a blessed man." She smiled.

"I like to think—" He stopped, noticing the corners of her mouth quiver. She'd forced the smile. "What's going on, Catherine? Are you angry at God?"

She shrugged. "I don't want to be angry at God . . . or anyone. It's just . . ." She shook her head. "Never mind. I don't want to begrudge anyone who is following God's leading. Even though—"

He couldn't let something this serious go. "Even though what?"

She lowered her head. "Even though it hurts to know that God directed you where you should go—*who* you should marry."

Lord, I ask that You please prepare Catherine's heart. I want her to understand why I married Edwina and why it took me so long to return home after she passed away. I believe it wasn't by accident that Catherine and I bumped into each other at the bus depot, but I don't know that she feels the same way. Lord, I ask that You make it obvious to her, or take the blinders from mei *eyes and show me that I'm wrong. In Jesus' name I pray. Amen.*

"I'm sorry I hurt you, Catherine."

"I'm sorry I brought it up. After all"—she closed her eyes—"we called a truce." She wiggled in her seat. "Wake me up when the bus stops again."

Elijah studied her heart-shaped face, prominent cheekbones, and slightly up-tipped nose. Except for the line between her brows, her creamy skin hadn't aged in six years. She hadn't lost her youthful glow despite the bitterness that had turned her heart to stone. He wouldn't recapture her friendship, let alone her love, if he didn't explain his past actions. But would her heart be receptive? Would she listen, or would she shut him out of her life forever?

He wasn't tired, but Elijah closed his eyes. His mind replayed the first encounter he had with Catherine alone. His family hadn't lived in Posen long, and their first winter was proving to be much like what he'd been used to in the Upper Peninsula. Given permission by the Glicks to cut ice from their pond, he was tasked with filling the *icehaus*.

Arriving at the pond, he spotted an Amish woman skating gracefully over the very slab of ice he was there to cut and haul away. He crossed the shoveled section of the ice, the soles of his boots sliding over the smooth surface. The long-legged beauty appeared lost in thought as she went into a graceful spin. Studying the way her honey-colored hair glimmered in the afternoon sunshine rendered him speechless. He'd never seen someone skate so well.

Her arms suddenly flailed, and her feet slid out from under her.

As the woman lay sprawled on the ice, Elijah rushed toward her. Only he struggled to gain traction. He fell face-first, sliding across the smooth surface on his belly, and stopped within inches of her. Before he could scramble to his feet, the woman stood and extended her hand to him.

"I was supposed to help you up." He pushed off the ice a little too fast and had to teeter for balance at the expense of listening to her chuckle.

"It's easier on skates." Hands clasped behind her back, she circled around him.

"Sure it is." He made his way over to the edge of the rink and stood on a patch of snow. "You'll want to get off the ice before I start cutting."

She skated toward him full steam, then stopped abruptly just shy of the snow-bank, shaving the ice in the process. "Can't you take the ice from the other side of the pond?"

"It's too dangerous for the horses." He hiked up the small incline and stopped at the flatbed wagon parked under a large oak. He was setting up the tools when she came tromping up the hill, deep lines forged between her eyebrows.

"This pond is on our land," she hissed.

"Sorry, but our *icehaus* is low on ice." He whistled to himself as he grabbed the hand drill and pick, then stopped long enough to assess the twentysomething woman with sparkling blue eyes before him. She was a sight to behold, standing tall in her skates with her fisted hands planted on her hips. Taken by her rosy cheeks and the way her foggy breaths hovered around her bow-shaped mouth, he forgot how much he disliked moving to Posen.

She skated away quickly, gaining more speed as she looped around the rink. Scraping the ice, marking her territory with every lap.

"Okay," he called. "You leave me no choice but to let your *daed* deal with you."

She raced toward him and came to an abrupt stop. "You don't know what you're talking about." Her words came out with a wheeze.

He eyed the graceful beauty before him and for a split second regretted having to ruin her fun. She was a good skater and obviously came here a lot.

"*Mei daed* wouldn't have given you or anyone permission. He's passed on."

"It was *mei daed* who made the arrangements with, I assumed, your *daed*. George Glick offered us the ice for our *icehaus*. I'm sorry about your *daed*."

"He's been gone over ten years," she said softly. "Heart attack."

She skated away, but not before he noticed her eyes dim. He hadn't meant to stir up painful reminders of her father, but the way her blades were scraping the ice with increasing speed, she was working something off. Her labored breathing reminded him of Edwina. Only his longtime best friend from back home sounded that way without exertion.

"Did *mei bruder* really give you permission to cut on this side of the pond?"

"According to *mei daed*, George said to take all we need. Have you had your breathing problem looked at by a *doktah*?"

She scrunched her nose and cocked her head as though puzzled.

"Every time you take a deep breath, you hiss." Mimicking the noise, he watched her confused expression morph into a narrow-eyed glare.

"I don't have breathing problems."

"Whatever you say, *Cat.*" He playfully exaggerated a hiss and this time made a clawing motion with his hand.

"Very funny."

He recalled how it had taken most of the afternoon to cut a few slabs of ice. In the end Cat stopped sulking and helped him attach the chains to the plow team. They were good friends after that. On the following church Sunday, he had asked to drive her home after the youth singing, and from that evening on, he was no longer homesick for Badger Creek.

The constant hum of the bus engine had lulled Elijah to sleep. Sometime later, the bus made its next stop. He didn't have to nudge Catherine's arm; she was already awake.

"Your stomach's been growling the last hour. I'm surprised it didn't wake you." She reached for the bag on the floor, opened it, then smiled at the contents inside. "I packed extra sandwiches. Would you like one?"

He returned her smile. "I never turn down food."

Once the other passengers had disembarked, they made their way off the bus. Elijah pointed to a picnic table next to the building where they could sit and eat.

Footsteps had beaten down a pathway to the picnic area, but once they reached the table, he discovered melted snow puddled on the benches and opted not to sit down. "You won't find melting snow up north this time of the year."

"That's for certain. Zach's horse had a difficult time making it through some of the drifts on our sleigh ride." Her sweet gaze swept the area. "Northern Michigan is much more picturesque with its snow-covered forests."

She probably had no idea the spark of jealousy she ignited by mentioning Zach. He would do his best to avoid that subject.

Catherine placed her tote bag on the table long enough to remove two foil-wrapped sandwiches. She handed him one.

"*Danki.*" He unwrapped the sandwich and took a bite. The location might not be ideal in her eyes, but he wasn't about to complain.

"Seems like we've been on the bus all day, yet it's only been a few hours," Catherine said.

"*Jah*, we're *nett* even out of Michigan yet." Although he wouldn't mind if it took a few extra days—even a week to get to Florida. He enjoyed her company—getting to know her again after being apart for so long. He wolfed down the sandwich in a few bites. "I guess I was hungrier than I thought."

"Would you like another sandwich? Or cookies?"

"Cookies sound *gut*."

Catherine dug her hand into the tote and came out with a tin of cookies. "They're nothing fancy." She offered him the tin. "Julie and I made a batch of peanut butter cookies, and Gwen and Leah made the chocolate chip and sugar cookies."

He chose peanut butter. "I take it Julie is George and Gwen's daughter. How many *kinner* do they have *nau*?"

She opened her mouth to take a bite of her sandwich but stopped short. "They have three. Leah, Jimmy, and Julie, who just turned five."

Catherine's eyes dulled. Either she was already missing her family or his asking about the number of children George and Gwen had reminded her of how long Elijah had been gone. He wished he hadn't brought up the subject. "When you write home, please tell little Julie how much I liked her cookies." He tapped his stomach. "Tell her they hit the spot."

"*Jah*, she'll be happy to hear that news." Her voice cracked.

"You miss her already, don't you?"

Catherine nodded. "She and I have a special bond. Upstairs, her bedroom is next to mine.

When she's unable to sleep, which lately has been most *nachts*, Julie *kumms* into *mei* room and sleeps with me."

"And you're worried how she's going to get along without you."

"It's foolish, I know. I'm *nett* her *mamm*, but we are very close."

Hearing the longing in her voice, he wanted to reach out and take her into his arms.

Catherine's attention drifted toward the parking lot, but she didn't seem to be looking at anything in particular. "I hope I made the right decision," she muttered.

Her doleful mood suggested something deeper. Perhaps she was sad she wasn't a mother. Or was she having second thoughts of leaving Zach behind? The cookie dried in his mouth, and he had to swallow hard to force it down his throat.

"Why are you really going to Florida, Cat?"

"To help *mei* cousin in her bakery. Why?" She nibbled on a cookie.

"Your decision to leave seems . . . like it's on the cusp of a failed relationship. Are you sure you're *nett* running away?"

She studied the cookie a moment, then slowly wrapped the uneaten portion in a handkerchief and returned it to the tote. When she caught him watching her, she said, "Twenty-nine is a little old to be running away from home."

"I'm wondering why you're worried you might

have made the wrong choice." *About leaving Zach?*

"I was feeling a bit melancholy about being away from home the first time, but I'm fine *nau.*" She placed the uneaten portion of her sandwich on the foil, wrapped it up, then slipped it back into the bag. "And I don't want to talk about Zach and *mei.*"

He handed her the cookie tin for her to put in the bag. "Would you like to take a short walk before we have to get back on the bus?"

"Okay."

Elijah took the quilted bag and slung it over his shoulder. His face might have heated if he were carrying the girly bag back in the district, but here he didn't care what people thought. He jostled the weight to his other shoulder. "How many sandwiches do you have in here?"

"A few. I also packed a few books, my knitting supplies, and stationery for letter writing, to name a few things. I wanted to make sure I had stuff to keep me busy on the trip."

He decided not to ask who she had planned to write letters to, but the question hung on the tip of his tongue. They walked around the perimeter of the parking lot in silence, the winter breeze numbing his fingers. He fisted his hands and blew warm air into them. "I didn't figure I would need gloves in Florida, so I didn't pack them."

"We're *nett* in Florida yet, silly," she teased.

"I'd offer to knit you a pair of mittens, but I think we will reach warmer *wedder* before I get them done. Dawn wrote in one of her letters that it'll be in the seventies or eighties on most days. Have you ever been to Florida?"

He shook his head.

"They don't have horses and buggies." She giggled.

"Oh." He almost commented that her laughter was music to his ears, but thought better of it. He didn't want anything to squash them getting along.

"They use bicycles to get around."

"That'll be something new." Hopefully his cousin still lived in Sarasota and had room for company. Elijah wouldn't mind sleeping on the floor if it meant staying longer in Florida and not having to say goodbye to Catherine.

"Looks like people are already lining up to board," Catherine said. "Do you think we have time to use the restroom before we leave?"

"*Jah*, but we'd better hurry. Otherwise the bus might leave without us."

Chapter 12

Catherine stared out the bus window at the passing scenery. Large city buildings cluttered the landscape for as far as she could see. "I feel sorry for the people who live in the city," she told Elijah.

"Why is that?"

"They don't ever get to watch the sun set across a field of barley or corn."

"Most of those office buildings overlook other offices. I suppose they catch a golden glow reflecting on the metal, but that's about it." He leaned slightly her way and set his gaze on something out the window. "It's interesting how different our lives are from city folks' lives."

"I'm sure some of them think our way of life is boring. Do you remember *mei* cousin Olivia Pinkham?"

"Mordecai and Irma's daughter?"

Catherine nodded. "She jumped the fence a little over a year ago. No one's heard from her. Leaving the way she did saddened her family, especially *Aenti* Irma. It would be very hard to know your daughter was out in the world but *nett* know her whereabouts or how she's doing."

"*Jah*," he said softly, sadness clinging to his words. "I always thought suffering the loss of a newborn, especially for the mother, would be the most difficult pain to endure, but at least one could have peace knowing the child is with God. Whereas losing older *kinner*, who know right from wrong and still choose to leave the flock, the parent doesn't have that same comfort."

Catherine's throat tightened. "You sound like you speak from experience. Did you lose a newborn? Elijah, did your *fraa* and child die at the same time?"

He closed his eyes and shook his head slowly. "We didn't really have a marriage, *nett* in the sense of . . ." His face pinched together. "We were married in name only."

"I don't understand."

"Edwina was the friend I had gone to visit in Badger Creek. I didn't go with plans to marry her. I fully intended to return home before the pond froze over to take you skating."

"You remember your promise?"

"Like it was yesterday."

A bucketload of questions sprang to mind—why would he marry in name only? Had someone twisted his arm to agree to such an arrangement? *Pray, just pray.* Catherine lowered her head. *Lord, give me Your ears to hear and the wisdom to understand . . .*

"I never meant to hurt you, Cat. I was broken by the decision I made."

Feeling her insides crumbling, she kept her head down, her eyes focused on her folded hands in her lap. "I believe you," she whispered.

He let out a heavy breath that apparently he'd been holding and went to reach for her hand.

Catherine withdrew her hand. "Why did you mislead me? I thought . . . we had something special—then you marry someone in name only?"

"We did, and I hate that I ruined everything." His face pinched for a brief second as he prepared his thoughts. "Growing up, Edwina was always frail. She could never run and play like the rest of us, and she was often left out of activities. Her lungs weren't strong enough to keep up, and I used to tease her playfully—until I learned she had cystic fibrosis. After that, we became *gut* friends. When the other kids were busy in the yard playing hide-and-seek or tag, we were inside playing board games so pollen didn't trigger her allergies and clog her already-limited breathing. I didn't mind. Our families were close—still are. We made plans to go to the youth singing together when we were old enough, but *mei* family fell on hard times and we were forced to move."

He turned silent a moment. "In Posen I made new friends, but Edwina and I continued our friendship through letters. Eventually, I talked you into courting me."

Catherine licked her dry lips. "Did you tell her about me?"

He shook his head slowly. "I wanted to, but I thought it'd be like salting a sore. I didn't want her to view her life as standing still when mine was moving forward."

"I see."

"I'm sorry, Cat. When I received the letter about how she didn't have much time to live, I had to go see her one last time."

Had to . . . ? Catherine glanced up and caught him wiping his bloodshot eyes with his hands. It wasn't difficult to figure out the rest of the story. Maybe he would spare her having to listen to the details of reuniting with his childhood love and getting married.

But he continued in the same melancholy tone, and she didn't have the heart to cut him off when it was painfully obvious he had something to get off his chest.

"We had a *gut* visit, and I tried to leave . . . once. But then she told me her biggest regret in life was dying unmarried. According to Edwina, marriage is every *maedel*'s dream."

Catherine understood too well how *maedels* are brought up to cook and clean and care for their younger siblings, all in preparation for becoming someone's *fraa*. Marriage was every *maedel*'s dream—she could certainly attest to that.

"Visiting with Edwina and her parents, I couldn't stop thinking about everything her family had done for mine. We would have lost the farm if they hadn't helped us financially. I don't know what came over me. I'm sure that wanting to please her parents and mine had something to do with proposing to Edwina. She didn't have long to live, and I wanted to give her the opportunity to die without any regrets . . ."

In a strange sort of way, Catherine admired his sensitivity. He stuck by a dying friend. *Jah*, she still believed Elijah was a good man with a good heart.

"The wedding itself was a short, family-only ceremony. Edwina wasn't well enough to leave the *haus*." He removed a hankie from his back pocket and dried the corners of his eyes. "I prayed that you would understand when I came back to Posen after—well, after I explained everything. I had no idea her *mamm* put the wedding announcement in *The Budget*, and for that I'm truly sorry. You shouldn't have had to read about it in the newspaper."

Catherine blinked tears off her lashes. Over the years she'd come up with a dozen or more reasons why he ran off to get married. Why he didn't—and Zach didn't—believe she was marriage material. Never once had this type of scenario played out in her mind. But why would it have? He'd never spoken of Edwina. How would she have known he was fulfilling a friend's dying wish—being a hero for someone else—while at the same time crushing her heart?

Catherine took a short breath and staunched the bitterness from seeping into every fiber of her soul. "How long did you have with her?"

"Three months."

"Months?"

Elijah gulped, his Adam's apple bobbing.

It wasn't until he nodded that the time span really sank in. A chill settled into her bones that no words could defrost.

He eyed her intently, as if studying her icy reaction for some form of hope or maybe forgiveness. If he was able to rid himself of the guilt, clear his conscience, what would it matter? She couldn't shake the feeling she'd been jilted—again—hornswoggled into feeling sorry for him. If he'd only been married three months, why did it take six years for him to come back to Posen? Her chest grew heavy as a thought crept into her mind. If it hadn't been for his grandmother's one hundredth birthday, would he have come back—ever?

Don't ask. Finding out the truth would only drive a stake deeper in her heart. *Think of other things.*

She turned and looked out the window. Street after street of dilapidated houses hugged the concrete wall divider, separating the tiny yards from the busy interstate. The noisy traffic would make it impossible to sleep in one of those houses. It made her appreciate the farm, even living under her brother's roof.

She'd grown tired of feeling constantly underfoot, invading George and Gwen's space. Catherine had made it clear to those who would listen that it was time for a change, and thankfully the opportunity arose to help in her cousin's bakery. She hoped the houses weren't close together like this in Florida.

Not long after they had crossed into Ohio, Elijah tapped her hand. "You're awfully quiet."

"Just thinking about what it'd be like to live in a noisy city. I don't see how people can sleep with this much traffic noise."

"Their brains eventually tune it out. City folks would probably have a difficult time adjusting to living in the country and listening to crickets chirping all night."

"Howling coyotes too." She recalled summer nights on the farm and how peaceful it was to listen to the livestock through the open window. "I wonder if I'll get used to Florida."

"If you can sleep on this crowded bus, you'll do fine." He winked. "You could always rest your head against *mei* shoulder and practice sleeping."

She widened her eyes and heat flushed her cheeks. Catherine reached for the tote bag at her feet and removed the partially eaten sandwich from earlier. She unwrapped it from the foil. "Are you getting hungry? There's another full sandwich and plenty of cookies."

"You know me. I can always eat."

Was it true? Did she really know him? He was correct in that he did used to have a healthy appetite. He always went back for seconds on anything she made for any district gatherings. Truth be told, she was glad to have someone on this journey to share meals with.

Catherine handed him the sandwich. "I'm glad you came with me on this trip." Her thoughts slipped from her mouth unchecked, and her face heated. "Not *with* me per se, but—"

He winked, and her cheeks burned all the more.

"Me too." He held her gaze several seconds.

"Did you want cookies?" She redirected her attention to the handbag.

"Maybe one." He selected a treat. "Don't forget to tell Julie these are *gut*."

"Gwen and Leah made that one."

"Tell them too." He took a bite.

Catherine nibbled on the sandwich, but with so many questions rumbling in her mind, even peanut butter tasted sour. "So why did it take you six years to *kumm* back to Posen?"

Sourdough bread clogged the back of Elijah's throat, and it took several attempts swallowing hard to get it down. He expected her to have questions, but her bluntness caught him off guard.

"You said you were only married three months."

"That's true." He set his sandwich down on the foil wrapper. "Before Edwina died, she had asked me to stay in Badger Creek and help her *daed.* He had been working long hours in the sawmill to pay medical expenses, and he needed help through harvesttime, so I agreed. I owed her family that much."

He paused to give her opportunity to speak, but she said nothing.

"I found out later that while the Troyers were helping *mei* parents put food on our table, they were struggling and having to go without. So knowing they needed *mei* help with harvest, I wanted to stay a few more months."

"And one harvest led to another five—I understand. Edwina had a *schweschaler*?"

"*Nay*, she didn't! And I don't think you do understand. About the time the *first* harvest had ended, I heard you and Zach had started courting. I didn't have any reason to return."

"You were misinformed. We weren't courting then."

Crushing heaviness filled his heart. *Lord, was it Your will to keep us apart? Why? I don't understand.* Elijah glanced at Catherine. *Please don't ask who misinformed me.*

She shifted her back toward him and stared out the window. *Was she questioning God too?*

Elijah pinched the bridge of his nose and squeezed his eyes shut. Conversations and laughter buzzed from all around except between Catherine and him. For them it was as if they were traveling separate directions.

Then a toddler in the seat ahead of them broke the silence by popping up with a toothy smile. "Hi." She wiggled her fingers in a wave.

Catherine's smile returned as she waved back at the child. "*Hiya.*"

Having their attention, the little girl covered her eyes with her hands, then pulled them away with a giggle. Catherine was quick to mimic the action, and soon a new friendship was formed as the two went back and forth playing peekaboo.

Elijah sighed. This was the Catherine he remembered. Warm, friendly, playful with children.

"Isn't she a sweetie?" Catherine said after a while of repeating the same gestures. "She reminds me of Julie as a toddler."

"You're very *gut* with *kinner*."

"I've always wanted a large—" She clamped her mouth closed.

Zach, you fool. You should have opened your eyes sooner and proposed long ago.

Elijah pretended not to notice her unwillingness to share her hopes and dreams, and focused on the little girl instead. He covered his eyes, but the moment he peeked between his fingers, the child's bottom lip trembled. Her sweet face puckered into what looked like a shriveled apple, and big fat tears rolled down her cheeks.

Elijah tugged on his oversized, floppy ears and crossed his eyes, but none of his silly faces stopped her crying.

When the girl's mother pulled the child into her lap, Elijah glanced over at Catherine and shrugged. "I don't seem to have the same effect as you on *kinner*."

"Takes practice. And it's probably past the child's bedtime. I'm a little tired myself." She shifted into a slouched position and leaned her head against the seat.

"You can use *mei* shoulder as a pillow."

"*Danki*, but I'll be fine." Her eyelids blinked heavily and finally stayed closed. After a few minutes of silence, she muttered sleepily, "Why didn't you write?"

Because foolishly he'd wanted to tell her everything in person—but he waited too long. She had moved on with her life. "Go to sleep. We'll talk about it later."

Thankfully she'd fallen asleep. Had Catherine been awake, she would have insisted on knowing and understanding everything, but even he couldn't explain why he never sent all the letters he'd written.

He studied her high cheekbones, heart-shaped

face, and perfect lips. She took his breath away, and she wasn't even aware of her power over him.

Catherine moved around in her seat with her eyes closed. After a moment her head bobbed heavily, then her cheek came to rest against his shoulder. Listening to her soft exchanges of air, Elijah closed his eyes. He wanted to savor this moment as if it were his last. *No more regrets.* If he had a chance to rekindle their relationship, he was going to. But first he had to find out about Zach. Was she planning to marry him or not?

Catherine wiggled again. This time she moved closer into his waiting arms. A smile filled his face as he, too, drifted off to sleep.

Jarred awake, Elijah braced for impact as the bus fishtailed, then finally swerved to the side of the road and struck something that brought them to a hard stop.

Chapter 13

Unexpectedly thrown forward in the seat, Catherine jolted awake. She hadn't registered what had happened when Elijah's strong arms pulled her back against his chest and held on to her with a crushing force. Still dazed, she didn't move.

Cries of frightened children and chatter of panicked passengers filled the bus cabin. Spots of lights from electronic devices and phones began to glow as some of the travelers made phone calls; others just held up their phones facing the front, recording whatever they could capture on video.

Someone held up a bright light and flashed it at people in nearby rows. Its beam landed on them. "You guys all right?"

"*Jah*, thank you," Elijah replied.

The light moved to another row.

Catherine pushed off Elijah's chest, turned, and peered out the window at nothing but darkness. "What happened?"

"I think we hit something." Illumination from various portable devices lit the area, revealing Elijah's concerned expression.

The overhead lights flickered on, then the speaker system squawked. "Folks." The driver waited for the murmuring to die down. "Please stay seated while I . . . check out—"

Catherine and Elijah exchanged glances when the man stopped midsentence. Passengers ahead of them stood, making it difficult to see what was happening at the front of the bus.

"The driver collapsed!" a man from farther up shouted.

"Is there a doctor on board?" A different man spoke into the crackling microphone, his voice wobbly with worry.

A lanky man from the back of the bus pressed his way down the aisle. "I'm a first responder," he called out, moving to the front.

Lord, please heal whatever is wrong with the driver, and watch over him and all of us on the bus. A strong odor filled the cabin. Catherine tilted her head up slightly and sniffed something steamy . . . mechanical, or did it smell sweet?

"Is something wrong?" Elijah asked.

She breathed in through her nose again. The pungent mixture was definitely new and out of the ordinary. Heated mechanical oils and steam filled her senses, making her light-headed. "You don't smell anything?"

Elijah tipped his face. "Nothing unusual."

Sirens blared as the police and fire rescue arrived. Catherine strained to see two men in reflective gear place red flares that illuminated the road and two more officers waving big flashlights to reroute traffic.

Soon after the ambulance arrived, the crew placed the driver on a gurney and took him away. Catherine listened as other passengers speculated that the driver suffered a heart attack and the bus hit the guardrail.

She turned her attention to what was happening outside her window. The driver was being lifted into the back of the ambulance, his mouth and nose covered with an oxygen mask. A flash of memories took her back to when her father lay dying on the barn floor. When he didn't come in for breakfast, her mother had sent her out to the barn to fetch him. Only she couldn't wake him.

Elijah nudged her with his elbow. "You okay?"

She nodded, more interested in the officer who had entered the bus and picked up the microphone. "If everyone could sit down and give me your attention, please." The officer waited for the chatter to settle. "Is anyone else hurt?"

"I can't move my shoulder and my fingers are numb."

Another man held his hand to his neck and complained about pain radiating from the back of his head, along his spine, and down to his lower back.

As the officer radioed for additional assistance and a second ambulance, Catherine immediately began praying for those injured and for the bus driver's heart.

Elijah leaned closer to Catherine. "Are you hurt?"

"*Nay*. What about you?"

He shook his head. "Looks as though we're going to be here awhile." He tapped his shoulder. "You can go back to sleep if you want."

"*Danki*, but I, ah . . . I don't think that's a *gut* idea."

"Sleeping isn't a *gut* idea, or using *mei* shoulder as your pillow?"

Heat infused her face as she recalled how he offered his shoulder earlier, and although she had refused, she ended up pressed against his chest. *Strong arms.* Gut *reflexes. Don't think on those things, foolish* maedel.

She directed her attention to the officer and first responder assisting the man with the shoulder injury. Even looking away from Elijah, she sensed him studying her with a puzzled expression. But one sideways glance at him told her otherwise. Elijah was grinning, obviously amused by her sheer embarrassment. The words tumbled out to wipe that smile off his face. "I won't allow myself to get . . . close to you again."

She won't allow herself. Catherine sounded *too* determined. Elijah raised a brow. "You still don't trust me?"

She narrowed her eyes. "It's *nett* something—"

More sirens shrilled through the air as multiple ambulances arrived, cutting off the rest of whatever Catherine had been about to say. The man with the neck and back injury was taken off the bus first, followed by the person who complained of not being able to move his shoulder.

Worried that Catherine's resoluteness had something to do with her pledge to Zach, Elijah decided not to revisit the subject of her trusting him, nor did he tease her anymore about using his shoulder as a pillow.

The police officer took the microphone. "Does anyone else need medical attention?" Even though plenty of people were groaning, no one spoke up. "Your driver has been taken to the hospital, although I'm unable to share details regarding his condition. We've informed Budget Bus of what happened, and they have a representative en route. Until then, I ask that you remain in your seats."

Catherine leaned forward and held her hand over her lower back.

"Are you sure you're *nett* hurt? Should I flag the policeman?"

"*Nay*, I'm only stretching." She flopped back against the seat. "I wonder if anyone knows what time it is."

Elijah leaned toward the man seated on the

opposite side of the aisle. "Excuse me. Do you have the time?"

The man glanced at his phone. "Two thirty-five."

No wonder he was starting to feel stiff. It had been hours since their last stop. He thanked the traveler, then turned his attention to Catherine. "Did you hear that?"

"*Jah*." She pinched the bridge of her nose.

"Do you have a headache?"

"*Jah*, it's horrible."

Lights from the emergency vehicles flashed in a nauseating rhythm that churned his own stomach. Elijah fought the urge to place his arm around her shoulders and encourage her to lean into him. They still had a long way to go on this trip, and these bright, rotating lights would be brutal for someone with a headache. "I have some water left in *mei* bottle. Would it help to take a drink?"

"Maybe." She accepted the container, removed the cap, and took a long drink. "*Danki*." She handed him back the bottle, then rested her head against the back of the seat and closed her eyes.

Facing her, he rested his cheek against the seat cushion a few inches from hers. "I did write you letters. After Edwina passed away."

She kept her eyes closed. "I didn't receive anything from you."

"I never mailed them," he admitted regretfully. When she didn't say anything, he continued.

"After I wrote the first one, I, ah . . . I didn't think it was right to start a correspondence with you so soon after Edwina's death—while living with her parents." The corner of her mouth twitched, and he cringed. He'd hurt her again. *Lord, will her heart ever mend enough to forgive me—completely?*

A female voice came over the loudspeaker. "Ladies and gentlemen, on behalf of Budget Bus, I would like to thank you for your patience." The woman didn't look much older than him. Her rumpled blonde hair flopped in front of her face, and she pushed her bangs aside. She apologized for the unforeseen circumstances surrounding their delay, then she broke the news that the bus they were on was out of commission and that arrangements had already been made for new transportation.

"I assure you, we're doing everything we can to get you to your destinations." The representative spoke into the microphone over the crowd's murmurs. "I've arranged for a local van service to transport you to a nearby twenty-four-hour diner. Your meals will be provided by Budget Bus." The idea of receiving a free meal didn't seem to calm anyone, as passengers continued to complain about the delay.

"Please take any personal items with you when you leave. You will not be returning to this bus."

"What about our luggage in storage?" a person from the back shouted.

"You do not have to worry about your checked bags. Someone from Budget Bus will transfer the luggage and see that it reaches your final destination. To repeat," she said when the volume of chatter rose, "please take your personal items with you. As you leave, I will issue a reboarding pass that you will need to give to the next bus driver. Do not lose your reboarding pass, as another one will not be reissued . . ."

Catherine checked her tote for her original packet of tickets. "Do you have yours?"

"*Jah*." He tapped his coat pocket and yawned. The initial jolt of the bus hitting the guardrail had awakened him, but now he needed coffee to stay awake. The spokeswoman's instructions droned on until the first transport van arrived. "Again, I appreciate your continued patience as we work to rectify this situation." She handed out passes to the passengers who had been seated in the first few rows as they left the bus.

Catherine reached for her tote bag on the floor and set it on her lap. "Don't forget your duffel bag in the overhead compartment, Elijah."

"I'll grab it when it's our turn to leave."

The shuttle process began, taking the front rows to the new location first. Several minutes later, it was Catherine and Elijah's turn. He stood aside to make room for Catherine to exit. Outside the flares and emergency vehicles illuminated the front of the bus, which was embedded in the crumpled guardrail. Engine fluids puddled on the pavement. The engine no longer steamed, but the sweet scent of radiator fluid still lingered.

Elijah managed to snag a window seat for Catherine in the cramped ten-passenger van. Most people opted to hold their personal items on their laps. The dashboard compass indicated they were traveling northeast. The clock read 5:00 a.m., about the time he usually headed to the sawmill. They hadn't been driving long before it started to sleet. Someone asked the driver if the road was slippery. Elijah was much more concerned about Catherine.

She watched the scenery outside in the blue-black haze of predawn as they drove into town. "The buildings have bars on the windows."

Detecting a hint of fear in her statement, he would keep to himself how bars on the windows usually meant a high-crime area. He gazed over her shoulder at the run-down buildings. This area wasn't anything like their little Posen village. He doubted the spokeswoman had researched the area where the diner was located. Something told him it would have been safer to stay on the bus.

If the bulbs all worked properly, the sign would read *Jake's Diner*. Catherine found the old brick building not only uninviting but eerie because of the way the overhead sign creaked, swaying in the rainy morning breeze.

As the van driver pulled away from the curb, Elijah took her cold hand with a firm grip. “Stay close.”

“Don’t worry. I’m *nett* leaving your side.” They fell in line behind the other van passengers about to go inside. If Elijah hadn’t accompanied her on this trip, she would have been stranded—alone. She tightened her grip on his hand.

Concern etched Elijah’s face. “We’ll be back on another bus soon.”

She nodded.

“You hungry?”

She shrugged. “I suppose I oughta be. It’s free.” Catherine spotted a scrawny calico cat licking itself near the entrance of the building and frowned. Not begging for food, the cat probably just ate a rat.

Walking inside, they met the familiar faces of fellow Budget Bus travelers. Some already dug into their breakfast while others were looking at menus.

“Sit wherever you like,” a pudgy man wearing a white T-shirt under a stained apron said from behind the service counter.

Elijah scanned the room, then headed to a small table for four close to the door. “How’s this?”

“*Gut*.” Catherine set her tote bag on the chair, then removed her cloak. Sitting next to the door might get drafty, but for now she'd leave it off. Ohio wasn't nearly as cold as Michigan.

A waitress handed them each a menu. "What can I get you to drink?"

Catherine smiled at the woman. "Coffee, please."

"I'll take the same," Elijah said, opening the menu.

"If you're unsure what to order," she said, "I suggest the hungry man's omelet." She leaned over his shoulder and pointed her pen at the menu.

"Sounds *gut* to me." He closed the menu and handed it back to the waitress.

The woman jotted his selection on her notepad, then turned to Catherine. "And for you, hon?"

"I'll have eggs over medium, sausage, and home fries, please."

"You got it." The waitress left the table long enough to give the cook the order, then returned with their coffees. Despite the sudden surge of unexpected customers, it didn't take long for their food to arrive.

The last vanload of travel-worn passengers entered the diner and filled the empty tables. A few minutes later the spokeswoman entered the building and sat on a stool at the counter.

The waitress buzzed around handling the flow. Catherine recalled how The Amish Table had filled to capacity and even had several names on a waiting list after the food critic's review appeared in the *Detroit News*. She had never cooked so fast for so many that season. But things settled back down to a more manageable pace. Now The Amish Table was closed until spring. That worked out perfectly. Otherwise she wouldn't have gone on this journey—this new adventure.

"Don't you like the food?" Elijah said.

"*Jah*, it's *gut*." She set her fork down and leaned forward. "*Danki*."

Elijah peered up and smiled. "For what?"

"For being here." Her eyes began to water, thinking about what had happened over the last few hours. The commotion on the bus, being shuttled to this dingy diner, and how difficult it would have been without him. She cleared her throat. "When I bought *mei* ticket, I was feeling brave. Leaving town, going all the way to Florida was a new adventure." She paused to collect her thoughts, and Elijah must have sensed her needing a moment to think, because he remained silent.

His kind eyes probed hers, and she continued. "Leaving town was something I was sure I could do alone. I thought I would get on the bus in Rogers City and get off in Sarasota. But nothing has been as simple as that. And though I was prepared to sit for long hours, I wasn't prepared to change buses in the middle of the *nacht*. I was wrong to think I could make this trip alone. *Narrish* for sure and for certain. If you hadn't *kumm* along, I'd be hiding in some corner, shaking in *mei* shoes."

"You're *nett* crazy." His eyes twinkled when he twisted his lips and pretended to rethink his statement. "Well, maybe a smidgen *narrish*." He winked. "But I like that you're brave and somewhat foolishly independent."

"Somewhat?" She cracked a smile. He always had a way of cheering her up.

"Mostly I like that we're on this new adventure together."

Catherine picked up the paper napkin and used it to dab the corners of her eyes. "Me too."

For the few seconds he held her gaze, something flickered in his eyes. He picked up his fork. "How else would I have had the opportunity to eat an omelet at Jake's Diner?" He leaned forward. "And, by the way, they're *nett* using farm-fresh eggs. I can taste the difference."

"*Jah*." She chuckled. "But I wasn't going to complain about free food."

"Oh, I'm *nett* complaining." He jabbed his fork into his runny omelet. "Eating here is certainly an adventure."

"Sure is." Catherine sipped her coffee.

"Can I have everyone's attention?" the spokeswoman announced from the front counter. "I've just received confirmation that a southbound bus with several empty seats is due to arrive in a few minutes. For those of you still eating, another bus is scheduled to pick up the remaining passengers within the hour. On behalf of Budget Bus, I want to assure you that we will do everything possible to get you to your final destination within the shortest time possible. However"—she paused for emphasis—"these buses will reroute you."

The crowd of weary travelers bombarded the spokeswoman with questions. "What type of compensation is Budget Bus offering? What about our checked baggage?" The questions continued.

The woman raised her hands to calm the people. "If you'll allow me to address the questions raised." She waited for the commotion to settle. "I'm not the person who decides compensation. My goal is to assist you in reaching your destination. As for your checked baggage, it's being expedited to its final terminal and will be kept secure until you arrive to claim it."

Several more people voiced complaints, and the spokeswoman did her best to address their concerns.

"Let's try and get on the first bus," Elijah said. "This area of town seems a little shady. It wouldn't surprise me if someone off the street came in with a gun."

Just the mention of someone having a weapon made Catherine's heart pound harder. She didn't want anyone to experience what Faith had at The Amish Table last year. An image of a masked man holding a gun against Faith's head flashed through her mind. The robbery took place in the blink of an eye.

Catherine's face must have blanched, because he immediately apologized for upsetting her. She rolled her uneaten sausage links in her napkin, knowing full well his gaze was on her.

"If you're *nett* done eating—"

"I am. This is for the cat." She glanced at the handful of people heading toward the exit, then looked out the window at the people hunched over under the diner sign being pelted with sleet. "I think several of the other passengers would agree with your observation and appear as anxious to get back on the bus as we are. They're already lining up on the curb."

"So I see." He pushed away from the table and stood. "Hopefully we won't have to wait outside long for the bus." He slung his duffel bag over his shoulder.

She put on her cloak, grabbed her tote bag and the napkin full of sausages, then followed Elijah out of the building. Sleet hitting her face was bad enough, but the freezing air sent shivers down to her toes. Catherine looked around for the cat. "Here, kitty-kitty."

A soft meow coaxed her to the side of the building. Spotting the cat taking shelter next to a Dumpster at the front of the alley alongside the diner, she walked a few steps over, then knelt. "There you are." The cat meowed. If this was Posen, she'd be tempted to take it home.

"Catherine!"

Elijah's tone was sharp, and his irritation was as plain as daybreak. "I'm giving the sausage to the cat."

"You wandered off into an alley—alone." His bark made the cat puff up and hiss as he loomed next to her.

"It's okay, kitty." She left the meat for the cat. As she started to stand, someone ran up from behind and pushed her over, then raced away. Stunned by the abruptness, it took her mind a few seconds to register that the man had stolen her tote bag. She pointed at the disappearing figure. "He—he—"

Elijah shoved his duffel bag into her arms. "Get on the bus," he instructed as he took off running after the fleeing thief.

"No! Elijah," she called in a frantic voice, but he failed to respond. Catherine rounded the corner of the building. The bus had arrived and was accepting passengers. She rose to her tiptoes and craned to look down the city block. *Elijah, come back.* She let a man and woman go ahead of her, disregarding Elijah's instruction. Still searching for him, she inched closer to the bus door.

"Last call for boarding," the driver announced, agitation in his tone. "Miss. If you're getting on, I need you to do so now. I have a schedule to keep."

No, she wouldn't leave without Elijah.

"Miss?"

Catherine shook her head as she stepped backward from the curb. She made it back inside the warmth of the diner and returned to their once-occupied table, from which the dishes had been cleared. She glanced out the window just as the bus was pulling away from the curb, and someone running alongside it hit his fist against the side.

Air left Catherine's lungs in a whoosh. The man the bus driver had stopped for and was now allowing to board was Elijah.

Chapter 14

Winded from running to catch the bus, Elijah paused at the head of the aisle. He needed to find Catherine, fall into the empty seat beside her, and sleep for a few hours. He scanned each passenger's face as he made his way down the aisle. After not finding her in the front of the bus or the middle, panic infused his veins. He rushed to the back of the bus, apologizing as he bumped into people's shoulders along the way.

Where was she? He never should have left her alone in the alley. "Catherine?"

Wary travelers peered up at him with puzzled expressions.

"Did you see an Amish woman get on the bus? She's wearing a blue dress." He made a motion with his hand to his head. "She's wearing a *kapp*—a head covering."

Several passengers shook their heads, while others just looked away, indifferent to the growing panic ripping his heart. He turned and made his way to the front of the bus as the driver pulled away from the curb. "Stop the bus. Please. I have to get off."

"Sir, I don't make unscheduled stops." The driver scowled at him and gestured toward the seats. "You need to sit down."

His heart pounding, Elijah hung on the railing. He had to convince the driver to stop. Maybe if he explained. The words rushed out: he'd been a fool to leave Catherine alone in the alley, and someone as naive as Cat shouldn't be traveling by herself, but he didn't realize he was speaking in Pennsylvania *Deitsch*.

The driver peered at him in the rearview mirror with narrowed eyes. "If you're not going to sit down, I'll have to throw you off this bus," he barked.

"Yes, please." Elijah breathed a sigh of relief as the bus driver applied the brakes.

The driver opened the door and pointed to the steps. "Get off." His face flared with anger. "Why do I get all the looneys?"

With a quick word of thanks to the driver, Elijah bounded down the steps, his feet barely reaching the pavement before he heard the gears grind as the bus pulled away. He probably had sounded as though he'd lost his mind, going on in another language like that. But he achieved his purpose. The driver stopped the bus a few blocks away from the diner, but he was off the bus nonetheless.

Snow mixed with sleet numbed his face. Elijah tugged his coat, pulling the collar higher to cover his neck. In between buildings, a haze of pinkness lit the eastern sky. Even in daylight, the barred windows and boarded-up buildings were uninviting.

The thug who had made off with Catherine's bag proved to be a much faster runner who had an unfair advantage of knowing the area. The man had darted down an alley and disappeared before Elijah could catch up. Forced to abandon his pursuit, Elijah had to run hard to make it back to the bus on time. He hoped Catherine wasn't carrying anything important in her bag. Yarn and needles were easy to replace, and he'd brought enough money with him that she wouldn't have to worry about purchasing food or drinks. The image of her fear-stricken expression when the bag was stolen burned in his mind. Elijah increased his pace.

The alley where she'd fed the cat was empty. He rushed into the diner, his gaze immediately drawn to the table where they had eaten breakfast. Empty. His pulse quickened as he scanned the room and the faces of strangers.

"Sir?" A woman's voice drew his attention, and he turned to his left to see a woman in her midfifties with short salt-and-pepper hair smile. "I saw your wife go into the restroom."

He released a pent-up breath, some of the tension easing out of his body. Catherine was here and safe. "Thank you."

"Are you Amish or Mennonite?" the helpful woman asked.

"Amish." He kept his gaze glued to the door of the woman's restroom.

"I've read all about the Old Order Amish in Pennsylvania. Once I even went to visit Bird-in-Hand. I found the horses and buggies fascinating . . ."

He caught the inflection change in her voice and glanced at her. "I'm sorry. Did you ask me a question?"

"I wanted to know how fast you can go, traveling by buggy."

"With a *gut* horse, upward of eight miles an hour." He motioned to the back of the room. "Do you know how long she's been in the restroom?"

"Not too long. She looked so frightened and upset, I almost followed her in to see if she needed me to help with anything. I suppose you two don't travel much. Are you from Pennsylvania?"

"*Nay*, Michigan." He smiled politely in an attempt to dilute the curtness in his tone from reaching her ears. The woman was only trying to be friendly, and compared to other well-meaning *Englischers*, she wasn't all that intrusive—yet.

"I didn't know Amish lived in Michigan." Her mouth gaped momentarily, then curled into an even bigger smile. "Whereabouts?"

"There are several settlements throughout the state. We're from Presque Isle County." He needed to check on Catherine. "It's been nice talking with you." He aimed his gaze at the bathroom door and headed in that direction. With some of the people already gone, the room wasn't as crowded. Still, he had to step aside for the waitress to pass between tables with the coffeepot in hand.

"Sit anywhere you like," she said. Apparently overwhelmed by the rush of customers, she'd forgotten that she'd already served him.

He squeezed into an empty chair off to the far side just to get out of the foot traffic. Depending on how long it would be before the next bus arrived, maybe Catherine would like another mug of coffee. Elijah had just barely sat down when he glimpsed Catherine coming out of the restroom, his duffel bag slung over her shoulder. She blotted her eyes with a tissue. From where he sat, she looked dazed. Elijah stood and waved, but she'd put her head down as if to avoid eye contact with everyone.

Before he could call her name, the spokeswoman for Budget Bus stood. "If I could please have your attention. In ten minutes another bus should arrive. Seating is limited. However"—her voice rose above the commotion of chairs sliding across the tile floor as people stood—"a third bus will pick up those of you who are remaining.

As I mentioned before, you will be rerouted."

Catherine fell into the mix of people working their way to the door.

Elijah lost her in the swarm. Feeling the panic of losing her again, he began whistling.

Her head bobbed up. "Elijah?"

The moment he caught sight of her red-rimmed eyes, his insides melted. In spite of her emotional state, she looked as beautiful as ever. "Catherine." He waved, heading toward the throng of travelers exiting the building.

She broke through the crowd, dropped the duffel bag on the floor, then surprised him by stretching out her arms and pulling him into a tight hug. "I'm so thankful you came back for me," she said, half weeping, half rejoicing. "When I saw you getting on the bus, I didn't think I would see you again." Her eyes glistened.

"You can't get rid of me that easily." He squeezed her tighter, not caring that they were in the middle of the restaurant, creating a spectacle of themselves. He'd been taught that public displays of affection were never warranted, but today he was changing those rules. Having almost lost her, he wasn't about to let her go and risk them being separated again. And for however long she clung to him, her face buried in the crook of his neck, he would savor the wisps of her warm breaths.

• • •

Catherine took a few calming breaths and mentally let go of every thread of apprehension she had about being in Elijah's arms. The wall she'd built to protect her heart from falling in love with him again crumbled like the walls of Jericho when Joshua led the Israelites around the city blowing horns.

His strong hands pressed her tighter against his chest. The world around her could fall apart, but she'd be safe. Breathing in the woodsy scent on his coat, she wanted to block out the bustle of people moving about the room.

But they needed to make the bus. She didn't want to stay in this town one minute more than they had to. She lifted up her head and looked into his eyes, a bit taken aback by the depth of his stare. Her eyes automatically closed as he leaned down and kissed her lightly on the forehead, leaving her body showered in shivers.

"We'd better go," he said, his voice husky.

She nodded.

Elijah reached for the duffel bag and swung it over his shoulder. "How did you know it was me whistling?"

She laughed lightheartedly. "If you only knew how off-key you are, you wouldn't have to ask how I recognized you."

He lifted his brows. "That bad?"

Nay, that *wunderbaar*. She grinned. "At least you caught *mei* attention."

"So you say." Elijah twined his fingers with hers and led her outside into the freezing drizzle.

The bus filled immediately with those ahead of them, and they were among a handful of others turned away.

"Another bus will *kumm* shortly," Elijah reassured her. "Let's go back inside."

But Catherine didn't need reassuring when she had him. She wasn't nearly as eager to get to Florida as she had been at the beginning of the journey. In fact, she was enjoying this trip—besides the misfortune of having her bag stolen and the panic of seeing Elijah getting on the other bus. She hadn't felt this blissful in a very long time. Dare she dream of a new future, joy that would last?

Elijah had said he was going to Florida to visit his cousin, but he hadn't indicated how long he planned to stay. Catherine hoped she wasn't so busy at the bakery that there wouldn't be some free time to spend with him.

Her thoughts shifted to Dawn. Somehow she needed to let her cousin know about the delay. Was it too early to call the bakery?

Elijah opened the diner door for her to enter. Inside, she scanned the room for a pay phone. Then, remembering her address book with the bakery's phone number was in her tote bag, her enthusiasm dimmed and she let out a heavily weighted sigh.

"You must be tired." He pulled a chair out from the table.

"A little." She sat in the chair opposite him. "What about you?"

He shrugged. "I could probably sleep," he said, nonchalantly, adding, "standing up" with a head tilt and the crossing of his eyes.

She smiled. "You're *narrish*."

"I'll take crazy over dull."

Catherine ignored the dig at Zach. She could argue Zach wasn't dull when it came to things he was interested in, like his clockmaking, but sadly she'd have to admit that his interest had excluded her. There was no denying Elijah was night-and-day different.

Her thoughts flitted to the instant she recognized his off-key whistling and the goose bumps that developed as she molded into his arms. Squeezing him the way she did had elicited a sharp gasp from him. Zach would have peeled her away for showing that much emotion in public.

A shadowy figure appeared in Catherine's peripheral vision, and she jolted.

The waitress stood before them, coffeepot in hand. "Do either of you need to see a menu?"

"Could I have a glass of water, please?" Catherine asked.

"Nothing for me, thanks." Elijah watched

the waitress walk away, then looked back at Catherine. "I think you fell asleep with your eyes open."

She shook her head. "I wasn't sleeping, just . . . deep in thought."

"About what?"

She should have expected him to ask. Her face warmed. "I think it's gotten warmer in here." She fanned her face, hoping it didn't look as on fire as it felt. "It'll sure be nice to get out of this *kalt wedder* and make it to Florida. How many hours do you think we're behind schedule *nau*?"

He looked at her strangely. "Close to six. Why?"

"I wanted to get word to *mei* cousin that I'll be arriving later than expected, but I don't have the phone number for her bakery."

"If you know the name of the business, we can ask the operator for assistance." He swept the room with his gaze. "I don't see a pay phone. We'll have to look for one at the next stop."

"I hadn't thought about the operator." Catherine breathed easier knowing he had it all figured out. "You're a smart man, Elijah Graber. You know exactly what to say to ease *mei* mind."

"I have more things I want to say—" He clamped his mouth closed as though he'd already spoken too much, which spiked her curiosity.

"What do you want to say?"

"I'll tell you later." He jutted his chin in a

forward nod toward people leaving the building. “The bus is here.”

They made their way back outside and didn’t have to stand in the drizzling icy rain too long.

She climbed the bus steps but halted when the driver put his hand out.

“Your reboarding pass, please.”

Catherine spun to face Elijah, her jaw fallen slack. “Mine was in the tote bag.”

Chapter 15

W*hat else can go wrong?*

Elijah positioned himself between Catherine and the beefy driver, whose soft belly hung loosely over the belt of his uniform trousers and rubbed against the steering wheel. "Sir, if you would allow me to explain. Catherine's bag was stolen—"

"No time to listen to ex-plan-a-tions. Just need to see your reboarding passes." His rough voice sounded like he was chewing gravel when actually he was trying to talk around a wad of chewing tobacco lodged between his yellow-stained teeth and cheek. "Ya got one or not?" He certainly wasn't as friendly as their first driver, and his manners left much to be desired. He used his shirt sleeve to chase away a dribble of dark-tinted saliva that escaped the corner of his mouth when he talked.

Lord, we need Your favor. This area is dangerous, and we must get on this bus. We're both road weary, Father. This will take a miracle for the driver to overlook our shortcomings.

"Well?" the driver growled.

Elijah swallowed dryly. The words of the woman representative rang in his head. *"Keep your personal items on you at all times. Reboarding passes will not be reissued."* No denying they'd been warned, but who could have foreseen a theft?

Catherine sidled up a step closer and gripped his arms with trembling hands. If he glanced at her now, he would, no doubt, find her shrouded in fear. He dreaded having to tell her they were stuck at the diner until other arrangements could be made.

"This is the last bus. We have to get on it." He'd hoped to appeal to the man's sympathy, but the driver pointed at the door and grunted, "Off."

"You can't leave them here." The woman who had asked him the Amish questions pushed up from her seat and strode to the front. "These people were on the other bus," she insisted.

"I don't make the rules. No ticket, no ride."

"Her ticket was stolen." Elijah wasn't about to mention he'd given his ticket to the first driver and had forgotten to ask for it back when he got off the bus.

"You two out!" The driver pointed to the exit, then twisted in his seat to address the helpful *Englischer*. "Ma'am, take your seat or get off with them. This bus is leaving. I have a schedule to keep."

"I'm reporting you." The woman pulled out

her phone from her purse. “Don’t underestimate me. When I set my mind to something, I know how to get an audience. TV, newspaper, social media—should I go on?” She continued talking as she pressed the buttons on her phone with her thumbs. “I think I’ll call it: Driver leaves helpless Amish passengers at an undesignated location.”

“Lady, get off my bus!”

The woman’s thumbs stopped, but she ignored the driver and instead directed her attention to Elijah and Catherine. “Is this your first time riding Budget Bus?”

“*Jah*, it is.” Elijah glimpsed the driver. His narrowed eyes were hooded by heavy brows, and as red as his face was growing, he looked about ready to explode. Perhaps irritating the man wasn’t the answer.

“Lady, I’m warning you,” the driver growled.

“What are you going to do, kick me off the bus for trying to help these people?”

“For getting on my nerves.”

“You’ll have to drag me off the bus. Last I knew we had freedom of speech in this country.” Appearing even more determined, the woman moved her thumbs over her phone faster.

Elijah couldn’t let this situation escalate to violence. He turned to Catherine, who was wiping tears from her eyes, and laid his hand on her arm. “We’ll have to trust God for another way to get to Florida.”

Catherine nodded and started to turn.

"No, wait." Extending her arms, the woman aimed her phone toward the driver, then panned over to them. "This is coming live from Budget Bus number 1248 where first-time Amish passengers—it is your first time, right?"

Elijah nodded.

"Where first-time Amish passengers are being denied entry onto the bus." She rattled off a brief explanation of how they ended up at the diner, stressing its location being an undesignated bus stop. "Can you explain what happened to your tickets?"

Aiming her phone at Elijah, she smiled and waited for his reply. Early childhood teachings had taught the Amish to avoid cameras and to cover their faces when an *Englischer* tried to take their photograph. This had to be different. "Catherine's ticket was in her handbag, but it was stolen." He hadn't noticed that several of the other passengers were pointing their phones at them as well until one shouted to look their way.

Elijah moved in front of Catherine. She certainly didn't need to be part of this. Answering the question, he'd exploited her himself. *"Thou shalt not make unto thyself a graven image."* The biblical teaching caught in his throat.

Passengers on the bus began to chant. "Let them on. Let them on."

Elijah glimpsed Catherine's lowered head and

rounded shoulders. Subjected to this form of embarrassment, she must have wanted to crawl under a rock. He placed his hand on her back between her shoulder blades and was about to direct her off the bus when the driver grunted.

"Find a seat. But I'm only taking you as far as the next bus station."

"Thank you," Elijah breathed in relief. At least at a bus station, he could plead his case to an official. Left at the diner, at a place other buses didn't stop, he had no idea how they would get to Florida.

As he made his way down the aisle, he noticed one empty seat toward the front and directly across from the *Englischer* who had spoken up for them. Glancing farther down the aisle, the other seats appeared to be taken. "Catherine, take that seat."

"But—"

The driver barked for them to sit down, leaving neither of them any choice. Elijah continued to make his way down the narrow aisle as the driver put the bus in gear and they rolled away from the curb.

Finally he plopped down on an empty seat near the back of the bus as the overhead speakers squawked.

"For those of you who are new, welcome aboard bus 1248. I'm sorry for the delay, ladies and gentlemen, but with a few rerouting adjustments and weather permitting, we should be able to make up the time and still reach West Virginia by Saturday afternoon. In the meantime, please relax and enjoy the ride."

West Virginia. How much longer would it take to get from there to Florida? Elijah hated being separated from Catherine, but for now at least they were safe. Perhaps later someone would kindly offer to switch places so they could sit together.

He glanced at the passenger seated next to him. In his early twenties, the man wore a black T-shirt with a skull on the front and ripped jeans, and he had wires hanging from his ears. Slumped against the window, his eyes were open yet he gave no indication he was aware Elijah had sat beside him. Perhaps it had something to do with his loud music. Even Elijah could hear thumping sounds coming from the man's earbuds.

Elijah yawned. He hadn't gotten much sleep, but he couldn't allow himself to fall asleep on this leg of the journey either. Not with Catherine so far away. Using his feet, he pushed his duffel bag under the seat ahead of him as far as he could, but it still left no leg room with his seat mate's oversized bag jammed under there too. *Just be thankful.* They were safely on the bus, once again heading south. How was Cat getting along? With her sensitive nose, was she as repulsed by the pungent scent of urine as he?

• • •

Catherine sank into the seat, relieved the driver had finally allowed them to get on the bus.

Seated across the aisle, the woman who had come to their rescue extended her hand. "Hi, I'm Thelma Marshall. I met your husband earlier at the diner. I'm sorry to say I bent his ear asking so many questions."

Catherine considered correcting the *Englischer* about her and Elijah's marital status, but what was the use? Doing so would be like swatting a hornets' nest with a broom. She'd be swarmed by more questions she didn't want to answer. "It's nice to meet you. I'm Catherine Glick."

"It's a blasted shame how poorly you and your husband were treated. To think that driver was going to abandon you at that diner—it makes my blood boil, is what it does."

Catherine smiled. "We really appreciate your help."

"I figured you needed someone to speak up for yas. I know your people are kind and meek and all that." She leaned closer. "By the way, I was bluffing the driver. The only thing I've ever organized was a community yard sale." The woman chuckled.

"I think you had everyone fooled." A giggle bubbled up within Catherine, unraveling tension that had balled up her nerves. She leaned into the aisle and looked toward the back of the bus for where Elijah was seated but couldn't see him.

"Third row from the back," the man sitting next to her said. His deep voice sounded musical to her ears.

She glanced over her shoulder at the elderly man. "Excuse me?"

"Your traveling friend. He's seated on the aisle, three rows from the back."

The man had on a large floppy hat like the type she'd seen men wear at The Amish Table after fly-fishing. The way he had the hat pulled low and the brim flopped in front of his face, she wondered how he noticed where Elijah had sat. But when she looked again for Elijah, she spotted the tip of his straw hat exactly where the man had said. "How did you . . . ?"

"You located him?" He smiled warmly.

"*Jah*, thank you." She returned his friendly smile, hoping it came across as genuine, because inwardly she was wishing he was Elijah. The sun shone brightly through the window, but Catherine hadn't felt so mentally and physically exhausted in her life. She would close her eyes and try to sleep some if she knew she wouldn't absentmindedly use the man's arm as a pillow as she had Elijah's.

Catherine turned over in her mind the conversations she'd had with Elijah on the journey so far. *"We were married in name only. Three months."* Had Elijah mentioned who told him she and Zach were courting? *No.* Elijah had omitted that tidbit of information, but why? He'd been misinformed. She and Zach were friends. They shared a few walks together, but they weren't courting—then.

She recalled the ground was covered in frost the morning Zach had stopped by the house. When he arrived, he used the excuse of needing to speak with her brother, but a short time later, he was asking to court her.

"Is it true the Amish only go to school through eighth grade?" Thelma asked, pulling Catherine back to the present.

"*Jah*, it's true. We are finished with our book learning by then, but we continue to learn useful things such as cooking and sewing." Catherine politely answered a slew of questions. Even the *Englisch* customers at The Amish Table hadn't probed their plain lifestyle as much as Thelma did.

"How do you keep food cold if you don't have a refrigerator or freezer?"

"We have an *icehaus*. And the root cellar stays *kalt* too."

The woman's questions continued, and Catherine wasn't sure if Thelma would ever get her fill of information. But their conversation did pass the time.

"What happened to your ticket? Did I hear it was stolen?"

Catherine nodded. "I was feeding a piece of sausage to a stray cat, and a man came out of nowhere and took *mei* bag." Her thoughts flitted to Elijah running after the hooded man. The brazen bag snatcher could have been carrying a gun or knife.

"You poor thing. You must have been frightened to death."

"It all happened so fast." *Thank You, God, for protecting Elijah when he ran after the crazed man.* Catherine leaned into the aisle and turned to search for Elijah. Not seeing him, she leaned her back against the chair and closed her eyes.

When she opened her eyes again, Thelma's head was tilted up, her mouth was hinged open, and she was making irregular, raspy sounds with intermittent snorts that would almost wake her up.

"That's sleep apnea," the man next to Catherine said. "She doesn't listen to her doctor and lose the extra weight that would make her sleep better."

"You know her?" Catherine whispered.

"Not directly."

Catherine kneaded her hands together, wishing she had her crochet hook and yarn to keep herself busy. At least the inquisitive woman had fallen asleep, and the older man beside her wasn't too talkative. She glanced beyond the man and gazed out the window at the rolling snow-covered hills. It must be a beautiful sight in the fall when the trees were full of reds and yellows and oranges. As it was, the sky was darkening with snow clouds.

"First time traveling?" the man asked.

"*Jah*, do you know where we are?"

"People refer to this area as Ohio's hill country. It's part of one of the oldest mountain ranges, the Appalachian."

"Are you from around here?"

"Oh no, child. This isn't my home. I'm just passing through." He glanced out the window. "We're going to get rain."

"You don't think those are snow clouds?"

He shook his head. "Clouds are low. It'll be rain mixed with ice crystals." He turned to her. "Would you like to sit by the window since this is your first time traveling?"

She wanted to gaze at the new landscape, and even though he offered to trade seats, she still didn't wish to impose. "That's kind of you to offer, but I'm fine here."

"How far are you traveling?"

"To Florida." Should she have shared that information with a stranger?

"Following the sparrows south, are you?"

Catherine straightened a wrinkle on her dress. "Joining them, I suppose."

"Yes, that's right." The man scratched his bristly white whiskered jaw. "The birds have already flown south for the winter."

An image of the lone sparrow she'd seen perched on the fence post came to mind. *Not all of them went south.* Pondering God's promise of providing for the sparrow, Catherine decided she wasn't much different. Here she was sitting on the bus—without a ticket—out of her element of comfort. She was grateful she only had a few dollars in the bag when it was stolen. She had sewn most of her money into the hem of her dress, although it wasn't enough to purchase a new ticket. Like the sparrow, she, too, would have to rely on God's provision.

Icy rain splattered the window, making long streaks across the glass. Inside the bus turned dim from the loss of sunlight. Gloomy days such as this were best spent putting a puzzle together with her nieces and nephew or relaxing by the woodstove with her needlework. She wrung her hands, stopped, then found herself absently wringing them again.

With a sense of foreboding, she lifted up from the seat a little and strained her neck to look out the front windshield at the road. The back-and-forth movement of the wiper blades, working hard to clear sleet away, made her nauseated. As the bus traveled fast around a winding hillside, her body automatically leaned into the turn. The driver had said something about making up time, but was it really necessary to go this fast?

Another sharp corner. *Focus on something*

other than the sleet hitting the windshield. But it was no use. The wipers whooshing from side to side as the bus rumbled along the narrow road caused her stomach to roil. Acid coated the back of her throat. The passengers' chatter muffled into the background.

She closed her eyes, inhaled deeply, then slowly exhaled, letting the calming breath relax her tightened muscles. The fragrant scent of lilacs filled her senses as she drew in another deep lungful of air.

Horns blared.

Someone screamed.

Oncoming headlights breached the fog—the only warning she had.

Chapter 16

The screeching sound of brakes engaging and tires locking preceded the powerful impact that sent Elijah airborne, along with several other passengers, various electronics, and a cascade of overhead luggage, during the 180-degree whip-lash spin.

Elijah landed with a thud in the adjacent row; his right shoulder thwacked the window. With no warning, flying debris pummeled him; blood oozed from the side of his head. At the same time, another passenger collided with him and something rammed into Elijah's back, striking his left kidney with a mighty blow that left him gasping for air.

An eerie half second of silence fell over them as the bus came to a stop. Elijah lay perfectly still, crumpled at the bottom of a heap, twisted in ways his body shouldn't go, and waiting for the other person or maybe people to come to their senses and move.

"Where's my baby!" A frantic mother's chilling scream pierced the air.

Whimpering and moans echoed throughout

the bus cabin. More glass shattered. The scent of burning rubber filled his nostrils and brought tears to his eyes. He had to get out from under the pile so he could find Catherine, but even the slightest movement seared his shoulder with what felt like the pointed end of a red-hot fire poker.

He tapped the arm of the man who had pinned him against the floor but didn't get a response. Had the man stopped breathing? Elijah gave him a harder nudge. No response.

Warm blood trickled down Elijah's cheek and pooled in the corner of his mouth. He licked his lips, the metallic taste bitter on his tongue. His nose, cheeks, legs, and hands were cold. A numbing sensation blanketed him like morning fog covering a field.

The mother was still searching for her baby, her cries grating on his ears. Others tearfully called out their loved ones' names.

He joined the chorus of voices. "Catherine Glick!" A piece of luggage dropped from an overhead bin onto him and triggered a chest spasm that stole his breath. He panted shallow breaths, his lungs crackling like burning logs. Holding his breath, he squeezed his eyes closed and bit back a yelp.

A few seconds later he mustered enough strength to call out again. "Catherine?" He winced. *Lord, I need You. Catherine needs You.*

Is she unable to respond? I don't hear her. Please, help me find her.

"It's gone!" someone shouted. "The front of the bus is gone!"

"Sir, please return to your assigned location. Sir?" a voice shouted over the chaos.

Elijah ignored the emergency worker's instruction. The area where he'd been assigned, based on the green identification tag around his wrist, was set up along the mountain side of the road.

Dazed after the accident, he couldn't recall how he made it off the bus, just that he did. Perhaps the lapse in memory was some sort of protective mechanism God had designed to stave off hysteria in times like this. Those able to move around searched for loved ones in the same trancelike state.

"Catherine Glick?" he called out.

A bystander tapped Elijah's arm. "Sir, I'm Garnet, a first responder for Rescue Unit 442. Can you tell me your name?"

Elijah's eyes went in and out of focus on the uniformed man's face. Attempting to stand in place, his body swayed as if the ground was moving.

"It'd be best if you lie down."

"*Nay*, I have to find Catherine." He shuffled a few steps but stopped when an emergency vehicle arrived on the scene.

Garnet positioned himself in front of Elijah, blocking his path. "Let's move to the other side of the road so we don't hinder the ambulance crew from their work." He motioned to the mountain side of the road where other passengers were seated along the curb.

Elijah's ears rang. Everything was spinning. His knees buckled and he collapsed. He was sucking air when the man aided him into a lying position on the cold, wet pavement.

"I need a backboard over here."

Elijah willed his body to move, but his muscles refused. Pain rippled along his nerves, and he cried out as two men logrolled him onto a sturdy board.

"I'm going to do a quick assessment," Garnet explained, opening the toolbox he'd been carrying. "Is that okay?"

Elijah reluctantly agreed.

Garnet took his blood pressure and pulse, flashed a bright penlight into his eyes, and asked him questions as he touched places on Elijah's body that caused him to flinch.

"Can you tell me your name?" The man's hands surveyed his head and neck.

"I have to . . . find . . . Catherine," Elijah rasped. "Have you . . . seen her?"

"I haven't treated anyone named Catherine, but we have several crews on the scene. Let me check you out, then I'll see what I can find out."

"Thank you."

"Can you tell me your name?"

"Elijah Graber."

"Do you know where you are, Elijah?"

"On the—" He shied away from the man when his hands touched a tender spot on his ribs. He squeezed his eyes closed and panted a few short breaths to defuse the ripple of pain spreading over his body.

"Keep talking to me, Elijah." Garnet pressed on Elijah's hips first from the top, then from the sides.

"Elijah? Where are you?"

"On the side of the road?" he finally said, forming his reply into more of a question. He had no idea the name of the road or, for that matter, what state they were in. Pain shot through his right leg.

The man's hands moved down his left leg, his ankle, foot. "Does this hurt?"

"A little." He lied.

"I'll need to inspect it further." Garnet retrieved a pair of scissors from his emergency tackle box, then snipped the seam of his blood-soaked pant leg, exposing his flesh as far up as his thigh.

"Can you tell me what day it is, Elijah?"

"Friday . . . or Saturday maybe. I don't know." He was more concerned with the amount of blood the wound was oozing. He hadn't felt the sting until the gash was exposed to air.

Garnet opened several packages of bandages and applied them, along with pressure, to the site. After a long, uncomfortable moment, he wrapped Elijah's leg with a tight bandage, then addressed the gash on his forehead. "What bus were you on?" he asked, while securing the gauze on his head with a piece of tape.

"Where's Catherine? Have they found her?"

"The rescue squad is still sorting patients."

"Budget Bus. I have to know if Catherine is all right." Elijah tried moving, but shards of pain tore through his leg and now his arm. It was then that he noticed his shoulder, separated from its socket, dangling like an appendage on a cloth doll.

"Keep as still as you can." The worker placed two fingers over Elijah's wrist, studied his watch half a minute, then pinched his fingertips. "I'm going to immobilize your arm with a sling. You have a strong pulse and good circulation, but you'll need to tell me or one of the EMTs if your fingers start to tingle or go numb."

"Okay."

Once the sling was in place, the man made a few notes on the back of a small card, then attached the green tag by a string to his sling. The tag read: Triage Priority 3.

"Elijah, I have more patients to treat." Garnet closed his emergency tackle box. "It might be a while before an ambulance is available to transport you to the hospital, but someone will check on you periodically. It's important to remain as still as possible. You most likely have a few broken ribs, and they could potentially puncture your lungs if you move around."

While the first responder had been fussing over him, wrapping tape around his rib cage, a fleet of fire trucks and ambulances had blocked his view of the ravine and, more importantly, of the other passengers being treated. A wavering panic hit Elijah as Garnet picked up his medic box. "What about Catherine? How will she know where I am?"

"If I'm able to locate her, I'll be sure to let you know."

If? Elijah's nerves couldn't handle the uncertainty, but he thanked the man, then waited for him to walk away before pushing up from the wet ground. Too restless to wait for news to get back to him, he set out to find her himself. First he checked the "green zone" without success. Next he limped between two fire trucks to get closer to the heart of the crash site.

The bus that had hit them lay on its side, partially dangling over the side of the cliff and emitting death groans that made the hairs on his arms stand on end. Men wearing reflective rain gear and helmets worked steadily to fasten the vehicle's chassis with thick belts and chains to stabilize its teetering. Meanwhile, a mixture of agonizing cries filled the air.

Over to his right, a dozen or more bodies lay sprawled over broken glass. Tagged with blue identifiers, Elijah wondered if they'd been left to die. The emergency crew members were concentrating their efforts on another large group of people.

He canvassed the area. Some bodies were missing limbs, others were covered in blood, their faces swollen and unrecognizable. A woman's sob summoned his attention. He couldn't be certain it wasn't Catherine, so he followed the wailing voice drowning out all the others. He found the woman sitting down and rocking back and forth against the crumpled guardrail, sobbing uncontrollably.

Elijah stopped one of the caregivers. "Have you seen a woman named Catherine?"

"No, sorry."

In the chaos of suffering and utter bewilderment, one man with a bandanna wrapped around his head was more interested in emptying suitcases than addressing the chunk of flesh flapped open on his cheek. He went through two pieces of luggage, pocketing whatever treasures he could find.

Elijah continued searching for Catherine. He made it a few feet and froze when he spotted a piece of blue material sticking out from under a sheet-covered body. The same blue shade that matched the dress Catherine had been wearing. His mouth went dry.

No! God, please nett *Catherine.*

Elijah stared at the covered body.

Right size, shape—No!

His mind screamed denial even as he forced himself to draw nearer. He lowered himself to his knees. Hands trembling and tears burning his eyes, he reached for the corner of the sheet.

"Excuse me, sir." A hand came down on Elijah's uninjured shoulder. "I have to ask you not to . . . disturb—" The man wearing a uniform with an EMT patch on his shoulder turned as white as the sheet itself. He swallowed dryly, the shape of his face warping as his Adam's apple moved down his throat. Then, regaining his composure, he said authoritatively, "I need to take you back to your designated area."

"I have to know if this is—" He couldn't bring himself to say her name—not in relation to a corpse.

Feeling the weight of the man's hand coming under his armpit, gently prompting him to rise, Elijah refused. He pulled the covering away from the woman's battered face and let out a cry—a blend of sadness and relief mixed with guilt.

"Sir, let me help you up."

Elijah stood on his own, but pain shot through his leg and shoulder, rendering him woozy on his feet. He took a few staggering steps, then felt an arm go around his waist.

"I've got you," the man said.

Feeling the trickle of something warm going down the side of his face and neck, he used his good arm to wipe his face. It wasn't sweat. His bandage needed changing. He straightened his posture. "I think I'm all right *nau*." He wasn't, but didn't want to be ushered back to the green zone. He needed to find Catherine.

Ambulance sirens screamed as they left the scene. Over to his left, machines with oversized clippers grabbed on to a section of the bus and peeled its metal back like it was opening a can of tuna fish. Workers systematically began removing passengers from the wreckage.

"Ward, we can use more help over here."

"Be with you in a sec." He aimed his thumb sideways in Elijah's direction. "Got a walking wounded to take to the green staging area."

"I don't need help," Elijah said. "I can find *mei* way back to *mei* designated area."

The worker hesitated. "I'll stay with you. I'd hate for you to pass out."

Elijah couldn't stomach the idea of tying up this man's time when he could be helping people with greater critical issues. If the blue-tagged people were left unattended, surely he didn't need personal assistance to walk back to his zone. He headed toward the designated area, and when he discovered the worker had jogged off to help the people from the other bus, Elijah veered toward the bus he and Catherine had been on.

Approaching the battered vehicle, he somehow managed to evade emergency personnel. A quick evaluation told him the bus had been struck somewhere around the fifth row. Catherine's row. But where was the severed section?

Elijah bent at the waist and vomited. His head pounded, his throat was raw, and every muscle in his body ached. He would find her before someone escorted him back to his area. Elijah wiped his mouth with his shirt sleeve.

Looking down, he caught sight of what looked like skid marks, not from tires but from metal, stretching across the pavement. At first he thought the markings were made from the other bus because they led to where the bus was dangling off the cliff. Then another possible scenario jumped into his mind, along with a sinking sensation in the pit of his stomach.

The thought sent him stumbling toward the wreckage of the dangling bus, hoping he was wrong and it wasn't Catherine's section that had been pushed over the edge by the other bus.

Chapter 17

Without taking his eyes off the scattered bus remnants at the bottom of the ravine, Elijah ambled alongside the guardrail, searching for the best place to cross, an area that wasn't so steep. He stayed mindful of the other bus dangling over the forty-foot drop. He didn't want to find himself under it if the chains didn't hold.

"It isn't safe to go down there," said a deep baritone voice behind him.

Without looking at the man, Elijah replied, "I have to," and kept going.

"That bus isn't safe. If even one chain snaps, it might launch the remaining portion over the cliff."

Exactly why I'm distancing myself from it. Elijah ignored the man's warning and straddled the guardrail. He sucked in a breath, then dragged his injured leg over the barricade. He wasn't about to turn back.

Lord, give me strength. Elijah tested the ground, his boot sliding on the compacted snow. Maneuvering downhill with his injured leg and shoulder would be difficult enough, but not knowing how deep the snow was in places or where he was stepping was probably suicide. In the moment, the possibility of living without Catherine wasn't an option and justified his actions. He took another step.

Please, let me find her alive, Lord. To keep from sliding, he grasped hold of a low-hanging needled branch of an eastern hemlock and used it for support, but the branch snapped and sent Elijah free-falling down the slippery embankment. After a jarring somersault, he tumbled the rest of the way until slamming against a fallen log near the bottom of the ravine.

He released an agonizing cry that echoed back to him, unable to feel his fingers on his injured side. How would he be able to get Catherine and himself back up the slope? He should have thought this through better. He drew in a deep breath and released it in another cry as he pushed himself up.

Elijah took another step and dropped down again. Wet, cold, and in horrific pain, he belly crawled, digging his good elbow into the snow while dragging himself forward inch by inch until his body refused. Sharpness seized his lungs. He couldn't breathe. Darkness shrouded him.

Vaguely aware he was being lifted off the ground, Elijah peered up at the hovering helicopter. Two men wearing reflective coats and oversized pants stood beside him as the wire-basket system he was lying in began to rise slowly.

"They're going to take good care of you at Shepard Hill." The man with the neatly trimmed mustache patted the cage.

"Where—?"

"Try not to talk. You're going to a hospital in Columbus, Ohio."

"Where's Catherine?" he mumbled. The words sounded like gibberish, and he opened his mouth to speak again but was silenced by a calming pat on the shoulder.

"Just relax. You're starting to feel the effects of the morphine."

Strapped to a long wooden board, he couldn't move his hands to signal them to stop. The basket lifted higher, swaying like an infant's cradle as it rose above the rescuers' heads, above the tops of the trees.

A cloth strap placed over his forehead prevented him from turning his head, but he managed to work it free with a little wiggling. In the distance he glimpsed scattered pieces of metal, then just as he was lifted out of visual range, he spotted a heap of smoldering ashes with charred trees surrounding its perimeter. Men searched the wreckage. His eyelids became too heavy to keep them open.

Lord . . . let them find Catherine alive.

• • •

Voices whispered—voices Elijah couldn't recognize. He pried his eyes open, but blinding overhead light forced them closed. Flashes of white spots filled the darkness. Once the polka dots faded, he opened his eyes again, this time only a slit, then waited for his vision to adjust. He attempted to raise his hand to block the blaring light aimed directly at him and winced when pain seared his muscles.

A woman wearing blue scrubs approached the bed rail and smiled. "You won't be able to move your arm for a while. Your shoulder was dislocated and the circulation was obstructed, but the doctor will need to explain the extent of your injuries." Her straw-colored hair was pulled back in a ponytail that flopped forward as she leaned in. "I'm Candice. I'm the nurse taking care of you today. Can you tell me your name?"

"Elijah Graber." His throat was dry and scratchy. Lifting his uninjured hand to grip the handrail, he noticed the IV tubing running fluid into his body. Again he winced. Even the slightest movement caused pain to cross over from his uninjured shoulder to his injured one. He touched his immobilized shoulder, the ache starting to wane the longer he kept it still.

"It's nice to meet you, Mr. Graber. Do you know where you are?"

Elijah read the employee badge clipped to the woman's shirt pocket: Shepard Hill Memorial Hospital. "The hospital."

Beep. Beep. Beep. The piercing noise came from the right. His gaze traced the source of the alarm to the machine hanging from a pole at the side of his bed. If he'd done something to trigger an alarm by moving his hand with the tubing attached, he hoped it wasn't serious.

"Don't let the alarm worry you." Her reassuring smile helped ease his anxiousness. She pressed a few buttons that terminated the noise. "The alert was sounded to let me know your antibiotic had finished infusing."

"How long—?" His words strained. He swallowed hard to help moisten his throat, then licked his lips.

"Would you like a sip of water?"

"Yes, please."

She picked up a small plastic pitcher on a rolling stand, then poured water into a Styrofoam cup. After placing a straw in the cup and bending it forward, she held it close to his mouth.

The sip of cold water soothed his throat. He released the straw from between his teeth. "Thank you."

"I'm going to set this on the bedside stand, but if you need help reaching it or if you need help with anything else, you can press the nurse call button." She set the cup down, then pointed out the buttons on a remote. "These buttons control the TV. This one the volume and the other one the channel. The red button is the one you'll push to call the nurse. When it's pressed, your room number lights up and beeps at the nurses' station. Don't be surprised if someone answers over the loudspeaker."

"How long have I been here?"

"You were brought into the emergency room two days ago."

He groaned. He couldn't recall anything between the time he'd been airlifted from the hillside to right now.

"Elijah?"

"I'm sorry. Did you ask me a question?"

"I'd like you to rate your pain. One being mild to ten being severe."

"Will you find out if Catherine is here in the hospital? She was on the bus—we were traveling together. Only we weren't sitting together, so I don't know if—if . . . I don't know how badly she was hurt." Tears pricked his eyes. He'd promised to watch over Catherine, and he'd failed. "Will you find her for me? Her name is Catherine. Catherine Glick." Talking made him short of breath.

"Just relax, Mr. Graber. You've had surgery to repair your punctured lung."

"I have to find her."

Her hand was steady on his uninjured shoulder.

"I understand. You said her name is Catherine. Are the two of you related somehow?"

"We're *nett* married . . . yet."

The tiny lines across her forehead softened. "I can't make any promises. Security has been heightened with the media swarming to talk to the passengers."

Elijah swung his leg out from under the cover but hit the tray table and sent it rolling. Sharp pains rippled through his leg, and he gasped.

"Mr. Graber, please. Allow me to get the water for you."

"I'm *nett* trying to get water." He glanced at the flimsy gown he was wearing, and his face immediately heated. "I need *mei* clothes."

"You're in no condition to be getting out of bed. Your lungs are not strong, the chest tube was only removed recently, and you need more antibiotics. Besides, there's still a chance you'll need surgery on your shoulder—"

"I told you." Clutching his bandaged ribs, he puffed out short breaths to relieve some of the pain as he pushed himself upright. "I have to find Catherine."

She angled her head to make eye contact. "I understand." The warmth of her smile told him she really did understand. "I'll see what I can do to locate your fiancée. Okay?"

Catherine and he weren't exactly engaged, but he needed help. If he corrected Candice, her willingness to help might diminish, and if that happened, he might never get to tell Catherine everything he wanted. He'd lose her again.

Besides, it wasn't like he could leave the hospital without his clothes. As shaky as he was, he couldn't even get out of bed at the moment. Plus, he'd have to detach himself from the tube connecting him to IV fluids. And even if he accomplished all that, would anyone even talk to him about Catherine if they knew he wasn't a family member or her soon-to-be spouse?

"Mr. Graber?"

Seated on the edge of the bed, he glanced up at Candice.

"Your IV alarm is going off. I'll need to check the tubing." She went to reach for his hand connected to the fluid, but he jerked his arm away. "If you will get back into bed and finish your course of treatment, I'll do everything I can to find out if your Catherine is a patient here."

"Everything?"

Chapter 18

Elijah slowly opened his eyes. The hospital room was dark except for the light spilling into the space from the hallway. His gaze lingered in a corner of the room. If it weren't for the side effects of the pain medicine that had him groggy even hours later, he would have sworn someone was lurking in the shadows.

He rubbed his eyes with the back of his hand, and the tape from where the IV was placed scratched his eyelids. Elijah blinked away the sting, then reached for the handrail and attempted to pull himself up.

A shadowy silhouette moved toward him. "How are you feeling, Mr. Graber?"

"Better, I think." He didn't recognize the man's voice, nor could he get his eyes to focus on him.

"I'd like to ask you a few questions if you're feeling up to it."

"Okay." He had a few questions for the doctor himself, one being when he could leave.

"Do you mind if I turn on the light?"

"*Nay*, go ahead." Bracing for the flood of brightness, Elijah closed his eyes, then slowly reopened them after he heard the hum of the fluorescent bulb. The man wore a black woolen overcoat, not a white doctor's coat as Elijah had expected. His leather hat was pulled down low over his forehead, the brim worn from years of wear.

"Are you *mei doktah*?"

"No." He stepped forward and removed his hat, exposing a receding hairline. "My name is Alex Canter, and I work for the law office of Rulerson, Markel, and Boyd."

"How do you know *mei* name?"

He bowed his head shyly. "I confess. I'm paid to snag new clients. Most people describe my calling as being an ambulance chaser. Granted, it's not a glamorous depiction of my work, but I've got to do something to put food on my table."

Based on the man's girth, it was evident that business was thriving. His jowls reminded Elijah of the lazy hound he had once owned.

"I overheard someone say you were one of the bus accident victims, and"—he shrugged—"I took a peek at your wristband while you were sleeping. Were you on the bus carrying the theater group? *Fiddler on the Roof*, right?" He made a hand gesture of a beard to his shadowy jaw and smiled. "You look the part."

Elijah glanced at the plastic band fastened around his wrist with his name, a barcode, and a string of some sort of identification numbers stamped on it. “I was a passenger on Budget Bus.”

Mr. Canter had no qualms admitting to the unscrupulous manner in which he obtained his information, but just because he confessed to being here without permission didn’t mean he should be trusted. Having second thoughts about agreeing to answer more of the man’s questions, Elijah reached for the remote and positioned his thumb over the nurse call button.

“You might want to hear what I have to say before you summon the nurse, who will undoubtedly call for security and have me banished from the building.”

“Sounds like you’ve been escorted out of other hospital rooms.”

“A time or two.” The man shrugged again. “But, hey, I’m not here to cause problems—just the opposite.” He slicked back a few strands of thinning hair with the palm of his hand. “In fact, I want to help you. I’ve already spoken with several of the victims from Budget Bus as well as from the private charter company. It isn’t official who was at fault, but either way I’m certain we’ll have a strong case.”

“You’ve spoken with the other passengers?” Elijah sat up higher in bed but regretted the sudden move as pain caused the nerves in his body to sizzle. Once he could muster the strength, he restated the question more directly. "Did Catherine send you to find me?"

Alex stared blankly. "Nobody sent me. Well, my managing junior partner did, but who is Catherine?"

"She's . . ." Elijah shook his head. "I don't think it's a *gut* idea to talk with a . . . an ambulance chaser."

Alex crossed his arms. "Did someone from Budget Bus tell you to say that? The only thing they're trying to do now is damage control."

"I don't understand. The damage is already done."

"Exactly. So, we're on the same page. That's cool." The visitor slid a chair closer to the bed, then opened a briefcase and removed a portable device that looked like the same instrument people used on the bus to play video games on. He pressed a few buttons and the screen lit.

Elijah frowned. "Are you going to play a video game *nau*?"

"Oh no, sir. I use this to take notes. My handwriting is illegible. Plus, it holds all of the forms I need to fill out. I can link it to a portable printer, and it also works as a camera. Have you seen the new tablet yet?"

"*Nay*, and I'm *nett* sure this is a *gut* idea."

"Look, Mr. Graber. The group of attorneys who employ me are ruthless, which is good news for you, because at Rulerson, Markel, and Boyd, we go above and beyond to win huge settlements for our clients. That means your hospital and doctor bills will be paid in full, and that's in addition to the lofty settlement you'll get for your pain and suffering. Our firm will put Budget Bus in a choke hold and squeeze every dime from their big pockets. How does that sound to you?"

Elijah thought several moments. Over the years, Edwina's hospital and doctor fees had put a hardship on her parents. If he had any chance of marrying Catherine, he wouldn't be much of a provider if he was strapped with unpaid medical bills. Still, lawsuits went against everything he believed.

Alex placed his elbows on his knees and leaned forward in the chair. "What's causing your hesitation to make a big chunk of change?" He chuckled nervously. "Have you already won the lottery?" He continued without giving Elijah a chance to reply. "Your injuries are a windfall waiting to be paid out. You don't want to miss out on what's *due you,* if you know what I mean."

"Right *nau*, I don't care about money. Sure, it'd be nice to have *mei* hospital bills paid for, but all I care about is finding Catherine. We were traveling to Florida together."

Alex quirked a brow. "So, she's another passenger?"

Elijah nodded. "I have to find her."

"Absolutely." Alex poised a soft-tipped pen

over his device. "I'll jot down some information and see what I can do to find her for you. How would that be?"

"You think you can find Catherine?"

"It's what I do. I found you, right?"

Elijah nodded.

"Okay then, don't worry. I'm the best." He looked down at his machine. "Does she spell her name with a *C* or *K?*"

"Catherine with a *C*. Her last name is Glick. Will you tell me right away if she's here in the hospital?"

"Of course." He smiled reassuringly, then proceeded. "Can I get your cell phone number so I'll be able to contact you?"

"I don't have a phone."

"Sorry, I wasn't thinking. You probably lost it in the accident. We'll skip that section for now. Where are you both from?"

"Posen, Michigan." He wasn't going to confuse Alex with a long explanation of how he'd moved away from Posen and hadn't technically moved back.

"Describe her for me. What's her age, eye color, hair color, approximate height and weight. Any tattoos?"

"*Nay*, tattoos. We're—" Elijah debated if he should tell the man they were Amish. If he knew anything about their way of life, he would know they didn't believe in lawsuits. Something told

Elijah that the man was only interested in finding Catherine to sign her as a client too. But if he was the best at finding people . . .

"Catherine's beautiful. She's twenty-nine and of average height—five six maybe. I'd guess her weight to be around 140. She has long honey-colored hair and bright blue eyes." Excitement swelled within Elijah as Alex transcribed the information. At least he seemed motivated to help. Elijah hoped he really was the best at finding people.

Alex glanced up from his notes. "Do you have a picture of her in your wallet?"

Guilt niggled at Elijah for not being totally upfront. "We're Amish," he blurted. "We don't believe in having our image engraved, such as in photographs."

"Interesting" was all the man said before continuing with more questions. "So you were on your way to Florida for a once-in-a-lifetime vacation?"

"*Nay*." Elijah wasn't sure why it mattered, but he answered anyway. "Catherine was supposed to work in her cousin's bakery for a few months."

"Loss of work," Alex muttered happily while typing.

"Catherine's a very *gut* baker."

"I'm sure she is." Alex smiled. "What about you? Were you also going to Florida for work?"

Elijah shrugged. "I hadn't made any definite

plans. I was . . ." *Hoping Catherine gave me a reason to stay.* "I planned to train and sell horses once I returned to Michigan." He was too embarrassed to admit that he'd had those plans for over a decade and nothing had materialized. He hadn't found a place to settle down and call home—had no interest if it didn't include Catherine.

"That's okay. We don't necessarily have to prove loss of work. Obviously, the injuries you've suffered have diminished your potential to earn an income."

Elijah's thoughts drifted to the dreams he and Catherine once shared about owning a horse farm, raising buggy horses, and training up a houseful of children. An image of her smiling brightly as she held up the bag of peanut butter cookies she and her niece had baked for the trip flitted across his mind. He licked his dry lips. Earlier he had no appetite. Now just thinking about Catherine's cookies had awakened his stomach.

Reaching for the bedside tray, he rolled it closer, then picked up the Styrofoam cup of water and tilted the straw toward his mouth. The ice had melted and the water was lukewarm. When he took a sip, the water left a metallic taste on his tongue.

"I think I have enough information to get started." Alex slid the tablet into his briefcase and stood. “I am going to find her for you, Mr. Graber.”

“Thank you.”

“But I’d like your word that you won’t sign with another law firm. I usually don’t work on a case without first having the client’s representation in writing. I’m making an exception for you, but I hope you will refuse to entertain another firm’s spiel of what they can do for you. Rulerson, Markel, and Boyd will take good care of you—and Catherine.”

Elijah nodded. “When do you think you’ll know something?”

“I’m going to get started working on this immediately.” He fished his hand into his shirt pocket and removed a card. “You can reach me day or night at this number. Anything you need.”

The only thing Elijah needed was proof that Catherine was alive.

Chapter 19

"I thought we would go for a walk today."

Elijah groaned at his nurse's suggestion. Ever since Candice had told him that Catherine's name wasn't on the hospital census, he'd lost hope. Ambulance chaser Alex hadn't been back to see him—hadn't called with any updates either as he said he would.

"You need to get up and move, doctor's orders." Candice handed him a hospital robe. "Do you need help?"

"*Nay*." Even if he did need help, he would figure it out before being stripped of all his dignity and having to admit he needed assistance. He struggled with the flimsy material, his face growing hotter. The hospital gown was made of soft, thin material. But up until now he had been hidden under the covers. Now she wanted him to walk down the hall. He had a notion to refuse to move even if it was a doctor's order.

"Here, let me help you. This can be a little tricky." She undid a row of snaps, then refastened them around his injured shoulder. She opened the garment the same way for the side with the IV so the long tubing wasn't caught up in the sleeve.

"How long have I been here?" Pain meds had made him so loopy he spent most of his time sleeping.

"This is your fourth day."

The nurse had been kind enough to let him use her cell phone yesterday to call Catherine's cousin at her bakery and tell her about the accident. Since they should have already arrived in Florida, he didn't want Dawn worried. Plus, he didn't want her sending a letter back to Posen inquiring about Catherine's whereabouts. He hadn't wanted to call Catherine's family until he had news to share about her condition. As far as her family was concerned, he and Catherine were in Florida. He hated not telling them, but there wasn't anything they could do from Michigan.

The nurse was at his side, arms guiding him as he lowered his socked feet onto the floor and pushed off the handrail to stand. His knees wobbled. Endless hours of lying in bed had all but crippled him.

"Easy," she said.

"Sorry, but I don't think I'll be very *gut* company."

"Don't you worry about it. You're pleasant to be around compared to some patients I've had. You won't take a swing at me, will you?"

He stopped. "Someone has swung at you before?"

"More than once." She placed her hand on his back and didn't move it even when he tensed.

He ambled forward. "Doesn't sound right. Why would someone do something like that?"

"Most of them don't know they're being combative, especially the inebriated ones. I take it all in stride."

"It takes a special person to do that." He blew out a few quick breaths to ward off the burning sensations traveling up his spine with every step.

It took several minutes to reach the corner of the hall. He was ready to turn around, but she motioned him to continue down another corridor.

"Can you go a little farther?"

"I don't know." He was telling the truth. His legs were beginning to feel like Jell-O.

"There's a woman in the surgical wing at the end of the hall," she whispered.

"Is it Catherine?"

Candice looked side to side, then glanced over her shoulder. If he had more strength, he would have followed her gaze. As it was he had propped himself against the handrail that ran the length of the blue wall and was holding on tight in fear his legs would buckle.

"From what I understand, she was brought in from the accident and was rushed into surgery. She's registered as Jane Doe, but I thought maybe . . ." Candice bit her bottom lip hard enough that when she lifted her teeth, her lip had the indentation. "We should get you back to your room. Your face is washed out, and I can see you're in pain."

"You thought maybe what?"

Candice gave him a once-over with her eyes, and for a moment he was sure he'd be ushered back to his room without further conversation. Then her eyes lit with enthusiasm and she lowered her voice to barely above a whisper. "I thought once we get down the hall you might need to rest on the banister outside of her room." She gave him an exaggerated wink.

He picked up on the hint and headed down the hallway with remarkable speed. By the time he reached the room, stabbing pain had rendered him winded. He clutched the banister to catch his breath and wait out the spinning going on inside his head.

Candice tipped her head and opened her mouth to speak, but he used every ounce of strength to lean into the open doorway and peer into the room.

A nurse seated in the corner of the room stood. "May I help you?"

Elijah disregarded the nurse and approached the bed. The woman wasn't wearing a prayer *kapp*, but she shared the same honey-colored hair as Catherine.

The woman stirred. Her gentle eyes locked with his.

• • •

"Well?" Candice had waited until she and Elijah were several feet down the hall.

"*Nett* Catherine." The woman who had been staring at him had brown eyes. Besides that, when she stirred the covers, he'd noticed a butterfly tattoo just below her ear. The Jane Doe wasn't Catherine.

Tears burned his eyes as he limped back to his room. Spying on the woman with her mouth wired shut had made him that much more determined to find Catherine.

"I'm sorry," Candice said. "I was hoping for a better outcome."

"Me too." He returned to his room, short of breath as shards of pain burrowed into his bones. He crawled into the bed, pulled the covers up around his neck, and sank his head into the pillow, a defeated man. He couldn't even walk a few yards without breathing heavily and breaking into a sweat, and that was while holding on to a handrail. His mind was telling him to get back up, sign himself out of the hospital, and search for Catherine, but his body refused to cooperate.

"I'll get you something for your pain." Candice left the room, then returned a few minutes later with a syringe. After injecting the medicine into the IV port, she asked, "Would you like me to turn the TV on for you?"

"*Nay*, thank you." He didn't give her any

reason why or explain his beliefs. Most of the time outsiders didn't understand the Amish plain way or their convictions.

"I feel bad for getting your hopes up." Candice's sullen expression seemed to match his own. "The other patient's jaw had been shattered in the accident, so she wasn't able to communicate prior to surgery. Then when she came out of the operating room, her mouth was wired shut and she was under anesthesia . . . I should have waited until she was able to communicate her name before I involved you."

"Thank you for *nett* waiting," he said drowsily.

"I'll let you rest." She went to the door and paused. "I'll come back later to check on you." She slipped out of the room and closed the door behind her.

The room fell silent. Lonely.

It wasn't long before his muscles relaxed completely and his body molded into the mattress. He closed his eyes.

"Elijah! Elijah, help me." Catherine's voice echoed, but she was nowhere to be found. Emptiness surrounded him. He stumbled over wreckage, ignored the faint moans and cries coming from other victims, and ambled toward the edge of the cliff.

"Catherine! Where are you? Catherine?"

A gentle shake on the shoulder woke him. He

winced when the overhead light hit his eyes. The woman's image at his bedside slowly came into focus.

"You were having a nightmare," Candice said.

He was still dazed even when she wrapped the blood pressure cuff around his arm. He swallowed hard. "*Mei* throat's dry."

"Probably all that yelling," she said with a smile. "I'll pour you a cup of water once I take your vital signs."

"I hope I didn't disturb any of your other patients."

"Oh, I doubt you did. Most of them have their televisions on, and besides, these walls are thick." She adjusted the blood pressure cuff over his arm, then pressed the button on the machine. "Try to stay still and not talk."

The cuff inflated, squeezing his arm until his fingers started to tingle. It deflated. Elijah fisted his hand, opened it, then fisted it again to return circulation. "How is it?"

"Normal."

"Am I going to be able to leave soon?"

"That will be up to the doctor." She swiped his forehead with a wand-like instrument, then recorded his temperature in the computer. "Are you in any pain?"

He shook his head.

"Would you like to go back to sleep?"

"*Nay*. I keep having the same nightmare. I hear

Catherine calling for me, but I'm never able to find her in the wreckage." Normally he wouldn't share his fears with a stranger, but Candice was a good listener; she no longer seemed like a stranger to him. "I'm afraid I might never see her again."

"Isn't it the enemy's plan to get you all knotted up with worry? He'd like nothing better than to make you feel hopeless and to feed you with lies so you believe the worst. You can't let him deceive you. This is the time to stand in faith."

"You're right," he admitted.

"I'm glad to hear you say that. I took the liberty of asking one of the on-call chaplains who was in the hospital visiting another patient to stop by your room. Of course, you can decline the visit, but I think it might be helpful to talk with someone."

"Instead of you?"

"In addition to me. Someone with . . . spiritual insight."

Candice's insightfulness about standing in faith had encouraged him. He didn't need to speak with a chaplain.

"He's a new chaplain who only recently started volunteering on our floor. I think you'll like him. He's easy to talk to."

Elijah wasn't about to disappoint Candice, one of the only people who had shown interest in helping him. The ambulance chaser hadn't paid him another visit. For all he knew, Alex could have researched the Amish way of life and figured out they didn't believe in lawsuits. Based on the man's money-hungry demeanor the other day, Alex probably focused his attention on finding other injured passengers to recruit and forgot about looking for Catherine.

"Should I send him in?" Candice motioned with a nod toward the middle-aged man loitering outside the door.

Elijah sighed. "*Jah*, okay."

"Chaplains are used to dealing with situations like yours. They're trained in what to say to someone who's lost . . . who's suffering from grief." The nurse waved the man wearing a stiff-looking button-down shirt, a bright yellow tie, and tan trousers into the room.

"Elijah, this is Mr. Fisher, and Mr. Fisher, this is Mr. Graber."

"Call me Paul." The man approached the bed and extended his hand.

"I'm Elijah." He shook awkwardly with his left hand.

"It's nice to meet you, Elijah."

Candice poured a cupful of water and placed it on the tray table, then rolled it closer to the bed so the cup was within reach. "I have some other patients to check on, so I'm going to leave you two alone." Candice rolled the blood pressure machine toward the door. "I'll come back to check on you before my shift ends."

"Okay." Elijah found himself wishing her shift wouldn't end. Admittedly, he liked having company. Candice was someone who understood his desperation to find Catherine. A romantic at heart was what she'd called herself. He'd spotted tears in her eyes earlier in the day when he was talking about how Catherine and he met.

The chaplain motioned to the chair next to the wall. "Do you mind if I sit?"

"Please do."

"I understand you were one of the passengers on the bus involved in the accident."

Elijah nodded.

"Sometimes it helps to talk about what happened, but only if you feel up to it. No pressure."

"It all happened so fast . . . No time to react . . ." *Would Catherine have seen the other bus coming and had time to brace for impact?*

"That must have been frightening."

"I'm frightened more *nau*," Elijah explained. "I still don't know what happened to *mei* friend Catherine. She and I were not able to find seats together, and after the crash I couldn't find her anywhere. Have you talked with any of the other passengers? Perhaps you've seen or spoken to Catherine—Catherine Glick."

"I'm sorry, I haven't. Are you sure she's here?"

Elijah sighed. "I'm *nett* sure of anything."

Paul removed a pad of paper from his pocket. "I'll jot her name down and check with the other members on the clergy staff. I don't cover all of the floors, so maybe one of them has spoken with her."

"That would be great, thanks." Candice had already said Catherine's name wasn't on their hospital census, but it wouldn't hurt for Paul to double-check the list. Maybe at the time the nurse looked, the list was incomplete. Maybe Catherine had been admitted since then, or maybe her status was updated from Jane Doe . . . maybe.

"Where are you from?"

"Michigan. Both Catherine and I are from Posen. Well, I haven't always lived in the same district." Elijah spoke nervously fast, telling Paul things about his past. How he'd grown up in Badger Creek, moved to Posen as a teenager when his father wasn't able to make a go of it in the lumber business, and then fallen in love with Catherine.

Elijah found Paul with his nonjudgmental nature easy to talk to. In the end Elijah had shared more than he wished. He even told the clergyman how he'd felt pressured by his parents and Edwina's parents to get married, and how he'd broken Catherine's heart in the process.

"I was following her to Florida in an attempt to win back her heart." Tears clouded his vision. "We weren't supposed to be on that bus. Our driver had to make an emergency stop. He had a heart attack, or at least that was the rumor."

Paul handed him a small box of tissues from the nightstand.

"Thank you." He tugged one from the box and blew his nose. "What if I missed God's warning? Neither of us had tickets, and the driver of this last bus had tried hard to keep us from getting on."

Paul's brows drew together, forming an A shape over the bridge of his nose, but he said nothing.

"Catherine's bag, which held her ticket, was stolen, and I ended up giving mine to another driver, thinking Catherine was on that bus. It's a complicated story." He plucked another tissue from the box and wiped his eyes. *What a nightmare.*

"Why do you think you missed God's warning?"

Elijah shrugged. "The only reason the driver ended up letting us board was because another sympathetic passenger took up our cause. She argued with the driver about leaving us stranded, and it wasn't a nice part of town either. But I had allowed her to video us—something I'm totally against . . ."

"But she was helping you?"

Elijah nodded. "To get on a bus we should never have been on. I went against *mei* beliefs, and here I am—stuck in a hospital bed, and worse, I don't even know if Catherine is alive or dead. We should have stayed at the diner." Elijah's frustration came out in his tone. He took a deep breath and let it out slowly. "Ever wish you could relive a day?"

"Sure, but then I remind myself that God knows the beginning and the end."

Elijah nodded in agreement. God knew Catherine's whereabouts too.

"Have you contacted your family or your friend's family yet?"

"*Nay*." He glanced at the phone sitting on the bedside stand. "The nurse explained how to place a call, but it's long distance. I would have to reverse the charges."

Their *Englisch* friend Beverly Dembrowski would accept the call, and he would be sure to reimburse her the money once he returned home, but something else was stopping him. What would he say about Catherine being missing?

Paul removed a cell phone from his pants pocket and handed it to him. "I have free long distance."

Elijah swallowed hard. "I was supposed to look after her on this trip."

"Don't let guilt eat away at you. The accident wasn't your fault."

"I don't know what to say."

"Trust God to give you the words. Don't you

think it's better that your families know?"

"*Jah*, I know you're right." He still didn't dial the number.

"God is merciful. His arms are open to the brokenhearted."

Lord, give me the right words. Elijah tapped the numbers on the keypad and waited for Beverly to answer.

Midafternoon the following day, Alex called Elijah's hospital room. "Were you a stowaway?"

"What?"

"Don't try pulling the wool over my eyes. Tell me the truth. Did you belong on that bus?"

Taken aback at the man's clipped tone, Elijah considered hanging up the phone. But Alex had said he could locate anyone. "*Jah*, sorta. We weren't stowaways."

"What do you mean sorta? Budget Bus has no record of you or a Catherine Glick being on that bus, so did you have a ticket or not?"

"We purchased one-way tickets from Rogers City, Michigan, to Sarasota, Florida. With everything that's happened, I'm still a little confused about the date." Elijah started at the beginning, but hearing heavy breathing on the other end of the phone line, he skipped ahead.

"After our driver had to be taken to the hospital, we were placed on another bus. But while we were waiting, Catherine's bag was stolen with her ticket in it. We were eventually allowed on without boarding passes based on other passengers vouching for us. So that's why our tickets were *nett* scanned into the system. We didn't have them to give. You can ask the driver. He should remember us. The other passengers made quite a ruckus, chanting to let us on."

"The driver's dead."

A gasp escaped Elijah's mouth. He closed his eyes, but images of bodies sprawled out on the pavement etched in his mind. His stomach roiled as he recalled the different-colored tags and those who had been covered with sheets.

"You still there?" Alex asked after a few moments of silence.

"*Jah*, I'm here."

"We'll get the mess sorted out. Budget Bus is just being hard—" He growled under his breath. "Difficult donkeys is what they're being at the moment."

At the moment Elijah wasn't concerned about Budget Bus's stubbornness. He had more important questions on his mind. "What about Catherine?"

"She's not a patient where you're at. I've been told there were seventy-eight passengers total between the two buses. At least three different hospitals received patients. I still don't have a count of how many went where, and from what I understand, the authorities have dogs searching the ravine, which tells me they still have passengers unaccounted for. But nobody's talking, so I have no idea how many people are still missing. I'm on my way to Community General to see what I can dig up. Has the doctor said how long it'll be before you're released?"

"*Nett* yet. Why?"

"If I hit a brick wall—and I've been known to scale some pretty tall barriers, so I'm not afraid of heights—we might have to go about it from a different angle and eliminate the unclaimed Jane Does first."

"What do you mean?"

"Frankly, I wish there was an easier way of saying this other than to just spit it out. Hopefully it won't come down to having to search the morgues, because to be blunt, if her body needs to be identified, I can't do it."

Elijah's eyes burned with tears. "You said something about dogs searching the ravine. Do you think those people will be found alive?"

"They could be, sure. As of this morning, reporters are still calling it search and rescue. I have no idea when the authorities will change the status to search and recovery. Have you been watching the news?"

"*Nay*."

"Channel 10 has been doing regular updates. If you hear anything new, let me know. I'll do the same." He ended the call with "Goodbye."

Silence taunted Elijah. After only a few minutes, he picked up the remote. Despite his deep convictions to remain separated from the world, his desire to be informed of any updates warred with his willpower and won. He pressed the On button and flipped to channel 10. A red banner trolled the bottom of the television screen: *Action 10 Breaking News.*

Elijah recognized the hillside road even though the buses had been removed.

A news reporter holding a microphone stood next to the mangled guardrail, turning slightly inward when a gust of wind blew his thick mop of dark hair. "A few short steps behind me, at the bottom of this forty-foot ravine, lies the dismembered section of Budget Bus's fifty-two-passenger streamline, which was involved in Friday morning's accident with Custom Ride, a private charter bus service carrying forty-eight passengers from an off-Broadway theater group.

"It is not yet known which of the two buses is to blame for the fatal accident that has taken the lives of fourteen people so far and sent numerous victims with varying critical injuries to surrounding hospitals." The reporter went on to tell about the theater group's recent *Fiddler on the Roof* production and its sold-out tour, then focused his attention on the number of search-and-rescue dogs combing the area as the camera angle shifted to the deep ravine.

Elijah leaned forward, studying the television screen with keen eyes. Patches of snow, snapped trees, the broken-down bus, but no sign of survivors. The camera shifted back to the reporter. Elijah dropped back against the mattress.

The reporter placed his hand against onc car. "I'm being told now that Sheriff Bailer will be making a statement to the press shortly. No word yet on what information he plans to share. Search-and-rescue teams have been canvassing the site well over one hundred hours."

The camera view cut to three officers, and the larger man in the center stepped up to the microphones.

"On Friday morning, two buses traveling in opposite directions collided on River Ridge Road, resulting in at least fourteen deaths and leaving several critically injured. Upon notification to the Muskingum County Sheriff's Department by Budget Bus and Custom Ride that six passengers were still unaccounted for, search-and-rescue teams were dispatched. As of this time none of the missing passengers have been recovered. My thoughts and prayers are with each of the victims and their families. Thank you."

Reporters shouted questions barely picked up on the news channel's microphone. Elijah turned up the volume on the television.

"Can you tell us which bus company is to blame for causing the accident?"

"When will a list of passenger names be provided to the public?"

"It's been four days. At what point will the search-and-rescue efforts be changed to a recovery mission?"

The sheriff lifted his hand and the questions stopped. "The accident remains an ongoing investigation, and therefore I am not at liberty to discuss any details. Both bus companies are cooperating fully and are working to compile a list of passengers. However, that list will not be made public until family members of the deceased are contacted. As for the question regarding a rescue versus recovery status, we are still viewing this as a rescue mission at this time. As you probably know, when and if the temperature drops below zero, chances of survival diminish."

He lifted his hand when the reporters shouted out blizzard forecast predictions for the southeastern area. "Until the weather changes, we will continue to search for the missing passengers. That's all the time I have."

The reporter recapped the sheriff's message for those just joining them, then ended his on-site coverage with "For Action 10 news, I'm Calvin Dover."

Elijah lowered the volume. His eyes burned with tears as he wondered if Catherine was among the missing.

A soft knock sounded on the door. Candice entered the room, her face drawn with concern. In the short time since he'd known her, he learned to read her expression. He turned off the television. "What's wrong?"

"I heard your TV on. Are you okay?"

He shook his head, afraid if he spoke with a lump in his throat his words would come out garbled.

"It won't be long before you're released from the hospital." She handed him a box of tissues.

Elijah agreed. He'd already made up his mind—he was leaving the hospital today.

Chapter 20

"What, may I ask, are you doing in your street clothes?" Candice stood in the doorway of Elijah's hospital room with her stethoscope draped around her neck and her hands planted on her hips. "I didn't see any discharge instructions in the doctor's progress notes."

"I haven't been released technically, but I can't stay here and do nothing." Elijah fumbled with the hook and eye on the front of his tattered shirt. With his arm immobilized in a sling and the thick bandages holding his ribs in place, even simple things were difficult to do.

"Let me help you." Candice fastened the hooks, then adjusted the arm sling. "How's your pain?"

"Manageable."

Candice smiled. "I have to advise you that you shouldn't leave until the doctor discharges you. Your lungs are still weak, and your ribs haven't healed. Your head and leg have stitches that need to be removed. And your shoulder needs physical therapy. Plus, there's a good chance of infection."

"Advice taken." He touched his temple where

it had been sewn back together. The stiff thread was knotted at the ends, and the stitches along his inner thigh had already started to itch. But stitches weren't difficult to remove. He'd done it before when one of the mares he was training sliced open her leg. Couldn't be that much different to remove his own.

But he'd forgotten about the emergency workers cutting his pant leg up to his thigh until he put on his pants. He made a spectacle of himself with the flopping open pant leg that left him exposed. Too bad his duffel bag with his extra clothes was lost somewhere in the wreckage.

"Does that mean you'll stay?"

"Nope." He found his socks balled up in the bottom of the bag that held his pants, shirt, boots, and suspenders.

Candice sighed. "I'll be back in a few minutes. Please don't leave while I'm gone."

"It'll take me that long to put on *mei* socks and boots," he said as Candice left the room.

Elijah sat on the chair next to the wall and readied the first sock. Hopefully she wasn't planning to rally reinforcements to convince him to stay. It wouldn't work. If he stayed it would only prolong reuniting with Catherine, and that wasn't something he was willing to put off any longer. Too much time had already lapsed between them.

Candice returned with a clipboard and pen. "Any chance you changed your mind?"

"Nope."

She handed him the clipboard. "In that case, I need you to sign some forms stating you are choosing to leave against medical advice."

"Where do you want me to sign?"

Candice pointed to the line. "I wish you would wait until you're stronger."

"I can't. I have to go *nau*." He signed where she indicated and handed her back the forms. "Thank you for your *wunderbaar* care."

"I was just doing my job."

"If I'm ever in the hospital again, I hope you're *mei* nurse."

"And you might end up readmitted if you don't take it easy." She tore off a copy of the signed document and handed it to him along with a packet of other papers. "You'll need to come back to have your stitches removed in a week. Make sure you follow these patient instructions. It's important to keep your wounds clean. Inside the information packet is a list of things to watch for. Be sure to read it. If you become short of breath, you must go to the emergency room. Remember, your ribs are still broken."

"*Jah*, I will." He folded the papers and tucked them into the plastic bag marked Patient Belongings.

"This is something from me." She handed him an envelope. "It isn't much."

Elijah stared at his name scrawled on the front, not sure how to respond.

"Open it."

Peeling it open, he eyed the cash. Elijah lifted his gaze to hers. "This is very generous. But you can't give me money. You work hard for this. Here." He tried to give it back, but she took his hand and folded it around the cash.

"You'll need this," she said, her eyes aglow with kindness. "I don't do this with all my patients. Actually, I've never done this before. I believe God prompted me to give you this money, and I also believe God will bless me for being obedient. So don't you dare steal my blessing by giving it back, you hear?"

Elijah smiled. Before leaving Posen, he'd only pinned a few dollars into the waistband of his pants. The rest of his money he packed in his duffel bag, which was somewhere lost in the wreckage. Not that he had a lot of money. He'd counted on picking up odd jobs once he got to Florida.

"I don't know what to say. You've blessed me already. You've not only taken care of me, but you tried to get information about Catherine's whereabouts, and now you give me this. Thank you so much."

“It’s a gift from God, so don’t thank me. It’s all about Him.”

“*Jah*,” he said, feeling put in his place. “I stand corrected. All *gut* gifts are from God, aren’t they?”

“Absolutely.”

He lowered his head. *Father,* danki *for this gift. I pray You will bless the giver and meet all of Candice’s needs according to Your will.*

“Oh, I almost forgot.” She dug her hand into the front pocket of her shirt and removed a handful of safety pins. “These should help keep your pant leg closed.”

“*Ach*! *Danki*—thank you,” he said, relieved to have something to close his pant leg. The woman was an angel.

“I put my address inside the envelope. Will you drop me a note and let me know when you find Catherine?”

“*Jah*, I will for sure.”

“I’ll be praying for you, Elijah.”

“Keep Catherine in your prayers too.”

“Absolutely!” She walked over to the bedside table and picked up the phone. “Where do you want the cab driver to take you?”

The presence of several news vans had caused a traffic backup along River Ridge Road. With so many of them leaving the accident area, Elijah’s pulse quickened. Surely they wouldn’t leave until all the lost passengers were found. He shifted on the back seat of the cab to get a better look outside.

"This road has been jammed ever since that accident the other day." The driver looked at Elijah in the rearview mirror. Recognition dawned in his expression. "That's how you injured your arm and why you have those stitches in your head, ain't it? You're one of the passengers."

"*Jah*," Elijah admitted reluctantly. He never liked drawing attention to himself.

"I knew it." The driver smiled in the rearview mirror at him. "I noticed the bloodstains on your clothes and how you had your pants pinned up the seam."

And he'd been picked up at the hospital. "Do you think they've found the missing passengers and that's why so many news vans are leaving?"

"My guess is they're chasing another story. If they found any of them, they'd still be filming."

Elijah's excitement withered. He hoped they weren't leaving because the search had been called off. Would they do that? It wouldn't be dark for a few more hours, and the sky didn't look as though a storm was brewing.

The driver stopped the car several yards from where the accident took place. "How long are you going to be here? You want me to wait?"

"*Nay*, I'm joining the search." He paid the driver, then slid out from the back seat.

The driver rolled down his window and stuck his hand outside. "Here's my card. Call me if you need me to come pick you up. Once they look at you all bandaged up, I doubt they'll let you volunteer."

"Thank you." Elijah took the card out of politeness. With no phone he had no means of contacting the man.

He limped down the road, feeling the hard pavement with every step. He managed to slip past a lingering news van and make his way around a row of parked trucks with empty dog pens in the beds of the vehicles. He spotted a tent set up under a stand of pines several feet away and froze as the words of the cab driver replayed in his mind. What if the cab driver was right and the authorities didn't allow him to stay? Where would he go? As winded as he was now, he wouldn't get far if he was sent away. He wouldn't even make it to a pay phone to call the cab driver back—that's if there were pay phones around here.

It didn't matter if they turned him away; he wasn't leaving. He would find Catherine on his own.

Elijah slipped off the arm sling, shoved it under his shirt, then tucked the shirt into his pants. He headed toward the tent and the group of people milling around the area drinking from steaming Styrofoam cups.

A man wearing a bright orange hunter's coat and matching hat turned in Elijah's direction and acknowledged him with a nod. "Good afternoon."

"Good afternoon to you too." He scanned the small gathering of men and women. "*Mei* name is Elijah Graber, and I would like to join the group of volunteers searching for the missing accident victims." Eyed by several in the batch, Elijah straightened his shoulders and tried to mask his pain with a smile.

"Looks like you've taken quite a blow to your head recently." The man looked Elijah over, his line of vision stopping on the safety pins holding his torn pants together, then moving up to meet Elijah head on. "I've been down to the bottom of the ravine and it's a difficult undertaking."

He'd been down to the bottom once too. "I can do it."

The man with the orange coat looked at the others standing with him, then back to Elijah. "Do you have dogs?"

"*Nay*, but I'm a hunter and a *gut* tracker."

"See Officer Bennett inside the tent," the man in the orange coat said. "You'll need to show your driver's license in order to sign the volunteer roster."

Elijah swallowed hard. He didn't have a driver's license or any other proof of identity, for that matter. "Has anyone been found yet?"

The man shook his head.

Another man in the group whose downtrodden expression reflected the grave situation said, "It's beginning to look like the bodies might have gone through the ice, and if that's the case, the undercurrent would have swept them away." He took a drink from his cup, then tossed it into the trash can next to the tent. "It's sad. We might not find them till spring."

No, God, please . . . say it isn't so. Elijah's throat swelled. *Catherine did not go through the ice. She didn't drown.* He turned and coughed into his hand, trying to dislodge the lump obstructing his ability to swallow.

One man whistled and three dogs jumped down from the bed of a nearby truck. "I'll take my team down the east side and work toward the river." He pulled his knitted hat over his face, covering everything but his eyes, nose, and mouth, then made a hand signal to his eager bloodhounds, and they were off.

Not wanting to waste any more time, Elijah went to the tent, pulled back the tarp, and stepped inside.

The man seated behind the table glanced up. "I'm Officer Bennett. May I help you?"

Elijah moved closer to the table. "I'm here to help with the search."

"Have a seat." The officer motioned to an empty chair opposite his.

Elijah eased onto the chair. It felt good to

sit. His facial expression must have given his thoughts away, because Officer Bennett's brows drew together.

"I'm guessing you were a passenger in that accident?"

If he was reading the officer's expression correctly, he was about to be asked to leave. He couldn't let that happen. Elijah tilted his head slightly off center and pretended to be confused. "Excuse me?"

"You held your breath every step you took, and you look like you've been through battle. Which bus were you on?"

Elijah lowered his head. "Budget Bus."

Denied volunteer placement on the search team on account of his recent injuries and determined not to let anyone stop him, Elijah ambled toward the road, then when he was sure no one was watching him, he cut through a small stand of trees toward the ravine.

He crossed the guardrail and began easing down the slope.

Elijah's foot slid on a patch of snow. He grasped a nearby tree limb and hung on long enough to catch his breath. Maneuvering the terrain with his ribs wrapped and a useless arm that should be in a sling was much more difficult than he expected.

"You could puncture your lungs again or rip

your stitches open. Infection . . ." The nurse's warning played in the back of his mind.

Slow and steady. Stay focused. Don't hurry. If he took the wrong step, he might find himself at the bottom of the forty-foot drop incapacitated with more broken bones. Then he would hope the bloodhounds found him. Although he'd probably be counted as one of the lost.

He climbed down a few more feet. Finding a level spot to rest, he calmed his breathing. His hands were raw and sticky from pine sap. At least the white pine trees' branches were flexible and forgiving. He didn't trust the branches of a birch not to snap under his weight, and he'd made the mistake of grasping a wild raspberry bush, and its thorns pierced his hand.

He continued to inch down the steep incline. A sheet of snow moved under his feet, and he fell. Tumbling out of control, he was sliding headfirst, belly on the ground with no use of his injured arm and not finding anything to grab hold of with his free hand.

His chest hit a large rock and stopped him. "Lord!" Pain riveted him to the spot. For a long moment he didn't move and silently assessed his injuries. A spasm in his rib cage stole his breath. He wouldn't have long if he punctured his lung again, exactly what Candice had warned him about.

Dogs barking echoed in the distance. The

chopping sound of helicopter blades became louder. He couldn't let them delay their search for survivors working on him.

Elijah clenched his teeth and continued. Wet and shivering, he reached the bottom of the slope, rested a few minutes, then pushed off the ground and lumbered along the edge of the ravine toward the wreckage.

By the time he reached the area where the treetops had been cropped, Elijah's legs were wobbly and threatening to buckle. Then he glimpsed something reflective shining a few feet away. He limped toward the metal object. Drawing closer, he realized it was a panel of the bus. Glass littered the ground. He trudged through a swampy area, finding more remnants of the bus on his way.

The moment he saw what was left of the mangled bus lying on its side, tightness filled his chest and he gasped. The way the front section was crushed, it had probably rolled several times. His eyes brimmed with tears as he gingerly approached the torn metal. The ground turned slushy. Melting snow—no, melting ice. Until now, he'd been so focused on getting to the bus, he hadn't paid attention to the surrounding cattails dusted with snow, nor had he considered the marshy wetlands where they grow. He'd reached the river, and the bus had landed partly on it.

Elijah stepped gingerly toward the metal

structure, acutely listening for sounds of ice cracking.

"The one you have come to find is not here."

The deep baritone voice startled Elijah. He paused and listened for the voice again but didn't hear anything. Elijah made his way around the massive heap lying on its side and stopped at the opening. Peering inside, his attention was immediately drawn to the hole in the ice where windows had been blown out and sheet metal curled up. He climbed inside.

His stomach roiled, hearing the lapping sounds of water movement. Counting the number of seats, acid rose to the back of his throat. Catherine had been seated at what looked like the point of impact—where water was now seeping into the cabin.

With every morsel of breath in him, he cried out, "Why, God? Why Catherine? Why *nett* take me?"

"It isn't for us to understand the mind of God, child. Some things are only revealed in time."

Elijah turned and faced the stranger. A ray of sunlight illuminated the older man's features. His bright red hair and the gold specks swimming around the man's pupils, in particular, captured Elijah's attention. He blinked a few times and pushed the tears away from his eyes with his sleeve.

"Don't look for her here. She's gone, Elijah."

How does he know mei *name?* He's a volunteer. Someone from the top probably saw him go down thc ravine and radioed the others.

"It isn't safe to be here," the man said. "The ice is already fractured."

"I'm *nett* ready to leave." Elijah turned his back to the redheaded stranger. He stared hopelessly at the hole, his eyes burning with tears. *How can I go on?* Bowing his head, he sobbed. His entire body shook, the movement sending sharp pains down his injured side, which he ignored.

He remained in the bus several minutes, grateful for the time and that the stranger had respectfully left him alone. Over and over, he asked the Lord "why" while at the same time, scriptures from the book of James crossed his mind: "Now listen, you who say, 'Today or tomorrow we will go to this or that city . . .' You do not even know what will happen tomorrow. What is your life? You are a mist that appears for a little while and then vanishes."

"Lord, You are the giver of life. You alone decide the number of breaths. Even so, Lord, help me to understand Your will. Your love . . ."

A few minutes later, Elijah climbed out of the bus. He spotted the man standing off in the distance. He lowered his head and walked toward the stranger. Once he reached the man at the base of the ravine, he stopped long enough to look back at the bus. "Is it true the authorities are assuming the people who are missing are underwater?"

"Yes," he said solemnly.

"And the bodies." He cleared his throat, finding it hard to think on these terms. "When will they be . . . found?"

"Not until spring."

Elijah tilted his head toward the sky, tears pooling. *God, I need You. What am I supposed to do? I don't want to accept that she's gone.*

Barking dogs drew closer. Elijah opened his eyes as a pack of hounds circled around a large oak a few feet away and began clawing at the trunk. His gaze traveling up the tree, Elijah's jaw fell slack. Several feet up, a woman was tangled in the branches.

Chapter 21

Trackers caught up with the dogs within a few minutes of the hounds surrounding the tree. They praised the dogs for their good work, then with a few hand-gestured commands, the dogs stopped barking and moved away from the tree.

As more rescuers arrived, Elijah stood a safe distance away so as not to be in the way of their work. Thankfully the woman dangling in the tree was not Catherine, but from where he stood, he wasn't sure if it was the same woman who had talked the bus driver into letting them board—the woman who had been seated across the aisle from Catherine.

One man scaled the tree, ropes slung around his shoulder, while the others watched. Elijah drew cautiously closer, overhearing snippets of conversation between the men.

Looking upward, the youngest man of the group shielded his eyes with his cupped hand. "Any chance she's alive?"

"Maybe."

"Doubt it. Hank picked up the scent first. Didn't ya, old boy?" The orange-vested man patted the hound's head. "Hank here is my top cadaver dog."

Another man scratched his whiskered jaw. "If she did survive, it'd be a miracle."

"Let it be so," Elijah muttered, inching closer. He pushed a limb aside and stepped into the clearing where the rescuers were gathered. The dogs spotted him first and perked their ears. *Easy. No sudden moves.* Normally dogs didn't frighten Elijah. He'd raised a few over the years, but dogs in a pack were different.

He scanned the crowd for the redheaded man with kind eyes whom he'd spoken with inside the wreckage, but the man wasn't anywhere to be found. Instead he met the hardened stares of unfamiliar faces and dozens of slanted brows.

The man who had bragged about his cadaver dog spoke up first. "Where did you come from?"

"I, ah—"

"Ken." The person standing next to Hank's owner elbowed the man's side. "I think he's one of them there lost souls from the accident, aren't ya, mister?"

Elijah opened his mouth, but before he could respond, a man off to his right pointed up at the tree. "Randy made it up." He diverted everyone's attention to the climber.

Elijah, along with the throng of rescuers, watched as the climber eased down on the limb and scooted toward the woman. After a short evaluation, the climber shook his head. Everyone on the ground had the answer—the woman was dead.

With heads lowered, silence shrouded them all. Elijah not only grieved for the woman whom he'd met only briefly, but he grieved for Catherine and the others still missing. It didn't take long for the man in the tree to secure a harness around the woman. He used the ropes to carefully lower her down while the other men eased her onto the ground.

For Elijah, everything moved in slow motion, like a terrible nightmare. Only this wasn't something he could wake himself up from or could erase—nothing after today would ever be the same.

Once the man climbed down from the tree, the men worked together to place the woman onto a black body bag someone had produced from his backpack. Watching them zip it up made it all so final. A collective sigh hung in the air. Elijah blinked and tears slid down his face.

Catherine, where are you?

The rescuers quickly decided among themselves which four men would carry the body back to camp while the others continued to search the wooded area. Elijah took a few steps backward, not wanting to draw attention to himself. He planned to follow the trackers, invited or not.

The four men chosen to return to camp each grabbed a corner strap on the body bag and began the uphill hike. The others attended to their dogs.

"We're going to lose sunlight if we don't get moving soon," the large man everyone called Ken said to the men around him. He left the group and approached Elijah. "I didn't catch your name?"

"Elijah Graber." He stood up straighter even though his throbbing back muscles rebelled. "Catherine Glick and I were both passengers on Budget Bus when it crashed, and *mei* friend Catherine is still missing."

The man pulled a cell phone out of his coat pocket, pressed a few buttons, but instead of making a call, he studied the screen, repeating Catherine's first and last name under his breath. "I don't have her on the list. You sure she's missing?"

"She was seated next to the woman you just pulled down from the tree. Earlier, I was inside the severed section of the bus. It's on the ice." He motioned with a nod in the general area. "Beyond those cattails."

"I'm familiar with its location."

"The side of the bus with the greatest amount of damage, which I'm assuming was the point of impact, was where Catherine had been seated." His throat tightened and he fought a wave of nausea, recalling the hole in the ice. "Do you think she's in the river?"

"No, I don't." Ken's brows puckered as he eyed Elijah with concern. "Mr. Graber." He spoke slowly, although not in a degrading way. "Your friend's name isn't on the list of missing passengers." He cocked his head. "That means her whereabouts has been accounted for somewhere."

"Where is she?"

Ken shook his head. "I don't have that information." He looked beyond Elijah and made a hand gesture to one of the other workers. "I'm going to have Mitch take you back to camp."

"But I—" Another wave of nausea roiled his stomach.

The man who had climbed the tree came up to them. "Did you need something, Ken?"

"I'll be right back," Ken told Elijah, then motioned for the climber to follow him. They stopped a few feet away. "I want you to make sure Mr. Graber gets back to camp all right." He pivoted slightly, turning his shoulders inward, and lowered his voice.

Straining to listen, Elijah picked up only parts of the conversation.

"He's one of the accident victims and in no shape to be down here in the ravine. Make sure you have your radio on, and take the backpack with supplies."

"You don't think he'll make it up the hill? How did he get down here?"

"I don't know." Ken glanced over his shoulder briefly and smiled at Elijah. "I've told him twice now that the person he's searching for isn't on the list. Either he's delirious or in denial."

Delirious? Maybe. Elijah had pushed himself hard just to get down the steep slope, then trudging through the rough terrain had aggravated every muscle in his body, including his stomach muscles, which were sore from dry heaving. But how could he be in denial? Catherine was missing—no denying that.

Mitch nodded at something Ken said, and then he went back to the group and grabbed one of the backpacks leaning against the tree. He rejoined Ken and Elijah.

"Mitch will make sure you get back to base camp safely," Ken said.

"Catherine's name might not be on any list. We lost our tickets. The driver didn't want to let us board without them, but he ended up letting us. So our tickets wouldn't have been scanned into the system."

"I wouldn't know anything about that." Ken turned to Mitch. "When you get back up to base, put Mr. Graber in touch with Officer Bennett."

"So, there is a chance Catherine is in the river." Elijah crossed his arms. "I want to stay."

Ken shook his head. "That isn't in yours

or Catherine's best interest. If the number of passengers originally reported isn't accurate, you'll need to make Officer Bennett aware. Unless he updates the list to add her, no one will know to keep looking once we find the others. You need to tell him everything you've told me."

Elijah sighed. He had already reported the ticket mix-up to the officer when he stopped at the tent to sign up as a volunteer. Officer Bennett had promised to contact the bus authorities, and Elijah was to wait until they responded.

"Waiting is always the toughest part," Mitch said, adjusting the shoulder straps of the backpack.

"More like torturous," Elijah grumbled.

Mitch placed two bottles of water in the backpack side pockets, then nodded at Elijah. "Ready?"

He took a deep breath and released it. "I suppose I don't have a choice."

Mitch smiled sympathetically, then led the way, taking them in a different direction than the route Elijah had taken. He plodded along, dreading having to scale the upcoming hill with one arm in a sling. It had been difficult enough going downhill with adrenaline pushing him forward.

Mitch glanced over his shoulder. "How are you doing? Need to stop and rest?"

"I'm okay." It seemed like they'd been on the trail a long time, but at least the gradual incline was easier on his joints. On a different day he would have enjoyed listening to blue jays chirp. The sun warmed his face. Melting snow had turned the path into a mixture of slush and mud. "How do the dogs do when everything is melting?"

"It doesn't change their ability to follow a scent, if that's what you're asking." Mitch hiked a few more yards and stopped. He removed the two bottles of water and handed one to Elijah. Then he removed a Snickers bar from another pocket and broke it in half.

"Thank you." Elijah uncapped the bottle, took a drink, then peeled the wrapper off the candy bar. Until now he hadn't thought about eating or drinking.

"I overheard you say your friend was seated up front."

"*Jah*, the area where the bus was hit."

"What's her name?"

"Catherine Glick."

Mitch grimaced. "Have you checked the area hospitals?"

"I was told Shepard Hill is the nearest hospital." Elijah shook his head. "She wasn't taken there."

"In cases of mass casualties, patients are transported to multiple facilities. I know helicopters were airlifting patients out of the ravine." He took a bite of the snack and stopped chewing when Elijah said he'd been one of them. The man's gaze assessed him more closely, stopping on his stitched head, then moving down his pinned pant leg. "What kind of injuries did you have?"

"Broken ribs. Punctured lung, I think the *doktah* called it a pneumothorax or something, but whatever it's called, it hurt like crazy, so did *mei* dislocated shoulder. And some lacerations," he said matter-of-factly before popping the last bite of chocolate into his mouth.

Surprise registered on Mitch's face. "And you were released from the hospital already?"

Elijah shook his head. "I left on *mei* own accord."

"That wasn't wise."

Elijah shrugged. "Catherine's alone—somewhere. She'd never ridden a bus before, never gone on a trip . . . I promised to take care of her." Lowering his head, he focused on his muddy boots. "I failed her in so many ways."

"You can't beat yourself up over it. The accident wasn't your fault."

He hadn't caused the accident, but he was the reason they were on that bus. Had he not chased after the purse snatcher, they would have been on the first bus. He'd wanted to earn her love or at least her respect by getting her bag back. He recalled how her downcast expression changed into joy when their eyes met across the crowded diner. She had weaved around the other passengers to reach him, then collapsed against his chest, burying her face in the crook of his neck. In that moment everything was right.

"I don't want to rush you, especially if you're in pain." Mitch glanced at the horizon. "We should get going. Once the sun goes down behind those trees, the temperature will drop and we'll be hiking in the dark."

"I'm ready." Elijah recapped the bottled water.

"First, I'd better wrap your arm. I see that you've been favoring it." He knelt and unzipped his backpack.

"No need." Elijah reached under his shirt and removed the sling. "I have this."

"Now why doesn't that surprise me?" Mitch helped immobilize Elijah's arm before they continued the hike.

His ribs were sore, and the stitches pulled the skin on his leg with every step he took, but he kept moving, not wanting to be a hindrance.

Mitch was patient. He slowed his pace when they reached rocks that, because of their size and slipperiness, were difficult to maneuver over. The last several yards of the journey took them straight uphill. The sun was lost in the forest, making it difficult to see. Elijah wasn't sure he could have reached base camp if Mitch hadn't been there to give him a hand. But somehow they made it to the top.

A throng of reporters surrounded the back of an ambulance as the men who had carried the dead woman's body lowered the black bag onto a waiting stretcher.

Mitch's radio squawked. "We're calling it for the night," the man on the walkie-talkie said.

"Anything?" another male voice asked.

"No. We're heading up now."

Mitch turned the volume down on his radio. "Officer Bennett's tent is over here."

Elijah wasn't keen on talking with the man who earlier had denied him access to join the search. He plodded along, conjuring up an explanation for his actions in his mind.

"Hey, over here! It's one of the missing passengers," someone shouted.

Elijah turned, only to realize the reporter calling for everyone's attention was pointing at him.

A bright light attached to a large camera propped up on someone's shoulder landed the beam of light on his face. "I'm *nett* one of the missing passengers." He shielded his eyes with his good arm.

"Come on, guys, leave him alone," Mitch said. "Elijah helped with search efforts today, and that's all we're going to say at this time."

Even as Mitch and Elijah headed toward Officer Bennett's tent, the questions continued. "How many people are still missing? Can you tell us the name of the woman you recovered from the ravine?"

Mitch pushed the flap open on the tent, then addressed the reporters as Elijah went inside. "No comment."

Officer Bennett glanced up from his paperwork and, making eye contact with Elijah, frowned.

"Sir, this is—" The radio in the tent and Mitch's walkie-talkie squawked in unison.

"We located another person. This one on the northwest ridge, midway up."

"If you two will excuse me, I'm going to see if they need help." Mitch left, and Elijah was quick to follow him out of the tent.

"I'd like to go too."

Mitch shook his head. "It'll be dark soon, and we'll need to work fast. Besides, that's the steepest side of the ravine. I'm not sure how involved this recovery will be." He turned without giving Elijah a chance to speak and headed toward the ridge.

Elijah caught up. "Will you tell me if it's Catherine? She's twenty-nine, has long golden hair, and was wearing a blue dress."

"Find me afterward." He disappeared down the embankment just as a reporter asked if another person had been found.

The reporter made a quick hand wave, and another man aimed his oversized camera down the hill. Elijah leaned around the reporter to get a look at what the cameraman was filming, but trees blocked his view.

"Who was wearing a blue dress?" the reporter standing next to him asked.

Elijah stared straight forward.

"I know you were a passenger on the bus. Obviously, you were separated from someone who's very important to you."

"*Jah.*"

"I've been covering this story since the beginning. You've probably seen my updates on Channel 10." He paused a half second, plastered on a toothy smile, then adjusted the cuff of his sleeve under a thick red sweater. "Is she a relative of yours? The reason I ask is because I plan to do a personal-interest piece. It'll run over a few segments. Nothing too big, but it'd be good PR for your theater group."

"What?"

"I've interviewed several survivors. What's her name?"

Elijah studied the man's flashy smile, which was too perfect, too forced to be sincere. Cat wouldn't have talked with him or any reporter. Then again, if the man was as persistent with his questions as he'd been with Elijah, she might not have been able to avoid him. "Catherine—her name is Catherine Glick. Have you seen her?"

"Maybe. Like I said, I've interviewed several from your theater group."

"I'm *nett* in a theater group."

The man eyed Elijah's tattered clothes. "You're not part of the *Fiddler on the Roof* cast?"

"*Nay*, I'm Amish."

The reporter touched his chin with the pads of his fingers. "Interesting."

Dogs barking drew their attention. The hounds came running up the hill and didn't stop until they were next to their master's truck. A few minutes later, the men arrived. First the ones carrying the body bag, followed by the other trackers.

Elijah spotted Mitch in the group, his face long with sorrow. Elijah sucked in a breath. *Don't let it be Cat.* Nett *in a body bag. Please, Lord.*

Mitch looked straight at Elijah and shook his head. Then stopping next to him, Mitch whispered, "Male."

"*Danki*, Lord." Elijah exhaled heavily. Relief lasted only a moment before he was torn with guilt. Someone's life had been tragically lost, and inside he was celebrating because it wasn't Cat. *Forgive me, Father.*

Officer Bennett stepped out of the tent and waved in Mitch and Elijah's general direction.

"I think he wants to talk with you, Elijah. Maybe he's received some updated news."

Chapter 22

A rhythmic hissing sound blotted out the ability to decipher the conversation going on around her. Two voices, both women, spoke barely above a whisper. Strangers had spoken to her before, asking her to squeeze their fingers if she was in pain. Her body throbbed, every fiber, yet her muscles refused to move. A strong antiseptic scent filled her senses. A moment later, despite her inability to communicate her level of pain, warmth seeped into her veins. Her mind went numb. The pain was gone. Locked in a drug-induced state, she had no concept of time or place.

Sometime later a soft, unfamiliar voice sounded muffled. “Is she waking up?”

“Yes, I believe so. Will you page Dr. Gleeson and let him know, please?”

Did she know a Dr. Gleeson? It hurt to think, to concentrate. Her mind went blank. More whispers. So distant, unrecognizable. She tried turning her head in the direction of the voice but for some reason couldn’t move.

Footsteps crossed the floor, a door creaked

open, a phone was ringing somewhere, then the door closed and the outside noises were gone.

"Good morning," greeted the woman who had given the orders to the soft-spoken one. "I'm Amy, charge nurse for the surgical step-down unit at . . ." The nurse's words garbled together, and the name of the hospital was lost to muffled noises that reminded her of trying to hear deep underwater.

Something prevented her from opening her eyes. Just making an attempt to view her surroundings increased the pressure around her eyes. The rhythmic hissing noise coincided with air rushing into her lungs, expanding her chest cavity. Moving her arms was impossible. Something was tied to her wrists, keeping her pinned to the handrails of the bed. Trapped, as if cocooned in cement.

"Try and stay calm." The voice was closer now. "You're in the hospital."

Pressure in the back of her throat kept her from responding. Her airway . . . She couldn't . . . breathe. Panic infused her veins. She pulled against the wrist restraints, but to no avail. Unable to speak—to see—to swallow. Why wasn't the person trying to help? Couldn't she see something was wrong?

Please, someone look at me. Help me! This was a dream, a bad dream.

An alarm blared. The repetitive piercing scream

cut through her skull with what felt like shards of glass, crippling her thoughts. To deaden the intensity, she needed to cover her ears, but her hands were strapped down.

Seconds later the blaring stopped. But even after the alarm was silenced, a dull ringing in her ears remained. In the background the rhythmic hissing continued, expanding her lungs every few seconds.

"Just relax, sweetie, and try not to fight the breathing tube." A warm hand grasped hers. "Dr. Gleeson is on his way."

Moments later heavier footsteps clacked into the room, then stopped at the side of the bed. The bed railing rattled, and she sensed the male newcomer leaning over her. "I'm Dr. Gleeson, the surgeon who's been monitoring you these last few days."

"She's restless, Doc."

"Vitals?"

"BP: 120/78. Heart rate: 94. Respirations: 14 with intermittent independent breaths. Electrolytes, hemoglobin/hematocrit, and blood gases within normal limits, and respiratory therapy has initiated the weaning process per your criteria with spontaneous breathing trial success."

"Good. Let's remove the ventilator and see how she does on her own." As if he had redirected his position so he was closer to her, his voice grew louder. "How does that sound to you?"

Did he really expect her to answer with a tube stuck in her throat? *Yes, take it out.*

"If we need to," the doctor said, "we can always reinsert it. Your face is bandaged, and I know you're unable to see me, but Nurse Amy and I will explain things as I go."

Once again the nurse took her hand, wiggling her fingers against Catherine's palm. "Squeeze my finger if you need to. Removing the tube will feel a little strange."

Something tugged at the back of her throat.

"Cough if you can," the doctor instructed.

She couldn't. Even so, the breathing apparatus moved through her throat smoothly and was out. She rasped a few sharp breaths, the dry air irritating her already-raw throat.

"I'm going to listen to your lungs," Dr. Gleeson said as something cold landed on her chest. "Take a deep breath for me."

Inhaling even a little hurt, but every time he moved his stethoscope, she did her best to comply.

"No rales. No rhonchi. Lungs sounds are equal." He removed the instrument from her skin. "Your respiratory muscles are going to feel sore, and that's normal. Think of your lungs as unused muscles. After a long period of immobility, the first few stretches are painful, but like your muscles, your lungs will recover."

"Okay." She cleared her throat. Her weak

voice came out strained and hoarse sounding, barely above a whisper, and not because she was trying to talk low, but it hurt to talk. She went to feel for a bulge but couldn't lift her arms more than an inch or two. The bed rail rattled as she pulled against the strap pinning her down.

A large, rougher hand took hers. "Easy," Dr. Gleeson said comfortingly. "We had to restrain you for your own protection. You were trying to pull out the respirator. But now that the breathing tube has been removed, I don't see any reason to limit your movements." Dr. Gleeson gave her hand a gentle reassuring squeeze, then let go. "Okay, Amy. Go ahead and remove the restraints."

Her muscles relaxed as apprehension faded. The band holding her head in one place came off first, followed by the straps around her wrists. Finally free to move her hands, she touched the bandages on her face, covering her eyes.

"It's important that you don't disturb the bandages," the doctor said, taking her hand and guiding it down to her side. "We need the gauze dressing to stay clean and in place."

Questions jumbled in her mind, but before she could form any words, the doctor spoke first.

"You've been in a serious accident. I'll explain your injuries and the treatment plan, but first, young lady, can you tell us your name?"

• • •

"Can you tell us your name?"

The doctor's question shouldn't have required so much thought. But her mind was blank. Except for what she'd been told about being in an accident, and that her face was damaged enough that it required extensive bandages, she couldn't recall anything, including her name or anything about her past.

"I don't . . ." Her throat dry and scratchy, she touched her neck. Even with the breathing tube out, her voice box was stubborn.

"Amy, would you get her a cup of water? Her throat is probably sore."

Raw. Off to her right side, water was poured. A moment later a straw touched her lips.

"Take small sips," the nurse instructed.

She opened her mouth and took a drink. The room-temperature water helped soothe her throat some. When she finished drinking, she tried to communicate but was unable to push her voice above a strained, hoarse whisper no matter how hard she tried. Growing frustrated, she touched her throat again, and the nurse offered her more water.

"Do you want to try again?" the doctor asked once she had taken a longer drink.

She shook her head. It was no use. Not only did her voice not want to cooperate, but she couldn't answer his question. Her mind was numb—empty.

"Let's give your vocal cords some rest and try this again later," Dr. Gleeson suggested.

She tightened her grip on his hand, not wanting to let him leave before he explained why her eyes were bandaged. Was she blind?

"I made a few phone calls as promised regarding the bus passengers." Officer Bennett stood with his shoulders squared, his hands clasped in front of him, and his unwavering gaze fixed on Elijah. He offered no indication if the news he'd received was good or bad.

Elijah steeled his nerves. "What were you able to find out about Catherine?"

"Nothing concrete."

Despair and fatigue merged on Elijah, and his shoulders wilted like a plant with no water. He needed answers. "So no one knows where she is? Not even the police or rescue workers?"

Officer Bennett sighed. "Please understand that in cases of mass casualties, a large number of patients are unconscious. They're separated from their loved ones, as in your situation, and they don't always have identification on them. As for Budget Bus, they have no record of her boarding the bus."

"And I explained how we had lost our tickets." Elijah shifted his weight to his unhurt leg, the physical demands beginning to take a toll.

"Please, have a seat. You look like you're in

pain." He waited for Elijah to sit before continuing. "I know you mentioned the bag her ticket was in was stolen, but the ticket that has me puzzled is yours. According to bus records, you boarded a different bus. Your boarding pass was electronically scanned."

"*Jah*, I did board that bus. I hopped on it thinking Catherine had already boarded, but shortly after, I discovered I was wrong. She wasn't on board. So I convinced the driver to let me off, and he did. Only I forgot to get my ticket back." Noting skepticism in the officer's bent brows, Elijah said, "Neither one of us tried to cheat the bus company. We paid for our tickets in Michigan, and we should have already arrived in Florida."

"No one is accusing you of cheating the system," Officer Bennett said. "Unless the bus company plans to deny your claim, which you'll be able to fight in court. I was merely stating the facts. Budget Bus doesn't have either of you listed as passengers, which means they have no reason to believe Catherine is missing."

"Are you saying she's at the bottom of the ravine or"—he gulped—"in the river?" He prayed it wasn't the latter.

"I would be wrong to say there isn't a chance. However," Officer Bennett added sternly, holding his palm up when Elijah opened his mouth. "Before you set your mind on joining the search, you'll need to check the patients listed as Jane Doe—which I found out is many—and check the morgue, as the number of deaths has increased."

She's nett *in the morgue. I refuse to believe she's dead.* What was he going to tell George? Elijah had promised to call with an update.

"I jotted down the toll-free number assigned to passenger information." Officer Bennett handed him a slip of paper. "Someone at this number should be able to assist you in reporting Ms. Glick as a missing person. I have her information in my record, but you'll still need to fill out the necessary paperwork with the bus officials. Be assured, my men will continue to search even though the official count hasn't been changed yet. I believe your story, and we're going to do everything we can to find her."

"Thank you."

"Also, I made a list of the hospitals in the immediate area that received patients from the accident. The list of John and Jane Doe patients are too many to match with your description over the phone, but I've contacted each facility, and one of their representatives will be available to assist you. You'll have to check in with security. Unfortunately, I don't have data on how many patients were treated at one facility and transferred later to another. Again, call the eight-hundred number and file the report. I hope you find her."

"Thank you. I hope so too." He scanned the information he'd been given. Community General Hospital, Mercy Regional, St. Luke's Hospital, Shepard Hill Memorial, and Muskingum County coroner's office. His gut wrenched reading the latter. Elijah looked up from the list. "I don't have a phone."

The officer removed his cell phone from his pocket and handed it to Elijah. "Use mine."

His fingers trembled as he pressed the number keys. The line rang, then rang again before an automated voice came on the line guiding him to press one if he was searching for a passenger. "Please be advised that we are experiencing a heavy call volume at this time. All of our representatives are currently busy . . ." He covered his hand over the phone. "They want me to leave a message—yes, hi, I'm looking for information on Catherine Glick," he said after the beep. "She was a passenger on Bus 1248, seated in row five. I don't have a callback number. I'll have to try again when you're *nett* busy." As Elijah disconnected the call, one of the rescuers entered the tent.

"We're all packed up," the worker said.

"Very well," Officer Bennett replied. "Tell the crew we'll regroup at sunrise."

A sense of despair shrouded Elijah. Was

Catherine in the ravine . . . in a hospital . . . in the morgue? If he called the number again, would anyone be able to answer his questions? He pressed redial on the keypad but heard the same automated message. What should he do next?

As he tucked the paper into his pocket for safekeeping, his fingers touched the cab driver's business card. The man had offered to pick him up. "Do you mind if I make another call?" he asked once the worker had left. "I'd like to call a cab."

"Yeah, go ahead. Do you know the number?"

"The driver gave me his card earlier." He placed the call, then handed the officer back his phone. "He's on his way."

"I don't do this for everyone." Officer Bennett wrote something on a pad of paper. He tore off the page and handed it to Elijah. "This is my cell number. If you want to call me tomorrow afternoon, I'll be able to tell you if there've been any changes. And please, let me know if you find her."

"Thank you, very much. I'll be sure to call."

By the time Elijah lumbered out from the tent, it was dark. Most of the trucks with the dog boxes were gone. *Lord,* mei *body aches and I'm weak. Would You bless me with a double portion of strength? Please.*

Chapter 23

She awoke with a gasp, her hands automatically going to her throat. Her airway wasn't blocked—the breathing tube had been removed yesterday. Yet she was choking. *Relax. Take a deep breath.* She focused on the large volume of air entering and expanding her lungs.

The nurse had talked her through the same calming exercises when panic struck the last time. It worked then, but this time was different. She was alone—surrounded by darkness—and haunted by an endless void in her memory.

Yesterday Dr. Gleeson had taken time to explain her injuries and the reason her head was bandaged. Shattered facial bones had caused her face to swell, but that wasn't the worst of the damage. According to the surgeon, it still wasn't known if she would lose her right eye. Reconstructive surgery to fix the fractured orbital socket wasn't possible until after some of the swelling went down, and that wouldn't be anytime soon. Based on the extent of her other facial fractures, the doctor had said he was cautiously optimistic about the amount of damage to her optic nerve and eye ligaments, although to her ears his tone held more hopelessness than optimism. Her eyesight would never be normal again. At best her vision would be double or blurred. But she was alive—whoever she was.

"You are a child of God," a voice within her said.

A tingling sensation spread throughout her body. Not all of her memory had been lost—deep down she knew God. He was part of her past. Thrilled about her recent recollection, her outlook brightened, then dimmed. Perhaps it wasn't a memory from her past at all. Perhaps that knowledge was something innate to every believer. God was past, present, and future all in one—that she remembered.

A soft knock at the door pulled her attention. She had learned the sounds of the door creaking open, the light-footed padding of the nurse walking to her bedside.

"Did you need something, sweetie?"

She recognized Nurse Amy's voice and mumbled, "No," through the small opening in the badges.

"Hmm. Let's see why your call buzzer went off at the nurses' station. Sometimes it gets wrapped up in the blankets and is accidentally pressed."

A slight tug on the cord told her she had inadvertently rolled on it. "I'm sorry to trouble you."

"Don't be silly. This happens all the time, and besides, it's time for your antibiotic. I'm wrapping the remote around your handrail." As the nurse worked around the equipment, she talked in general. "It's bright and sunny out today. I wouldn't be surprised if some of the snow melts. I'm good with that."

Amy giggled. "I've never been a fan of winter. Too cold. I've done some cross-country skiing. One of the old golf courses near my apartment makes a ski trail as a way of making extra money during the off-season. Truth be told, their golf course is a little dated and not always kept up, so I think they do better in the winter." She continued chatting as though they were longtime friends.

At the moment Amy was her only friend.

"I need to scan your wrist bracelet. Now the Zosyn. Good. Now I'm piggybacking the antibiotic tubing to your IV fluids."

Amy's step-by-step explanations always put her at ease.

The nurse's nails clicked against the computer keyboard. "I see it's been over four hours since your last dose of morphine. How are you doing?"

"Okay." The dull overall body ache was manageable at the moment.

"That's good to hear. I'm going to let you rest for now. I'll be back in an hour after your antibiotic is infused. If the pain returns before then, please don't hesitate to call the desk." Amy left the room humming an upbeat but unfamiliar tune.

The room went silent. Loneliness struck once more.

"God has not forsaken you. Talk to Him."

The male voice was gentle sounding, but it wasn't someone she recognized. "Is someone . . . in the room?" Her throat quivering distorted her tone. Reaching for the handrail, she blindly felt her way to where the nurse had strung the remote. Controller in hand, she pressed every button.

The TV blared. "Again, a second body has been recovered from the ravine off of River Ridge Road at the site of Friday night's multiple bus accident involving a total of 102 passengers and drivers. This brings the current number of fatalities to 16."

"What's wrong, sweetie?"

With the television volume up high, she hadn't heard Amy return. "I can't—" She pressed the buttons, frantic to silence the noise before it disturbed the patients with rooms next to hers. Instead of turning the audio down, she pressed the wrong button and the volume went up.

"Here, sweetie, allow me."

Within seconds of releasing the remote to Amy, the television was adjusted.

"I didn't know what I was doing. I couldn't see the buttons." Efforts to mask her frustration failed.

Amy patted her hand. “Try to relax,” she said soothingly. “I know this is hard.”

“Is someone else in the room?”

“No.”

“I heard someone. A man. His voice was deep.”

“In your room?”

“Yes. Like he was standing next to the bed.” *Or possibly in my head.* Everything was too confusing. Her head hurt. Pain shot across her cheekbone and her nose. Pressure behind her eyes made it feel as though her eyes had a pulse of their own. Her muscles tightened and she clenched her teeth.

“Sweetie, are you in pain?”

She couldn’t speak, couldn’t move her head to nod.

“I’ll be right back.”

In the short time Amy was gone, the eye pulses turned into a stabbing sensation as the pain intensified.

“I’m giving you morphine,” Amy said. “You should feel better in a few minutes.”

“Thank you.”

“Can you describe what you felt?”

“Stabbing. No, first pressure behind my eyes. Then it turned into feeling like something sharp was stabbing me. What’s wrong?”

“I’m not sure, but when I get back to the desk, I’ll page Dr. Gleeson and let him know what you're experiencing. Meanwhile, the morphine should help the pain and hopefully help you to relax some."

"Can I bother you for a sip of water? My mouth is cottony."

"You're not a bother."

Hearing water poured into a cup made her even thirstier. The straw touched her lips, and she opened her mouth. Cold. Refreshing. She was already starting to feel better. "Thank you."

"My pleasure. Is there something you would like to watch—listen to?" she corrected. "I can change the channel and put on something other than news."

"It doesn't matter."

"Okay, I just thought hearing about the accident might—"

"You've been in a terrible accident." The doctor's words replayed in her mind. He hadn't said what type of accident. Only that amnesia wasn't all that uncommon in traumatic situations. "Was I in a bus accident? Is that what happened? How I ended up in the hospital?"

"Yes. Are you starting to remember what happened?"

"Dr. Gleeson . . . terrible accident . . . memory loss." The numbing effects of the morphine made it difficult to talk.

"If you're concerned about the amnesia, I'll have Dr. Gleeson explain everything again."

Words refused to form. Her mind—same as her memory—went blank.

Catherine's eye pain wasn't completely gone, but she thanked God anyway. *Lord, thank You for reducing my pain enough for me to sleep. I pray that You will heal my body. Please forgive my unrest. I believe You hold me in Your hand, but I still worry. Am I blind? Is my memory loss temporary, or is my past erased permanently? I have so many questions. Is it wrong to question Your will? Why has this happened to me?*

"'Draw near to God and He will draw near to you.'"

"Who's in here?" She turned her head first to the right, then the left in an effort to hear better, but she couldn't detect where the stranger was located in the room. Maybe the medicine had something to do with her hearing things. She'd experienced strange dreams—maybe the medicine could have induced the voice in her head.

"If you were able to consider your past ways and the toil of your hands, would you want to go back to chasing the wind?"

Toil of her hands. Chasing the wind. "Who's in here!" The silence that followed had her once again questioning her state of mind. If she were delirious, would those be words she would use? Would she be able to reason or rationalize if she were delirious?

Pray.

"You have this time alone with God. Rejoice and be glad in it." The deep voice belonged to a man. Her mind couldn't possibly be conjuring up all this. *Focus.*

It was true that she'd been consumed with *why* things had happened, and she'd begged God to heal her body and give her back her memory. *Lord, are You trying to get my attention? Is that why I'm blind—isolated in darkness—to bring me closer to You?* Perhaps, in her past, she had only known *about* God but hadn't made Him Lord of her life.

Father, forgive me. I've been foolishly whining about being afraid and lonely all while You were here by my side. I am a child of the Most High King. I don't need to know what my future holds, for I will trust in You. Even if the healing never comes and I remain blind. In my darkness, Your light will shine on my path. My feet will not stumble. I will go where You lead. Your Word I will place upon my heart. Let it be that You find me faithful. Amen.

For the first time since waking up in the hospital, her mind, body, and soul were at rest. *To God be the glory!* Her pain was gone—she was healed.

Confident her healing was complete, she touched the bandages on her face and considered removing them—at least the area covering her eyes. She wanted to see. Moving her fingers over the gauze in search of the end of the bandage, she hadn't heard the door open.

"Sweetie," Amy said with a gasp.

She wished the nurse had knocked as she had every other time before entering.

"Please, don't pull on your dressing. It's important to keep it intact so your wounds stay clean."

She brought her hand down to her side. "Is there someone else in the room?"

"No," Amy said cautiously.

"Are you sure?"

"I've been sitting at the desk, so I would have seen if someone came in or out."

She fell silent.

"What's wrong, sweetie?"

"A few minutes ago a man stood at my bedside. I heard his voice as plain as day. Are you sure no one came into my room?"

Amy placed her hand over hers. "Pain medicine can sometimes cause hallucinations. I'm sorry you were frightened."

"Would you want to go back to chasing the wind?" She cleared her throat. "I wasn't afraid."

Chapter 24

The sign posted on the information desk in the lobby of Community General Hospital read Closed and listed 7:00 a.m. as the time when the desk would reopen. Having no place else to go, Elijah roamed the main floor of the hospital, praying God would send someone to help him find Catherine.

"You lost, mister?" a man pushing a housekeeping cart stopped to ask. "I noticed you circled this area a few times. I figured I'd ask."

"I'm looking for a patient. Catherine Glick. Do you know her?"

The man shook his head. "I'm just the man who picks up the trash at night, but I do know visiting hours are over."

"*Jah*, I noticed the information desk is closed."

"Opens at seven." He pushed the cart a few feet, then stopped and looked back. "Don't you have no place to go till then, mister?"

Elijah shook his head. The last time he checked the wall clock in the lobby he only had a few more hours to wait. If he were in Badger Creek, he'd already be up milking cows.

"I'm supposed to tell people that this here area is closed. Gonna wax the floors shortly."

"Okay. I'll stay out of the way." Elijah returned to the lobby. He paced the floor, afraid if he sat on one of the cushioned chairs, he might fall asleep. He read the posted signs and took his time gazing into the glass cases at the various trophies and awards the hospital had received. Time dragged by.

The man he'd seen in the hallway rolled his cart up to him and stopped. "I thought you could use a cup of joe." The worker handed Elijah a Styrofoam cup of what smelled like strong coffee.

"Thank you." He'd been running on fumes since leaving Shepard Hill Hospital yesterday and going straight to the accident site. Elijah took a drink and cringed.

"Yeah, it'll grow hair on your chest. It was brewed last night at the beginning of my shift. Hope you don't mind a few grounds. Reminds me of campfire coffee. Ever have it?"

"*Nett* camping." Elijah's mother had to watch their old stovetop coffeemaker closely. Otherwise the grounds would end up in the water if it percolated too long. "But this tastes *gut*. Thanks again."

"I best get back to work. You take care now." The wheels of the cart clacked as the man left the lobby.

The strong coffee mixed with the different hospital scents aggravated Elijah's senses. He stepped outside for fresh air and got a glimpse of the dawn's light blue sky in a little section of horizon he could see between the buildings. The scenery looked drab compared to the sunrise over the pasture. He'd give anything to be sitting on a porch swing sharing a pasture view with Catherine as they had done in the past.

He followed the sidewalk to the front of the hospital, where he sat on a bench a few moments to collect his thoughts. Resting his elbows on his legs, he buried his face in his hands and closed his eyes.

"Lord, I miss her so much. I keep thinking about the past, and it makes me miss her all the more. I want her back. Father, please lead me to Catherine. I don't know how to go on without her."

Someone nearby cleared his throat. "'Trust in the Lord with all your heart and lean not on your own understanding; in all your ways submit to him, and he will make your paths straight.'"

Elijah vaulted up from the bench, his heart hammering hard against his chest. He rubbed his eyes. "I didn't see you . . . sitting there."

"Yes, I believe your eyes were closed when I sat down." He tapped the bench. "You can sit back down. I won't be staying long."

Elijah sat and wrung his hands nervously as he

tried to place the man's familiar voice. But Elijah was tired and not thinking straight. The people's faces, including the passengers on the bus, the hospital workers, reporters, and emergency rescuers, all blended together.

"Your help comes from the Lord."

Elijah nodded, then glanced sideways to catch another glimpse of the redheaded stranger. Gold flecks shimmered in the man's eyes as if a ray of sunlight had lit them internally. Elijah rubbed his face. He would splash himself with cold water if he were near a faucet.

"You probably haven't had much sleep, have you?"

"Hardly any." He'd seen those gold flecks before, not glowing to this degree, but he'd seen this man somewhere. *Inside the bus—the disappearing man from the ravine.* Elijah turned toward the stranger. "We've met before. Yesterday."

He smiled warmly. "You were searching for your friend."

"Yes, that's right." At least his mind wasn't totally addled—except the eye-glowing part. Now, taking a closer look at the man, Elijah saw that his eyes appeared normal. *Lord, I need sleep.*

"Elijah!" A man wearing a dark suit and tie approached. "It's Alex Canter with Rulerson, Markel, and Boyd." He extended his hand. "Good to see you again. I tried to contact you at the Shepard Hill Hospital but was told you had left."

"*Jah*, I signed myself out."

Alex cringed. "Hate to hear that. Well, it is what it is. Was it bad care? I can make a case that you felt your life was in jeopardy under your doctor's or nurse's care and that was why you left."

Elijah shook his head. "They took *gut* care of me. I left to find Catherine."

Alex glanced at the red-haired man, then back to Elijah. "Would you like to talk inside? I'm meeting another client in the lobby in a few minutes, but I'd like to go over a few things with you first."

Elijah glanced at the stranger sharing the bench. "It was nice seeing you again." He went inside with Alex.

Alex found a place for them to sit so he could see the door. "So, is Catherine a patient here?"

"I don't know yet." The attorney opened his briefcase and removed a folder. "But she's on the top of my search list. See?" He flashed a sticky note toward Elijah, which Alex held just enough for him to read Catherine's name, age, and the brief physical description Elijah had given him when Alex visited him at the hospital. "I'm making progress with Budget Bus."

"And they know where she is?"

"No, but they have other passengers still

missing too. Up until this morning, she wasn't on their official list, but they are investigating. Trust me, the company isn't eager to add another one to the count, but they'll have to sooner or later."

Elijah noticed a woman wearing a striped vest take a seat behind the information desk, then turn the sign. "I need to talk with the desk clerk."

Alex stood and straightened his tie. "Why don't you let me talk with her. You want to know if Catherine is a patient here, right?"

"*Jah*. I was told they had some patients listed as Jane Doe."

"Give me a few minutes." He strutted toward the blonde.

Elijah sat on the edge of the cushion. Alex would know the right words to use. He was definitely more social in these situations, noting the large smile on the woman's face. A few moments later, Alex waved him over.

"We have to go through security for permission, but I don't think that will be a problem. According to the helpful desk clerk, the hospital has been eager to help family members identify their loved ones." Alex redirected his attention to the woman. "Thanks, Megan. We really appreciate your help," he said with a wink.

"Your help comes from the Lord." Elijah heard the words as though the man from the bench was standing next to him. But a quick scan around the

room told him otherwise. He rubbed the back of his neck. *Stay awake.*

Thankfully it was only the matter of a few minutes before the security officer met them in the lobby. The officer, who had a shaved head, stood feet shoulder-width apart with his hands clasped in front of him. "I'm Officer Perkins. I understand you're searching for someone from the bus accident?"

Elijah stepped forward. "Her name is Catherine Glick. Is she here?"

"Let's talk more in my office." The uniformed man looked at Alex. "You look familiar. Where do I know you from?"

"I'm Elijah's legal representative." He elbowed Elijah's arm. "Tell him."

He grimaced, rubbing his arm. Next time he'd stand with his injured side away from the man. "Alex is helping me find Catherine."

"I'd like to ask you to wait in the lobby," Officer Perkins told Alex in a tone that implied his order wasn't negotiable. "At this time, we are only allowing immediate family members access."

Don't say anything. Please, Lord, close his mouth. If the officer knows I'm only a friend— Elijah sucked in a breath and held it.

"Why do you think my name is Julie?"

"When I stopped in your room last night to say

goodbye, you were talking in your sleep," Amy said.

"What was I saying?"

"You were mumbling mostly. Something about George."

"George?" *Did she know someone named George?*

"You don't know who George is?"

She pushed up on the bed. "No. Should I?"

"You told me last night he was your brother."

"I did?"

"It's okay if you don't remember. I think you were still asleep. Your speech slurred, and you called George your *bruder*." Amy patted her hand. "Sometimes our unconscious mind reveals things we aren't aware of yet."

Could I have hallucinated again? She hadn't heard any more voices in her room . . . "Shouldn't I remember something? Shouldn't I know if my name is Julie—and *if* I have a brother? What exactly did I say?"

"George is calling." When I asked you *who* he was calling, you replied, 'Me.' You mumbled mostly after that, saying things I couldn't make out. But when I prompted you to tell me why George was calling you, you said, 'It's supper-time. We must go inside.'"

"Julie." She rolled the name over in her mind. "It does sound familiar. I wish I knew for certain."

"I have a call into the investigational team

handling the accident and missing people reports. They've been compiling data, so I'm sure we'll know more shortly. Until then, is it okay if I call you Julie?"

"It's certainly a pretty name." Having a name would make it easier for the nurses. Julie sounded better than *hon, sweetie,* and *dear.* Not that she minded Amy referring to her as sweetie, but several of the other hospital staff members seemed to stumble over *what* to call her, which only led to feelings of awkwardness. "*Jah*, I'd like to be called Julie."

Someone else entered the room. Soft footsteps usually indicated another nurse. "Excuse me. You have a phone call at the desk, Amy. An Alex Canter."

"Ooh, that's probably the person I've been waiting to talk to. I need to get it," Amy said. "Sandra, meet Julie."

Sandra neared the bed, her voice booming with excitement. "Your memory came back? That's wonderful!"

"Hopefully, after this call we'll know your last name too," Amy said. "I'll be back."

"Amy," she called before the nurse's footsteps disappeared from the room. "Will they know if *mei* family—assuming I have family—has tried to find me?"

"I'm sure they have good records of every inquiry."

She swallowed. “What if I don’t remember them?”

“Have faith,” Amy said. “It’ll all come together in time. You’ll remember everything.”

“You really believe that?”

“God’s capable of making the impossible possible.”

Elijah followed the security officer down the corridor, debating whether to confess the truth about Catherine’s and his relationship but decided against it. After all, he was the only family she had at the moment.

The officer opened the door marked Security and acknowledged a younger man seated at a desk in front of a group of wall monitors with a nod.

Elijah scanned the black-and-white images on the different screens. He noticed Alex looking at something on his cell phone on the monitor labeled Lobby.

Officer Perkins led Elijah into a smaller room and motioned for him to sit in the chair opposite the desk.

“As you are probably aware, our patients who haven’t been identified are either in critical condition or, for whatever reason, are unable to communicate. We’ll start by calling the intensive care unit.” The officer picked up the phone. “I’ll place the call, then you can give the nurse a description of—good morning, Regina. This is Officer Perkins, and I have Elijah Graber with me. He is searching for a passenger from the bus accident. Are you able to talk with him?"

He glanced at Elijah and nodded. "Great, I'll put him on the line." As he turned the call over to Elijah, he said, "Give the nurse a description of your friend, and she will assist you."

Elijah held the phone to his ear. "Hello."

"Hi, I'm Regina, the charge nurse for ICU. I understand you are searching for someone from the bus accident?"

"Yes, that's right. Her name is Catherine Glick."

"Can you tell me her approximate height, weight, age, hair and eye color, and if she has any unique identifiers such as birthmarks, moles, or tattoos?"

"She's twenty-nine. Probably five foot six, and maybe 140 pounds. Her hair is honey colored and her eyes are bright blue." He closed his eyes, and an image of Catherine's warm smile came to mind. "She doesn't have any birthmarks or moles on her face, but I wouldn't know about the rest of her body. As for tattoos, no, she wouldn't have one."

"I need to put you on hold for a moment while I check with the other nurses."

The nurse's voice was replaced with a recorded announcement. Elijah placed his hand over the receiver. "I'm on hold," he told the officer as the speaker listed a series of accolades given to Community General for their leadership in patient safety, followed by an advertisement for various imaging services.

"Mr. Graber." The nurse came back on the line. "I'm sorry, but we don't have any patients fitting the description you've given me. I wish I had better news."

He sighed tiredly. "Thank you for your time."

"I can give you the toll-free number to call for passenger information."

"Okay, thanks." He jotted down the number even though it was the same as what Officer Bennett had given him yesterday—the number with an answering machine on the other side.

"I wish you the best of luck with your search."

"Thanks." Elijah lowered the phone to its cradle and sighed.

"Nothing?" the security officer asked.

Elijah shook his head.

"We have another place to look." Officer Perkins opened the side drawer on the desk and removed a set of keys. "Come with me."

They took the service elevator located in the hospital lobby to the basement, walked down a deserted hallway, and stopped in front of an unmarked room.

"This is the morgue. If you don't feel up to going inside, I understand. I've had a few interns with queasy stomachs over the years."

“I’ll be fine,” Elijah said, even though his stomach churned, coating the back of his throat and tongue with bitterness. He should have declined the coffee.

Keys jangled as the officer unlocked the door. Thc room tcmpcrature reminded him of the *icehaus* at home. Not a place to linger. The frigid air numbed the tip of his nose and earlobes, and white clouds marked his heavy breaths. The windowless room wasn’t oversized by any means. Stretchers with sheet-covered bodies lined the wall with little space to walk between.

A wave of nausea washed over him as the officer checked the different toe tags.

“This one is an unidentified female.” He slowly peeled back the corner of the sheet to reveal the woman’s face.

Don’t pass out. Breathe. Breathe. Oh, thank God! He shook his head. The pale, lifeless corpse wasn’t Catherine.

The officer lifted the sheet on another body, and Elijah shook his head the moment he noticed short, dark hair. Sweat formed along Elijah’s brow despite the freezing temperature. His legs wobbled. Having to identify a loved one was torturous. The officer showed him one more nameless person, which thankfully Elijah was able to dismiss immediately.

“That’s all the females we have,” he said solemnly. “Sorry.”

Elijah wasn't sorry. At least she wasn't in the hospital morgue. He followed the officer to the elevator and pressed the button for the lobby.

Alex met him the moment he stepped off the elevator. "I take it you didn't find her?"

Elijah shook his head.

"I just received news that the authorities have finished cataloging the personal items recovered from the accident scene, and they have been made available for the owners to claim. We can stop by the warehouse if you'd like to look for your belongings."

"I'd rather check Mercy Regional first."

"I, ah . . ." Alex rubbed the back of his neck while rolling his shoulders, as if trying to loosen tension.

"What are you *nett* telling me?" The man's eyes hooded with what appeared to be his first genuine expression of sadness Elijah had ever seen. "Do you know something about Catherine?"

"While you were with the security officer, I called Mercy Regional. A woman at the nurses' desk said their last Jane Doe was identified. Her name isn't Catherine."

Elijah lowered his head as tears pooled. Nau *what do I do, Lord? Mercy Regional was the last hospital on the list.*

Chapter 25

False alarm," Amy said.

"My name isn't Julie?"

Amy approached the bedside. "That wasn't the call I expected. One of the other nurses picked up the line by accident before I got out to the desk, and in talking with him, I discovered Alex Canter was an attorney."

"You sound disgusted."

"I don't like the way some of them do business. Reputable attorneys don't chase ambulances."

"I don't understand."

"It's a term used as an underhanded way lawyers sign up potential clients. After the accident, administration set up a call system designated for people searching for victims, and those calls are routed to a toll-free number at a centralized location manned by law enforcement officials. Yet even with a workable system in place, we still get outside calls from smooth-talking lawyers, but let's talk about something more important, Julie."

"What's that?"

"Your next step." Amy lowered the bed rail. "It's time for us to take a walk."

"*Nay*! How am I suppose to go anywhere when I can't see a thing? I want to wait until the bandages *kumm* off."

"Sorry, but it's doctor's orders. You don't want to get pneumonia or bedsores. Besides, your muscles will atrophy if you stay in bed too long. So you see, there are too many reasons for you not to get up."

"I don't *see.* I'm blind."

"Your face is bandaged. Now, for the tough love." Amy peeled the covers back. "The best way to do this is to hold on to my shoulder as you swing your legs to the side of the bed."

"I thought you were *mei* friend," she grumbled.

A man outside the warehouse entrance stopped Elijah and Alex at the door. "Name, please."

"Elijah Graber."

Alex stepped forward. "Elijah was a passenger on Budget Bus, and we're here to collect his belongings."

"Stop at the first table, and someone there will issue you a pass."

"Thank you." Elijah stepped into the building, which was large enough to hold several buses. He headed toward the first table. "I was told to stop here first," he told the officer seated in front of a computer.

"May I have your name?"
"Elijah Graber."
The officer typed on his keyboard, and a few seconds later, a printer spit out a label with his name on it. "The tables are arranged by type of article. Laptops, tablets, phones, and other portable devices are along the far wall. Clothing, shoes, and miscellaneous personal care items are in the middle section. And over by the far wall on the left is the unclaimed baggage. Sensitive materials such as wallets, purses, and handbags will be released on an individual basis by an officer in the back. Please note that all items are sealed and will require you signing for their release. If you're unable to locate your belongings, please notify one of the officers at the back table. Do you have any questions?"
"I don't think so." All Elijah had to find was his duffel bag.
"Very well. Next."
"Alex Canter, I'm not looking for anything. I'm with Elijah."
The officer requested the spelling for Alex's last name, then typed it into the computer and handed him a visitor's pass.
"Where do you want to start?" Alex asked once they were past the gated area.
Elijah scanned the building. A mob of people, most of them weeping, milled around the tables. "I'd like to find *mei* duffel bag." *Then get out of*

here. He pointed to the area where the luggage was located, but Alex's attention was on the electronics crowd.

"I'll catch up with you in a few minutes." Alex veered off in the opposite direction.

Fine by me. He needed a few moments to collect his thoughts and steady his nerves. Besides, Alex wouldn't know what his duffel bag looked like. Elijah's mind wandered. With Alex having checked Mercy Regional for Catherine, all the hospitals on his list had been checked off. He wasn't prepared to give up his search—*ever.* He also wasn't prepared to sort through the recovered items of strangers.

Elijah looked through the various pieces of luggage twice but didn't find his bag. He described the navy canvas duffel to the worker in the area, but even he wasn't able to locate it. The worker directed him to the lost claims area but didn't offer much hope since the crash site had been searched carefully.

After thanking the man, Elijah headed toward the back of the building where he'd been directed. He described the bag and filled out the form. Only he didn't have a phone number to leave for them to contact him.

"I can see if someone can look through the records for a bag that fits the description," the friendly gray-haired woman at the counter said. "Everything logged in should have a number associated with it, and if someone else claimed it by mistake, we should have the person's name."

"Okay, thank you." Elijah recalled a man with a bandanna on his head going through luggage not long after the accident had happened. Obviously the man hadn't been pilfering his own stuff.

Elijah scanned the room for Alex and spotted him in the center of a small gathering, most likely drumming up more business, and probably the reason he suggested they come. Elijah ambled between the long row of tables holding baby bottles, toys, stuffed animals, makeup bags, miniature-sized bottles of shampoo, hairbrushes, a single shoe. Where was its mate? He moved down the row, scanning the different clothes scattered about. Nothing was organized according to size, nor was anything neatly folded. His gaze stopped on something he recognized.

Catherine's prayer *kapp*.

Bloodstains marred the white material. A lump formed in his throat as he picked up the delicate hand-sewn *kapp*.

Mei *dear, sweet Catherine.*

Elijah's vision blurred. He weaved through the crowd and made his way to the restroom. How was he going to tell George? He'd promised to call with an update. Acid coated the back of his throat. He barely made it inside the men's room and over to the trash container before he vomited. Once his stomach was emptied of its contents, he stood there a moment, his ribs aching and body shaking. "Lord, help me."

I've checked the hospitals and the morgue, and I even climbed down the ravine. Now what—wait till spring? Wait to see if her body washes up downstream? Her kapp *is bloody. I don't want to believe she's gone, but I need some mustard seed of faith* nett *to lose hope.*

When Elijah finally looked up, he glimpsed a man's reflection in the mirror and spun to face him. He recognized him immediately as the person who had sat next to him on the bench.

"You've done everything within your power to find Catherine. You've relied on man's help to point you in the right direction," the red-haired man said. "Child, isn't it time you put your trust in the Lord? Rest in His strength."

"I trust God, but I—" Elijah swallowed hard. He lifted the bloody prayer *kapp*. "This was Catherine's."

"Turn around and look at yourself in the mirror."

Elijah furrowed his brows but turned anyway. "I have dark circles under *mei* eyes, *mei* hair is a matted mess—what?"

"Your shirt is bloody from the gash on your head, isn't it?"

"*Jah*, and I don't have a clean shirt to change into either."

"But you're alive, right?"

Elijah nodded.

"Head wounds bleed profusely. Catherine's alive."

"I wish I believed that." Elijah cringed, admitting his deepest fear out loud.

"I wish you did too. The Word teaches to be anxious for nothing, but in everything by prayer and supplication, with thanksgiving, let your requests be made known to God; and the peace of God, which surpasses all understanding, will guard your hearts and minds through Christ Jesus. It is up to you to cast all your anxiety on He who cares for you." The man placed his hand on Elijah's shoulder. "Jesus wants all who are weary and burdened to come to Him. He will give you rest."

"*Jah*," he said matter-of-factly. He'd grown up studying the Scriptures, even quoted the same "be anxious about nothing" verse when Edwina had fretted about her family's financial well-being. But hearing it now, in this situation, he wasn't sure how to lay his burdens at the feet of Jesus. Maybe once he found Catherine . . .

"Do you not trust the one who called you by your name? The one who sends the angel of the Lord to encamp around those who fear him, and deliver—"

The bathroom door swung open, and Alex entered. "You all right, Elijah?"

"I'm fine." Elijah glanced apologetically at the

red-haired man. "I'm sorry. You were saying?"

Before the man could speak, Elijah glimpsed Alex in his peripheral vision. The lawyer's brows flicked, and concern webbed his forehead as he looked around the room. "You sure you're okay? What's that in your hand?"

"Catherine's prayer *kapp*." His voice choked again. "I need a few minutes—*please*."

"Yeah, sure. Hey, did you find your bag?"

"*Nay*." He ground out the word between clenched teeth.

"I'll wait for you out here." Alex moved to the door. "Don't worry about your bag. When we leave, we're definitely getting you a change of clothes."

"Your friend sounds concerned," the older man said once Alex left.

"I don't know him well enough to call him a friend. He's a lawyer, and yes, he's helped look for Catherine, but I thought he was rude not to at least acknowledge you were in the room."

"Not everyone can see what you see. Some people are too self-absorbed to look beyond their own gain."

"You're probably right." He turned on the faucet, cupped cold water in his hands, then took a drink. "It seems I've gotten myself into a pickle."

"How so?"

"I lost sight of *mei* beliefs. I thought I needed

Alex's help in order to find Catherine, when all along I should have trusted God. *Nau* I'm mixed up in worldly matters."

"Come with me." He opened the door. "You need a place where you can find rest for your soul."

There was something so soothing in the man's tone, Elijah followed without question. He held his breath as they headed toward the exit. Alex was too busy handing out business cards to even notice him leave the building.

The fresh air felt good against his face. He looked for a place to sit down and rest, but the red-haired man led him to a cab parked next to the curb. "Give this note to the driver."

Elijah hesitated to take the folded piece of paper, and when he did, he still didn't move. Shouldn't he have some sort of gut reaction—warning alarms going off inside his head?

"Elijah, where are you going?" Alex flagged him with a wave. "You still want help finding Catherine, don't you?"

Elijah nodded. He didn't want anyone to stop searching for her.

"Okay, I'll take that as a verbal agreement for representation. You won't be sorry."

Now alarms were sounding. Elijah climbed into the back seat and scooted over for the red-haired man, but the man shook his head.

"God permitting, I'll see you again soon."

Chapter 26

Elijah watched closely as the mileage added up and the fare ballooned on the cab meter. At the same time, he kept a mental tally of how much money he would have left once they reached the destination—if it didn't run out before he arrived. Perhaps he should tell the driver to stop.

"Be anxious for nothing, but in everything by prayer and supplication, with thanksgiving, let your requests be made known to God; and the peace of God, which surpasses all understanding, will guard your hearts and minds through Christ Jesus." Elijah repeated the same scripture over several miles. But it seemed every time he attempted to cast his worries, he ended up mentally reeling them in. *Clear your mind. Dwell on what God has in store for those who call on Him. Worry is the opposite of faith. And faith is what moves the hand of God.*

Lord, forgive me. I've been making so many mistakes. First trusting the lawyer and now trusting a stranger in the restroom. Have I run from one problem to the next? I haven't made many rational decisions lately. Otherwise, I wouldn't be in the back seat of a cab going to an unknown location. What if—?

Elijah drew a deep breath. Even while praying he was fretting. *Forgive me, Father.*

The driver turned up the volume on the radio as the newscaster reported heavy snowfall over the next several hours. Travel advisory warnings were issued for the central and southern regions of the state. "Sounds like the roads are going to be a doozy," said the driver, who had earlier introduced himself as Frank. "You'll want to stay put until this snow front moves through."

"How far are we from the ravine on River Ridge Road?"

"Where those buses crashed last week?"

"*Jah*, that place."

"With the amount of road construction in some spots, it'll be at least an hour."

What had he done? "Will you stop? Please." Panic laced his words. He couldn't go that far away from the accident scene. He needed to be close.

The driver pulled over to the shoulder and stopped the car. He looked at Elijah through the rearview mirror. "Something wrong?"

"I made a mistake. I'd like to go to the ravine. I want to join the search team."

"Search and rescue were called off earlier due to high winds. My cousin and his dog are part of the canine group, and he thinks it'll be called off indefinitely. That's if this storm drops the amount of inches everyone's predicting."

Elijah leaned back against the seat and slouched down out of sight of the rearview mirror.

"I can't drop you off at the ravine in good conscience. It's already starting to snow, so we need to make a decision quick." He lifted the slip of paper with the address Elijah had given him earlier. "Do you want me to continue?"

Elijah glanced out the window. It wasn't snowing hard, but if Ohio was anything like Michigan, that could change in a matter of minutes. "*Jah*, I suppose."

A few minutes later, the driver stopped the cab in front of a small stone and cedar shake cabin tucked under towering maples. Fresh snow covered the roof, and long icicles dangled from the eaves. With the driveway drifted closed, the home looked as though it hadn't been occupied in months.

"Hope you don't mind getting out here. I don't want to chance getting stuck in that driveway," Frank said.

"*Nay*, I don't mind." He leaned forward to check the final meter reading but discovered the machine had been cleared. "How much do I owe you?"

"The fare was just paid in full, including the tip, so you're all set."

"Just paid? How could that be?"

"Payment was made online." Frank lifted his phone and pointed to the screen, but Elijah wasn't close enough to read the details.

He thanked the driver and climbed out, then trudged through the snow to the cabin. The redheaded man hadn't said anything about a key. Houses in his district were seldom locked, but most *Englischers* were not as trusting. Some of them were even known to padlock their barns, sheds, and pasture gates.

At least here the cabin's windows were not boarded up. Elijah climbed the steps to the front porch. He turned the doorknob, and it opened.

The rough plank walls, oak floors, and stone fireplace gave the place an inviting atmosphere. The wood box held enough wood to heat the place for several days. He crossed the room and checked out the kitchen area. Curtain-fronted cabinets L-shaped the walls. A small countertop hand pump was next to the sink. Elijah spotted an oil lamp and Bible on the kitchen table and smiled. The red-haired man had said he would find rest for his soul, and Elijah was already feeling more at peace. A note next to the Bible caught his eye.

> Welcome home!
>
> You'll find canned goods in the cellar and more wood in the shed next to the barn.

> May you feel the love of Christ Jesus and the presence of the Holy Spirit, and find rest for your weary soul. Stay as long as you like.

Julie . . . Julie who? From where? She had pondered her name multiple times since learning of it last week. Not that it did any good. She was a stranger to herself.

A knock sounded at the door, followed by two sets of footsteps entering the room. She'd become familiar with the lighter, soft-heeled steps that belonged to Amy. The heavier, hard-soled steps belonged to one of her doctors. Her neurosurgeon, Dr. Gleeson, wore musk-scented cologne, and Dr. Edwards, her primary care physician, walked with a slight drag of one foot, although she wasn't sure if it was his right or left.

Between those doctors and the plastic surgeon who rebuilt her eye socket, she was checked on multiple times a day. More so over the last four days. Her facial swelling from the accident had gone down enough to do the second surgery to reconstruct her face.

The musky scent grew stronger. Dr. Gleeson talked slowly. "Good morning, Julie. How are you feeling today?"

"Okay," she said hoarsely. Her throat dried. On the opposite side of the bed from the doctor, her hand was grasped. She recognized Amy's soft hand clasping hers before the nurse spoke.

"Julie," she said in a cheerful tone, "Dr. Gleeson is here to remove your bandages. Isn't that great?"

"Yes" was all she managed to say. Prior to the last surgery, her bandages had been looser fitting. The swelling had gone down, and she could talk without much difficulty. But following the second surgery, everything was different. The bandages were tighter, movement was severely restricted, and her throat was constantly parched. Communication was limited to one-word sentences and hand signals, which Amy called charades. Even asking for ice chips had become frustrating. She ended up spending countless hours in silence.

"I'm going to remove your bandages," Dr. Gleeson said. "You may feel a slight tug as I work the scissors under the different layers of gauze. Try not to move."

She lay as still as possible, holding her breath as he guided the scissors upward from her neck. Snipping around her ears tickled, and she fought back a giggle.

Once he reached the top of her skull, he stopped cutting. "Now for the other side." He changed places with Amy and repeated the process.

Room air brushed against her chin and cheekbones, sending a shiver from the back of her neck down her spine.

He stopped cutting. “Try to hold still, please. I’m almost done.”

“Sorry,” she said, then willed herself to stay calm by stiffening. Would she recognize herself after the bandages were off when she looked in the mirror? It would be nice to finally put a face to the workers’ voices. She pictured Amy short and petite.

A few moments later, the doctor announced that he was finished.

“That’s it? I can’t see.” Her voice strained. She went to touch her face, but the doctor’s large hand stopped her.

“I decided not to remove the bandages around your eyes. You still have some swelling, and I think we’ll wait another day or two.”

She relaxed some, but trying to hide her disappointment in a smile, she winced.

“Julie, is it painful to smile?”

“A little.”

He placed his hands on both sides of her jaw and pressed his fingers over the bone.

She jerked back and automatically reached for her face when he touched the joint area.

He waited for her to relax, then placed his hands on the area again, only this time he didn’t press down. “Can you open your mouth for me?”

She followed his instructions until her joint locked. A burning sensation traveled along her nerves, webbing her face in electrifying pulses and bringing tears to her eyes. She didn't need a tissue; the bandages absorbed the wetness. Finally she was able to close her mouth, but that didn't stop the surrounding muscles from trembling. How would she be able to chew food without the use of her jaw?

"You did good, Julie." Dr. Gleeson gave her a friendly pat on the shoulder. "It's normal for your muscles to be sore."

"Do you plan to make dietary changes now that the bandages are off, Doctor?" Amy asked.

"We'll need to reintroduce food gradually. She's been receiving her caloric and nutritional needs intravenously since arrival, and we don't want to bombard her digestive system. Let's start her on protein drinks and applesauce and see how she tolerates it. How does that sound to you, Julie?"

She appreciated his attempt to include her in the conversation and decided a lighthearted response was better than worrying if she would get any better. She pressed through pain to smile. "Do I like protein shakes?"

Amy chuckled. "No time like the present to find out. Would you like to try the chocolate, vanilla, or strawberry flavor first?"

Up until this moment, she'd had no appetite.

Now she didn't know which to choose. She licked her dry lips. "Surprise me."

"Just a few more steps. You're doing great, Julie," Darla, the physical therapist, encouraged.

"Forty-eight more steps." This was her second trip down the hall today, and while she was getting better at listening to her surroundings and counting the number of steps to the nurses' desk, she wasn't thrilled about roaming the halls. She could only imagine how bad she looked to those who saw her coming down the hall wearing a hospital gown and tapping the floor ahead of her with a long walking stick.

Maybe it was better she couldn't see the strange looks on people's faces. She hated to think that bystanders pitied her. "I'm sure for a normal person the nurses' station isn't that far. I'm taking baby steps." *Shuffling.*

"It'll get easier. You'll be recounting in another week when your stride changes."

"From the bed to the bathroom is eight steps. Last night I made it in six and didn't have to turn on the light."

"Do you normally turn on a light?"

Julie smiled. "It was a joke."

Darla chuckled. "You got me on that one."

She shuffled a few more paces and stopped to listen for voices. She could pick out Amy easily. The other two were a guess. “Is that Amy, Claudia, and Alex?” She sniffed. “Dr. Gleeson is either here or recently left.”

Darla gave her arm a gentle squeeze. “You’re doing really well using your other senses. Listening for audio clues and recognizing scents can be a great help.”

“Amy’s voice is soft, and I can detect Dr. Gleeson’s musk cologne. And I hear the volunteer before she reaches my room. She’s always lugging around a book and magazine cart with rickety wheels.”

“Yes, Ms. Arleen’s a sweet lady.”

Julie agreed. “She reads to me some days. *Wuthering Heights*. The story doesn’t sound familiar, but I suppose that’s one benefit of memory loss—all things are new again.”

“Think of it as a new adventure every day.”

“I’m sure that once these bandages come off and I can see, I won’t be afraid.” Her thoughts flitted to all the different people she’d met so far. She’d learned a great deal about all of them and yet had learned only one thing about herself—her name was Julie—nothing more.

“Julie.” Amy’s voice rose above the others at the desk. “The ophthalmologist’s office just called. Dr. Mosley is on the way to the hospital. Maybe he and Dr. Gleeson will remove your bandages.”

She didn’t want to get overly excited. Her

doctors had postponed the removal three days in a row due to swelling, but heading back to her room, anticipation brimmed to the surface. She lost count of her steps.

Chapter 27

Elijah had never experienced cabin fever in all his years of living in northern Michigan as he had the last four days of living in a stranger's cabin. He was grateful God had placed it on the redheaded man's heart to offer his place to stay during the storm. Elijah had found canned food in the cellar as the note had mentioned and enough wood chopped and stacked inside that he didn't have to fight whiteout conditions to search for anything. The Bible he'd found on the kitchen table kept him company.

In the past he'd been busy with chores or had other things on his mind when he did his daily reading. Sometimes it seemed as if reading was another chore added to his day. But these past days had been different. As he spent time reading the Scriptures, the words spoke to him. He found comfort like none other in those moments when he quieted his own thoughts and drew closer to God.

Elijah awoke before dawn to feed the woodstove. The floor was cold against his socked feet as he padded out to the living room, a sure sign the fire had died out completely during the night. He opened the side compartment of the cast-iron stove. The embers were red and glowing. He added a few smaller pieces on the bottom, then a larger log to last a few hours.

Elijah went to the window and pushed the curtains aside, but it was too dark to tell if it had stopped snowing. Not that it mattered. He had no place to go. He considered going back to bed but opted instead to make a pot of coffee and read.

Once the percolator was prepared and on the stove, he sat at the table and opened the Bible to where he'd left off yesterday. But before he began, he folded his hands and bowed his head.

"Father, I come to You today thankful that You are with me. I am not alone. You've blessed me with this place of refuge, with Your Holy Word to breathe life into these dry bones. I hunger for You, Father. Let Your Word resonate within me and penetrate my heart so I might draw closer to You." He stopped praying and sat for a moment in silence. A new warmth—a warmth only God could provide—spread head to toe over him.

Julie sucked in a breath as the final gauze covering her face was clipped. She kept her eyes closed, awaiting either Dr. Gleeson's or Dr. Mosley's instructions.

"Okay, Julie. Go ahead and open your eyes," Dr. Gleeson said.

At first her lashes felt as though they'd been glued down. The sudden brightness was blinding. She closed them, then reopened her eyes again, this time slowly. "I see spots. Moving spots."

"Are the spots black or white?" Dr. Mosley asked.

"White." Feeling dizzy, her stomach roiled. She closed her eyes to make it all go away and held her hand over her stomach. "I think I'm going to be sick."

Amy was quick to place an empty basin on her lap. "Use this if you have to vomit, sweetie."

"Thank you." She hoped she wouldn't need it. Keeping her eyes closed helped.

Dr. Mosley waited patiently, giving her a few moments for the nausea to pass. "When you're ready, Julie, I'd like you to open only your left eye."

She'd been told the ophthalmologist had worked on her eyes during surgery and she vaguely remembered him asking her questions about pain after surgery, but she wasn't as familiar with him as she was Dr. Gleeson, who came by her room daily to check her progress. Not wanting to keep either doctor waiting long, she placed her hand over her right eye, then opened the left.

A white foggy haze filled her vision. It cleared after a few seconds, but things were distorted, wavy. "Hot pavement," she muttered as a memory flashed of a long country road. “It looks like heat rising from pavement on a hot summer day,” she said with growing excitement.

“Look to your right and tell me what you see.”

“A chair.”

“That’s great, Julie!” Dr. Gleeson said.

“I can only make out its shape. I wouldn’t have known what it was if I hadn’t used it to feel my way to the bathroom a few hours ago.”

Dr. Mosley used an instrument to shine a bright light into her eyes. “You can close your eyes and give them a few seconds to rest.” After a moment he instructed her to open her other eye, the one Dr. Gleeson had said was bandaged to keep the injured one from movement.

But that eye too was weak to respond. *Lord, I’m afraid. Please heal my eyes.*

As her eye regained focus, she automatically opened the other one. Her vision wasn’t perfectly clear, but she could see better, which was all that mattered. “Thank You, Jesus. You gave me back my sight.”

Dr. Mosley continued the exam. “How many fingers am I holding up?”

She had to turn her body to glimpse him standing next to her, and even then she couldn’t bring his fingers into focus once the wavy lines returned. “Three,” she guessed.

“Let’s try it again without turning your head.”

A dark mass filled her peripheral vision. “I can’t even see you, let alone your hand. It’s like I have horse blinders on. I can only see what’s straight ahead.”

“That’s not uncommon after the type of surgery you had.”

She turned her head to face him. “Will it get any better?”

“Probably not.”

Her eyes were dry and itchy. Rubbing them aggravated them more, and blinking only helped to moisten them some.

Dr. Mosley’s face pinched with concern. “Do your eyes feel dry?”

“Yes, and itchy.”

“Nurse, bring me a bottle of artificial tears, please.”

Amy crossed the room, her blonde ponytail swinging with her quick steps.

“Try not to rub them,” the ophthalmologist said. “You could have debris in your eyes, and rubbing them could scratch your cornea.”

“Okay.” She dropped her hands to her sides. “I certainly don’t want to cause more damage.” Tears spilled over her lashes and rolled down her cheeks, a warmth she hadn’t felt in weeks. By the time Amy returned with the bottle of drops, Julie no longer needed artificial tears to wet her eyes; the dryness had disappeared.

Dr. Mosley placed two drops in each eye anyway, then instructed Amy to instill more drops every four hours as needed. "Julie, I'll see you again tomorrow." A blurry image of him walked out of the room.

As the drops absorbed, Dr. Gleeson stepped into her line of vision. The deep wrinkles in his forehead came into focus. He was older than what she had expected. Kind blue eyes studied her from behind wire-rimmed glasses. His thick hair and bushy eyebrows were completely gray, and his hands were speckled with brown age spots.

"The good news is that your brain is receiving messages from your eyes. You were able to recognize the chair against the wall."

"I guessed. I could only make out its form."

"The signal your brain received and registered was a good impression. Neurologically, you're recovering nicely." He took her hand and gave it a pat. "I don't see anything hindering you from being released soon."

The thought of leaving knotted her stomach, but she returned his smile. Surely he wouldn't release her without a place to go.

"I have another patient I need to see," he said, excusing himself from the room.

She was finally able to put a face with the voice or the footsteps of her caregivers. Amy's small frame matched her light footsteps. Her blonde hair was pulled back into a ponytail, and her eyes were as blue as the cornflower-blue hospital scrubs she wore.

Amy plucked a few tissues from the box and handed them to Julie. "I, ah . . . I received some news, and I—well, I've been debating how to tell you."

"Your face is about as whitewashed as a sun-bleached fence. Just say what you're gonna say. Is it *mei* eyesight? You need to tell me *mei* brain won't heal?"

"It's not your eyes or your brain. Remember how I told you I had contacted the bus companies about a passenger named Julie?"

"*Jah*. My name isn't Julie, is it?"

"That's still unclear. But I was able to find out that neither bus had a passenger listed under that name. I tried different variations too. Julian, Julienne, even Joann. I also tracked down the ambulance crew who brought you into the hospital and spoke with the paramedics. They didn't find you with the rest of the passengers. Someone told them a woman was lying by the side of the road several yards away from the accident scene. Had the man not stopped them, you probably wouldn't have survived with your head injury."

"I'm *nett* sure what it all means."

"There's a chance you were never on the bus. We assumed you were a passenger because you came in with all the rest, but what if you were hitchhiking? When the buses collided maybe a piece of flying debris hit you."

"If I was hitchhiking, I could be from anywhere—running away from something or someone." Of course that held true as a bus rider too. Why did this news feel more uncertain?

"You've been through so much, but you're strong. An overcomer. You've learned your way around the hospital in total darkness, and now you can see."

"Can I get out of bed now?"

"That's the spirit." Amy's cheerful smile matched her encouraging tone. "I'll walk with you. Where do you want to go?"

Julie wasn't so eager to leave the room. She merely wanted to find a mirror to look at herself. Hopefully it would trigger her memory.

Standing in front of the kitchen window, Elijah gazed outside at the clear blue sky. He'd been waiting for a break in the weather, eager to refill the woodbox. The supply inside the house had dwindled, and he would need more before nightfall.

Elijah slipped on his boots at the door and grabbed his coat. Outside, the sunny blue sky was a bit deceiving. The brisk air nipped at his nose and cheeks the moment he stepped onto the snow-covered porch. He fisted his ungloved hands and blew air on them, but they still stiffened. Using the side of his boot, he swept some of the snow off the porch steps. He'd look for a shovel in the shed and clean off the steps later.

Snow compressed under his feet as he made his way toward the barn. As he neared the large structure, a horse's neigh caught his attention. He searched the area and finally discovered the young gelding on the opposite side of the barn, caught in the barbed-wire fence.

Elijah approached the horse with caution. Young horses were easily spooked, and one caught was even more unpredictable. "Easy, boy."

The horse's ears perked, then twitched. Aware of Elijah, the gelding stomped his hoof and snorted. Elijah went to reach for the halter, but the skittish horse sidestepped, tangling himself in the wire even more.

"Easy, boy." Elijah let the horse sniff his hand, then stroked its neck, its winter coat thick. "Where did you come from?" More importantly, how long had he been tangled? Fresh cuts marked his chest and places along his legs. He left the horse long enough to search for wire cutters in the barn.

The wooden barn had seen better days. Slates were missing and snow had blown inside. He located several shelves along the back wall loaded with equipment such as currycombs, hoof picks, bridles, harnesses, and other horse-exercising equipment. Discovering a cutter inside a rusty toolbox, he headed outside to free the horse.

"Easy, boy." Elijah took the horse's halter with a firm hand, but the gelding jerked its head and, in doing so, stretched Elijah's shoulder muscles until they burned. He buried a painful cry in a groan. Sweat beaded on his forehead as he worked to get the beast stalled.

The horse stomped and snorted while Elijah rubbed his shoulder joint. Elijah searched the shelves for something to put on the horse's cuts. Finding an unmarked jar, he removed the lid and smelled the contents. The strong iodine-based ointment would help heal the wounds. Hopefully it hadn't sat so long that it had lost its potency.

"Hello, boy." He eased open the stall door. Elijah slipped inside. "I'm not going to hurt you." He talked softly as he inched toward the horse.

He'd trained plenty of high-spirited horses, some with meaner temperaments, but he'd had full function of his arm and shoulder. Candice had warned him about his shoulder freezing up if he didn't move it. Wonder if she would approve of how he was moving it now?

Elijah reached out and stroked the horse's neck, which seemed to calm him some. He applied a generous amount of medicated salve to the horse's chest, then moved down each leg. The Standardbred's muscles had good form. His owner—whoever that was—had taken care of him well.

"You need something to eat, don't you, boy?" The breed was typically used for pulling buggies. But Elijah hadn't seen any Amish farms on his ride to the cabin. He couldn't remember any road signs denoting horse and buggies in the area either.

He slipped out of the stall, making sure to secure the gate latch. A quick search in the hayloft yielded nothing. The grain bins were empty too. Elijah had to find the horse something to eat. He hiked back to the house, went down to the cellar, and scavenged a grain sack full of carrots and another sack filled with apples. He collected the bags, then grabbed a bucket and filled it with water.

The horse refused to come near the stall door even when Elijah waved the carrot. When he finally did, he stood out of reach and stretched his neck. He nibbled on the end but then moved to the back of the stall.

Elijah waited him out. He had nothing else to do, and spending time with the horse took his mind off Catherine. Feeding the horse one carrot at a time, Elijah soon had the horse trusting him. The animal no longer snorted or stomped his hooves, and by late afternoon he was eating pieces of apple straight from Elijah's hand.

Inspecting the barn further, Elijah discovered

an old horse blanket hanging on a nail. It was moth-eaten, but it would help keep the horse warm through the night. Tomorrow he would see about finding the owner, although he had no idea where to start.

Leaving the barn, Elijah made his way to the small shed a few feet away. Thankfully it was filled with chopped wood. He collected an armload and headed to the house. He'd made it halfway across the yard when he heard heavy steps pounding the snow.

"Whoa, Ginger." The rider pulled back on the reins, and the horse stopped a few feet from Elijah.

"*Hiya*," Elijah greeted the Amish boy.

An older man riding a much older horse plodded up the driveway.

Elijah greeted the newcomer with a friendly smile. "*Welkum*. I didn't know there was an Amish community nearby. I'm Elijah Graber from Posen, Michigan."

"I'm Titus Zook, and this here is *mei sohn*, Joshua. Michigan, you say. You're a long way from home." The older man looked around the area. "I didn't know anyone was living here. It's been closed up for years."

Years? The carrots and apples weren't that old. Thrilled to have company, he motioned with a nod toward the house. "Would you like to *kumm* inside and warm up by the fire? I could put a pot of *kaffi* on the stove. I'd love to hear about your district."

"*Danki*, but maybe another time. We're looking for a horse, and we don't have much daylight left."

"Hold on a second." Elijah went to the porch and dropped the armload of wood, then swept the bark off the front of his coat. "I think you'll want to take a look at what's in the barn. I found him tangled in barbed wire earlier today." He led them to the barn once they tied their mounts to the fence post.

The young boy's elation claimed the stray. "Pickles!"

The horse tossed his head up and down and stomped his hoof.

"Should have named him Spitfire," the older man said with a huff. "I bought him last year, and he's too much beast to fool with. I plan to sell him come auction time."

"He spooks easily. I agree." Elijah unlatched the stall gate and slipped inside. "Easy, boy." The horse tossed his head and snorted as Elijah came close, but then he sniffed at his hand and settled down.

"You have a way of gentling a giant," Titus said.

Elijah patted the horse's neck. "He gets frightened easily and needs reassurance. I don't doubt he'd make a *gut* buggy horse. He has good form."

"That's what I thought when I bought him." Titus studied the horse a few seconds, then shook his head. "I could use a mug of that *kaffi* you offered."

"Sure." He gave Pickles a final pat, then exited the stall.

"Do you know Menno Zook? He's from Posen."

"*Jah*, he's our bishop."

"Small world," Titus said as they left the barn. "Menno's *mei* first cousin. We both grew up in Holmes County. His family ended up in Michigan, and mine helped to start this community in Hopewater."

The three of them left the barn and headed to the house.

"How long are you planning to stay?"

Elijah was taking it day by day. He didn't want to wear out his welcome at the stranger's cabin, but he also had no intentions of going back to Michigan without Catherine. "Probably until spring."

Titus smiled. "I might have a job for you."

Chapter 28

Julie stared at herself in the mirror. *Ugly stranger.* One cheekbone appeared much larger than the other, and bluish-purple blotches colored her skin. Her brow was shaved, and stitches surrounded her eye. Looking at her head, she noticed big square patches were shaved down to the scalp. How could she identify with this distorted image—with the monster in the mirror? She should have listened to Amy when the nurse tried to warn her. Now when people looked at her with shocked expressions, there would be no denying how deformed she was.

Amy's arm came around Julie's shoulders. "You're beautiful."

"No, I'm *nett.*" Julie flipped off the bathroom light switch. "I don't ever want to look at myself again."

"Don't say that. You're still healing."

"My head is shaved. I have hardly any hair to pull down over my face, and I have no idea who I am or where I belong. For all I know *mei* name isn't Julie."

"I know this is hard. You've gone through so

much. Is there another name you would rather I call you?"

"No—I don't know." She blew out a breath. "Julie's a nice name, I suppose. It's better than 'hey you.'"

"As for your hair, the doctor had no choice. He had to relieve the pressure on your brain. A subdural hematoma is very serious—deadly."

"I know. I've heard it all before. I'm lucky to be alive. Only I don't know who I am, so how lucky am I?" She moved out from under Amy's arm over her shoulder and turned toward the bed. "I'd like to lie down now."

"Sure. Can I get you a protein shake or some applesauce?"

"Maybe later." She wanted to crawl under the covers and never surface again. "Do you mind leaving me alone?"

"Um, sure. I have some charting I need to catch up on at the desk. I'll stop by your room before I go home." She opened the door to leave but came back to the bedside. "I have a friend who's a police officer. He mentioned running your fingerprints—you'd have to give consent."

"They can figure out who I am based on my fingerprints?"

"Maybe. But there's a catch. You might find out who you are but not like the results."

"What do you mean?"

"If you're a wanted criminal or there's a

warrant out for your arrest, he would arrest you."

Julie kept silent.

"You don't have to make up your mind now. I'll leave you to think on it." Amy left the room.

Julie slipped under the covers and closed her eyes. What if she was a criminal? The thought hadn't crossed her mind. *Lord, who am I?*

She spent the remainder of the day in bed, and as Amy had promised, she stopped by at the end of her shift, only Julie kept her eyes closed and didn't answer when Amy asked if she was awake. It wasn't until after Amy had gone that Julie opened her eyes and found the vase of yellow roses.

Tears streamed down Julie's face as she read the card.

> "Therefore I tell you, do not worry about your life . . . Look at the birds of the air; they do not sow or reap or store away in barns, and yet your heavenly Father feeds them. Are you not much more valuable than they?"
>
> Don't be discouraged.
>
> Your friend,
> Amy

Julie gazed at the front of the card. Why did the sparrow perched on the fence post look so familiar?

• • •

"I found out we have something in common," Elijah said to Pickles as he fastened the harness around the horse's girth. "We've both been in a bad accident." Elijah patted the horse's neck.

The long hours he spent with Pickles over the past few weeks had helped him bond with the horse, and his shoulder muscles were slowly getting back in shape. He'd gained the gelding's trust—until it came to hitching him to the buggy. Pickles still panicked. Elijah understood the horse's fear. The thought of riding a bus again gave him nightmares.

Elijah had worked with the horse every day in exchange for a few home-cooked meals at the bishop's house. Elijah had gotten the better part of that deal. His wife was a good cook—so was his eldest daughter. It didn't take long to feel at home in the district.

Once Titus had learned why Elijah wanted to stay in Ohio until springtime, he'd taken an interest in helping him find odd jobs. He chopped wood for a widow, who in turn had sewn him a new shirt. He saved it to wear on Sundays. He shoveled driveways, helped with milking, and did pretty much anything to fill the void. Other members in the district had supplied him with pants, a hat, and a pair of warm winter gloves. They didn't ask too many questions about his past, and Elijah suspected the bishop had something to do with that.

He still couldn't get through a conversation about Catherine without getting choked up, especially after learning that the authorities had called off search and rescue indefinitely. Informing George of the news was the hardest letter he'd ever written. Even then he spared her brother the part about finding her bloody prayer *kapp*.

Elijah stood behind him and tapped the reins. Pickles sidestepped, then refused to go. He wouldn't hitch him to anything today. After the failed attempt last week, he had to start the training over, even getting the horse used to wearing blinders.

Once Pickles moved, he immediately pulled for more rein, but Elijah was able to hold him back. Traipsing through the snow behind the horse was difficult at a slow walking pace, but he couldn't let Pickles go any faster. He directed Pickles across the eighty-acre pasture that separated the cabin where Elijah was staying from the bishop's farm. His boots sank into the snow. By the time he reached the bishop's house for supper, Elijah was chilled to the bone.

"*Kumm* inside. You look like you're freezing," the bishop's daughter Rebecca said. The twenty-two-year-old placed her hands on her hips, her dark eyes locked on Elijah's snow-covered boots.

He stomped off the snow on the porch, then

stepped into the warmth of the home and removed his coat. "Something smells *gut*."

"Beef stew and biscuits. Hope you're hungry."

He smiled. "*Jah*, starved." He hung his coat on the wall peg, then removed his snowy boots. Balls of icy snow had collected on his wool socks. He plucked them off so they wouldn't melt and make a mess on the floor, then opened the door and tossed them outside.

Rebecca poured him a mug of coffee, then handed it to him with a smile. "*Daed*'s in the sitting room."

"*Danki*." He rubbed the side of his head and winced when the stitches tugged the skin.

Rebecca leaned closer, her gaze locked on the wound. "Why do you keep scratching—*ach*! Those have to *kumm* out."

"*Jah*, I've been meaning—"

"Sit down." She pointed to the chair.

"*Nau*?"

The bishop's wife, Lynn, came up from the basement, carrying a jar of preserves in each hand and breathing heavy. "Oh *gut*, you made it," she said, looking at Elijah. "We'll be eating shortly." The stout woman handed the jars to Rebecca's younger sister, Betty. "Titus is reading the newspaper," Lynn told Elijah, motioning to the sitting room.

"He needs the stitches in his head to *kumm* out. He left them in past their stay."

Lynn examined his head. "*Jah*, they sure do. Let's have the scissors, and bring me the bottle of peroxide."

"Do they look bad? I was going to clip them, but I couldn't find a pair of scissors at the cabin."

"I've seen worse."

Rebecca handed her the scissors, and Lynn snipped the thread. The sting from her tugging on the thread made his eyes water, and he had to blink several times to hide his tears from the womenfolk. He didn't need them teasing him over something so minor as a few stitches.

Once Lynn dabbed some peroxide over his wound, he stood. "*Danki*." He grabbed his mug and took his coffee into the sitting room. Elijah sat in the rocking chair next to the bishop's.

"How was your day?" Titus flipped to the next page of *The Budget*.

"Before your *fraa* ripped stitches from *mei* head, gut."

Titus chuckled. "So that was the ruckus?"

"*Jah*, it hurts more when you wait too long." He sipped his coffee.

"I'll remember that. Are you making any progress with Pickles?"

"Very little."

As Titus did every evening, he passed a section of the newspaper to Elijah. "What kind of price do you think he will fetch at the auction?"

"In Michigan he'd go for a thousand easily."

Titus frowned. "Less than what I paid."

"I haven't lost hope in being able to train him." He'd already lost hope in so many things. He couldn't lose faith in rehabilitating Pickles. The horse was traumatized. He needed time to heal.

Elijah opened the paper to the Posen section. His stomach wrenched as he read the opening line: "Catherine Glick is still missing. A love offering is being collected for George's transportation to Ohio."

Julie moved away from the window as Amy entered the room. Since she'd been moved to the rehab wing of the hospital, Amy was no longer her nurse, yet she came by to visit every day after her shift ended.

"I spotted a robin today," Julie said.

"You know what that means. Spring's around the corner. And Easter is next week. Can you believe how fast time is flying?"

Not for everyone. Julie's life had stalled. Even meeting once a week with a psychologist hadn't triggered any memories.

"I want to invite you to church next Sunday. I've already spoken with Dr. Gleeson, and he's willing to issue a day pass. He thinks the outing would be good for you too. In fact—and you didn't hear this from me—he's planning to discharge you."

No wonder the social worker had been bringing

housing applications in for Julie to fill out. The same ball of fire erupted in her stomach as it had the last time anyone talked about her leaving. Medically there wasn't anything else any of the doctors could do. Her eyesight wasn't great; she saw double when she was overly tired or stressed, and she'd learned how to cope without peripheral vision. According to the doctor, she could even learn to drive a car, although the idea frightened her.

"I have nothing to wear to church," she said.

"I've got that covered." Amy sat on the edge of the bed and patted the mattress.

Julie plopped down beside her.

"I want you to meet my fiancé on Sunday."

"You're getting married?"

"This June." She showed Julie the ring on her left hand. "He asked me last night."

"I thought he was away in the military."

Amy nodded. "He finished his tour in Afghanistan and wants to settle down."

"I'm happy for you."

"So, please tell me you'll go to Easter service with me." Amy made a pouty face with her lips until Julie agreed, then pulled her into a hug.

Over the following week, Julie fretted over going out in public. She hadn't looked in the mirror again, but judging by the stares she'd gotten from strangers she met in the hospital hallways, her face still shocked people. Anymore, she felt more comfortable wearing a scarf as a head covering. Thankfully the dress Amy had loaned her for the Easter service had a purple scarf to go along with it.

Throughout the service Julie fidgeted with the folds on the dress. She didn't like that her knees were exposed. Perhaps she was just self-conscious being outside of the hospital. Her dress wasn't any shorter than what all the women were wearing. Julie tried to focus on the sermon. The message of Jesus dying on the cross and rising from the dead stirred her heart. In the end she was glad Amy had invited her to church.

Amy's fiancé, Brett, was tall and handsome with his hair cut short, and he was wearing an army uniform. Her friend looked happy, and Julie was happy for her.

"Will you give us a minute, Brett? I want to introduce Julie to someone."

Julie tried to object, but Amy tugged on her arm. "It'll only take a minute."

Julie pulled her scarf down more on her forehead, fanning out the sides to shadow her face.

"Dr. Wellington," Amy called while crossing the church foyer. "I want you to meet my friend."

Julie wasn't sure why Amy was introducing her to another doctor, but once she met the older gentleman, she felt at ease.

"Dr. Wellington, this is Julie, the friend I was

telling you about. Julie, Dr. Wellington owns a children's ranch."

"It's nice to meet you, Julie. Was today your first time here?"

"Yes, it was. I enjoyed the service." Making small talk was awkward. She lowered her head and studied the green carpet.

Amy filled the gap in conversation. "How many groups of children are you expecting to come to the ranch this year?"

"The summer and fall are already full. I have a couple groups coming as early as May. Did you hear we have a new indoor riding arena?"

"No, but that's great. The children must love being able to ride during the bad weather," Amy said.

"You'll have to drop by sometime." Dr. Wellington turned to Julie. "It was nice meeting you."

"You too." Julie waited until the doctor ambled away before facing Amy. "I hope you weren't trying to play matchmaker in church."

"Oh, heavens no." Amy lowered her voice. "He's old enough to be your father."

"Then what was that about?"

"He might have a job opening."

Panic threaded Julie's veins. "You're going to quit the hospital?"

"No, for you."

Julie opened her mouth to decline, but Amy

spoke first. "We can talk more about it later." She rose to her tiptoes, searching the crowd. "Looks like Brett is ready to leave."

"Do you mind if I skip Easter dinner? I'd like to go back to the hospital."

Amy's brows knitted. "Are you sure?"

"Positive." Going to church was enough of an outing. She didn't want to impose on Amy's family gathering. Especially since Brett had only recently returned from overseas.

The three of them walked across the church parking lot to Brett's car. Julie climbed into the back seat. On the drive back to the hospital, Julie couldn't help but notice the way Brett looked at Amy. Had there ever been anyone who looked at her the same way?

"What if I can't cook?" Julie paced the length of the hospital room, her stomach twisting into knots.

"You probably won't have to," Amy said. "The children's ranch has a head cook. You'll be her assistant."

Julie shook her head. "I'm not ready to leave here. I'm still in therapy."

"About that . . ." Amy's lips formed a straight line.

"What were you going say?"

She sat on the edge of the bed and patted the mattress. "Come sit with me."

Julie eyed her friend a half second, then plopped down on the bed. "What are you not telling me?"

"Dr. Gleeson wasn't able to convince administration to extend your stay. He'll be here shortly to tell you that you're being discharged."

A lump formed in her throat. "But I still don't know who I am." They'd all drawn the conclusion months ago that she either didn't have family or was estranged from them. Otherwise someone would have come looking for her.

"You'll be safe at the ranch. Of course you won't get paid much, but you'll have room and board."

She was safe *here* in the hospital. Julie pinched the bridge of her nose, but she couldn't stop the tears from collecting. *Lord, help me.* "My face will frighten the children."

"They're blind."

Julie sniffled.

"Maybe the reason you spent so many weeks with your eyes bandaged was God preparing you for this job," Amy said softly. "You'll be able to relate to what the children are going through."

"I never thought about that possibility." Julie had asked why so many times. She thought God wasn't listening.

"There's one more thing I need to tell you," Amy said. "Your fingerprints were not on file. It's good news really. You're not a wanted criminal."

"When you look at it that way, it is *gut*. But nothing's changed. I still don't know who I am or where I belong."

Elijah dreaded the long drive into town, and thankfully the bishop wasn't talkative today. Elijah needed time to mentally prepare before reaching the police department. With the warmer weather the Muskingum River would have thawed. The runoff of melted snow would have raised the water level, and that meant the water would be rushing downstream at a faster pace.

The buggy wheel dipped into a muddy puddle, and he was unexpectedly jostled.

"You sure you feel up to going into town? You're looking a little pale, Elijah."

"I'm sure." He'd stopped at the police department at least once a week when he went into town with Titus. Sometimes he thought the bishop created a reason to take a drive just so Elijah could be reassured that nothing new had developed. Elijah wiped his moist palms on his pant legs and gazed out the window at the budding trees—nature's evidence of spring.

"I suppose you want me to drop you off at the police station," Titus said when they entered the city limits.

"Please." He pulled a hankie from his pocket and blotted his forehead. He should be praying, but lately he hadn't found the words. If praying that Catherine was found meant her body washing ashore, he couldn't pray that he'd find her.

The buggy rolled to a stop next to the curb in front of the police station, and Elijah slid off the bench. "I'll meet you at the market, or are you going to the feed store first?"

"Try the market first."

"Okay, thanks." A gust of wind lifted his straw hat, but Elijah was able to hold it in place. He hurried into the building.

The window clerk, Brooke, looked up and smiled as the bell buzzed. "How are you today, Mr. Graber?"

He shrugged. "Nervous."

She picked up the phone and pressed extension 58. "Mr. Graber is here. Is there anything I need to tell him?"

He'd been in the office so many times over the past few months that they all knew his name and the reason for his visit.

She put the phone down. "Nothing's come over the wire. Officer Rhodes said he would pay you a visit if and when he hears something."

"I know, but I was coming into town anyway. I thought I would stop in." Their conversation was always the same. "Thanks for your help."

"Anytime."

After the first few times he'd gone in to see an officer, Brooke had teased him that she had worked for more than twenty years for the department and had never had an Amish person in the building until he moved to town. Elijah had laughed at her joke, but inwardly he wished he had no reason to go inside.

Elijah shot up a quick wave and headed to the door. "See you next time." A sense of peace washed over him as he hiked the half mile to the market. Lowering his head to block the wind, he hadn't noticed anyone walk up until someone touched his coat sleeve.

"Elijah? Is that you?"

It had been months since he'd seen Alex. "*Jah*, it's me. How are you, Alex?"

"I'm doing great. The case against Budget Bus is getting closer to being resolved. I can't say for sure, but everything is leaning toward reaching a settlement out of court. However, if they don't meet our demands, we don't have any problem letting a jury decide." He reached inside his coat pocket and removed his cell phone. "How can I reach you? We'll have to schedule your deposition sometime soon."

"I'm living in Hopewater district, but I would rather *nett*—"

"The Amish settlement off of Hill Side Drive?"

"*Jah*, but I'm *nett* interested in going to court or testifying. I've had time to think it over and—"

"What about Catherine? You didn't say if you've found her. Unfortunately, it's too late to add her to the suit. I could probably arrange another firm to take her case."

"She wouldn't be interested. And *nay*, I haven't found her yet. I have to go." He pointed to the market. "I'm meeting someone."

"Oh yeah, don't let me keep you. I'll be in touch."

Please, don't.

Chapter 29

The children's ranch was massive. A long, narrow driveway with board fencing on both sides led to the two-story main home constructed out of cedar logs and a stone foundation.

Amy stopped the car in the circular driveway and turned off the engine. "So what do you think?"

Julie gazed in awe at the majestic surroundings. "It's certainly in the middle of nowhere."

"Doc owns a thousand acres." Amy opened the car door and got out.

Reluctantly, she climbed out of the car, then grabbed the brown paper bag from the back seat, which held all her worldly belongings. A few changes of clothes, a brush, and toiletries that Amy had generously supplied. Gazing at the house again, she took a deep breath. Tension knotted her muscles despite the sense of peacefulness the place emanated.

"Julie." Amy wove her arm around Julie's elbow. "Once you're adjusted, trust me, you'll never want to leave."

"If I don't earn my keep, Dr. Wellington might ask that I leave."

Amy tugged her elbow, drawing her in tighter. "Don't you worry about that. You're going to do fine."

They followed the sidewalk to the front steps.

Amy's eyes lit. "Don't you just love this big porch?"

"Impressive." The covered front porch spanned the length of the house, and various wooden chairs made it an inviting space to watch the sunset. She noticed a plaque near the door and touched the raised bumps.

"It's Braille," Amy explained. "Welcome to Hannah's Henhouse."

"Henhouse?"

"Odd, isn't it?" Amy chuckled. "This place reminds me of the resort I stayed at in Montana." She rang the doorbell. "Hannah was Doc's wife. She passed away a few years ago. I think he used to tease her about being a mother hen."

The door opened, and a woman who appeared to be in her early sixties greeted them with a smile. "May I help you?"

"My name is Amy Sawyer, and we're here to see Dr. Wellington."

"Oh yes. He's expecting you." She opened the door wider.

The foyer held a large round table in the center,

which held a tall iron vase of birch tree limbs bluntly cut.

"Hi, I'm Cynthia Hunt. You must be Julie, my new helper."

"It's nice to meet you, Ms. Hunt. I, ah—" She shifted the bag with her clothes to her opposite arm and extended her right hand. "I look forward to working with you."

"Same here," she said, shaking her hand. "Please, call me Cynthia."

The woman's friendly smile eased some of Julie's nerves.

"Let me show you to your room first so you can drop off your belongings." Cynthia eyed the brown sack. "Then I'll take you on the grand tour. Are you a fan of horseback riding?"

"I'm not sure if I've ever ridden a horse before."

The woman's brows angled curiously, and her head tilted to one side.

"Julie was in a terrible accident," Amy explained.

"I lost my memory." She chewed her lip, trying to decide if she should tell her everything. She needed to make a good impression; she needed the job. Her hospital bill was enormous. When Amy had contacted the bus companies to file a claim on Julie's behalf, a claim couldn't be processed without the required information—full name, photo identification, and proof of purchase by either a copy of the credit card statement or receipt.

Amy cupped Julie's shoulder with her hand. "She's undergone multiple surgeries and almost lost sight in one eye."

"Oh my." The woman pressed her hand to her chest.

"Truth is," she blurted, "I don't even know if my name is Julie." Acid clawed at the back of her throat. Would the woman still want to work with her?

"I see." Cynthia forced a smile she couldn't hold. Her shoulders straightened and spine stiffened. "Is Dr. Wellington aware?"

Amy nodded. "He is."

Cynthia turned away from Amy. "Do you require any special assistance, Julie—should I call you Julie?"

"I'll answer to anything, but yes, Julie is fine. And no, I don't need assistance. I'll be your best worker."

Cynthia eyed her hard. "Your memory loss explains why I didn't receive a copy of your background check."

Julie stole a glance at Amy, whose brows had arched. "I thought Doc said everything was worked out."

The woman continued to scrutinize every inch of her. "You'll only be around the children under direct supervision. It's for the safety of the children."

Julie nodded. "I understand."

"And you'll abide by the rules?"

"Of course." Julie hated to believe she might be a danger to the children, but how did she know if she even liked children—she couldn't even vouch for herself.

"Julie had her fingerprints run through the FBI program, and nothing came back," Amy said. "She *volunteered* to have her prints checked, hoping it would lead to finding her identity. What more does your background check involve?"

"I call former employers, check personal references."

"I'll vouch for her. I've known her almost four months, and I've never seen a kinder, gentler soul."

Julie would have described Amy the same way.

Cynthia's expression warmed. "Julie, you're fortunate to have such a wonderful friend like Amy."

"I'm blessed," Julie replied.

"Your room is in the west wing." Cynthia made a nod toward another room and started walking. "Our days begin early. Sometimes before sunrise . . ."

Julie glanced over her shoulder at Amy and mouthed, "Thank you."

As Cynthia led them through an empty sitting

room where leather chairs flanked a matching L-shaped couch, Julie inhaled the wood-burning scent coming from the fireplace and smiled. She looked forward to spending time in this room. Perhaps she would be able to borrow a book from one of the floor-to-ceiling shelves. The volunteer at the hospital had loaned her several books from her cart. Some of the stories were better than the others, but they served the purpose of passing the time.

Her bedroom was much larger than the hospital room. Brighter too. The lemony yellow walls complemented the blue-and-white checked curtains. She placed her belongings on the bed, then walked over to the large window. The big red barn caught her attention. Situated a few feet beside it was a long paddock with six stall doors, all closed. Not far from it sat a massive pole barn.

"That building to the right is the indoor riding area. The children love being able to ride during the winter." The woman frowned. She shook her head, making a *tsk-tsk* sound with her tongue.

Following the woman's gaze to the muddy pathway that led to the different buildings, Julie said, "I'll keep the floors mopped."

Cynthia smiled. "Oh, bless you, child. We're going to get along perfectly."

Julie smiled. Mopping was a chore she could certainly do. She'd make sure the floors were shiny enough to eat off them.

Cynthia motioned toward the door. “Ready to see the rest of the house?”

“Sure,” Julie replied.

Cynthia explained whose bedrooms were where without opening the doors. As they neared the front door, Amy stopped.

“If you don’t mind, I’m going to leave.” Amy glanced at her wristwatch. “I changed shifts with one of my coworkers today, so I need to get going now or I’ll risk being late.”

Julie’s breath hitched. Even though Amy had said on the way there that she wouldn’t be able to stay long, Julie wasn’t ready for her friend to leave. She was fine. Cynthia was kind, a sweet motherly type. *Relax. Breathe.*

“I’ll stop out on my next day off,” her friend said reassuringly.

Julie nodded. She trusted Amy. Her friend wouldn’t leave her somewhere unsafe. “Thanks for bringing me. I look forward to seeing you soon.”

Once Amy left, Cynthia continued the tour. The house was larger than it looked, with its various sitting areas, studies, and multiple kitchens on the main level and in the basement. The walls in the basement were finished with rough-cut timber from what looked like an old barn, and rafter beams sectioned off an area that housed a pool table. A leather love seat, couch, and chairs were around an oversized coffee table made from what looked like a massive tree slab. The shiny finish on the top brought out the rings of the old oak beautifully.

Drawn to the french doors, Julie gazed outside at the barnyard. A herd of horses trotted up to the fence, where a man was spreading hay on the ground. Some of the horses had spots; others had patches; some of their wintery coats were various shades of brown; others were black or white. Mixed in the group were several ponies with their long manes past their necks and bangs that covered their eyes; their big, rounded bellies were quite a sight. Her gaze flitted from the four-legged creatures over to the redheaded man feeding them.

Why does he look familiar?

Chapter 30

Over the following week, Elijah kept himself busy by reading the Bible and praying continuously for Catherine, as well as for direction for his life. He had no idea how long he would stay at the cabin. He didn't want to wear out his welcome even though he hadn't seen the red-haired man again.

Rain had melted the snow, and with the yard mostly muddy, he was careful not to push Pickles too hard for fear the animal would stumble on the slippery soil and injure himself. But limiting the horse's training meant Elijah had too much time on his hands. He'd replaced the missing slats in the barn siding and walked the fence line yesterday, inspecting it for needed repairs. Now, sitting inside the cabin, idly watching drizzly raindrops make rings in the puddles outside the window, his mind conjured up an image of Catherine smiling, and for a split second, he heard her laughter. Tears brimmed his lids, and he swiped them away. *She's gone.*

Elijah shot up from the chair. *This is crippling.* He had to do something. He shoved on his boots, snatched his coat from the hook, and put it on as he walked to the equipment shed. Hard work had always been therapeutic. Who cared if it was raining.

After finding a hoe, rake, and wheelbarrow in the shed, he crossed the yard to a spot that had good sun and would make a good place for a garden. He swung the hoe with all his might, taking out his pent-up anger over missing Catherine on the soil. As he turned over the ground, rainwater mixed with tears spilled into the trenches. By the time exhaustion set in, he'd cleared a larger area than he originally intended. He hoped the cabin owner would be all right with what he'd done. He should have asked permission.

Elijah gathered the dead leaves and the weeds he'd pulled, and placed them in the wheelbarrow. As he emptied the last load on the compost pile, the sun had completely faded. Dirty, exhausted, and aching all over, he decided it was too late to make supper with the bishop's family. He wasn't hungry. Besides, he wouldn't be much company anyway.

He washed up at the sink, then put the kettle on the stove for coffee. Maybe later he'd fry an egg or two if he felt hungry. He'd been blessed by the members in the district with quart-sized jars of milk and fresh eggs every day. The women had also spoiled him with pies and cookies.

When the coffee was ready, he poured a mug, then fished out a tasty treat from the cookie jar. The first bite of sweetness awakened his stomach; it growled for more. Elijah removed a frying pan from the cabinet, and as he tapped an egg against the countertop, someone knocked on the back door. Startled by the knock, he somehow crushed the egg. Yolk drippings went down the front of the cabinet and splattered on the floor.

He toweled his hands as he went to answer the door. With the visitor holding a lantern down at his side, it was difficult to make out who was standing on the stoop.

"*Guder* evening, Elijah."

His jaw went slack. He recognized Zach's voice before his eyes had a chance to adjust to the darkness.

Zach lifted the lantern higher in one hand while drawing his attention to the plate covered with foil in his other. "The bishop's *fraa* wanted me to bring you this. She thought you might be hungry. You never made it to supper."

"*Jah*, time got away with me—what are you doing here?"

"You gonna invite me in?"

Elijah opened the door wider. "Sorry, I didn't mean to be impolite. I wasn't expecting—"

"Me. You weren't expecting me."

Zach's controlled tone and probing stare caught Elijah off guard. It wasn't until his friend gave the plate of food a deliberate thrust against his chest that Elijah sensed Zach's wrath. Behind his friend's tight-lipped smile, he was clenching his teeth.

"Have a seat. I'll pour us some *kaffi*." Elijah turned his back to him and placed the plate of food on the table. "When did you get into town?"

"A few hours ago."

Elijah removed a mug from the cabinet. "I sent word to George that there hasn't been any news about Catherine."

"Your letter said *nett* to *kumm* until after spring. Something about waiting until after the river thawed."

"*Jah*, that happened a while ago." Needing something to occupy himself with as the coffee reheated, Elijah cleaned up the mess he'd made cracking the egg. *Lord, Zach has traveled a long way for a reason. Please, give me the right words.*

Julie still hadn't seen Dr. Wellington—or the redheaded hired hand—and she'd been on the ranch for two days. Cynthia had hinted at Dr. Wellington's aloofness as Julie washed down the breakfast table. "Don't take it personally. This isn't a good time of the year for Doc. He usually holes up in his office or takes long walks alone. We don't bother him, and he usually snaps out of it in a few days."

Does Amy know about his odd behavior? Her friend had called both of the days she'd been staying on the ranch, but Amy's work schedule was such that she didn't have a day off until Sunday, on which she promised to spend some time with her.

Julie filled the sink with hot water and swished her hand, causing dish detergent bubbles to foam on the surface. She didn't have many dishes to wash; the day camp children had yet to arrive. Julie had learned from Cynthia how over the years the number of campers had dwindled. Between insurance hikes and the costly updates needed to stay in compliance with state regulations, tuition was increased to offset the operational costs. For some of the out-of-state groups, it was no longer feasible.

Julie scrubbed the plate with the dishrag. She was grateful for the job, but only a fool would not see that she wasn't needed. Cynthia handled the meals with ease. The long-term employee was a hard worker and someone Julie wanted to model her work ethic after.

Cynthia fixed a plate of chicken casserole, green beans, and a roll, then covered it with foil. She'd done the same the night before, but the food had gone uneaten. She placed the plate in the refrigerator, then grabbed a clean dish towel from the drawer. "It's been such a treat having you here." She picked up a plate to dry.

"The pleasure is all mine. I can finish the dishes and sweep and mop the floor if you'd like to sit and rest. You've been on the go since daybreak."

The older woman chuckled. "Sweet girl, I—I'm going to take you up on that." She removed her well-worn apron and hung it on a hook inside the broom closet, then retrieved the covered dish she'd just put in the refrigerator. While waiting for the meal to heat in the microwave, she glanced over her shoulder at Julie. "You can leave any dishes that you're not sure where they go on the counter, and I'll put them away in the morning."

"Okay."

Cynthia grabbed a set of silverware from the drawer, poured a glass of milk, then left the kitchen.

Julie finished the dishes and did her best to find where everything went. She scrubbed the stove, washed down the countertops and sink, then swept the floor. She had already mopped the floor twice today. Once after the children finished their lunch and shortly again after the hired hands had come in from the barn. Boots had left a trail of mud from the kitchen back door to the table. No wonder Cynthia hated the rainy season. Julie wanted to make a good impression, so she filled the bucket with soapy water and scrubbed the floor on her hands and knees with a stiff brush.

Cleaning the floor and baseboards, Julie worked up a sweat. She took a short break to inspect her work, and without getting off her knees, she straightened her posture and pressed her hand against her lower back.

Dr. Wellington rounded the corner of the kitchen and stopped abruptly, and the milk glass he'd been balancing on his plate fell and shattered into tiny pieces. His forehead furrowed with deep-set lines. "I'm sorry. I didn't see you there. I hope you didn't get hit with flying glass."

"No, I wasn't hit." She rose to her feet. "I didn't mean to startle you."

"It's my fault entirely. I wasn't paying attention." He set the plate and silverware in the basin, then crossed the room as she was removing the broom from the closet. "Please, allow me."

Cynthia had stressed more than once to Julie that the doctor wanted to be alone at this particular time of the year. Julie didn't want her new boss upset with her. "I don't mind, Dr. Wellington. Really."

He held out his hand and smiled. "I insist on cleaning up my own mess."

She released the broom but held on to the dustpan.

He swept the floor. "Everyone calls me Doc."

"I'm Julie . . . Amy's friend."

He stopped and turned to face her. "I apologize

for not greeting you when you first arrived. I had completely forgotten what day you were supposed to start. I think Cynthia, bless her heart, screens my visitors or, in your case, new hires."

"I understand."

He resumed sweeping. "How is everything going so far?"

"Very well, thank you. You have a beautiful place."

"Thank you. Has anyone shown you around the farm?" He gathered the glass into a pile.

"Not yet." She bent down and angled the dustpan. "Cynthia's been busy training me on inside chores."

He nodded. "Cynthia's allergic to hay. She avoids the barns, even going outside on a windy day. Can't say that I blame her. Once she starts sneezing and her eyes start itching and watering, she's miserable for days. Antihistamines don't seem to work for her either."

"That sounds miserable." *Am I allergic to anything?* She couldn't even be certain she'd ever been in a barn. Julie emptied the glass in the trash can, then put the broom and dustpan away.

"After breakfast tomorrow, I'll show you around myself."

"Oh, I don't want to bother you. Cynthia said you—" She clamped her mouth closed, noticing his face pinch. She didn't know him well enough to know if the expression meant he'd been struck with sadness or if he was trying to hide being upset.

He sighed heavily. “I’ve known Cynthia for a number of years, and let’s just say she can be a little overly protective.”

She hadn’t learned everything about the ranch operations, but it was obvious that Cynthia cared a great deal about her employer.

“Please don’t take that wrong,” he said. “Cynthia is the one person I trust to keep this place running with or without me. Lord knows I would be lost without her.” He paused, then shook his head as if to clear his thoughts. “I’ll show you around the barns after we eat breakfast in the morning. If there’s anything you need, please let me or Cynthia know.”

“Yes, I will. And thank you again for allowing me to stay here.”

“Wish I could pay you more.” He ambled toward the kitchen entrance and stopped. “One more thing. I’m glad you’re here. I hope you feel at home. Good night.”

“Good night . . . Doc.” She crossed the room. “You don’t have to pay me. A place to stay is all I need.”

He smiled warmly. “We’ll talk about it another time. Sleep well.”

Julie waited until he left the room before inspecting the floor a final time for stray pieces of glass. She didn’t want one of the children accidentally getting cut. She swept the floor, then washed, dried, and put away the dishes he'd left in the sink. Standing at the light switch, she glanced around the room, smiling with approval. Tidy and ready for tomorrow—*a new day.*

For the first time since she had woken up in the hospital without an identity, she wasn't afraid to face tomorrow. *Thank You, Jesus, for providing me a place to stay—a place to call home.*

Chapter 31

Elijah placed the mug of coffee on the table in front of Zach, then took the chair opposite. For several seconds the tension thickened as neither of them spoke.

Zach outlined the top of the mug with his finger. "I heard the accident was bad."

"*Jah*, it was." Elijah looked down. It was easier to study the coffee grounds floating on the surface of his drink than to make eye contact.

Silence returned.

Guilt ratcheted Elijah's throat. Even turning and coughing into his fisted hand did little to lessen the constriction.

"I haven't stopped looking for her." Elijah's thoughts spilled out. He lifted his gaze to Zach's. "I check for new updates every time I go into town. The authorities know she's still missing. I won't let them forget."

"That's what Bishop Zook said."

"Bishop Zook of Posen district?" As he asked the question, he caught sight of the foiled plate. *"The bishop's* fraa *wanted me to bring you this. You never made it to supper."*

"Of Hopewater—your next-door neighbor,"

Zach clarified sharply. "Imagine *mei* surprise when I heard *your* woes told to me by the bishop. You lost the love of your life—only you failed to tell him that you lost Catherine six years ago."

Elijah swallowed hard.

Zach pushed away from the table and stood. "How did you happen to be going to Florida at the same time as Catherine? Did you two plan to leave together?"

"*Nay*—well, she didn't." Elijah's gaze followed Zach as he paced to the door and back. "Catherine had no idea until I boarded the bus."

Zach's jaw muscle twitched.

Elijah motioned to the chair. "Please, sit down. Let's talk this over."

Zach grumbled under his breath something Elijah couldn't decipher, but he plopped down on the chair and crossed his arms. "Talk."

"I ran into Cat at the bus station when she was there to purchase her ticket. I found out she was going to Florida, and I changed my ticket. She didn't know. At the time . . ."

"What?"

"She was hurt—humiliated really. That *nacht* in the barn when she asked you to marry her, you—you stomped on her heart."

"So did you when you ran off to Badger Creek and got married. You don't think that devastated her?"

Elijah closed his eyes. "I know it did."

"Did you know I proposed to Catherine the *nacht* before she left?"

His friend's words cut to the marrow, and rightfully so—he'd been betrayed. Elijah nodded. "She told me." His stomach twisted. He'd known about the proposal and pursued her anyway. Perhaps it had been wishful thinking at the time, but something told him that she wouldn't have gotten on a bus heading to Florida—for an extended period of time—had she accepted Zach's proposal. "Why did she go?"

"*Mei* proposal didn't change her mind about spending the winter in Florida. She had promised her cousin she would help in her bakery and—" Zach shrugged. "I messed up. I should have tried harder to change her mind."

"She was only going to be gone a few months," Elijah said, shamefully recalling how he'd planned to use those months to woo Catherine and convince her to fall in love with him. Now he was sorry Zach hadn't tried harder. Had she stayed home, there would have been no chance for the two of them. She would be planning a wedding, but at least she would be alive.

His eyes moistened with tears and his throat clumped. "There's something I have to tell you. The authorities believe . . . she's dead."

Zach blinked a few times, and tears spilled down his cheeks. "When you said in your letter they're waiting until the river thaws . . ."

"I haven't given up hope."

Zach wiped his face. "In the morning I need to drop off a miniature grandfather clock I made for the Beacon furniture store, but then I'm planning to head back to Michigan. I think you should *kumm* back home. The *Englisch* driver I hired has plenty of room, especially after I drop off the clock."

"Did Beverly bring you?" She'd been very concerned about Catherine every time Elijah had called with an update.

Zack nodded. "She dropped me off at Bishop Zook's and is spending the *nacht* with her niece, but she'll be here first thing in the morning to pick us up—if you want to go back to Posen." He went to the door. "You can think about it and let me know in the morning."

Elijah didn't have to think about it. He wasn't leaving Hopewater. Posen would never feel like home again—not without Catherine.

"Dr. Wellington tells me that he's going to show you around the barns today," Cynthia said as she flipped a pancake on the griddle.

"He insisted."

"Yes, but what I want to know is, what did you say to get him out of his melancholy?"

"Nothing." She couldn't tell if Cynthia was pleased with her or ready to scold her for bothering the good doctor. Julie shook her head. “I was down on my hands and knees scrubbing the floor when he came into the kitchen with his plate. He must not have seen me at first, because I startled him enough that he dropped his milk glass, and it shattered on the floor. While we were cleaning it up, he asked if I’d had a chance to see the horses, and I said—”

“Shh.” Cynthia motioned with a nod toward the back door.

Dr. Wellington entered, a rolled-up newspaper in his hand. “One of these days I’m going to bribe that newspaper man to bring the paper to the house.”

“Nonsense,” Cynthia said. “That walk to the end of the drive every morning does you good. You said yourself it keeps your joints from stiffening.”

“Apparently my hips and knees didn’t listen.”

“It’s going to rain. I can smell it coming,” Cynthia said.

He sat at the table and unrolled the paper. “There’s not much accuracy in being able to smell rain.”

Cynthia turned and waved the pancake flipper at him. “Tell that to the American Indians.”

“You didn’t let me finish. There’s not much accuracy in being able to smell rain when you stay inside the house all day.”

Julie chuckled.

"I think Julie agrees with me," Doc said.

She covered her mouth with her hand.

"Oh, I would think before you two decide to gang up on me." Cynthia pointed the flipper from Doc to Julie, who was setting the table. "Especially if you want to eat pancakes today."

Black smoke rose from the griddle. Cynthia scrambled to remove the pan from the stove. "Now look what you made me do, Doc."

He chuckled and winked at Julie. "She can smell rain coming from miles away, but she can't smell something burning next to her."

"I heard that."

"I'd better hush before she feeds us cold cereal." He lifted his paper and gave it a snap. "In other news, the seven-day forecast reports sunshine and a high of forty-eight degrees."

"It'll rain."

Julie found the banter between them refreshing. She certainly wouldn't describe Doc's mood as melancholy today, and she guessed that had something to do with Cynthia's cheerfulness as well.

The back door opened, and a couple of the workers came inside, removed their cowboy hats, and sat at the table. Julie had spotted them leading horses from one barn to another when she was washing windows yesterday, although she'd been more interested in the beautiful horses.

Doc set the paper aside. "Julie, have you met Matthew and Quinn?"

"It's nice to meet you." She absentmindedly touched the scar on her face and lowered her head, horrified. How could she have forgotten her scarf?

"Nice to meet you too, Julie," Matthew, the lankier one, said.

The covering was hanging on a hook on her bedroom door. It would only take a minute to fetch it.

"Julie, why don't you ask the men if they would like coffee," Cynthia suggested.

"I'll take a cup," Matthew said.

"Me too."

So much for the scarf. She turned to Doc. "Do you need a refill?"

He tipped his mug and eyed the contents. "Maybe a little if there's enough."

The men were already engaged in conversation about horses and feed and fence lines when Julie set their mugs on the table. Thankfully they were kind enough not to stare.

Cynthia set the platter of pancakes in the center of the table, then went back for the plate of bacon and sausage. "Julie, if you could grab the butter from the refrigerator and syrup from the microwave, I think we'll be all set."

"Sure." She found the butter, but figuring out how to open the microwave was a challenge.

Cynthia came up beside her, pressed a button, and the door opened automatically. "Sometimes it gets stuck."

"Thank you." Julie reached inside for the container. "*Ach*!" She jerked her hand out and stuck the tips of her fingers in her mouth to reduce the burning sensation.

Doc stood. "Are you okay?"

She nodded. Heat spread over her face, realizing everyone had turned their attention to her sucking her fingers.

"I'll get this. Run some cold water on your hand," Cynthia said.

The cold water relieved the stinging almost immediately. Julie was the last to sit down, and once she did, Doc said the blessing over the food.

The food dishes went quickly around the table as everyone filled their plates. Most of the men's chatter was on complimenting Cynthia for how good everything smelled and how hungry they were.

A few minutes into the meal, Cynthia read the day's itinerary out loud. "We only have one group of children arriving today. Saint Christopher's School for the Blind. They should be here within the hour. Julie and I will serve lunch at 11:40."

"How many are coming?" Matthew asked.

"Ten. Ages five to nine. Two are first-time riders. The ten-and-up group will be here next week."

Matthew turned to Quinn. "We'll need Penny and Henry brought up from the back pasture."

Quinn shoved the last forkful of food into his mouth, washed it down with a gulp of coffee, then stood. "On it."

Matthew and Doc talked about sectioning off the training arena, using one side for beginners and the other for advanced riders. A few minutes later Matthew had finished eating. He pushed away from the table. "Thanks for the meal. Julie, it was nice to meet you. I'm sure I'll be seeing you around."

"Nice to meet you." She hoped Doc hadn't changed his mind about showing her the barn. Hearing them talk about the indoor arena, she was even more curious about the riding facility.

Julie wished she could watch the children interact with the horses and the excitement on their faces when they experienced sitting in the saddle. Julie recalled how frightened she was getting out of bed the first time when she couldn't see. But Cynthia, who was probably speaking for Doc as well, didn't want her around the children.

As Julie began to gather the dirty dishes, Cynthia set down her mug and pushed back her chair. "I have this." Julie motioned for her to sit back down. "Enjoy your coffee."

"Are you sure?"

"Yes, absolutely." Julie couldn't help but

notice the older woman's reluctance to relinquish any of the kitchen responsibilities, or maybe she wasn't one to sit long.

"Let her help you," Doc said.

The lines of tension in Cynthia's forehead faded. She picked up her mug and took a sip.

Julie rushed through washing the dishes.

Cynthia brought her mug to the sink and rinsed it out. "It's faster to load the dishwasher."

"I don't mind doing them by hand." Besides, she wouldn't have any idea how to load it correctly or turn on the machine.

"Let me know when you're ready to see the barn," Doc said, flipping through the pages of the newspaper.

An image snapped before her eyes like a photograph of someone sitting in a rocking chair, holding up a newspaper, and then the image was gone.

Doc lowered the paper enough to look over it. "Unless you'd rather wait and go another time."

"I do want to see it. The dishes shouldn't take much longer." She pulled the drain plug, then grabbed a clean dish towel from the drawer.

"Run along," Cynthia said. "But don't spend all day in the barn. I'll need your help preparing lunch."

Doc refolded the paper and placed it on the table.

Julie tossed the dish towel onto the counter. "Doc, do you mind if I grab something real quick?"

"No, go ahead."

She dashed out of the kitchen, went to her bedroom, and swiped the scarf off the door peg, then returned moments later with her scarf tied at the base of her neck.

Doc's white bushy brows pulled together. "You sure you want to wear that scarf? Looks mighty fancy to go out to the barn."

"It'll be all right."

Someone trounced up the basement steps. The door opened and Cynthia appeared, breathless and holding a pair of shin-high rubber boots. "You'll want to wear these."

"Good idea." The pair of sneakers Amy had given her were all she had. She slipped her feet into the boots. Her toes pinched.

Cynthia stood over her. "They look small. Do they fit?"

"Like a glove." Even tight, the boots were better than getting her shoes dirty. She bundled up in her wool winter coat, another necessity Amy had supplied.

Outside, the soft ground squished underfoot. The weather was much warmer than she expected, and her heavy coat felt cumbersome. They reached the paddock, and Doc held open the door. Julie took in a deep breath, filling her lungs to capacity with the scent of horses, then let it out slowly.

"You're smiling like you've gone to heaven," Doc said.

"I can't explain it, but I recognize this scent."

He frowned apologetically. "The stalls are normally cleaned every day."

"Oh, the odor doesn't bother me." She closed her eyes and inhaled and exhaled again. She reopened her eyes at the sound of a horse's neigh. "Aren't you a beauty."

"Be careful," Matthew said, leading a horse out of the stall next to her. "That nag bites."

She scratched the white star on the horse's head. "You're too beautiful to be called a nag."

"This is Star," Doc said. "And unfortunately, she is a biter."

Thwack. Hinges rattled. *Thwack.*

Julie gave the mare a final pat on the neck, then moved down the stalls, looking for the restless horse. Most of the stalls were empty. She stepped aside as Quinn brought a spotted horse out from a stall.

Thwack.

"Token's in another foul mood," Quinn told Doc as he walked the horse past them.

"He already kicked the gate off its hinges once. I found him in here roaming around the other day. He gave me a rough time putting him back too."

Julie had to see the horse they were talking about. She stopped in front of the stall and peered in at the giant. "*Hiya*, boy."

"Julie, no!"

Chapter 32

Julie stood very still. She didn't want to frighten the horse by her presence.

"Julie, don't go near that horse." Doc lumbered breathlessly toward her, but Matthew got to her first.

He looped her around the waist and curled her away from the stall and into his strong arms. He pushed her back and held her by the shoulders at arm's length. "Are you out of your mind! That horse is dangerous."

She winced at his harsh tone. Perhaps the accident had caused brain damage, but she wasn't about to admit it to him. "I don't think Token likes the way you're talking to me. Look at him; it's you that's stirred him up."

The horse reared, kicking his front legs outside the stall's half door.

"That could have been your head he kicked," Matthew hissed. "You want the other side of your face messed up?"

Julie straightened her spine. Hardening her glare, she pushed out from under Matthew's arms and repositioned her scarf. "Don't look at me if my face disgusts you."

Matthew turned a pleading gaze to Doc, who was leaning against the stall opposite Token's, rasping for air. "Tell her."

"He's right, Julie. Token isn't . . . a horse to mess with."

Noticing Doc's complexion change from pink to pale, Julie rushed to his side. "Are you okay?"

"I'll be . . . fine." He reached into his front pocket and removed a small amber pill bottle. "Open this for me."

"How many do you want?"

"One."

She shook the tiny tablet into her hand and passed it to Doc.

A few seconds later, his breathing wasn't as labored. Color returned to his cheeks.

"I didn't mean to cause problems. Really I didn't." Hinges rattled behind her, and she glanced over her shoulder as Matthew bolted the top half of the stall door shut. *Poor Token. Closed up in the dark.*

"I should have warned you about him sooner," Doc told her, then turned to Matthew. "The children are due to arrive. Are the horses ready?"

"That's what I was working on. Are you going to be all right?"

He nodded. "I've had chest pain before."

Matthew disappeared into another stall, then

left the barn with the black-and-white pinto.

Doc placed his hand on Julie's shoulder. "Why don't we go into the arena and watch the children for a while."

"I think we should go back to the house so you can rest."

"Hogwash." He started walking away, but in the opposite direction Matthew had gone. "You coming or not?"

She fell into step beside him. "I'm not leaving you alone."

Doc smiled as he led her through a small office that joined the paddock with the pole barn. Various trophies lined a shelf behind the desk. Pictures of horses peppered the wall, many with dusty ribbons hanging from the frames.

The door on the opposite wall led to the large indoor arena where sawdust covered the floor. A group of children were seated on a small bench at the long end of the barn. Quinn was talking to them, but he was too far away for Julie to hear his instructions clearly.

Matthew entered the barn with two ponies and tied them up along the wall next to the horses. The man seemed too gruff to be working with children, and blind children at that.

Doc motioned to a row of plastic chairs lining the wall. "Let's sit a spell."

She took a seat, her eye on the children. A boy and girl at the end raised their hands. "Those two must be the new ones Cynthia mentioned."

"Matthew will pull them aside and work with them the first half of the day while Quinn works with the others."

"It must be frightening for them. I know when my eyes were bandaged I stumbled just trying to find the bathroom. I can't imagine what it'd be like riding a horse."

"It takes a lot of trust and confidence, but children tend to be fearless compared to adults. Of course, the same confidence it takes to get up in the saddle can also get them into trouble. Both Matthew and Quinn are great instructors."

"Matthew doesn't come across as a patient man to me."

"He is with special needs children. You'll see."

Julie observed the training and held her breath as the first youngster in Quinn's group climbed into the saddle. Quinn helped the boy get his feet into the stirrups, then had the boy stand and sit back down.

Doc leaned toward her. "Balance is very important."

Julie nodded, remembering how easy it had been to get disoriented and feel off-balance both when she couldn't see at all and later when she had double vision. Thankfully the double vision had gone away. She motioned to the girl in the corner whimpering. "What's wrong with her?"

"Not all of the children are just blind. Kimberly was born to a mother addicted to crack who never sought prenatal care. As a result she's blind and also suffers from other issues, such as difficulty coping emotionally as well as developmental delays in speech and language. It's very common for her to revert back to a two- or three-year-old's communication level."

"But she's able to ride a horse. That's wonderful." She wanted to focus on something positive.

"Most of the time. Sometimes, like how it looks to be going today, she stands in the corner alone and cries."

Alone. How sad. "Do you mind if I go ask her to join us?"

"Usually when she's like that no one gets through to her."

"I'd feel awful if I didn't try."

Doc motioned with a wave of his hand. "Approach her slowly. She's also been known to hit people with her walking stick."

"All the more reason to show this child love." Julie stayed close to the wall as she made her way toward the child.

The girl had keen hearing. She stopped crying, and lifting her cane as if ready to whirl it, she faced Julie. "Who is it?"

"My name is Julie. What's yours?"

"I don't know Julie." Her grip tightened on the stick.

"I'm new here. I actually work inside. I help prepare the meals. How old are you?"

"Seven. Ten. Eight . . ."

Julie waited for Kimberly to finish rattling off the out-of-sequence numbers. "You like riding the ponies?"

"No. Yes. Yes. No."

"I do too." Something about the girl tugged at Julie's heart. How could someone be so addicted to drugs that they didn't care about their unborn child? She wondered where the child's mother was now. Locked up, hopefully. "You don't have to stand here alone. You can come sit with me."

The child rounded her shoulders and turned toward the corner.

"It was nice to meet you, Kimberly." Julie stood there a moment. "I hope we can talk again."

The child turned, jabbed her stick in the air, and started crying again.

Without thinking, Julie swooped down and gave the girl a hug. "I'm sorry you're sad."

Kimberly let out a high-pitched squeal and batted her arms against Julie's back.

Julie released her.

Matthew stormed up to her. "Could you please leave this arena?"

Julie looked at the child, then over to where Doc was sitting. At least her employer didn't look perturbed with her. Not yet anyway. She took a few steps toward the sitting area and felt something touch the back of her leg. Turning, she found Kimberly following her.

"I go, Jew-e."

Julie reached for the child's hand, and the two of them headed toward the sitting area.

The girl toddled beside her. "You mine?"

An odd familiarity left Julie speechless. Holding the child's small hand, she was reminded of someone by the special bond they had formed in a matter of minutes, but who?

Julie yawned as she climbed out of bed. Over the past several weeks since her arrival, she had fallen into the regimented routine of the ranch. She and Cynthia prepared breakfast every morning, then depending on the day of the week, they worked on general housecleaning or laundry. In less than a month, Julie had fallen in love with the ranch and the people, with the exception of Matthew.

He had voiced his objection that Julie didn't belong in the barns and made no qualms about sharing those thoughts with Doc. She'd learned to avoid the pole barn when Matthew was giving lessons, except when Kimberly's school was on the ranch. Then it didn't matter how many scornful daggers Matthew threw at her. She was determined to spend time with Kimberly.

Julie also disregarded Matthew's instruction to stay away from Token. Sure, the horse had a mean streak. He still wouldn't allow her close enough to touch him, but he also had a softer side when she had an apple or carrot in hand.

Not hearing any sounds coming from the kitchen, Julie smiled. Since staying on the ranch, she had yet to beat Cynthia to the kitchen. Julie glanced at the alarm clock on the nightstand. Six o'clock. She hadn't overslept. She padded out to the empty kitchen.

Standing at the window, filling the coffeepot with water, she gazed at the hint of pink on the horizon and the horses grazing on the lush green pasture. No rain. The start of a perfect day. Now that the fields weren't muddy, maybe she would steal away on a walk later this afternoon. She loved the dry and warmer weather and loved breathing in the country scent. She was pouring the water into the coffeemaker when Doc lumbered into the kitchen.

"Cynthia is ill," he said, his eyes hooded with exhaustion.

"Oh no. Is it something bad?"

"I'm sure it's the flu." He went to the sink and filled a glass with water. "How are you feeling? Any fever?"

"I'm fine. Is there anything I can do?"

"If you can handle making breakfast, that would help."

"I'll make lunch and supper and breakfast tomorrow too. Tell Cynthia not to fret about anything." Cynthia hadn't given her many responsibilities when it came to actual cooking—Julie mainly peeled potatoes or washed and cut vegetables—but she was willing to try.

"Thanks, that will be a big help."

Julie got to work. Although pancakes would be the simplest meal to make, the men had eaten them yesterday, and they probably wouldn't want a repeat. She opened the refrigerator and removed a couple of green peppers and onions, a slab of bacon, and a package of cheddar cheese. Julie set the bacon to frying, then diced the vegetables. By the time Doc came to the table and Matthew and Quinn came in from the barn, she had three omelets waiting and the last one on the stove.

The men helped themselves to the coffeepot as she served the food. Doc said grace as he always did before the meal, adding a request for Cynthia's healing.

"What's wrong with Cynthia?" Matthew asked.

"She's under the weather with the flu." Doc placed his napkin on his lap and picked up his fork and knife.

"Sorry to hear that," Matthew said between bites. He pointed his fork at Julie. "You made a good omelet."

"Yeah," Quinn echoed, shoving another forkful into his mouth.

Julie waited for his disclaimer, like the vegetables weren't completely cooked or it was too greasy, but it never came. "I'm glad you like it." She set down her fork. "I couldn't find the day's agenda that Cynthia always reads."

"Yeah, well, she did that for your benefit," Matthew said. "We know what we're doing."

"Would you care to fill me in?"

Quinn looked from Matthew to her, then back to his coworker, as if amused with the entertainment.

"It's Friday." He quirked his brow at her as if to say she should know what day of the week it was.

She did, but that didn't mean she knew the agenda. It depended on what school was on the schedule, and Cynthia had told her yesterday that a group had called to make a change. "What time do you want to eat lunch?"

"Eleven thirty." He turned to Doc. "The horse auction is coming up at the end of the month. I think you need to consider taking Token and Matilda."

"Why?" Julie blurted.

Matthew furrowed his brows. "Julie—"

Doc held up his hand to stop Matthew. "We can discuss it another time." He dismissed the conversation from going any further by pushing his chair away from the table and standing. "I'm going to check on Cynthia. I would appreciate it if you two could get through the day without bickering."

“Those two, ha.” Quinn lowered his head and excused himself from the table.

“We’ll get along,” Julie said sternly, staring at Matthew.

The back door closed behind Quinn, but it didn’t block out his laughter.

The moment Doc left the room, Matthew pushed away from the table. “Thanks for the meal.”

“You’re welcome.”

He shoved on his hat. “Stay out of the barn.” The door closed hard behind him.

Julie grumbled under her breath as she cleaned off the table. Then shaking the rag of crumbs into the trash, she caught a glimpse of the Saint Christopher’s School for the Blind van pulling into the driveway. *Oh no, I’m not staying out of the barn,* she thought, spotting Kimberly among the children climbing out.

Chapter 33

After considering Doc's request for Matthew and her not to bicker, Julie decided against going out to the barn. Instead she doted on Cynthia, making sure she had plenty of water to drink.

"I made you a bowl of chicken noodle soup," Julie said.

Cynthia smiled weakly. "It smells good, but I don't think I could hold it down."

She set the tray on the chest of drawers. "Are you feeling any better?"

"About the same as when you checked on me an hour ago." She patted the bed. "Will you sit for a moment?"

Julie eased down on the edge of the mattress.

"I appreciate your concern, but I don't want you worrying about me. I'm going to be okay."

"I hate seeing you so weak. You and Doc both mean so much to me. I don't know what I would have done—"

"It's okay, Julie. Everyone gets sick."

She hadn't wanted to tell Cynthia, but all day she had a sinking feeling that everything was about to change. "I don't want to lose you two."

"We're not going anywhere." Cynthia's voice strengthened. "Now, what are you making for lunch? I keep getting whiffs of something good, and it's not soup from a can."

"I don't know what it is. I just threw stuff together and put it in the oven."

"You save me some, and I'll have it for supper. I should be able to hold food down by then, and I heard wonderful things about your omelets. Maybe you should start doing more of the cooking around here—if you like cooking."

She shrugged. "I don't know what I like to do." That wasn't entirely true. She liked being in the barns with the horses, but if she brought that up, she would end up telling Cynthia about her and Matthew's ongoing squabble. Things were better off unsaid.

Julie sniffed the air and stood. "I'd better check the oven." She paused at the door and looked back at Cynthia. "I'll save you a plate if it doesn't burn."

Thankfully the room hadn't filled with smoke. Julie opened the oven and peered inside at the golden-brown concoction. Hopefully it would taste as good as it looked. She removed the dish and placed it on a pot holder to cool, then gathered the plates and utensils to take outside. Now that the weather was warmer, everyone ate on either the lawn or picnic tables, which was fun for the children because manners were not as enforced.

The children and school counselors filed out of the barn and marched into the house, where they took turns washing their hands. Kimberly was at the back of the line. The girl's lips were puckered, which usually meant she was either mad or in trouble, often both.

"Is something wrong with Kimberly?" Julie asked one of the counselors.

"She's having a bad day. Most of the morning she spent in time-out."

"Is it still all right if we sit together during lunch?"

The counselor nodded. "As long as she behaves."

Julie waited until her new little friend was closer. "Hello, Kimberly. Are you ready for lunch?"

"No." Her bottom lip quivered.

"Aren't you hungry? I am. My tummy has been growly all morning."

Kimberly cracked a smile.

Julie took the opportunity to take her hand. They went inside, washed their hands, then found a place at one of the picnic tables. "I'll be right back. I'm going to fix our plates."

Once the child had something to eat, her mood lifted. When she had trouble spearing an egg noodle with her fork, she giggled, whereas on other days she would have pitched a tantrum.

"Jew-e." Kimberly tapped the table for attention. "Me ride pony."

"You did! Was it fun?"

"Yes. No." She giggled again. "Yes."

One of the counselors seated across from them shook her head at Julie. "Kimberly, we talked about telling fibs. You didn't ride the pony today. You've been in time-out most of the morning."

"I bad girl." The child dropped her fork on the table and crossed her arms.

"Finish your food if you want to ride this afternoon, Kimberly," the counselor said.

Even if she had to leave the dishes soaking, Julie wanted to be there when she rode for the first time. "Can I come and watch you?"

Kimberly nodded. She patted the table until she found her fork.

When the meal ended, the children once again lined up. Julie talked with the counselor out of earshot of Kimberly. "I need to collect the dishes and take everything inside. Could she be one of the last ones to ride?"

"It's okay with me, but it'll be up to Kimberly not to get into trouble."

"I'll hurry." Julie gathered up the plates and utensils and took them into the kitchen, then went back outside to bring in the food dishes.

Doc came up beside her and picked up the

noodle dish while Julie grabbed the salad bowl and basket of garlic bread.

Once inside, he set the dish on the counter. “Where did you find my wife’s recipe for *yummasetti*?”

“I didn’t follow a recipe. I found egg noodles in the pantry, and tomatoes, meat, and cheese in the refrigerator, and put it together.” She opened a cabinet and removed the foil.

“It *iss appeditlich*.”

“*Danki*.” She spread the foil over the glass dish and tore off the section. “I’m going to put a plate aside for Cynthia. She thinks she can hold down a meal at suppertime. What do you think?” When he didn’t answer, she glanced over her shoulder. His stare was blank and haunting. “You don’t think she can hold it down, do you?”

Doc seemed to shake out of his deep thoughts. “We’ll see.”

She’d seen him heavyhearted before. He had the same glossy eyes when she first arrived. *Please don’t hole up in your study again. Cynthia needs you. I need you.*

“I’m going to take a walk.” His shoulders slumped as he headed to the door.

Did his dolefulness have anything to do with Cynthia’s sickness? Julie looked out the window and watched his uneven stride. His hips and knees were bothering him. An inner voice prompted her to follow him. He shouldn’t be alone. But

Kimberly would be disappointed if she wasn't there to watch her ride.

Julie plugged the sink drain and turned on the faucet, then put the leftovers in the refrigerator, her mind debating what she should do. She turned off the tap and raced out of the house. If she hurried, she could get back in time to see Kimberly.

A heavy scent of lilacs filled her senses as she followed a narrow path through the dense stand of maples. Brilliant shades of green leaves shimmered in the breeze. The trail led her around a pond and ended in a field of purple lilacs. For a moment, she was lost in the beauty and overpowering sweet scent.

Then she spotted Doc sitting on a bench, head bowed. *Was he talking to himself?* Inching closer, she stepped on a fallen branch. The snap gave her away.

Doc looked up.

"I'm sorry to bother you. I just thought . . ."

He slid to one side of the bench. "Have a seat."

She should have rehearsed what to say before she invaded his privacy.

Doc started the conversation. "I love this time of year when the lilacs are in bloom."

Julie wrestled with her thoughts until she just blurted, "Is Cynthia dying?"

"Why do you ask that?"

"I've never seen her sick before, and when I

mentioned making her a plate of food for supper, you got . . . weepy-eyed."

"It's nice that you care so much, but I assure you, Cynthia will recover. She has the flu. You'll probably get it next because of how close you've been working together."

"That's a relief. I thought she was dying."

"Technically, the moment a person is born, they start to die. Time on earth is short."

"Man is like a breath; his days are like a passing shadow." She pondered the words. "Do you think it's strange that I don't remember anything about my past, but I remember Bible verses? Sometimes repeating them is the only thing that brings peace of mind."

"I don't find it strange at all. God's Word speaks to your spirit, to your soul."

"Then why doesn't He tell me who I am?" She let her frustration out in a lengthy breath.

"It's better that you follow what the Bible says. 'Trust in the Lord with all your heart, and lean not on your own understanding; in all your ways acknowledge Him, and He shall direct your paths.'"

"I believe He's led me to your ranch. I just don't know the purpose for my memory loss."

Doc smiled. "But the good news is He has a purpose. Hold on to that truth."

She nodded.

"Sometimes trauma can affect the way our

brains work. I've seen people who have no physical reason for long-term memory loss, meaning their brain has not been injured, but it's as if something too painful in their past has shut down their ability to recall."

"You think my past is the reason I can't remember?" *It must have been awful.* Was this God's way of sparing her from the truth?

"Let's not get sidetracked with science. God has you, and He won't let go."

"Arms of mercy," she whispered.

"My wife and I used to come here every year when the lilacs were in bloom. We even planted several varieties so the blooming season would last closer to six weeks instead of the average two."

"They're my favorite flower too—I think—I mean, the scent is familiar."

"Hannah's favorite too, but you probably already guessed that." He stood up. "I'm going back to the house. Stay and enjoy this place, and if your heart is heavy, ask the Lord to show you your purpose." He took a few steps away and stopped. "And, Julie, you're always welcome on the ranch. I think of you like a daughter."

"Thank you, Doc." Julie lowered her head and closed her eyes, but words wouldn't come. After a moment of basking in silence, she finally whispered, "Lord, I will trust You."

A branch snapped. Julie opened her eyes

expecting to find Doc, but instead she found a redheaded man with shimmering flecks of gold in his eyes.

"The child you've come to love has lost her way. She's in danger—go to her."

Kimberly!

Julie sprinted back to the house. Distant shouts rang out as Matthew, Quinn, and the workers from the school were spread over the area, calling for Kimberly with panic-stricken voices.

Doc came out of the house. "Kimberly's missing." His breathing wheezed. "I just checked inside."

"She's lost her way. Go to her."

"She's in the paddock." Julie ran to the barn. "Kimberly!" If the child answered, she couldn't hear over the blood pulsing through her inner ears. She checked the stalls. Empty. Empty.

Thwack.

Token. His stall door was closed. Julie yanked open the top half of the door and found Kimberly crouched in the corner, waving her walking stick at the horse.

"Kimberly," she said in an even tone. "I need you to listen carefully and do as I say."

"Okay."

"Drop the walking stick."

She eased the door open and slipped into the stall. Token turned to her, nostrils flaring. "Easy, boy." She inched toward the corner. "No one's going to hurt you."

"Julie?" The girl's high-pitched screech agitated the gelding. He turned one way, then made a sharp turn in the opposite direction.

"Easy, boy." Julie bent down, gathered Kimberly into her arms, then slowly made her way out of the stall.

"Oh, thank God." Doc was midway down the center of the paddock, wheezing heavy breaths and staggering. "Thank You, Jesus."

Julie put Kimberly down and gave her shoulders a shake. "What were you doing in there!"

"I find you." The child sobbed.

Julie gathered her back into her arms. "You found me. Don't cry."

Kimberly buried her face in the crook of Julie's neck, soaking her with warm tears.

Matthew stalked toward them. "I told you that horse was dangerous."

"She's okay. He didn't hurt her," Julie said.

"The girl disappeared—to find you. When you make a kid a promise, you should keep it."

Doc came between them. "That's enough, Matthew."

"The only reason the girl went into the stall was to find Julie." Matthew glared at her. "Now do you believe me?"

Julie didn't answer. She merely walked away, carrying Kimberly in her arms.

• • •

Kimberly was banned from the ranch. The dean of Saint Christopher's made the decision based on the counselor's recommendation despite Julie promising to watch the child's every move and Doc putting a deadbolt on the office door leading into the pole barn. The dean's word was final—and horribly heartbreaking.

Julie hadn't spoken to Matthew since the near trampling, nor did she care. She stayed away from Token, the barns, even the children. To combat a longing in her heart she couldn't explain, she planted a garden. Sufficient time left in the growing season was iffy at best—this was already June. But it gave her something to do, and Cynthia and Doc encouraged her to plant the seeds and see what matured.

Julie pulled a handful of weeds and tossed them into a pile. She didn't hear anyone walk up the row until he cleared his throat.

"Do you have a minute?" Matthew asked.

She yanked another clump of weeds out by their roots. "What do you need?"

"I wanted to apologize."

She glanced up and squinted from the sun. "Did Doc put you up to it?"

"No." He kicked the toe of his boot into the dirt. "I feel bad for how I treated you and for the things I've said."

Forgive and forget. She held up her hand to

shield her eyes. He looked sincere. "It's okay."

"It's my fault that Kimberly isn't allowed to come back. The dean called and asked my opinion, and I told him she was disruptive and didn't follow directions."

"Do you even know her background? She was born to a mother addicted to drugs. Her emotional development and physical problems are not her fault. She was given no future to speak of, and the little bit of kindness from me, well, that doesn't compare to what—"

"I know. I have an appointment at the beginning of next week to talk with the dean. I'd go today, but he's on vacation."

"What are you going to say?"

"That I believe she deserves a second chance."

"Yes, I do too." Tears pricked her eyes. She wasn't sure what to make of Matthew's sudden change in attitude.

"It'd be nice if you make omelets again." He turned and stepped over the row of sprouting beans.

"Matthew," she said.

He stopped and looked over his shoulder.

"I think you're right about Token. Doc should take him to the auction tomorrow."

Chapter 34

Elijah shooed a fly away with his hand. The pesky creatures seemed overpopulated for this time in June, at least compared to northern Michigan. He shuffled toward Pickles's stall, then slipped inside.

"I'm sorry I failed you, boy." Elijah patted the gelding's neck. "If I had the money, I would buy you myself. You have potential. You just need a trainer with his head together, and unfortunately, that isn't me."

Admittedly Elijah hadn't been the same since the accident. He still went into town regularly to check for updates, and he was always relieved to hear that Catherine's body hadn't washed up downriver, but he didn't understand how someone could disappear completely. Would he ever be able to move on with his life? He'd heard before that time heals old wounds, but that wasn't the case for him—or Pickles. The horse wasn't over the accident he'd been in either. The skittish gelding still didn't trust people, and the progress Elijah had made with him hadn't been enough to make him into a buggy horse for Bishop Zook's son.

Bishop Zook trounced across the barn floor. "Mason is here. Is Pickles ready to load?"

"*Jah.*" Elijah clipped the rope onto the horse's halter. "I should have been able to turn him into a *gut* buggy horse. I feel awful that he's going to auction."

"*Sohn*, don't blame yourself. When I bought Pickles he was an angry horse on the way to the glue factory. I thought I could turn him into a buggy horse too. It just wasn't meant to be."

"But with more time—"

Bishop Zook shook his head. "I know it's hard for you to let him go, but the auction only comes around once a year, and frankly, I can't afford to feed a horse that doesn't work." He clapped Elijah on the shoulder. "You've done a *gut* job. I'm *nett* disappointed in you."

"That means a lot. *Danki.*" But Elijah was disappointed in himself. He'd put countless hours into working with Pickles and made little progress. How would he ever build a business training horses? He led the horse outside the barn to the waiting trailer. *Lord, let him go to a* gut *home.*

The driver closed the trailer door with a thud and attached the padlock. They all climbed into Mason's truck, Bishop Zook in the front seat and Elijah and Joshua in the second seat.

Joshua shifted on the seat with nervous energy

to face Elijah. "You think we'll find a *gut* horse today?"

Elijah shrugged. "I've never been to this auction."

Mason glanced into his rearview mirror. "You'll find a lot of horses, but it'll depend on your price range."

The young man's excitement deflated, and he sank back against the seat.

Joshua had just finished school a few months ago, and he was itching to have his own horse. Elijah hadn't bought his first buggy horse until he was old enough to court. He recalled how amazed Catherine's gaze was when she looked over his new mare for the first time. Her eyes sparkling with wonderment, she had asked all sorts of questions. The mare's name, her age, and the question he hadn't expected, *"When can I drive her?"*

Reminiscing about the time she had let the horse have free rein made the hour-long ride to the auction house go by quickly.

Joshua elbowed Elijah. "You want to check out the horses?"

"We need to unload Pickles and get him registered first," the boy's father said.

Elijah stayed with the horse as the bishop went to the office. Unloading wasn't too difficult, but releasing him to the holding pen was an emotional struggle for Elijah.

The metal building was hot even with the large overhead fans at full power. It would get hotter yet once the bleachers filled up. Bishop Zook wanted to make sure they found a seat, but Elijah was too anxious to stay in one place. “I’m going to walk through the holding area. I’ll let you know if I see a horse that looks *gut*.”

Joshua’s eyes widened. “Can I go?”

“It’s up to your *daed*.” Elijah would have liked a few minutes alone, but he also saw this as a good opportunity to give the boy a few pointers on picking out a horse. With the bishop’s approval, they were off. They came to the first holding pen. “First, you want to look at their feet.” He pointed to one limping. “The roan is probably going lame. The black one tied up doesn’t have a *gut* temperament with other horses. People probably irritate him too.”

Elijah moved to the next pen and looked over the stock. “I hate to be the bearer of bad news, but today’s *nett* the day to buy. Not many of these horses are trotters, and of the ones that are here, they’re either swaybacks or lame.”

“What about a saddle horse?”

“There’s a few sound-looking ones. Of course, you won’t have any idea if it’s broke until you get it home.”

“But you could train it, right?”

Elijah was hesitant to agree to that undertaking. He’d been praying about whether he should move back to Posen or not. *Am I ready to leave Hopewater? Or is this God's opportunity to stay?* "You would have to ask your *daed*. He might *nett* want you to get a saddle horse. But we can look them over."

The auction was in full swing by the time Elijah and Joshua finished looking at the horses. He'd found a few that looked promising, but he wanted to stand closer to the rail to watch their gait when they were brought into the arena. "Tell your *daed* I'll be standing down by the railing so I can view them up closer. I'll signal him if I see a *gut* one, then it's up to him if he bids."

"Okay." Joshua rejoined his father long enough to relay the message, then returned to watch the horses at the rail with Elijah.

As the horses paraded in front of them, Elijah explained what he was looking at. A black horse with good muscle tone came into the circle. The announcer gave the particulars about the gelding named Token.

Joshua elbowed him. "What about him?"

The animal appealed to Elijah for its form and gait, but the two men bringing him out had their hands full. "No."

A mare came out next. She, too, had issues, but biting was something he could correct. "You like that one?"

"*Jah*."

Elijah turned and hand-signaled the bishop. The

bidding went so quickly that Elijah wasn't sure who won until the bishop's paddle number was announced over the loudspeaker. "Looks like you got yourself a horse. You should go thank your *daed*."

Elijah continued to watch the horses. Maybe next year he'd be in a position to buy one himself. Pickles came up next, but he didn't watch the horse. He wanted to see the bidders. An elderly man on the second row on the opposite side of the ring won with the highest bid. The bishop should be pleased. He doubled the money he'd paid for the horse.

An inner prompting urged Elijah to warn the new owner of Pickles's skittish nature, especially if the older man bought the horse for the woman seated beside him. Pickles required a strong hand. If she was anywhere near the man's age, the horse wouldn't be a good fit. Elijah studied the couple, but because a scarf was covering most of the woman's face, he had no way of determining her age. *Buyer beware.*

Feeling his shoulder tapped, Elijah turned.

"Pickles fetched a *gut* price," the bishop said. "Thanks to your hard work."

"I'm glad things worked out." Elijah was happy for the bishop, but he couldn't shake his nagging conscience about warning Pickles's buyer.

"We're going to the office while the line isn't too long to settle up. You coming?"

“I’ll meet you at the pen.” He had something more pressing on his mind to take care of first. Elijah headed toward the opposite side of the arena, but as he made his way around the various sectioned-off gates, the new owners stood and climbed down the row of benches. He followed them to a standing-room-only area near the concession stands. The place was crowded, but Elijah broke through the throng of people.

“Excuse me, sir.” His gaze flitted from the man to the woman reading the menu who stood off to the man’s side. “May I speak with you about—” He looked at the woman again and gasped. It was Catherine. No doubt. She was wearing *Englisch* clothes, and her scarf covered part of her face.

“Cat?” He moved in front of the man and reached for her arm.

Her muscles tensed under his touch, and a wide-eyed look of horror filled her expression.

“Catherine?” *Why don’t you recognize me?*

“Doc!” she cried out, her entire body shaking. In one fluid movement, the older man curled her into his arms, protectively turned her away from Elijah, and guided her toward the exit.

“Catherine, it’s me. Elijah.” He started to follow, but another man wearing a cowboy hat stepped in his path. “Catherine, wait,” Elijah shouted. “Don’t leave.”

The cowboy’s black eyes pinned Elijah with a

stare. “Her name is Julie, and you’re not going near her.”

Elijah tried sidestepping the man but was shoved backward. “Her name is Catherine. She was in a bus accident six months ago.”

The man grabbed Elijah by the suspenders and jerked him up close, his breath heavy on his face. “It doesn’t matter. She doesn’t know you.” He tightened his hold. “You’re not going near her—do you understand?”

Elijah had no recourse but to agree.

The cowboy gave him a hard push that sent Elijah stumbling into a nearby group of people. He apologized profusely to the man who had dropped his drink in the commotion, and then he pulled a five-dollar bill from his pocket. “I’m really sorry.” He handed the man the money, then bolted toward the exit.

He searched the bleachers, the holding pens, and the office. Catherine was gone. Again.

Elijah shifted his weight nervously from one leg to the other, standing in the auctioneer’s office. “I have to know the person’s name who bought the horse numbered 214.”

The woman seated behind the desk tapped a few keys on her computer. “The sale hasn’t been satisfied yet. The buyer has twenty-four hours to complete the transaction and collect the horse.”

"There isn't anything you can do? Can you page him overhead?"

"Sorry, you'll have to check back later." She handed him a business card with the auction company's phone number.

This was already the third time he'd checked tonight. He stepped away from the counter. *Twenty-four hours.* What were the laws for staying overnight in an auction house? He exited the office and didn't have to go far before he noticed the No Loitering sign.

Bishop Zook approached. "What did they tell you?"

"Pickles hasn't been paid for yet. The new owner has twenty-four hours."

"Are you sure it was Catherine?"

"*Jah*, it was her." He couldn't imagine what had happened in the accident that had left her not knowing who she was—who he was. Her frightened image would be etched in his mind forever. "She looked straight at me . . ."

"It looks like they're closing the building, Elijah. We'll have to contact them in the morning."

He nodded. "Are Joshua and Mason with the new horse?"

"*Jah*, they've already loaded her into the trailer. I arranged for Mason to bring you back here tomorrow if it's necessary."

"*Danki*." Elijah walked back to the truck with

the bishop and climbed into the back seat. *Lord, I don't want to believe You allowed me to know without a doubt that Catherine is alive, only to take her away again. What's wrong with her? Will You please open her eyes and mind to me?* He battled the final part of the prayer. *If Your will is for me to let her go, I will.*

Later that night, he fell asleep repeating his plea and struggling with the idea of letting Catherine go. The following morning it was as if he were being tested. The auction company at first refused to give him any information, then after calling back multiple times, he was told the horse had been paid for through a third party. The business listed was a commercial ranch with a post office box for an address.

He turned down the Zooks' multiple invitations for supper and ended up moping around the cabin for days. He finally sat at the table to write a letter to George, but he was at a loss for words. What should he say? *I found your sister, but now she's* Englisch*—lost to the world.* He attempted to write something more than "Dear George" but ended up pushing the pen and paper aside.

Lord, I thought I could accept that she's gone, but I don't know how to release the pain. Lord, I need You.

A knock sounded at the door, and when he answered, Joshua rushed inside.

"Will you help me find *mei* horse? I think she jumped the fence."

"Give me a minute to get *mei* boots on." He needed a distraction, and he'd promised the boy he'd help train the mare. But so far he hadn't even walked into the bishop's barn to get a closer look at her.

The two of them split up to search the fields. Elijah finally found the mare drinking out of a pond a short distance away. He clipped a rope to her halter and led her back to the bishop's farm. While he had the horse out, he tied her to the fence, then cleaned each hoof with a pick, almost getting bit in the process. The hooves were shoed, trimmed, and in good shape.

It wasn't long before Elijah spotted Joshua plodding through the pasture, head low and shoulders rounded. "Joshua, over here."

The boy's shoulders straightened, and he began running.

Elijah untied the horse from the post.

"Where did you find her?"

"At the pond." He handed the boy the rope, then headed toward the bishop's house. "Training starts tomorrow."

Lynn opened the door and welcomed him inside. "We've been worried about you. You're staying for supper, *jah*?"

He smiled. "I was hoping you would ask."

The bishop's wife made him a mug of coffee,

and he sat with the bishop in the sitting room. This time he wasn't interested in reading the newspaper. "How do you trust God when you can't get past having to know why? Why didn't she recognize me? What kind of God do we serve that . . . that stands by doing nothing when His child—me—is hurting? I want to know why."

Bishop Zook set down his paper. "I don't have answers to any of your questions. The only thing I can advise you to do is not lose faith. Why was Joseph in the Bible sold by his brothers to be a slave? He was falsely accused and thrown in jail. Do you think he asked God why? We know Job asked God why he lost his family and livestock. Have faith, Elijah. Trust that God has everything in control. He is the great I Am."

Elijah nodded. *Lord, forgive me. Have mercy on me, Father.*

The bishop's wife poked her head into the sitting room. "There's someone here to see you, Titus."

The bishop stood. "I'll be right back."

A few moments later, Lynn came into the room with a dish towel draped over her shoulder. She plopped down in the bishop's chair. "It's Titus's *bruder*-in-law. I thought I'd give them some privacy."

"I don't remember meeting him at any of the Sunday services. Does he live in this district?"

She leaned closer and lowered her voice. "His

schweschaler Hannah married an *Englischer*. I'm surprised Titus agreed to speak to him. The hardest thing he's had to do was disown his *schweschaler*, but it was her choice. Nothing he could do. She chose to live in the world. There's been bitterness on both sides."

It wasn't long before Titus appeared at the entrance of the sitting room. "Elijah," he said solemnly, "there's a man here who would like to speak with you."

Elijah crossed the room. "He wants to talk to me?"

Bishop Zook nodded. "He's waiting for you in the kitchen."

When Elijah entered the kitchen, the *Englischer*'s back was to him. He rounded the long table and, seeing him face-to-face, realized he was the older man with Catherine at the auction. Elijah sat down.

"I have a few questions for you," the visitor began.

Chapter 35

Elijah clasped his hands and rested them on the bishop's table. *Lord, give me the right words. And let the words spoken be pleasing to Your ears.*

"First, let me introduce myself. I'm Dr. Wellington, but please call me Dennis. This is an unusual situation. I've been in prayer about it ever since we ran into you at the auction."

"Me too."

"Julie came to stay with us on the ranch a few months ago, and I've come to think of her as a daughter."

Elijah bit his tongue, stopping himself from correcting the man about her name. At the moment, it was more important to hear the doctor out.

"I know a lot about the Amish way. I know when a man gets married, he grows a beard. Is Julie your *fraa*?"

"*Nay*, I'm a widower. *Mei fraa* died of cystic fibrosis. Catherine is the woman I love. The woman you call Julie." He studied the man's expression but couldn't get a feel for what he thought about not being her husband.

"She was the one who told us her name was Julie."

Elijah shook his head. "I don't know why she would do that. She has a niece by that name. What else has she told you about her life?"

"Nothing, and that's what makes it so puzzling. As you're probably aware, her long-term memory has been, simply put, short-circuited. Sometimes the brain shuts down when there's been severe trauma."

"She was in a bus accident."

"I understand, and from what I read in the paper it was a bad accident. I wasn't her doctor, but from what I've heard, she came into the hospital with a subdural hematoma, which is bleeding between the skull and brain. The pressure builds, and it can be deadly. Fortunately for her, the doctors were able to release the pressure, and she recovered."

"Just not her memory."

"That's the troubling part. It should have returned, and bits of it has, only she didn't recognize it."

"What do you mean?"

"She made *yummasetti*. I recognized the dish as something *mei fraa* used to make. When I asked her about it, she had made it without a recipe. I told her it was delicious in Pennsylvania *Deitsch* and she replied in the same language automatically. So the memories are there, but that leads me to wonder what's hindering the rest. Was she running away from the Amish? Is that why she was on the bus?"

"*Nay*. We're from Michigan, and her cousin in Florida asked if she would come down and help in her bakery. I went along to make sure she arrived . . . safely."

"So you were in the bus accident as well?"

Elijah nodded. "And I've looked for her ever since that day. You can ask the sheriff's department how many times I've been there to see if there's been any news." Tears fell freely. "I love Catherine. I'm lost without her."

"I can see that."

"Catherine loves the plain way of life. She would never walk away from her belief. Never."

Dr. Wellington wiped the moisture away from his eyes.

"Please take me to her. I have to talk to her. I have to know she's all right."

The doctor was silent for several seconds. Finally, he nodded, and a rush of relief washed over Elijah.

"You have to understand," the doctor said. "I can't force her to remember you—and neither will you."

Seated on the front porch, Julie grabbed another potato to peel. "Cynthia, are you going to tell me what's been wrong with Doc these past few days?"

For days now Doc had been too quiet. It seemed he either locked himself in his study or went on long walks alone. He wasn't himself, that was for certain.

"He has a lot on his heart." Cynthia peeled the potato without looking up.

"That's why I'm so worried. It hasn't been that long ago that he had to take pills for his chest pain. Do you think he's having pain again?"

Cynthia finished the potato and tossed it into the bowl. She picked up another one, then set it and the paring knife on her lap. "What do you know about the doc's late wife?"

"Her name was Hannah. She was the one who wanted to make this place into a children's ranch." Julie shrugged. "Her favorite flower was lilacs, which is why there's a grove at the end of the pathway."

"Did you know she was Amish?"

"No." She stopped peeling and gave Cynthia her full attention.

"He used to treat a lot of Amish folks, and he hired her to work as a receptionist in his office. They ended up falling in love, and it created a lot of problems. She was shunned from the community and disowned by her family."

"That's sad."

"In some ways she was tormented by the separation, but she loved Doc."

"Did her family ever come around?"

Cynthia shook her head. "They would turn the other way when they saw her in town. When she was dying, Doc went to see her brother, but even knowing his sister wasn't going to live long, he refused to see her. Doc was devastated when she died. He went through all the stages of grief, only he never got over his bitterness toward the Amish. In some ways, I believe when he's thinking about Hannah, he automatically stirs up the anger pent up toward her family. He hated them for a while."

"That would rot anyone's heart."

Cynthia nodded. "I've prayed for years that he would forgive—for his own sake."

"I've been praying for God to heal his heart physically, but now I'm going to pray that God deals with his soul." Julie sighed. Now it made sense why Doc had shuttled her out of the auction so fast when the bearded man in suspenders called her someone else. Without peripheral vision, she had been startled when he grabbed her arm. She hadn't even noticed he was Amish until Doc whirled her into his protective arms and got her to safety outside the building.

Doc's truck pulled into the yard, and Cynthia was quick to start peeling again. "He's home. Let's not talk about Hannah anymore."

Julie focused on the potato she was working on and didn't look up until a second truck door closed.

"Looks like we have company," Cynthia whispered.

Amish company.

"Julie." Doc approached the porch steps. "There's someone who would like a few minutes of your time."

"I know who he is," she said.

The Amish man smiled.

"You grabbed my arm at the auction."

"I didn't mean to frighten you." The man was soft-spoken. Sincere.

She glanced at Doc and tried to read his expression.

"I think you need to talk with him." He motioned with a nod to Cynthia. "We'll be in the house."

Julie followed them with her gaze, but neither Doc nor Cynthia looked over their shoulders before going inside. When she turned her gaze back to the Amish man, he was on the porch.

He motioned to the chair Cynthia had just vacated. "May I sit down?"

"I suppose."

"*Mei* name is Elijah Graber." He paused as if she should recognize the name. "I understand you have some problems with your memory. So what I'm going to tell you might *nett* make sense, but please hear me out."

She took in a breath and held it.

"We were in a bus accident. January 17."

"We?" she rasped.

"*Jah*," he said softly. "Your name is Catherine Rosemary Glick. I call you Cat, which kind of bothers you sometimes." He grinned sheepishly but sobered again when she remained stoic. "The first time we met, you were ice skating—and upset with me because I was there to cut the ice."

"Why?"

A slow smile spread across his face. "We use the slabs to keep the *icehaus kalt*."

There was something very endearing about this man. He seemed sincere enough. *Lord, do I know him? Is what he's telling me true?*

"I've been searching for you since January. When I saw you at the auction . . . Well, you know what happened."

"I didn't see you. I lost my peripheral vision in my right eye."

"I'm sorry."

She slipped her fingers under her scarf and touched her scar. "I still have some fuzziness, but that usually happens when I'm overly tired." She wasn't sure why she was sharing about herself. She didn't know this man. Or did she?

"Your family back in Michigan are worried about you."

"My family?"

He nodded. "You live with your *bruder*, George, and his *fraa*, Gwen. They have three children—Leah, Jimmy, and Julie."

"Julie?" She stood and paced to the end of the porch. "So I *do* have a brother named George," she muttered to herself under her breath. Perhaps she'd been dreaming about her niece when Amy overheard her say "Julie." Images flashed before her eyes of a restaurant, Elijah running for a bus. She faced him. "Tell me why we were on a bus."

"Your cousin in Florida asked you to help in her bakery for the winter."

"I'm a baker?"

He nodded. "You're a cook at The Amish Table too."

She closed her eyes as bits and pieces flashed like snapshots before her. The bus. Headlights. Children crying . . . Golden eyes looking down at her.

Elijah stepped closer. "Are you remembering something, Catherine?"

"Will you excuse me?" She rushed down the porch steps and ran as hard as she could to the narrow pathway. She had to find the man with red hair. The man who told her about Kimberly—the same man who had carried her to safety after the bus accident.

She reached the lilac grove. Most of the blooms had fallen off the trees and now carpeted the grass with different shades of purple. Searching the area, she found that the redheaded man was nowhere to be found. She plopped down on the bench. "Who is he, Lord? An angel?"

A tap on her right shoulder bolted her off the bench, her heart hammering and lungs gasping for breath.

"I didn't mean to frighten you." Elijah lifted his palms out in a surrendered position. "I thought you saw me."

"*Nay*!" She pointed to her face. "I don't have full vision."

Color drained from his face. "Oh, Catherine, I'm so sorry. I forgot."

She grinned. "*Nau* who's the one with the failing memory?"

"Guilty." He shrugged.

His cheeks turned a rosy pink, which made his eyes more blue than gray. If everything he was telling her was true, she could see how she was smitten by him. She sat down, leaving him room on the bench to join her.

He motioned to the bench. "May I?"

She nodded.

"Did I say something to send you off running?"

"It wasn't anything you said . . . I had some images flash across *mei* mind that—that I wasn't prepared for." *A reappearing man with red hair and flecks of gold in his eyes. No, I can't tell Elijah about someone who showed up only to disappear again.* "Were you running to catch a bus?"

"*Jah.* Your tote bag was stolen in an alley outside a restaurant we had stopped at. I ran off to chase the thief, which wasn't wise."

"Sounds brave to me."

"*Nay,* I shouldn't have left you alone in the alley. The bus was coming and—" He shook his head. "It was a foolish thing to do."

"Maybe the foolish part was being in the alley in the first place."

His brows arched. "You remember?"

Her puzzled expression must have clued him that she didn't, because his brows dropped and his eyes lost their sheen. "So, why were we in the alley?"

"You insisted on feeding a cat your leftover sausage."

She tried to picture it all but drew a blank.

Elijah shifted on the bench. "Is that all you remember—me running for the bus?"

"I remember bright headlights and children crying and . . ." She cleared her throat. "You never said if you were injured badly."

"*Mei* lung was punctured, and I dislocated *mei* shoulder, but other than that, just a few stitches."

She studied him a moment, wishing her mind would cooperate and something would jar her memory. "I should get back to the *haus* and help Cynthia with supper."

"Oh." His shoulders dropped. He blinked a few times and forged a smile.

She couldn't describe the thoughts scrambling her mind, but suddenly she didn't want their conversation to end either. "Would you like to stay for supper? I'm sure Doc and Cynthia won't mind. I mean unless you have other plans."

"*Nay*—I mean *nay*, I don't have plans. I'd like to stay for supper. Yes—yes, I would." He blew out a breath and dialed down some of his eagerness. "I guess it's obvious that I want to spend more time with you."

She smiled. "I enjoyed our talk too."

Chapter 36

Elijah received a warm welcome from everyone at the supper table except the man who had pushed him into the crowd when Elijah tried to pursue Catherine at the auction. The cowboy merely grunted when Cynthia introduced them, but Elijah played like he didn't hear and smiled anyway.

Cynthia passed Elijah the meat loaf. "What type of farming do you do in Michigan?"

"Potato farms are popular in Posen." He took a second helping of meat loaf and passed it to Dennis at the head of the table.

"You grow your own hay for the livestock too, don't you?" Dennis asked.

"*Jah*, and depending on the year, we alternate crops of alfalfa and oats with winter wheat and barley." He glanced across the table at Catherine who had been quiet during the meal. She didn't look up from her plate.

Cynthia passed the bean bowl around. "When do potatoes come in season?"

"Harvest is in October. Usually it takes two weeks to gather, bag, and get them into storage."

"Does your district use tractors?" Dennis stopped eating to ask.

"Nay, we're Old Order. We don't believe in using modern equipment."

"Yet you rode a bus." Matthew snickered.

"True. It'd take a month of Mondays to get to Florida by horse and buggy."

"You mean month of Sundays." Matthew pushed away from the table. "Thanks for the meal, Catherine and Cynthia. Dennis, I'll check the new gelding before I turn in to the bunkhouse for the night." The man left the house.

Catherine cleared her throat. "Farming without the use of tractors sounds like laborious work."

"*Jah*. It's a lot of bending and lifting and crawling on your knees in the dirt. Your hands stay calloused. But at the end of the harvest, when all the fields have been gleaned, our district has a big get-together. The womenfolk usually have a cooking contest. You won the honors one year with your cheesy potato casserole."

"It sounds like Posen is a lovely place to live," Cynthia said. "Doesn't it, Julie—I mean Catherine?"

Catherine smiled, but it was the vacancy in her eyes that worried him. Without her saying anything, he suspected she didn't remember a bit of what he'd talked about. Would she recognize her family, the other members of the district—Zach?

"Well maybe you can have supper with us again soon, Elijah," Dennis said, pushing away from the table.

That was his cue it was time to leave, and he didn't want to overstay his welcome. Only he didn't want to leave Catherine. Today was the most alive he'd felt in a long time. He stood. "*Danki* for the meal. It was very nice meeting all of you."

"Give me a minute to get the truck keys, and I'll drive you home," Dennis said.

"Okay, I'll, ah . . . I'll wait on the porch."

Catherine stood. "Let me walk you out." She followed him to the door, and the moment they stepped outside, she said, "Did I like being Amish?"

"*Jah*. In fact, you mentioned how your cousin Olivia had jumped the fence and how sad it was that she had chosen to live in the world." Her silence tugged at his heart, and he had to ask, "Does the thought of living a plain lifestyle frighten you?"

She shrugged. "I just can't picture living anywhere but here."

Lord, would she think the same way if she remembered her life as Catherine? Please, give her back her memory. A distressed horse neigh captured his attention. *Pickles*. "Catherine, I'll be right back." Elijah ran toward the barn.

"You should be made into dog food." Matthew

slapped the horse's chest with a leather belt. "Blasted nag." He raised the belt again, but the horse reared and struck Matthew's arm with his front hooves, knocking the hot-tempered cowboy to the ground.

"Easy, boy." Elijah calmed Pickles with gentle words.

"Give him to me."

The horse pawed the cement floor and snorted. "He needs time to calm down." Elijah refused to release Pickles.

The cowboy raised his voice. "I said, give him to me."

Dennis stormed toward them. "Matthew, go to the bunkhouse."

"But—"

"I saw the whole thing. Go." The doctor's tone hardened. Then, once Matthew left the barn, he turned to Elijah. "Thank you."

"Pickles isn't a bad horse. He was in a bad accident and spooks easily, but with patience he'll be a *gut* horse." Elijah stepped out of the stall and closed the gate.

Dennis rested his arms on the half door and gazed at the horse. "Catherine said she and you had a nice visit."

"She doesn't remember me. She remembered bits and pieces of the trip and me running to catch the bus, but nothing about being Amish."

"Give her time."

Elijah nodded. He had no other choice.

"As for Pickles, I agree. He needs someone with patience to work with him. How would you like the job? It'd give you time to get to know Julie—Catherine—more."

"I'd like that very much. Thank you."

"You can start tomorrow. I'll have a talk with Matthew and make sure he doesn't give you a hard time. As for Catherine, you two could always make new memories."

Whistling came from inside Pickles's stall as Catherine approached carrying a thermos of ice water and a drinking glass. She stopped in front of the stall's half door and peered in at Elijah. "You're off-key again."

Again! She remembered something new.

"I thought you might be thirsty."

"That's mighty kind of you. *Danki*." He stopped cleaning the horse's hoof, took his work gloves off, and approached the stall door.

She poured a glassful of water and handed it to him. "I've teased you about that before, haven't I?"

"I liked to believe you loved *mei* whistling all these years." He took a drink and sighed. "Wait until you hear me sing."

Snapshot memories flashed of her sitting on a wooden bench among a crowd of women singing songs from the *Ausbund*. Elijah was seated across the aisle on the men's side of the barn. Catherine smiled. "Your singing is off-key too. I remember."

He lowered the glass from his mouth. "You do? You remember?"

"*Nett* everything." She had dreamed about her niece Julie asking to sleep with her, and it had been so real the dream startled her. "I know *mei* name is Catherine."

"And you know I'm a bad singer. That's a *gut* start." He winked.

"I'd like to know more about *mei* life. Were we . . . ?"

"In love? *Jah*, very much so."

The intensity in his piercing stare sent a shimmer of tingles down her spine. Unable to hold eye contact, she redirected her attention to the straw-covered floor. "What if *mei* memory doesn't fully return?"

Elijah brushed the silky hair away that had fallen in front of her face, then lifted her chin with his fingertips. "We can create new memories."

Tears pricked her eyes. If she believed in love at first sight, it would be with Elijah. She wanted to know everything about him—about their past together.

"I was planning to give Pickles a break. Would you like to go for a drive with me?"

"Let me make sure Cynthia doesn't need *mei* help first. I'll only be a few minutes." She raced back to the house. Was this how she felt the first time he'd asked to spend time with her years ago?

A few minutes later, Elijah helped her onto the buggy bench. Catherine gazed around at the simple boxy design.

He climbed inside and sat next to her on the bench. "What do you think?"

"Is it *kalt* in the winter?"

"A little, but most of the time you bundle up under a wool blanket." He clicked his tongue, and the horse lurched forward.

She gripped the edge of the bench as the box structure bounced on its springs when making the transition from the gravel road to pavement. "Where are we going?"

"I want to introduce you to some people," he said, speaking louder as a car passed them. "The rest of the way shouldn't be too bumpy *nau* that we're on pavement."

The rhythmic clip-clopping of horse hooves was like music to her ears. A familiar sense of peacefulness she couldn't describe washed over her as they continued toward town.

Elijah stopped the buggy along the curb, jumped out, and circled around to her door.

She noticed the Police Department sign in front of the building and crinkled her brows.

"I want you to meet some of the people who've been searching for you," he explained.

"I want them to know that you've been found."

Following him into the building, a woman seated at a desk looked up and smiled. "Hello, Elijah." She picked up the phone.

"I'm *nett* here to get an update." He placed his arm around Catherine's shoulder. "I came to give you an update. I found her. This is Catherine Glick."

The woman looked her over. "It's a pleasure to meet you, ma'am. I must say, you have a very determined fiancé. Elijah refused to give up searching for you, and he kept us on our toes too."

Fiancé? Catherine's mind went a zillion directions.

The room filled with several uniformed officers who seemed genuinely happy for her and Elijah. Catherine let Elijah explain how she suffered a head injury that messed up her memory, and how he'd found her at the horse auction by divine intervention.

"We won't keep you," Elijah said. "I know you have important things to do. I just wanted to let you know why I won't be coming in for more updates."

An older officer chuckled. "This is the best type of update." He turned to Catherine. "Elijah was a regular face around here."

"So I heard." She studied Elijah's face. The sparkle in his eyes—*his beard.* She took a step backward.

"You look like you're ready to go, Catherine," Elijah said. "Thanks again, everyone."

Catherine waited until they were both seated in the buggy. "You have a beard!"

Elijah scratched his jaw. "You're just noticing that?"

"Why didn't you tell me we're married?" Catherine gasped. "You have a beard—I know what that means."

Elijah wished they would have had more time together to build *new* memories before he had to explain his past to her. "I'm a widower. *Mei fraa* went home to be with the Lord."

"So we're *nett* married?" Maybe her mind wasn't totally scrambled. She would hope if she ever got married, she would never forget that day.

He shook his head. "I wanted to take you to meet Bishop Zook and his *fraa* if you're up to it . . ."

She wasn't sure why he shifted the conversation so quickly, but perhaps it was for the best. The whole idea of marriage—of proposing—was still confusing. "*Jah*, I'd like to meet the Zooks."

A few minutes later, Elijah pulled into the driveway of a large two-story farmhouse. He parked next to the fence and got out and tied the reins to the fence post.

Catherine took in the sweet scent of hay and

clucking sounds of free-roaming chickens. "It's beautiful here." She gazed at the large porch, the rain buckets next to the downspouts. "Have I been here before?"

"*Nay*, but your *bruder*'s *haus* has a big porch like this one." He opened a door that led to the kitchen.

Two women were abuzz with chatter while exchanging baked cookies for a pan of doughy ones ready for the oven.

"You're just in time, Elijah." The older woman set the hot pan on a pot holder and turned. "*Ach*, I didn't know you brought a guest. Hello, I'm Lynn Zook. You must be Elijah's Catherine."

"It's nice to meet you." Catherine's face heated, repeating Lynn's words. *"Elijah's Catherine."* She liked the sound of that.

"I'm Rebecca," the twentysomething woman said. "We've heard a lot about you." She motioned to the table. "Have a seat, please. Would you like a cup of *kaffi*?"

"Sure."

An older man lumbered into the kitchen, who Elijah introduced as the district's bishop, and a few minutes later, Catherine met the entire family when a younger boy ambled into the kitchen asking if the cookies were done.

After Catherine answered their various questions about her injures and how she had come to live with Doc on his ranch, Lynn asked, "Are you planning to *geh* back to Michigan soon?"

Catherine glanced at Elijah briefly, then shrugged. "I'm *nett* sure."

"Catherine's memory is just coming back," Elijah explained.

The conversation shifted naturally to the men talking about farming and horses, and Catherine talking to Lynn and Rebecca about gardening and canning. Catherine enjoyed the time they had spent together, especially when Lynn gave Catherine a tour of her home and showed her the different quilt projects in process.

Catherine touched the cottony fabric and studied the hand stitches. *"Keep your stitches even. You don't want lines that zigzag."*

"Are you okay, Catherine?" Lynn asked.

"Oh, I'm sorry. I was just remembering something *mei mamm* said to me about sewing. I, ah . . . I've been having these flashbacks and"—she wiped tears with the back of her hand—"they take me by surprise most of the time."

"Let's get you a tissue." Lynn led her back into the kitchen and handed her the box of tissues from off the counter.

Elijah stood. "Is everything all right?"

Catherine nodded, even though her heart was breaking and things were not all right. Had her mother really passed away? Was her memory correct?

"I think we should probably head back to the ranch," Elijah said. "I don't want Doc worrying about you, and I still want to work some more with Pickles."

"I hope you *kumm* back soon," Lynn said, following them to the door. "Maybe you could *kumm* for supper one *nacht*."

Catherine smiled. "That would be *wunderbaar*. *Danki*." She walked to the parked buggy alongside Elijah. "They're nice people. I really like Lynn."

He opened the buggy's passenger door. "They've been like family to me." As he climbed in the driver's side, he asked, "Why were you crying?"

"I had a flashback. Something *mei mamm* said about sewing, and then I remembered she passed away, and I missed her."

Elijah reached for her hand and gave it a gentle squeeze. "I wish all your memories would be *gut* ones and *nett* sad."

"You're a *gut* man, Elijah Graber. I see why I fell in love with you."

"Please don't ever forgot those words." He winked, then fell silent.

Catherine turned her gaze out the window. *Thank You, Lord, for guiding our paths. Only You could have brought us back together again.*

Elijah parked the buggy next to the barn.

"I'm going to work some more with Pickles."

"I should see if Cynthia needs me to do something." Catherine headed for the house but doubled back to the barn. She found Elijah in the horse stall with Pickles. "Would you like to stay for supper?"

"Sure. What time?"

"We usually eat around six."

According to the clock hanging on the barn wall, that gave him a couple hours to work with Pickles. "Sounds *gut*."

Catherine took a few steps away, then stopped.

"Is something wrong?"

"We were in a barn when I proposed. I remember putting a blanket on *mei* horse, Cocoa. It was *kalt* out. January?"

Elijah's Adam's apple moved down his throat, and his brows pinched together.

"I did propose, right? *Mei* mind isn't scrambled, is it?"

He nodded. "You did."

Her throat tightened, and tears began to well.

"Catherine." Elijah slipped out of the stall. "I should have told you—"

"Oh, Elijah." She fell against his chest and molded into his arms, nuzzling her face in the crook of his neck. "You've been so patient with me. I know why you didn't tell me. You wanted me to remember it on *mei* own. You didn't want to overwhelm me all at once.

You're a *gut* man, Elijah. God's given me a *gut* man."

He kissed her forehead. "Are you ready to go home, Catherine?"

Chapter 37

Y*ou're a* gut *man, Elijah."* Catherine's words haunted him throughout the night. He wasn't a *gut* man—he allowed Catherine to believe she had proposed to him. It had been so easy to withhold the truth at the time. Now the truth had his stomach twisted in knots. Sooner or later she was bound to remember it was Zach she wanted to marry. *How would she feel about him then?* Definitely *nett* as the patient man who didn't want to overwhelm her. No, he'd intentionally withheld the information, hoping somehow those memories were gone for good.

Elijah flipped to his other side on the mattress. He wasn't looking forward to the trip back to Michigan, but he had promised himself that he would see that she made it safely home. Once they were back in Posen, Catherine would take one look at Zach, and all those memories she had hidden would suddenly surface. Things would never be the same again.

Lord, give me strength. She's alive and that's all that matters. If she chooses to resume her life with Zach, help me to accept that decision. I am so grateful that You kept her safe and that I was able to spend this time with her. Lord, You know how much I love Catherine . . . Just please give me strength to let her go.

Dr. Wellington insisted on driving them to Michigan when Catherine started to have a panic attack about getting on another bus. She wanted to go home and see her family, while at the same time, she didn't want to leave those she'd grown to love in Ohio. Especially Kimberly. The child had just been cleared to return to the ranch, and if she learned Catherine had left, Kimberly might act out. Before leaving, she made Cynthia, Matthew, and Quinn promise not to tell her immediately, and to watch her closely when they did.

Everything felt right in an odd sort of way. She just wished she didn't feel like Elijah was holding something back from her. She trusted him. But he'd been quiet the last few hours—ever since they started seeing signs for nearby towns.

As they neared Posen, Catherine grew restless. "I remember this area. That's Lake Huron."

"The third largest of the Great Lakes, and it has the longest shoreline," Doc said.

"I've lived in Michigan *mei* whole life and never knew those facts." She chuckled. "Or maybe I did and I just don't remember." She glanced in the back seat at Elijah. "Did I know that?"

He shrugged. "I didn't."

She turned her gaze back to the deep blue water. "We're *nett* far *nau*." She wrung her hands. Would she remember everyone? Her brother and sister-in-law, and her nieces and nephew? She still couldn't visualize their faces or what the house looked like. But she also wouldn't have been able to describe Lake Huron before they came upon it.

Elijah leaned forward. "You'll want to turn at the next left."

Catherine knew the turn. In another mile they would turn again onto Leer Road. She rubbed her hands on the dress given to her by Lynn. It wasn't until she placed the prayer *kapp* on this morning that she figured out why she had felt comfortable wearing a scarf—she was used to having her head covered. Made sense. Everything was beginning to make sense again.

Elijah guided Doc in the right direction. She'd been too busy discovering all the changes. Her *aenti* Irma and Faith had put in a larger garden this year in preparation for Faith's upcoming wedding, no doubt. It looked like the Kings had a new horse in their pasture.

"It's the second driveway on the right," Elijah said.

Catherine stared at the big farmhouse. She searched out her bedroom window on the second floor. Same curtains. The lawn was freshly mowed. She gulped when all the parked buggies came into view.

"Looks like word got out," Elijah said.

"How did—?" She twisted in her seat to look at him. "Did you notify everyone?"

"*Nay*, just George."

The moment Doc parked the truck and turned off the motor, her heart raced even faster. Was she ready for this? Would she recognize everyone? Catherine drew a deep breath. *I can do this if Elijah is close by.* She glanced at Doc, who hadn't unlatched his seat belt. "You're coming inside, *jah*?"

"I booked a motel room in Rogers City," Doc said. "I'll stop by in the morning and say goodbye."

"*Nay*, please don't go. *Nett* yet," Catherine pleaded. "I'm sure *mei* family will want to meet you."

"They will," Elijah added.

Doc hesitated a moment, then unhooked his seat belt. "Okay. I'll stay long enough to meet everyone, but I don't want to impose. They want to spend time with you."

Elijah got out of the vehicle and stretched. He sidled up beside her. "Ready?"

She sensed his smile was covering something, but she didn't ask. Perhaps he was tired. It had been a long trip. She looked around the farm and took in a deep breath. "It's *gut* to be back, isn't it?"

"You remembering everything? The *haus* and barns?"

"*Jah*, everything."

The door swung open before they reached the top porch step. Gwen was first to come out, followed by George. Both greeted her in a warm hug. George and Elijah shook hands, then Elijah introduced them to Doc, as Catherine had become tangled in hugs from her nieces and nephew.

"I missed you, Catherine," Julie said.

Catherine bent down and gathered Julie into her arms. "I missed you too, sweetie." Tears streamed down her face, but not just tears of joy. At the same time she held her niece, she was shrouded with a dull ache. She missed Kimberly. Catherine set her down. "I think you've grown a foot."

Julie giggled, then wrapped her arms even tighter around Catherine's neck.

Inside the house a throng of people welcomed her home at once. Catherine was hesitant. She didn't recognize everyone at first. She had no clue who some of them were until they spoke, then she recognized their voices. Others, like her cousin Faith, she remembered immediately.

"I'm so glad to see you." Faith hugged her tight. "I've missed you so much."

Catherine pulled back after a minute of soaking in the joyful reunion. "Have you and Gideon set the date of your wedding yet?"

"We were married in April," Gideon piped up. "Faith was very sad after we heard about your accident, so I talked the bishop into marrying us sooner."

Faith frowned. "*Nau* I wish we had waited so you could have been a part."

"Nonsense." Catherine pulled her back into a hug and whispered in her ear. "I proposed too, you know."

Her cousin pushed her to arm's length. "You did? When?"

"In January." She chuckled. Someone else tugged on her arm. She turned only to get pulled into a suffocating hug by a short, gray-haired woman Catherine didn't recognize.

"It's so *gut* to see you. We were all so worried." The woman held her a long time, then pushed her out to arm's length. "Catherine, you've gotten so thin. If you're *nett* careful, a gust of wind will pick you up and carry you away."

"You think?" Catherine looked down at the baggy dress Lynn had given her to wear home. She hadn't had time to take in the seams.

Another woman came up beside her and wrapped her in a hug, then another unfamiliar face welcomed her home, then another. The walls in the room seemed as though they were closing in. So many people. Faces she didn't recognize. Names she didn't know. *Too much commotion. Too much unwanted attention. Where's Elijah?*

Catherine glanced around the room and found him embraced in a tearful reunion with his parents, and Doc was engaged in a conversation with George. In need of a breath of fresh air, she made her way to the back door. She hadn't been outside long before Elijah joined her.

He came up beside her. "Is everything okay?"

She nodded.

"You sure?"

She shook her head. "I don't know very many people, and I was beginning to feel smothered. Everyone thinks I'm too thin *nau*." She pinched the bridge of her nose. "I didn't expect coming home to be so hard. I miss Kimberly."

Elijah tipped up her chin with his thumb. "No one expects you to remember everyone. And as for your weight, you're perfect just the way you are."

She smiled. "I'm so glad I have you."

"Always."

She gazed at the area surroundings, taking in the green pastures and different outbuildings. Part of her missed Ohio.

"We should probably go back inside," Elijah said.

"Is it wrong that I don't want to? That I would rather spend *mei* time with just you?"

"It's *nett* wrong through *mei* eyes. I wish we could avoid the crowd too." He chuckled.

They strolled back to the house, and as they stepped inside, her longtime friend Mary was there to greet her with a hug.

"It's so *wunderbaar* to see you! We need to set a time when we can get together and catch up. I want to hear what happened."

Catherine wasn't sure she wanted to talk about the accident, but she didn't let those emotions show in her reply. "*Jah*, tell me when."

"Hello, Catherine. It's *gut* to see you."

She turned and recognized Zach's smile. "*Hiya*, Zach."

"You look . . . *gut*." His gaze seemed to focus on the scar around her eye. "Are you still in pain?"

She'd been so busy greeting family and friends, she'd forgotten about her scars, but now, standing before Zach, every one of her insecurities returned. Catherine pulled her *kapp* lower to cover more of her face. "How's your clock business?"

"You remembered. That's great. George said you lost your memory and might have difficulty remembering things. I picked up more furniture stores. I'm up to ten."

Numbness entered the top of her head and worked its way down her spine. Her memory had returned—even things she'd remembered wrong.

Catherine hadn't proposed to Elijah—it was Zach.

Another well-wisher came up on her blind side and pulled her into a hug, then someone else greeted her, until her body was as limp as a rag doll.

"This has probably been a bit overwhelming," Zach said. "Maybe you should sit down."

The only overwhelming part was not knowing why Elijah had led her to believe the two of them were in love. Her thoughts whirled. Once again the crowded room closed in and she found herself needing air. She pressed through the visitors and slipped out the back door. Catherine ran to the barn and found solace in the stall brushing her mare.

The barn door opened. "Cat?" Elijah came up to the stall. "Are you all right?"

"*Nay*, I'm *nett*." She whirled around and pointed the currycomb at him. "Why didn't you tell me that I was in love with Zach? I didn't propose to you—it was Zach."

His complexion drained of color as first he stiffened, then his shocked expression morphed into one of guilt. He bowed his head, not willing to look her in the eye. "I didn't want to confuse you."

"Ha."

"It's true. You did propose to him, but you also left town. Maybe your memory is still foggy in that area because—"

She straightened her shoulders. “Because I’m confused?”

He glanced up, but the moment he did, he looked back down. “Catherine, I brought you home so that if you want to be with Zach, you can be with him. He’s a *gut* man. But only you will know if you’re in love with him.” He turned and walked away.

Sobbing uncontrollably, Catherine brushed the mare’s coat, then dropped the brush and hugged the horse’s neck. She had no idea how long she’d been in the barn when the door creaked open.

Faith found her sitting on the floor, her back against the stall door. Her cousin sat beside her and reached for her hand. “You’ve been through a lot, and I want you to know that I’m here for you.”

Catherine leaned her head against Faith’s shoulder. “I still have some memory problems. When I told you I proposed, I thought I proposed to Elijah. It wasn’t until I saw Zach again that I knew it was him.”

“Zach will understand about your memory problems.”

“Will he understand that I haven’t sorted out that part of *mei* memory? I don’t know if I love Zach. Why did *I* propose?”

“You and Zach have courted several years. I know you were frustrated at times because it didn’t seem like Zach would ever pop the question, but then there were times you seemed content."

"Content, or was I settling for the status quo?"

"Only you can answer that."

"That's pretty much what Elijah told me too." Catherine sighed. She was back home and more confused than ever.

Faith pushed off the floor and reached for her hand. "*Kumm* on, you have a *haus* full of people who have all missed you."

Doc! Catherine scrambled to her feet. "Did you meet Dr. Wellington yet?"

"Your *Englisch* driver?"

"He's more than just a driver, but I'll tell you about him and his ranch later. I left him with George." Catherine rushed out of the barn, but his truck was gone. Once she went back inside, she searched for Elijah, but he was gone too.

Chapter 38

After a long night of praying for wisdom and direction, Catherine awoke with a clear head. It had only taken a moment to register how late it was by the amount of sunlight in the room. She tossed back the covers and shot out of bed.

Once downstairs, Catherine greeted her sister-in-law. "*Guder mariye*, Gwen. What time is it?"

"Almost one o'clock. The children wanted to wake you, but I didn't know how much rest you needed after your long trip . . . and since your accident." Gwen poured a mug of coffee and handed it to Catherine. "Would you like me to make you something to eat?"

Catherine shook her head. "I'll make a sandwich later."

"Your *Englisch* friend stopped by the *haus*. He asked that I didn't wake you when I told him you were still asleep."

Catherine sank into the kitchen chair. "I wanted to say goodbye."

Gwen brought her mug to the table and sat next to Catherine. "He's a very nice man. He and George talked for some time."

"*Jah*, he was very kind to take me, a stranger, in. I didn't even know *mei* name. I went by Julie. Apparently while I was in the hospital, the nurse overheard me talking in *mei* sleep and assumed *mei* name was Julie."

"I don't know how I would have handled it." She shook her head slowly. "It had to be difficult." Gwen was silent a moment, probably pondering a flood of what-ifs. "Elijah kept us up-to-date as much as he could. His letters always sounded so hopeful, but reading between the lines, we knew he was shattered. The authorities thought you'd gone through the ice and that you probably wouldn't be discovered until the river thawed. Even then, Elijah refused to accept that possibility. He refused to leave Ohio. Zach couldn't convince him either."

"Zach came to Hopewater?"

"He sold one of his clocks to a furniture store and wanted to deliver it in person so he could meet the owner and set up future business with his new account. Beverly drove him down. He stayed at Bishop's Zook's cousin's *haus*. Elijah was staying somewhere in the district, and Zach said he had tried to convince him to *kumm* home."

Danki *for the confirmation, Lord.* Catherine stood. "I have something I need to do." She raced out of the house, harnessed her buggy horse, and went to find Elijah.

Catherine stopped at his *mammi*'s house first, but the house windows had been boarded up. She went to his parents' place in the next township and knocked on their door. His mother answered.

"Catherine, it's so *gut* to see you again so soon. Elijah told us all about your memory loss after the accident. It's a miracle you both survived."

"God has been merciful, that is for certain. Is Elijah home?"

His mother shook her head. "He told me last *nacht* he was going back to Ohio. He's going to finally start training horses." She sniffled. "It's something he's always wanted to do."

"He went back?" The news struck her like a hard mule kick to the stomach. *Why did he leave without saying goodbye?*

"Didn't he tell you?"

Catherine's throat tightened. "*Nay*."

"Oh, dear child." His mother's arms came around her shoulder. "Elijah said he needed to leave in order for you to have a fresh start."

"That's *nett* true."

"It pains *mei* heart too. His father and I are to blame for pushing him to marry Edwina. We thought it was the right thing to do at the time, and . . . none of us measured the cost of what it would do to him to lose you. I shouldn't have interfered. I was the one who had told him you and Zach were courting. I thought if he stayed in

Badger Creek and helped his father-in-law that he would be better off. I was wrong."

Catherine swallowed down the lump in her throat. "Elijah never lost me—he's the one who found me."

Catherine cried the entire ride home, flooded by the same despairing thoughts she had before she left to go to Florida. Perhaps Doc had been right. Maybe her mind had somehow buried the past because too many aspects were painful.

Zach's buggy was parked in the driveway when she arrived. She slipped into the house and found him sitting at the kitchen table having coffee with George.

"Catherine." Zach stood. "I've *kumm* by to talk with you."

"Oh?"

He motioned to the door. "Can we go out on the porch?"

"Sure." She followed him outside. An image flashed of the expression of scorn he'd given her when she proposed. Why didn't she see it then? Perhaps she had but disregarded it. *Desperate.* "Why did you *kumm* over?"

"I've given it a lot of thought, and *nau* that *mei* business is doing well, I think we should get married. George agrees."

"Hmm. Do you know I'm partially blind? That I can't see anything on *mei* right side? Or that I might *nett* get *mei* memory back fully? A lot of things have changed."

"Are you saying you don't want to marry me?" A flicker of hope danced in his eyes.

"You want me to decline, don't you?" She smiled, already knowing the answer by the way he let out a long breath.

"I heard Elijah left town again. I figured you would be devastated, and I'm *nett* opposed to marrying you."

"He left town so we could have a fresh start. Only neither one of us wants a life together."

"I wish you well, Catherine," Zach said. "Are you going back to Ohio?"

Elijah learned on the ride back to Ohio that Doc Wellington owned the cabin he'd been staying in. His wife had inherited the property from her parents years ago, but because of poor relations with her family, Doc and she had never used it, nor were they willing to sell it to an *Englischer*. Doc had no idea who the redheaded man was who had given Elijah the address, or how it had been stocked with canned goods and chopped wood.

"God has a way of working all things to the good," Doc said, signing over the deed. "Had it not been for you and Catherine coming into my life, I might have gone to my grave with unforgiveness in my heart. Now those shackles have been removed." He looked around the area. "This place will make a nice fresh start. If Hannah were here, she would agree."

"*Danki* again." Elijah shook Doc's hand. "Please, stop by anytime."

"I'll keep in touch." Doc went to the door when a truck and trailer pulled into the yard. "You have a delivery."

"What?" Elijah followed Doc outside. "The driver must have the wrong *haus*. I'm *nett* expecting a delivery."

"I'm giving you Pickles. I bought the horse for Catherine. She thought he would make a good horse to pull a sleigh."

"I can have him pulling a sleigh by winter," Elijah said. "I think the children on your ranch would enjoy going for a ride."

"Maybe so, but not this horse. This horse is Catherine's. I'm just leaving him in your charge."

"But she's—" A car pulled in the drive, and when it stopped, Catherine stepped out. Elijah stared in disbelief.

"Go to her," Doc said. "She's traveled a long distance."

He didn't have to be told twice. Elijah sprinted to her. "Catherine!" He swung her into his arms and twirled her around.

"You were right about why I was going to Florida. The *nacht* before we left, when Zach asked me to marry him, I couldn't say yes. I wasn't in love with him—I was still in love with you. All this time *mei* heart was still searching for you."

"I love you, Catherine." He leaned down and captured her mouth in a soft kiss. Then fueled by years of waiting, he pulled her in tighter and deepened the kiss. He broke the kiss, needing air, but didn't move more than an inch. She felt too good in his arms to let her go so soon. He wanted to hold her in his arms forever.

"Your kiss is exactly how I remembered," she said, melting in his embrace.

Epilogue

Eighteen months later

Catherine climbed onto the sleigh bench and situated the wool blanket. She smiled down at her husband, who was bent down and tying Kimberly's scarf.

Elijah made a *brrr* sound and pretended to chatter his teeth. "Are you sure you're *nett* too *kalt* to take a ride?"

"No," Kimberly replied adamantly.

"*Hmm* . . . Let's see, are your ears *kalt*?" He touched her ears.

"No."

"What about your nose?"

The child giggled when Elijah swooped her into his arms. He placed her gently on the bench next to Catherine, then gave Catherine a wink before climbing into his spot.

With a click of Elijah's tongue, Pickles lunged forward. The sleigh glided over the freshly fallen snow.

Catherine made sure the blanket was tucked around Kimberly. She didn't want the state authorities for the foster care system accusing her of not properly looking after their soon-to-be daughter.

"We're going to have lots of fun," she told Kimberly. Catherine had checked the pond every day to see if the ice had thickened enough to skate.

A few minutes later they arrived at the pond. Elijah stopped the horse and set the brake.

Catherine tied the laces on Kimberly's skates. "Remember how we practiced walking on skates?"

"Yes. I glide."

Ever since she opened the package on Christmas Day, Kimberly had begged to wear them. Catherine laced them on her feet and taught her how to keep her balance with the blade protectors on, but that wasn't on ice.

Catherine reached for the girl's hand, and Elijah reached for the other. Together they stepped onto the ice.

"Glide, glide, glide," Kimberly said, doing remarkably well. Her laughter carried over the air like sweet music to Catherine's ears.

All three of them were exhausted by the time they got off the ice. Kimberly fell asleep on the sleigh ride home, and Elijah had to carry her inside.

"She's exhausted," he whispered.

Catherine smiled. "She's a happy little girl."

He placed Kimberly on the bed to finish her nap, then returned to the kitchen. "What about you?" He pulled her into his arms. "Are you happy?"

"Do you have to ask?" She threaded her fingers through his hair and leaned in to give him a kiss. "I've never been happier."

A knock on the door pulled Elijah away from her. The visitor introduced himself as Alex Canter, an attorney for Rulerson, Markel, and Boyd, and when Catherine told him her name, his eyes lit. "You're the famous Catherine Glick we've all been hunting for."

"I'm Catherine Graber *nau*, and I'm *nett* famous."

"She had a head injury and had lost her memory," Elijah explained, placing his hand on her lower back. "What can we do for you?"

Alex opened his briefcase and removed a long envelope. "I told you Rulerson, Markel, and Boyd are the best firm to hire." He presented Elijah with an envelope.

"What's this?"

"Your part of the settlement, minus our fees, of course."

"But I told you I didn't want to go to court."

"We had a verbal agreement for representation," he said. "Remember?"

Elijah wasn't sure what to believe. He had specifically told Alex he didn't want to go to court or make a statement, and he had never seen Alex again until now. Elijah stared at the envelope, then looked over at Catherine. "I have everything I need." All of their medical bills had been paid—his through Alex's law firm, and Catherine's had been paid thanks to a victims' assistance program. He handed Alex the envelope.

"If I take this back, the check will sit on our books until it's sent to the state as unclaimed funds. That money is yours."

"To do with as I wish?"

"Yes," Alex said. "Don't give it to the government."

"Can I give to it someone else?"

"Sure, I can arrange it."

Elijah went into the kitchen and removed a pen from the top drawer, then jotted a message. *This is a gift from God, so don't thank me.* He handed the envelope back to Alex with instructions for how to locate the nurse who had helped him in his time of need.

"You don't even want to look at the amount of the check?"

"*Nay.*" He glanced at Catherine and smiled. "God blessed me with finding Catherine. I have everything I need."

Alex turned to Catherine. "I'm sorry you weren't included in the settlement. Without having an agreement for representation, there wasn't anything I could do. However, you are entitled to—"

"I have everything I need too." Catherine sidled up beside Elijah. "God has been *gut* to both of us."

Alex sighed. "Okay, it's been nice working with you." He shoved the envelope back into his briefcase and shook Elijah's hand. "I'm glad everything worked out for you."

Once Alex left, Elijah brought Catherine into his arms. "I'm sorry. I should have asked you before giving that money away."

"Elijah," she scolded, "when I said I have everything, I meant it. And"—she stretched to kiss his cheek—"in, I'd say about eight months, we're going to be blessed even more."

"*About* eight months?" His jaw went slack. "We're having a *boppli*?"

She nodded.

"We're having a *boppli*!" He swooped her into his arms, carried her into the sitting room, then lowered her onto the couch. "Can I get you anything? A glass of water? Warm milk? We're having a *boppli*—a baby!"

"Hush *nau* before you wake Kimberly. I don't think we want to tell her this soon she's going to be a big *schweschaler*."

Elijah kissed her forehead. "You've made me the happiest man in Hopewater, Catherine Graber. Our little family is growing, *jah*?"

"Faster than you think." She patted the couch cushion. "You better have a seat. I don't want you to faint."

He sat on the edge of the couch and eyed her carefully. "I love you."

"I love you too." Smiling up at him, her face radiating with a joyful glow, she guided his hand to her belly. "The *doktah* said we're having twins."

"Two?" His mouth dropped open, and for a moment he just stared. "We're going to need to put an addition on the *haus*." He stood, then paced to the end of the room and back.

Catherine chuckled. "Elijah, don't wear out the floorboards. You'll have plenty of time to do that eight months from *nau*."

He returned to his place beside her on the couch, then leaned down and kissed her forehead. "I can't wait to see what our future holds."

Acknowledgments

Thank You, Jesus, for allowing me to finish another book and for placing great people in my life to help make my dream a reality.

I want to thank my husband, who sacrifices the most while I'm holed up in my office typing. It takes a great man to understand times when I'm lost in thought or when I'm carrying on conversations with my characters in my head.

Thank you, Lexie, Danny, and Sarah. You three are the best kids ever! Lexie, your help with social media has been such a blessing. God has given you a talent with photography and video editing, and I'm so proud of the work you've done. Danny and Sarah, this is your senior year and I'm so very proud of both of you. I can't wait to see what God has in store for you. Thank you for all the work you do around the house.

This book would not be possible without the tremendous dedication of my publishing family at HarperCollins Christian Publishing. I wish to especially thank Becky Monds, my wonderful editor, for her encouragement, support, and God-given editing skills. You are such a blessing to me! I'm also very grateful for Julee Schwarzburg, my line editor. I am so honored to have been able to work with you! A special thanks to Kristen Golden who works hard marketing my books, to Jodi Hughes who typeset *Arms of Mercy*, and to my publisher, Amanda Bostic, who allows me to be part of the HCCP family.

I want to thank my agent, Natasha Kern, for her ongoing support. I can't thank you enough for all the help you've given me while writing this book. I treasure your storehouse of knowledge!

To the folks who have so kindly agreed to be part of my Backroads Messengers street team—*thank you!* I so appreciate everything you do to help promote my books. God bless you all.

I also want to thank my Scribes critique partners: Jennifer Uhlarik, Michele Morris, G. E. "Ginny" Hamlin, Sarah Hamaker, and Colleen Scott. I love that within our group we are not only authors who understand each other but prayer partners. You ladies are the best!

Discussion Questions

1. As an Amish woman Catherine went against the grain when she proposed to Zach. Do you think Zach should have reacted the way he did? Was Zach's rejection reason enough for Catherine to leave town?

2. It's natural for an Amish man to want to have means to support a family before he gets married, but do you think Zach was too focused on growing his business? Was he missing out on the present by worrying about his future? How could his financial concerns be viewed as a lack of faith?

3. Catherine's reaction to seeing Elijah again was steeped in bitterness. Was her unwelcoming attitude justified? What reasons did Elijah have for rushing into marriage? How did his promise to Edwina and past obligations change his future? In what ways are Elijah and Zach different?

4. In Michigan, sparrows usually migrate south for the winter, so when Catherine spots a small bird sitting on a fence post in January,

she's worried. What passage in the Bible comes to mind? Has there ever been a time in your life when your needs were supplied supernaturally? What does Matthew 6:33–34 tell us to do?

5. The man with red hair shows up in several scenes of the book. Who does this man represent to you? How did the stranger help Catherine? How did he direct Elijah's path? Do you see other reasons for the red-haired man's involvement than just getting Elijah and Catherine back together?

6. Both Catherine's and Elijah's nurses were inspirational in helping them while they were in and out of the hospital. Did you see the nurses' help as God's way of supplying Catherine's and Elijah's needs? Have you seen God work through one person to provide for someone else? Do you believe God blesses both people in the process?

7. The conflict between Bishop Zook and Dr. Wellington stemmed from the loss of someone they both loved. Can you see how bitterness had taken root in their hearts? Do you think God planted Elijah and Catherine in their lives to bring the men to a point of forgiveness?

8. Kimberly was a victim of her mother's bad choices. What was your reaction when you read that her blindness was the result of her mother's addiction? Can you see how Kimberly would have emotional problems associated with being abandoned?

Additional Copyright Information

About the Author

Ruth Reid is a full-time pharmacist who lives in Florida with her husband and three children. When attending the Ferris State University College of Pharmacy in Big Rapids, Michigan, she lived on the outskirts of an Amish community and had several occasions to visit the Amish farms. Her interest grew into love as she saw the beauty in living a simple life.

Visit Ruth online at RuthReid.com
Facebook: Author Ruth Reid
Twitter: @AuthorRuthReid

Books are produced in the United States using U.S.-based materials

Books are printed using a revolutionary new process called THINKtech™ that lowers energy usage by 70% and increases overall quality

Books are durable and flexible because of Smyth-sewing

Paper is sourced using environmentally responsible foresting methods and the paper is acid-free

Center Point Large Print
600 Brooks Road / PO Box 1
Thorndike, ME 04986-0001 USA

(207) 568-3717

US & Canada:
1 800 929-9108
www.centerpointlargeprint.com